A NEW WOMAN

A NEW WOMAN

Elizabeth Shorten

Hodder & Stoughton

Copyright © 1997 Elizabeth Shorten

First published in Great Britain in 1997
by Hodder and Stoughton
A division of Hodder Headline PLC

The right of Elizabeth Shorten to be identified as the Author of
the Work has been asserted by her in accordance with the
Copyright, Designs and Patents Act 1988.

10 9 8 7 6 5 4 3 2 1

British Library Cataloguing in Publication Data

A CIP catalogue record for this title is available
from the British Library

Shorten, Elizabeth
A new woman
1. English fiction – 20th century
I. Title
823.9'14[F]

ISBN 0 340 68242 6

Typeset by Avon Dataset Ltd, Bidford-on-Avon, Warks

Printed and bound in Great Britain by
Mackays of Chatham PLC, Chatham, Kent

Hodder and Stoughton
A division of Hodder Headline PLC
338 Euston Road
London NW1 3BH

To my son Sebastian
for teaching me
about being a mother

and

To my mother Shelley
who always knew

My thanks to: my agent Patrick Walsh, my editor Carolyn Mays and her assistant Diana Beaumont, and Jeffrey Archer and Val Corbett for their valuable advice.

CHAPTER ONE

Maybe it was chance that she was still there when they came for her, that she had lingered over her paperwork instead of obeying her instincts and her watch and plunging straight out into the crisp February night air.

But Rebecca Carlyle did not believe in the accidental. She had read somewhere that chance favours only the prepared mind. Nothing had prepared her for the changes to come.

She looked at the three worried faces outside her trailer door. Putting down her coat and bag was a reflex, her limbs moving before her mind could intervene. 'You'd better come in,' she said.

They filed one by one up the narrow steps: Letitia, her partner and the other producer, jaw jutting in readiness for battle . . . Jeremy, her bright young director, a gangly bundle of nervous energy . . . and dear solid Terence, her production accountant, looking, as he always did, careworn and old.

'I know you're supposed to be going home,' Letitia ploughed in first, 'but this is a crisis.'

When wasn't it? Becky reflected wearily. Film sets were always a battleground. The point of taking on a partner was that, just now and then, you should be able to leave the damage limitation to somebody else.

'What's happened this time?' was all she said.

Jeremy could contain himself no longer. He ran a hand through spiky hair – roots dark, ends dyed a startling blond – that stood permanently to attention, and she felt an exasperated rush of affection for him and his passionate seriousness. 'It's Ross Piper,' he burst out. 'We're ready for him – have been for ages – but he's barricaded himself inside his trailer. Says he's too ill to shoot.'

'And what's the real story?'

'Drunk!' Letitia snorted, pacing back and forth, the narrow space too confining for the explosive anger packed into her slender frame. 'Plain old sozzled. According to his personal assistant, he's auditioning for lifetime membership of AA. Hit the bottle a couple of years ago and hasn't looked back. No one in the know will touch him with a bargepole.'

It was nice to be the last to know, Becky thought wryly. At least it explained why a star of Ross Piper's calibre had agreed to appear in their small budget British art film. When he'd accepted, Becky had flattered herself it was because he loved their script. Now she cursed herself for not looking deeper. 'Show me a man's weakness,' her father always said, 'and I'll show you his motive.'

'We can't afford to cancel,' Terence pronounced gloomily. 'Whether Mr Piper performs or not, we still have to pay the cast and crew. There's no room in the budget for extra shooting days . . .'

I know, I know, Becky wanted to scream, *but I have another life.* I'm supposed to go home and take care of my son so the nanny can have at least one night off. I'm tired of babying bolshy stars and rebellious crews when I never get the chance to use my mothering skills on the person who needs them most.

They were all staring at her, eyes glued to her face as though she could somehow magic the solution out of the air. It was one of the things she'd always liked about this job – the trust placed in her by the people she worked with, their complete faith that she would give every ounce of herself not to let them down.

But tonight she had nothing more to give. Tonight she wanted to go home to Rupert and Adam.

Full of resolve, she turned to Letitia. 'I'm supposed to be leaving you in charge. Can't you handle this?'

'You know I can't!' Letitia exploded. 'I haven't got your knack of . . . doing it tactfully.' She looked at Becky with grudging admiration. 'You can give someone a good dressing down and at the end of it they're so charmed they practically write you a thank-you letter.'

Becky stared at her with dawning understanding. Letitia, who struck fear into the hearts of lesser mortals, was actually afraid – afraid of Ross Piper's fame and his two Academy Awards and his formidable temper. But what made her think Becky wasn't?

They were all looking at her again. This time she didn't have the energy to argue. 'I'll see what I can do,' she said, 'when I've made arrangements for someone to take care of my son.'

Rupert picked up a mascara from Becky's dressing table and tried the effect of darkening his lashes. It might be fun, different, though his looks hardly needed enhancement. When the phone rang he answered it idly, his concentration on his reflection. 'Yes?' he drawled.

There was a small hesitation on the other end of the line, then he heard his wife's voice, soft and familiar. 'Rupert, I need a favour.'

'What's it this time?' She had some nerve, he thought, phoning from work with her lists of chores, as though he had nothing better to do than play the house-husband. He had a career too – even if it was temporarily on hold. An actor couldn't always be in work, especially when his own wife wouldn't pull the necessary strings to cast him in her films.

She had, it seemed, another crisis on set: a drunken star, a potential budget overrun. It wasn't that Rupert didn't understand these matters – after all, he was in the same business – but he was determined not to make it easy for her. 'Surely you don't think *I* can do anything?' he enquired with feigned amazement. 'I'm not the great producer.'

'Lolly's supposed to go off. I want you to look after Adam till I get back.'

Rupert examined his mascara'd lashes in the mirror. He'd lived with his looks too long to be surprised by them, but he knew the effect they had on other people. From the time he was twelve, women had been trying to seduce him. The excitement of using his physical powers to manipulate others had long since settled into habit.

His face had the symmetry of a matinée idol's, his eyes were the smoky blue of a late evening sky, his hair flopped over his brow, black and glossy and irresistible to the touch. When he made his entrance this evening, it would cause the usual stir.

'If it's a nanny you need, talk to Lolly,' he said shortly. 'I'm going out. It's all arranged.'

'Can't you cancel? Please, Rupert. I wouldn't ask if it wasn't important. Lolly needs a break, and I really wanted to talk to you . . .'

But *I*, thought Rupert, don't want to talk to *you*. Not if it's another lecture about the overdraft and the school fees and isn't it time you gave your liver a bit of a rest? Not when the drink makes me forget – and you make me remember – the last time I went for an audition and they actually gave me the part.

Besides, his buddy Todd would have left already for their rendezvous point. They were going to hit the nightclub circuit and check out the action. Rupert was in the mood to rock and roll. He had no intention of cancelling anything.

'Lolly doesn't mind doing a bit more overtime,' he said airily. 'She's making a bloody fortune off us. Tell you what – I'll ask her myself.'

'Oh, would you? You're a darling.' Becky sounded all relief and warmth. He could almost see her expression, the huge green eyes so alive they seemed to dance in her face. When he'd first met her, he'd been bowled over by the sheer, undiluted goodness of her, like a blast of pure sweet oxygen to his lungs.

'What if Lolly has other plans?' Becky was sounding anxious again. Rupert had no such qualms. He thought of how Lolly trembled when he accidentally brushed past her, and of the rush of blood to her cheeks when he paid her a compliment on those skin-tight little outfits she liked to wear, he suspected for his benefit.

'She'll cancel them if I ask her to,' he said, with a confidence born of never knowing denial.

'All right, then . . .' Becky paused. 'How long will you be out?'

He'd been seconds from a clean getaway. Why did she ask that question, when she knew how much he loathed having to answer it? He had to have space, room to manoeuvre. It wasn't that he wanted to hurt her, but his own horror of boredom was by far the stronger impulse.

'I'm sure I'll be tucked up in bed by the time you get back,' he soothed. 'But I'll be very disappointed if you don't wake me . . .'

His suggestive words didn't produce the expected giggle, but Rupert's mind had already wandered on to wardrobe decisions, and he didn't notice.

Becky knocked firmly on the trailer door. From within came the sounds of glass breaking. She winced. There were objects of value in there – the sort of perks a star could demand and get – in this case, a monitor with multi-system VHS so Ross Piper could watch his favourite videos on American format. The insurers would take a dim view of wilful destruction.

She knocked again, and when there was still no answer, she almost gave up and walked away. She was tired, too tired for this, and the beginnings of a headache were pressing against her temples.

But then the door was opened an inch by Sandra, Piper's assistant, a mousy girl with a long-suffering expression.

'Who's that?' a voice roared from within.

'It's the producer, Mr Piper.'

'Good – send him into the lion's den.'

With a helpless look of apology, Sandra stood aside to let Becky pass. Ross Piper, she reflected gloomily, must be very drunk indeed if he couldn't even remember the sex of the person producing his film. As she stepped into the half gloom, Becky felt very much like the unfortunate Daniel, facing unknown terrors.

The custom-fitted mobile home was a mess, empty bottles and broken glass strewn everywhere, but Becky breathed a sigh of relief when she saw the video system intact. She remembered the warning she'd been given by Piper's agent when they signed the deal.

'With Ross on board, I hope you have at least a hundred thousand dollars in petty cash for whims.'

'What whims?' she'd asked innocently.

She was beginning to find out.

In the midst of the wreckage towered the great man, his face as familiar as a childhood friend's – the clear blue eyes, the shock of salt-and-pepper hair. She remembered as a child of ten sitting in a darkened auditorium watching him in a biblical epic and believing fervently that God, when she eventually came face to face with Him, would look exactly like Ross Piper. And now she was going to scold him, like any recalcitrant child.

Becky raised her chin, her blond bob falling back from a face settling into lines of quiet determination, and looked him straight in the eye. Never before had she so regretted her five feet four inches of height.

'A *she*, eh?' he slurred approvingly. 'Thash more like it. Wouldja like a drink, m'dear?'

She squared up to him. 'I don't drink when I'm working, Mr Piper. Nor should you.'

'A feisty one!' He laughed uproariously. 'I like 'em with a bit of spirit. Spirit, eh? D'ya get it?'

'You sent word to the set that you're not well enough to work,' Becky said, pointedly eyeing an empty bottle of Scotch. 'Are the "spirits" for medicinal purposes? Wouldn't you be better off if we got you a doctor?'

The actor glowered at her, swaying on his feet. 'You're not being any fun. Come a little closer . . .'

'I don't think—'

'I got a tattoo on my dick. Wanna see it?'

In the periphery of her vision his hand seemed to be edging downwards, and suddenly the blood rushed to Becky's head, and with it all her pent-up emotions. She felt light, detached, no longer part of her own body.

In a movement she was scarcely aware of, she drew back her arm and punched Ross Piper full in the mouth.

Sandra gasped. Becky stood rooted to the spot. Ross Piper's face broke into a crooked grin. 'Bravo!' he declared – before pitching backwards onto a sofa and passing out cold.

'You did *what*?' Letitia shrieked.

Becky sat in a miserable heap on her trailer floor. 'He wanted to show me his tattoo.'

Letitia shook her cropped auburn head in disbelief. 'And this is a reason to *hit* the man?'

Jeremy was looking at Becky with an expression close to awe. 'Wicked!' he breathed.

No, Jeremy, her mind protested. She didn't want him to admire her for this. She had never condoned violence, never even believed in raising her voice. And now, with this explosion of anger that had come from nowhere, all her carefully constructed system of controls seemed to have evaporated. She had allowed something to break free inside her, and she was frightened because she didn't yet know where it would lead her.

'What are we going to do if this gets back to Stanley Shiplake?' Letitia demanded.

Becky pressed the balls of her palms against her eyes. If Ross Piper complained to their powerful backer, she didn't rate her chances of holding on to her position as producer of this film.

Weakly she said, 'We have to try and keep it under wraps.' That was wishful thinking, considering how many people knew already. 'I called the doctor . . .'

'For you or Ross Piper?' Letitia sneered.

'He said there won't be much of a mark. But he's passed out cold—'

'—thanks to you—'

'No, the drink. There's no chance of getting him sober enough to stand, let alone deliver his lines. We'll have to cancel tonight's shoot.'

Becky looked anxiously at Jeremy, expecting a furious objection, but he was still gazing at her with undisguised admiration.

'You never know,' he said, 'maybe he'll write you a thank-you letter.'

'If you don't shut up, Jeremy,' Letitia menaced, 'I'll make sure you're next on the casualty list.'

She flounced out, leaving Becky and Jeremy staring at one another, with all the shock of newly opened horizons.

Sir Humphrey Humes watched as Becky sat on the bed in his trailer, hugging her knees to her chest. He didn't like the way her eyes had glazed over, like a rabbit's caught in a headlamp.

'I can't even explain it to myself,' she was saying, 'but I wanted to try and explain it to you.'

'You don't have to,' Humphrey assured her. 'The damn fellow asked for it. The word "penis" might have been acceptable, "member" even . . . but "dick"!'

He was warming to his theme now. Sir Humphrey had an enormous contempt for all persons transatlantic, and those who were anything to do with the film industry in particular. He had trodden the boards of the British stage for forty years now, and his acceptance of screen roles like the current one was an evil necessitated by the more modest pay from what he considered his true vocation. Also, at seventy-eight, he had resigned himself to accepting what work he could get.

'I mean, damn it all, apart from their appalling bastardisation of the English language, look what sartorial outrages the Americans have inflicted on the world. The blue jean . . . the baseball cap . . .' Humphrey's personal taste ran to baggy suits and cotton poplin shirts with sewn-in gussets and large floppy polka-dot bow ties or paisley cravats.

'I don't think we can hold Ross Piper personally responsible,' Becky reasoned.

'Why not? I guarantee he *wears* the bloody things. They all do when they're trying to hide from the paparazzi. If I caught him at it, I'd pop him one on the nose myself.'

'Humphrey!' At least she was smiling now, a small grin that flashed momentarily through the pain like sun breaking through cloud.

'I know – I'm not being very helpful, am I? Too old, you see. Can't take any of it seriously, not with the old Grim Reaper waiting in the shadows.'

'Perhaps it *isn't* all that serious,' Becky attempted, not sounding too convinced.

Humphrey passed over a half-eaten box of after-dinner mints, the discarded wrappers neatly plugged into the empty holes. Chocolates, he felt, were a great source of comfort in times of distress. 'My dear, someone once said that most things don't matter at all, and nothing matters very much. I didn't believe it at your age, no more than you probably do, but now . . .'

'My father always taught me the value of common decency. He said people would let me down, but I could survive that as long as I never let myself down.'

Humphrey patted her hand. 'Your father must be a very good man. If he is, he must also know that to err is human.'

She gave him a wistful nod. 'I've got to tell Juliette next. Not the details, of course, just that we're cancelling tonight's shoot.'

Juliette Winters was their female lead, one of British cinema's bright young things. The industry grapevine had her pegged for a starring role in a big studio picture, and Becky was hoping to ride on the publicity. While not in Ross Piper's league, Juliette was developing a sense of her growing worth – and an ego to match it.

'Ah yes.' Humphrey stroked his chin. 'Our Miss Winters may cut up rough. Not because she's a star, but because she isn't one yet. I wouldn't take it too seriously.'

'But people expect me—'

'Let 'em all go to hell! You're worth the lot put together.'

She popped a mint into her mouth, and it bulged in her thin cheek like a hamster's stash.

'Thank you,' she said, 'for trying to make me feel better. But I know what I've done. If Ross Piper pulls out, so will the backers. And this film is putting food in mouths. There are a lot of people relying on me . . .'

'Yes,' Humphrey said gently, 'but only one of them is your biological child. Now you go on home to him and let the rest take care of itself.'

Becky fiddled with buttons, looking for something soothing on Radio Three – a little Mozart or Vivaldi for the night owls, like herself, still out on the road.

There was no point in flooring the accelerator. No matter how fast her wheels ate up the distance to her house at World's End off the King's Road, by the time she got there Adam would be long asleep, blond hair tousled, blue eyes tightly closed. She pictured him in his bunk, his dinosaur duvet kicked to one side. He was passionate about dinosaurs. When he grew up, he said, he wanted to be a paleontologist and a pop star.

It went so fast, a childhood. Six years had passed in the blink of an eye. Before she knew it, he *would* be grown up and she would have missed it all.

It was Lolly he went to with his nightmares and his first wobbly tooth, Lolly who taught him to balance on a bicycle and tie his own shoe laces. 'Look, Mummy,' he would say, 'I can do it now, watch me!' and she would smile and tell him what a clever boy he was, and bite back the anguish that she was never there for the first time.

Lolly was a darling, but Becky hadn't planned on handing over so much of the mothering. Not that Lolly couldn't cope, but the bubbly seventeen-year-old with a spring in her step who had won Becky's heart at the interview two years ago had long since vanished, overwhelmed by tiredness and overtime. In the end, it was Adam who suffered most.

The blame, she knew, lay with the treachery of her trade. Films were not a nine-to-five occupation, they were a vocation. If I can just get through this one, Becky vowed, get the footage safely in the can and the money securely in the bank, then I'll be able to make some changes. More time off for Lolly, more attention for Adam, more co-operation from Rupert . . .

Rupert! What would he say if he knew what she had done to Ross Piper tonight?

A Chopin Nocturne tinkled from the car speakers, and for a while she drove numbly, letting the music flow through her mind and empty it of its cares. But soon the unwelcome thoughts were back, flitting across her consciousness like malevolent ghosts. When, if she were honest with herself, was the last time she had truly confided in Rupert?

Once, they'd told each other everything. They'd met on a commercial shoot, she a humble production assistant, he an equally lowly extra. When she saw him for the first time, it was hard not to stare at the perfection of his features, but she'd never imagined he would notice her. Yet somehow they'd found themselves huddled over polystyrene cups of coffee, talking non-stop about how he wanted to be a serious actor and she wanted to produce feature films and what a success they were going to be.

Their talk had spilled over quite naturally into dinner at an Italian restaurant frequented by students and winos. They were still chattering about what it was like for him living on unemployment benefit between bit-parts when they found themselves on the sofa in his flat, facing a poster of a man in country tweeds sipping champagne on the bonnet of his Rolls Royce, which was parked outside the Department of Social Security. The caption read 'Poverty Sucks', and Becky laughed out loud from shock and admiration because he didn't care what anyone thought.

His flat was tiny, furnished with odds and ends from second hand shops, an incongruous background to some pieces of extraordinary beauty and value – first edition books and old maps and bits of Georgian silver – the few relics that had been saved from a life of privilege. His family, he said, had owned five thousand acres in Gloucestershire, and from the time he was four, his father would take him out on horseback and tell him, with a sweep of his hand, 'One day, son, all this will be yours.' Only when one day came around, his father had lost it all on fast women and slow horses.

Rupert made light of it, but she knew how it must have pierced his proud soul. He had been taught to expect a certain life as his birthright, and never been given the resources to cope when it was suddenly snatched away from him. As she reached up to tuck back a stray lock of his hair, she was filled with an overwhelming tenderness towards him.

When he took her to bed in the huge four poster reminiscent of bygone glories, she had poured herself out as never before, as though with the gift of her body she could finally make his present more rich than his past. And he had responded with a fierceness that frightened them both, hungry as even he had not known for his empty spaces to be filled with her love.

The next morning, Sunday, he had taken her rowing on the Serpentine, and she had watched the muscles cord thickly in his forearms and listened drowsily to the slap of oars against water and thought she would float, just float away on a tide of contentment.

He taught her, for the first time, to see, actually to *feel* the beauty of physical things. She had never really noticed her surroundings, never cared if her clothes were piled up on chairs or her sofas didn't match. But Rupert, with a genuine love of antiques inspired by innate good taste, made her appreciate what a chair could be, teaching her to recognise the elegantly curved cabriole leg of the Queen Anne period, the ornate 'French' leg with scroll foot of the Early Georgian era, the late Regency 'Greek' leg, bulging thickly at knee height and tapering to impossible slenderness. They prowled the corridors of the Victoria and Albert Museum, where Rupert showed her how to distinguish the suave grace of a genuine Georgian piece from the shamelessly 'improved' Victorian copies he despised, alerting her to often subtle differences in ornament, proportion and manufacturing technique. In lunchtimes they haunted the showrooms of Sotheby's and Christie's, possessing with their eyes for a few precious moments treasures they could never actually afford to own. They lived, it seemed, in a permanent feast of visual delights.

And then there was the sex, a constant surprise and wonder. It seemed there were whole days when they didn't get out of bed. She couldn't remember when she first began leaving a spare toothbrush and some suits for work in his flat, so she could stay in his arms till the very last moment. But soon it was crowded with her film books and computer and family photographs and stockings over the bath, and she was making enough money from her first movie for them to afford somewhere bigger.

Marriage didn't enter the equation till she was halfway through her second film and missed her monthly cycle. Her earnings were rising in leaps and bounds while Rupert's remained sporadic at best, but though they would all be dependent on her, it never occurred to her to give up the baby. They spoke, instead, of live-in nannies and a house in Fulham.

And if she had doubts, she kept them to herself, putting them down to pre-wedding nerves or the hormonal changes of pregnancy. And when she felt panic, as she sometimes did, at the inexorable march of events which seemed to have gathered a momentum all of their own, she sat down to write lists and plan menus and create for herself the illusion that she was still in control.

When the day finally dawned she felt perfectly calm, unable to remember what her fears had been about. The ceremony in the Kensington and Chelsea Registry Office was attended only by immediate family. Becky's parents, who had never met Rupert, flew in from their retirement villa in Tuscany and were disconcerted in equal measure by their new son-in-law's film star looks and uncertain prospects. Her brother Michael couldn't get leave at short notice from his bank in Hong Kong, but sent a video camera as a wedding gift so they could capture it for him on tape. Rupert's mother had passed away, deserted long since by his father for an older woman of property. He sent a telegram pleading prior commitments, and no wedding present. A handful of friends were invited to lunch at an expensive restaurant, a reflection of Rupert's preference for quality over quantity. Becky wrote the cheque.

But she was happy – happy to bursting – with Rupert beside her and his child inside her and the two simple bands of gold clasped round their fingers, and all of it accomplished without her being able to remember when any conscious decision had been made . . .

The throaty roar of a powerful engine made her glance across into the next lane. Behind the wheel of a red Porsche, a boy scarcely older than Lolly was giving her BMW the once over. Another one spoiling for a race, a war of wheels and nerves, and she knew from the confident thrust of his jaw that he believed he was unbeatable, immortal, death something that only happened to other people, old people. He was also probably several drinks over the limit.

Averting her gaze, she allowed her thoughts to drift back to Adam. How she had loved him, from the moment he emerged, squalling, into their world. How she adored being a mother, longed to plan a second baby.

But if she took the time off work, who would pay for the nanny and the private nursery school and their ever-growing collection of antiques, acquired from endless scouting trips to country auctions and tiny shops along their patch of the New King's Road, which were Rupert's permanent hunting ground? As her mind worried endlessly at the problem, a new fear began to seep into her soul, a suspicion that Rupert did not need success to bolster his innate sense of superiority. 'Try your best,' her father had said, and she always did. But Rupert had lacked any sound parental guidance, any preparation for the struggles ahead. So he took casting directors for long liquid lunches and flirted with the secretaries of important distributors a.id waited for the doors to open by virtue of his charm and breeding alone.

As her fears took shape, so Becky began to grow impatient of Rupert's past, to resent the hand-crafted rocking horse and painted tin soldiers that cluttered up Adam's nursery, relics of a world that no longer existed. Neither the Carlyle name nor its lost acres were any use to their son now. She wanted Rupert to be free of it, once and for all, to face the fact that it was over and start again.

But with the passing of the years, her hopes that he would embrace what had to be done, carve out a new place for himself in the world, had slowly withered and died, and with them, her dreams of a shared success, a partnership of equals, a house filled with children. And so she had resigned herself to what was, and had tried not to think of what might have been, had shouldered more than her share of the burdens and thought she was reconciled to it all, until tonight, in Ross Piper's trailer, when she had suddenly lashed out in fury against all that should not be expected of her.

As she pulled up at a red light on the King's Road, she noticed with irritation that the Porsche driver was still beside her. He grinned across at her, laying down the challenge. Impatiently, she wondered if he'd bothered to look in her rear window at the toys and sweet papers strewn over the back seat. True, speed was an

advantage in getting her to distant locations, but she'd really chosen
this model (a saloon, unlike his sports) because it was spacious in
the back with plenty of room for Adam and the paraphernalia that
always grew up around him.

The Porsche driver revved his engine, anticipating the green
light. As it changed, he roared off with a squeal of burning rubber.
Becky waited several seconds before cruising forward at a sedate
speed. She watched his tail-lights disappear, imagining the
disappointment on his face.

It wasn't that she didn't like a challenge. But she preferred to
save her energy for the ones that counted.

Becky eased into a space two blocks from her house, and warily
picked her way back across pavements glassy with frost. Fumbling
for her keys, she glanced up quickly at the primrose four-storey
façade, stuffed with all the belongings and the memories she and
Rupert had accumulated over the years. The windows were in
darkness.

As she opened the door, she breathed in the familiar, comforting scent of home – beeswax polish on wood and dog basket
and the fresh flowers she loved to pick from the garden but more
often grabbed from a roadside stall. From the kitchen she could
hear the thumping of Bogey's tail, but felt too tired to risk his
boisterous greeting. It was she who had picked this name for
Adam's wheaten terrier, and he, who had never heard of the film
star, latched onto it in delight because it was one of his favourite
'rude words'.

She mounted the stairs, by habit heading first for Adam's room.
The night light was on, the toys stacked neatly away in trays – the
hundreds of toys she bought him out of guilt that she hadn't
provided him with a brother or sister to play with. Quickly she
checked that he had remembered to feed the rest of his menagerie:
the goldfish Jekyll and Hyde hanging eerily in the water, eyes
open even in sleep, and the hamster Mischief treading endlessly
and mindlessly on her wheel.

Then she went over to him, her son, her cherub, face perfect in
sleep, duvet kicked off as usual despite the chill in the air. Carefully
she tucked it around him and bent her head to inhale the baby
sweetness of him, the heart-melting scent of warm puppy milkiness

that still clung around him long after the bottles had been thrown away. She kissed the soft curve of his cheek.

Heading for her own bedroom, she reached down to hook off her shoes, letting her feet sink soundlessly into the thick pile of the carpet. As her eyes grew accustomed to the dark, she saw, in the four-poster that had become for her a symbol of their married life, the mound of a sleeping form on Rupert's side of the bed.

Did she feel relief that he was home before her, or apprehension? She wasn't sure. 'I'll be very disappointed if you don't wake me up,' he had said on the phone . . .

Silently Becky slipped off her clothes and laid them over a chair. With infinite stealth, she slipped between the sheets, making quite sure not to cross the invisible boundary between her side of the bed and his.

As she drifted into a troubled sleep, the last thought that flashed through Becky's mind was that she was beginning to make a habit of avoiding sex with her husband.

CHAPTER TWO

By the kitchen clock, Adam was due at Launceton Hall in exactly nine minutes. Though it was only eight minutes' drive from the house in medium traffic, Becky wondered crossly why it was that, the closer you lived to your child's school, the later you left in the morning – with the result that you always arrived after the parents who had much farther to travel.

'Brush teeth, wash face, get bookpack,' Becky rattled off to Adam, who was still munching on a piece of toast. Somehow the strawberry jam, instead of going into his mouth, had managed to smear itself all around it.

'I haven't finished my breaf-kast,' Adam said stubbornly, continuing to chew.

'Do as I say!' yelled Becky. 'NOW!'

Lolly stopped clearing the plates and stared at her. Adam's lip began to tremble.

Oh God, thought Becky, I'm doing it again. What's wrong with me?

She sprang to Adam's side just as his face crumpled and he burst into loud wails. Becky clasped his jammy face to her clean pink sweater and tried to shush him. She felt wretched for making him cry, anxious in case his howls woke Rupert. Her husband did not like to be disturbed before nine.

I'm too tired, she thought hopelessly, I shouldn't have tried to get up this morning. But if I let Lolly take Adam to school as well, when would I ever see him?

The clock was edging closer to nine. 'We have to go,' Becky said, gently trying to disentangle herself, but Adam clung on fiercely until Bogey muscled in, licking the tears and the jam from his face. Adam transferred his grip to the dog, burying his face in its furry neck, from which they could still hear the odd muffled sob.

'Please get him to hurry, Lolly,' Becky pleaded. 'I'm going to bring the car to the front door.'

Lolly bore down with some wet kitchen towel. 'There now, silly. Who's a big cry baby, then? Mummy says it's time for school – you let go of that dog now, do you hear?'

Meek as a lamb, Adam peered out from Bogey's curls and raised his face to be sponged. How, Becky wondered, did Lolly manage it?

She pulled on a coat and some sunglasses, less to shield her eyes from the sombre day than to hide the dark circles beneath them. Then she ventured forth onto treacherous pavements.

Adam's teacher Miss Hungerford would not approve of his morning routine. When she'd been for her parent-teacher interview at the end of the previous term, Miss Hungerford had told her sternly, 'Adam's not as independent as he should be. Do you and his nanny do everything for him, or is he being taught to manage certain things by himself?'

'What sort of things?' Becky had asked guiltily, aware of how little time she had to teach Adam anything at all.

'Who gets him ready in the morning?'

'That depends how late we are!'

But Miss Hungerford was not to be deflected by her weak attempts at humour. 'Adam should be encouraged to dress himself and organise his own things for school. If you have no time in the morning, maybe you should get him to put out his uniform the night before.'

That was great in theory, but how many mothers were that organised? Becky wondered. Usually she was grateful just as long as everything got done – whoever was responsible.

When she pulled up in front of the house, Adam was ready and waiting, though Becky knew it was thanks to Lolly's efforts and not his own. Lolly fastened him into the rear seatbelt, and Becky took off with a squeal of rubber, much like the Porsche driver of the night before. If he'd encountered her this morning instead, he'd have had a far better chance of finding out what her BMW was really capable of.

'Are we late again, Mummy?' Adam demanded.

Becky fervently hoped not. If they were, she would get another of those dreaded little notes. 'It has come to our attention that Adam was late for school several times this week . . .' And of course it would go down in the end of year report. 'Number of absences: 30 (8%). Number of times late: 25 (7%).' It made Becky feel like a naughty child herself.

Glancing at Adam in the rearview mirror, Becky noticed that he was scratching with a finger in his wavy blond curls. 'Mummy,' he asked, 'what are nits?'

Becky slammed her foot on the brake harder than she had intended, narrowly avoiding being rammed in the rear by a Volkswagen Estate. 'Why do you ask? Is your head itchy?'

'Angus Mackenzie's mother had to fetch him early yesterday. Miss Hungerford said he had nits.'

Becky shuddered. The thought of those revolting creatures crawling over her son's scalp made her want to be sick. How was it possible that, in a modern hygienic society, with fresh running water and piped sanitation and regular rubbish collection, a child could come home from his nice private school full of nice middle-class children with head lice in his hair?

'You haven't told me, darling,' she beseeched. 'Is your head itchy?'

'I don't know. If I have nits, will you come and fetch me early too?'

Becky felt the stab of guilt, like a bird pecking at her entrails. Reaching behind her, she squeezed her son's leg. His expression in the rearview mirror was old beyond his years. He knew she would not come. It was Lolly who fetched him when they phoned from the office because he had a sore tummy or had cut his knee falling off the climbing frame.

Launceton Hall was looming up ahead. There was no time for empty words of comfort. There was never enough time . . . Becky screeched up in front of the school and stopped on a yellow line. Praying no clampers were about, she leaped out and freed Adam from his seatbelt. Clutching his bookpack, she set off with him at a run.

Miss Hungerford stared with amazement at the jammy fingermarks she had forgotten to wipe off her sweater when Becky delivered Adam to her at six minutes past nine. Then she handed

Becky a notice – an official warning that there were head lice in the school and all parents should check their children's hair.

As Becky drove home, she made a mental note that, sometime in today's frantic schedule, she must fit in a trip to the pharmacy to buy one of those nasty smelling potions promising to de-nit your child in only fifteen minutes.

Lolly used the good serrated knife to cut the oranges in half. Then she began to rummage patiently through the backs of drawers for the manual squeezer. She would leave his usual glass of fresh orange for Rupert to find when he came downstairs – just like she did every morning, when Becky had left to do the school run.

But this time she didn't want to risk waking him with the whine of the electric machine. He'd got in late last night, probably had a bit of a hangover. He might not want to get up at his usual time.

Her searching fingers closed around a bulbous glass shape. Triumphantly she withdrew it and ran it under the tap to remove the grime of long neglect. It looked grossly old-fashioned but she reckoned it would do the trick.

She placed the first orange half over the hump and began to twist it back and forth, till a thin trickle of juice ran down underneath. Her slender arms were taut with the effort. It was harder work than she'd expected, but she didn't mind.

Strictly speaking, her job only required her to prepare Adam's food. Becky had told her to leave her and Rupert to fend for themselves, but it wasn't right, really, a man having to squeeze his own breakfast juice because his wife hadn't the time. Men were no good at that sort of thing, in Lolly's experience. Men needed looking after.

Nervously, she glanced down at the tartan miniskirt and black tights she'd put on this morning, after a lot of agonising between them and the lycra pedal pushers with luminous green trim. She prayed she didn't look too naff. Rupert had such a good eye when it came to clothes, if he thought she looked silly, she'd just *die*.

Not that she *really* cared for his opinion. He was old – nearly thirty-two – what did he know about fashion? Becky was thirty-four, and she was always too busy to bother much about how she looked, but somehow it didn't seem to matter, she always dressed simply and right. And she had a good heart, really, even if she wasn't around enough for her husband and child. There weren't many employers, Lolly knew, who were as tolerant and kind as Becky.

The glass was almost full now, and her arm was aching. She was reaching over to pour in the last few drops when a hand closed over hers.

'Is that mine?' Rupert asked in her ear.

Her throat was too dry to answer. She kept her face turned away so he wouldn't see the tell-tale flush spreading up her neck and face.

'You're a good girl.' Rupert let her hand go and picked up the glass, but it was a whole two minutes before she felt her blush had faded enough to risk sneaking a sideways look at him.

He had been in the shower and the sheer physical presence of him, the aroma of his soap and aftershave, filled the room. He was wearing a thick sweatshirt with matching exercise shorts. Everything he wore looked so cool. Glancing shyly at the contoured muscles of his legs, she wished, would have given anything, if hers weren't so long and spindly. She must look to him like some skinny child.

'Excellent.' He put down his empty glass and smiled at her, a gleam of amusement in his eye. 'But why on earth did you use that ancient old squeezer? Haven't you heard of the labour-saving joys of electricity?'

Lolly mumbled something about having to make Adam's bed and fled from the room. He was laughing at her. He thought she was stupid. She just wanted to *die*.

Rupert required his daily life to have a certain rhythm. At Heath Park, the ancestral home, a bell had summoned the family to meals served at hours which never varied. The silver was polished religiously on Thursdays. Saturday nights the children were always allowed to stay up for an extra hour. The predictable ebb and flow of domestic routine had made him feel protected and secure.

With the loss of Heath Park had come restlessness and discordance till Becky had brought a new logic to his world. Not that Becky was either tidy or predictable. But she breathed a purpose into their existence which gave it a natural shape and path.

Now he had her and Lolly and Mrs Christos, their Brazilian

cleaning lady. Mrs Christos came every Tuesday and Friday. Between them they kept his surroundings ordered, his shirts cleaned, his orange juice squeezed fresh every morning. Behind every man, he believed, there should be three such women.

He always rose at nine. After his shower, switched to maximum so the hot, needle-sharp water drummed the tension from his shoulders, he went down for breakfast in the huge country kitchen that opened onto a garden filled with roses and flowering shrubs. It was a room always awash with colour, even on the dullest winter day, from the bright Clarice Cliff china on the Dutch dresser to the bunches of dried flowers hanging from the ceiling. Here family meals were eaten, family discussions held, here Adam curled up in the pile of cushions on the small sofa to hear his favourite stories, and Bogey slept in a tattered basket by the Rayburn. It was, Becky always said, her favourite room in the house and the one in which, when at home, she was usually to be found.

Breakfast for Rupert consisted of half a cup of muesli with plain yogurt and a drizzle of honey, followed by twenty minutes behind the pages of the *Telegraph*. He had just started on the editorial when Becky swept into the kitchen like a hat blown in on a breeze. 'Hi,' she said, 'it's bloody freezing out there.' She planted a cold kiss on his nose.

'Tone it down, would you,' he winced. 'You know how I loathe all that energy first thing in the morning.'

'Sorry.' She threw down her coat and bag in a heap on the floor. Rupert eyed them balefully. He couldn't bear mess, she knew that too.

When Mrs Christos came banging in with the brooms and the brushes, he was on the verge of losing his temper. Her scowl stopped him, as her eyes fell on his bare legs protruding from skin-tight exercise shorts. Her eyebrows snapped together into a solid black line like an exclamation mark as she muttered darkly under her breath in Portuguese.

It wouldn't do to upset Mrs Christos. Rupert swung the offending limbs under cover of the table and beamed the full wattage of his smile on her. 'Be a dear, Mrs C, go and start on one of the other rooms first.'

'Plenty to do in the kitchen,' she grumbled, eyeing the build-up from breakfast and the bits of chewed stick that Bogey had left scattered all over the floor.

'Of course, but the bedrooms are horrid as well,' Becky said, gently guiding her towards the door. 'We've been so longing for you to come and sort them out.'

'Hrrmph!' Mrs Christos snorted, appeased for the moment. Giving a final scowl at Rupert, she took up her brooms with a martyred air and scurried off.

'Better have a word with her about the sitting-room sofa,' Rupert said with an edge of irritation to his voice. 'There are dog hairs all over it again.'

'Oh dear. Naughty Bogey!'

The offending animal looked up with one eye at the sound of his name, and thumped his tail.

'Something has to be done about it, Becky,' Rupert insisted impatiently. 'That animal shouldn't be allowed in the rest of the house. I knew this would happen – I warned you against having a dog . . .'

He had, as Becky remembered quite well, but Adam was animal crazy and she had been determined he should have pets of his own to love. So Bogey had made his enthusiastic entrance into their lives, with the inevitable casualties to Rupert's collector's items. But Becky had no regrets, despite the many rows. Adam and Bogey loved one another with a blind devotion that compensated in some small way for the lack of another child in the house.

'I'll have another go with the obedience training,' Becky said placatingly.

Rupert watched her head for the coffee machine and her first caffeine intake of the day. He had long since given up trying to talk her out of her unhealthy habits. She just smiled in that sweet, absent way of hers and carried on doing what she'd always done. You couldn't win an argument, he'd discovered, when the other person never argued back.

She was looking peaky – dark smudges under the green eyes, milky skin a shade paler. 'Another bad night?' he enquired.

She gave a small nod.

'You should have woken me. I'd have found a way to relax you.'

'I tried to,' she said quickly, 'but you were sleeping too deeply.'

So that was how she was going to play it. He'd only just made it to bed himself when she came in last night, and he'd been waiting for her to reach out for him – till he realised she was deliberately keeping her distance. Sod her, he'd thought. He'd had a heavy night too. He could do without it if she could.

But he felt as though she'd thrown a stone into a calm pool, and ripples of doubt were spreading out into the once quiet corners of his mind. He'd grown so used to the fact of her love, her physical responsiveness, that he almost hadn't noticed, till her little white lie of a moment ago, how infrequent their actual love-making had become. Even so, he couldn't quite believe that she had begun not to need him any more.

Not that he needed her either, he told himself sharply. There were plenty of other fish in the sea. He remembered the blatant come-ons from a queue of creamy-skinned blondes and dusky brunettes at the club the previous evening. He pictured again the flush that had spread up Lolly's neck when he captured her hand. He was far from losing his touch.

'Did you sort out your little problem last night?' he asked coolly.

Becky shifted uncomfortably, like a worm on a hook. She didn't want to talk about last night, not without being sure of a sympathetic hearing. The trouble was, if she didn't tell him, someone else would.

She opened her mouth . . . and shut it again. Rupert raised an eyebrow.

'Do I take it Ross Piper's giving you a run for your money?'

'He was drunk. We had to cancel the shoot.'

'What rotten luck. Still, that's what you get when you'd rather work with Yankee has-beens than your own husband.'

'Rupert, that's unfair and you know it!' Becky exploded. He understood as well as she did how the game was played. To raise money for a film, you had to have a star attached – and because the US was the biggest market, that usually meant an American star. She didn't make the rules, and Rupert knew she wasn't in a strong enough position yet to break them.

And yet she longed to help him, to hold out a hand and pull him from the mire of bitterness and apathy into which he was sinking. 'Be patient,' she said, 'it won't always be like this. Next time . . .'

Her words died with the withering look on his face. He would not allow her to fob him off, to relieve her guilt with empty promises. But why, she asked herself, did she feel guilty – why was he so determined to lay his failures at her door?

'Do you have any idea,' he drawled, 'what the word "loyalty" means?'

This again – this, after all she had tried to do. 'It means,' she said coldly, 'that you disapprove of me working to keep a roof over our heads – unless that work is of direct benefit to your flagging career.'

In the long and ominous silence that followed, Becky bent her head and traced meaningless doodles in the butter with the scimitar blade of the knife. The dish was a piece of Worcester porcelain from the late eighteenth century, Rupert's favourite period, with a fat contented calf lying sideways to form the handle of the lid. They had found it on a trip to Devon, in those early days of being in love with the world and with their lives and with each other.

'You're not the only one with a problem,' she said finally. 'I also have a breaking point, and I may just have reached it. I'm doing silly things . . .'

'At least you're doing *something*.'

She felt dull with defeat. She had tried to reach him, to tell him of her transgression, but he wouldn't let her, and the moment had passed. In his current mood of resentment, she didn't feel up to facing his judgement.

Into the tense silence ambled a cheerfully grinning Todd, all easy good nature and vacuous goodwill. 'Hi, you guys. Lolly let me in – what a babe! Ready for action, Rupe?'

Bogey growled and raised his hackles, earning instant Brownie points with Becky. 'What's the action this time?' she enquired with more than a hint of sarcasm.

Todd looked at her with amazement, as though the answer were obvious. 'You know – the Riverside.' He was referring to a trendy Chelsea health club by the Thames, for which Becky paid the outrageously expensive family membership, though she seldom got a chance to use it. 'Coupla circuits, little sesh on the sunbeds.'

'Sounds like a heavy schedule!'

Rupert smiled at Todd with genuine warmth. 'Pull up a pew. Fancy some muesli?'

'No thanks.' Todd patted his washboard stomach. 'Gotta count the old calories. Swimsuit shoot in the Caribbean next week.'

'Lucky old you.' Rupert rose and gathered up his kit. 'I could do with getting away myself.'

Becky watched as her husband strolled out, one arm draped casually over Todd's shoulder, without giving her so much as a backward glance. She wanted to call after him to please buy the nit lotion but she didn't dare. Besides, he would probably forget.

Anthea Brockenhurst banged two liberal spoons of sugar into her coffee and stirred vigorously. Her wrists had the fine-boned strength of a woman bred to the rigours of riding excitable mounts to hounds.

'You did it,' she announced to Becky, 'because you really wanted to hit Rupert.'

'I did not—'

' 'Course you did. Most husbands want hitting. The day I floored Simon was absolute bliss!' The occasion in question was when Anthea discovered that the mistress he'd installed in the company flat – the third, it turned out, the well-qualified and well-endowed head of his credit management department – was carrying his love child.

'Just fancy,' Anthea marvelled at Becky, 'and I thought he loathed blue-stockings.'

She and her two children lived in the house next door to Becky's, where she occupied her time as a housewife and passionate amateur gardener. Simon had been packed off to the company flat and the antenatal breathing classes. The second thing Anthea had done, after dumping his bags in the discreetly furnished foyer of the bank of which he was a director, was to take a solo trip to Italy on his credit card. She came back laden down with souvenir statuettes of Michelangelo's David and assorted Roman nudes, and proceeded to chop off their private parts with a chisel. These mementos were now positioned at strategic points all over her house, on Chinese lacquered cabinets and Chippendale sideboards and Victorian wash stands.

'Don't you think it's a bit rough on Joshua and Hugo?' Becky had ventured, worrying about the effect on Anthea's teenage sons.

'Nonsense! I'd do it to them too, if I thought it would stop the rot. But they'd still have all those Y-chromosomes swimming round, so what would be the point?'

She rummaged in Becky's biscuit tin for something to dunk. 'Jaffa cakes. Heavenly! What do you think of my hair? I tried to do the highlights myself – Frederico will kill me.'

She looked, Becky thought, rather like a badger – wide blond streaks through dark grey. 'I know,' Anthea cried, 'you don't have to say anything – it's a fright. But I can't go spending a hundred quid right now, not till the settlement comes through. Simon's being simply beastly about it, of course.'

'It must be awful,' Becky said. 'I'm so sorry.'

'Don't be. He snored like a sawmill, you know. Let him keep Miss Credit Management awake every night – that'll teach her.'

Becky wondered what it would be like, not having Rupert beside her in bed. Was that the next step, after avoiding sex? Was that when your husband started looking at other women? It made her feel cold just thinking about it. She could not, would not believe their love for each other was in question. They were going through a period of adjustment, that was all. And she did *not* want to hit him.

'We're trying to make some silly arrangement about the house in the country,' Anthea was saying. 'Alternate weekends – that's the latest from the leeches' – her name for the lawyers. 'Imagine, I'll be tripping over pushchairs again when I got rid of mine ten years ago.' She paused to nibble at a Jaffa cake. 'Have you ever caught Rupert being unfaithful?' she asked suddenly.

Becky flushed, as though her treacherous thoughts had been uttered out loud. 'I'm sure he's never done anything like that.'

'Heavens, darling, they're all capable of it, and you give Rupert more opportunity than most. All those nights working late . . . and as for that little nanny of yours, she's far too young and pretty and I'm not going to say "I-told-you-so" but I did warn you before you ever took her on.'

Lolly chose that moment to wander through with a load of Adam's washing. Both women stole a glance at her endlessly long legs in black tights beneath the tartan miniskirt, and her abundant curly brown hair tied up in a ponytail above a perky face unlined by age.

As soon as she'd passed through into the utility room, Anthea hissed, 'Fire her today and get some middle-aged hag from *The Lady.*'

Becky laughed. And then, just as suddenly, she felt like crying. Because the people she loved and the job she loved had always made her world seem safe – but not any more.

* * *

Alex Goddard glanced out of the window of his book-lined office at the constant motion on the Strand down below. It was almost twelve thirty and he had been at his desk since six that morning. He shifted his weight to stretch cramped limbs, anticipating a brisk lunchtime walk and some fresh air to blow the cobwebs from his brain.

'Are you listening, Alex?' a petite and well preserved woman in her late forties demanded. She was poured into a tight-fitting skirt and bodice top which would have been a daunting challenge to a girl half her age.

'I always give you my undivided attention, Claire,' Alex said soothingly. On most days, it was true. Claire Kinghorn was theatre royalty, not a woman to expect anything less than complete concentration from her agent or her public.

'I mean, it's a magnificent role, and of course I'm flattered, but do you really think I look young enough to play Cleopatra?' She took out a powder compact and studied her English rose complexion in the mirror. It had undoubtedly worn very well.

' "Age cannot wither her" – that's how Shakespeare's Mark Antony describes Cleopatra. The same could be said of you, Claire.'

'Hmm.' She snapped the compact shut. 'In other words, I *am* old but I don't look it. Still, I'll take that as the compliment I assume you intended . . . Now, about the money they're offering . . .'

'Claire, this is the Royal Shakespeare Company,' Alex said reasonably. 'Money is not the only consideration.'

'Tell that to my bank manager,' Claire snorted.

Money and youth and beauty and ego, these were the burning issues Alex dealt with every day. What was the going rate per pound of flesh for an aging actress who could still deliver the goods? 'I'll go back to them,' he said, 'and see if they're willing to improve their offer.'

'You really are the best, darling.' She leaned forward, giving him more than a glimpse of what was still one of the finest bosoms to grace the British stage. 'I know you can talk them up a bit, I'm counting on you. Now I'll have to love you and leave you or I'll be late for my masseuse.'

As Alex closed the door firmly behind her, his stately old red setter, companion of many years, thumped his tail hopefully from his basket in the corner. He knew it was almost time for his midday walk. As Alex for once had no business engagement, he planned to do the honours himself.

Usually, if he had an important studio head or director to entertain, it would be lunch at the nearby Savoy Grill where the head waiter kept a table for him and knew which cuts of meat he preferred. If it was a young actor, a potential client, he would take him down to a bistro or Japanese sushi bar in the more bohemian Covent Garden. It charmed him, constantly enthralled him, to work in the heart of this great city, surrounded by so much choice.

He was born in a picture-pretty suburb of Los Angeles, where his work-driven father founded International Artists Management, the talent agency that had grown into a force to be reckoned with in the film industry. His mother, a would-be starlet, had lacked staying power when it came to both her career and her difficult husband, and ran off with the landscape gardener when Alex was eight. There followed a succession of East Coast boarding schools, whose rarefied and academic air had been sweeter to Alex's lungs than the brash and smog-filled atmosphere of his home town. At Harvard he studied officially for his Master of Business Administration, and unofficially lost himself in the histories of great and ancient civilisations: the Egyptians, the Incas, the Elizabethans . . .

When he passed with acceptable grades, his father welcomed him home, the heir apparent to his booming business. Alex had nothing against the film industry, but everything against the plastic paradise of his birth. He asked to make his start in the London office, and his father, though surprised, could think of no particular argument against it.

That was fifteen years ago, and Alex had long headed up what had turned into one of the most profitable arms of his father's empire. While Frank Goddard remained in good health and firm control of the Los Angeles head office, there seemed no particular reason to upset the current arrangement. Alex's father had long since stopped asking him when he planned on coming home.

It was not just England's past but the present way of life of these obstinate and idiosyncratic islands that had Alex in its spell. He adored the quirkiness of the people, when his own countrymen seemed somehow so homogenised, so equal. He loved the British backbone and earthiness. Life was more difficult than in Los Angeles, but it was also more real.

Unfortunately, his wife had not shared his enthusiasm. He had married, in the first flush of love, an aspiring actress named Lara Noble. His father disapproved, claiming that in the light of his own abortive attempt to mix matrimony and showbiz, Alex's plans were a triumph of optimism over experience. Perhaps, Alex was forced to concede later, he was only trying to replace his lost mother. Whatever the motive, the exercise was not a success. Lara did not take to the damp English climate or the reserved English ways, and booked a one-way ticket back to Los Angeles almost two years to the day after she had arrived.

Alex reached for Wellington's lead. The dog was beside him in a single bound, nuzzling wetly against his hand. If they took the route westwards, they would come to Trafalgar Square with its imposing structures of the National Gallery and Nelson's Column. A swing to the south would bring them to Whitehall and Downing Street. Accustomed as he was to these sights, Alex still felt a thrill of awe at the great ghosts of the past which they conjured up.

But Wellington preferred the route through the Victoria Embankment Gardens, where they could rest in the shadow of Cleopatra's Needle, and watch the boats ply up the Thames.

There was a discreet knock on the door and Belinda, his secretary, stuck her head around it. 'There's someone here to see you.'

Alex had no intention of seeing anyone who hadn't made an appointment. 'Who is it?' he enquired, fastening Wellington's lead firmly to his collar.

'Rebecca Carlyle.'

'Show her in,' Alex said without hesitation, unclipping the lead and ignoring the dejected droop of Wellington's tail.

'Don't act up,' Belinda scolded the dog. 'I'll take you out, you know I will.' She relieved Alex of both animal and lead, and went to fetch Mrs Carlyle.

He would take her to lunch at the Savoy's River Room, Alex decided, where the light glancing off the river would catch in the gold of her hair.

He had met Becky when she was casting her first film, and

came to Alex, inexperienced and eager, to enlist his help in securing one of his better-known clients as the female lead. It was the start of a friendship that had never faltered. Alex had wanted it to be the start of something more, but he had still been married to Lara at the time.

Then, when he finally woke up to find himself free of his complaining wife, Becky was living with Rupert and expecting his child. If success was in the timing, then Alex knew he had missed his chance. So he put aside his own regrets and resigned himself to friendship, and standing godfather to Becky's child, admiring as he did her stout heart and quiet determination, the way she took on the world and never complained if occasionally it got the better of her. In a business renowned for greed and treachery, she fought for her share but never took anyone else's. In another age, he could picture her as the captain of a great sailing ship, setting out in quest of unknown riches and unimaginable dangers, with nothing but her courage and her principles to sustain her. She was, Alex reflected, everything he admired about this country. She was pure gold.

'I'm not upsetting your well-planned day, am I?' Becky asked, taking a tentative step inside his room.

'I sure hope so.' He felt the smile on his face spreading right through to his heart.

Becky stared out at the glassy flatness of the Thames, reflecting a grey sky. Alex, as always, had managed to secure a window table with a view.

'I'm not expecting you to take my side,' she said. 'Ross Piper is your father's client, your loyalties must be with him. I just want you to help me put this right.'

Alex was gazing down at a pheasant breast in a pale golden gravy with little round crisp potatoes and an artfully arranged clump of greenery to one side. Since she'd started on her story, he hadn't touched it.

She wished he would look up so she could read in his eyes what he was thinking. Did he know, had he guessed, that what had happened was more than an momentary loss of control? That she had been throwing off her former acquiescence, rejecting the status quo?

He seemed so distant, so withdrawn from her, she could take a guess at his thoughts. She had shocked him. A temper – a capacity to strike out physically – had never entered into his picture of who she was.

'Don't,' she begged, wringing a pink napkin in her hands, 'don't be disappointed with me. I couldn't bear it. I'm so ashamed of myself—'

'It's not that.' He seemed to be fishing about helplessly for the words. 'It's the surprise . . . taking it in . . . I mean, are you OK?'

'Shouldn't you be asking if *he's* OK?' she countered, with a weak attempt at a grin.

'Oh, he'll live – I think we both know that. His ego's probably more bruised than his chin. But you . . .' He stared at her, eyes narrowing. 'You wouldn't have done something like that without good reason, no matter how badly he behaved. You'd have written him off as a jerk and walked away. What happened, Becky?'

If he kept on looking at her that way, with those kind brown eyes brimming with concern, she would burst into tears. He had always been so good to her, from the day she went trembling to his office, trying to sign up one of his star clients for her first film because, with a name attached, she would have some chance of raising the money. She was terrified, her head buzzing with industry jokes about fearsome agents like the late great Swifty Lazar. ('It's safe to go swimming in the ocean with Swifty. Sharks don't attack their own kind.') And Alex Goddard *had* been overpowering, but only because of the bigness of his heart. He had come through for her then, and she had got used to thinking he always would.

He would be forty next birthday, and he had the solid air of someone who had achieved much and was comfortable in his own skin. Even his good clothes seemed to mould easily to his form, taking on more of his own personality than the designer's. He was her touchstone and her best friend, and of all the consequences of this mess she had made, losing Alex's good opinion was the one she feared most.

She owed him an explanation of some kind. At least she had to try. 'It just felt, all of a sudden, like I'd been saying "yes" to people for too long, letting them get away with things they shouldn't get away with, and just once, I had to say "no".'

'I'm glad, then,' Alex said, 'if those were your reasons.'

'What do you mean? You're saying I wasn't wrong?'

'No, but it takes a lot of courage to admit being wrong – to face up to something inside you that's been telling you for a long time things have to change . . .'

'I don't know,' Becky said firmly, 'what you mean.'

He picked up his knife and began to play at cutting up the pheasant breast. 'OK, then, let's work on some damage limitation.'

Becky felt an overwhelming sense of relief. If this could be fixed, then Alex would fix it, without raised voices or histrionics, but with the quiet effectiveness that was his trademark.

'Ross might walk off the picture,' Alex said, 'or he might press charges. Both options will be pretty rough on you. But he won't do either till he's spoken to L.A.'

'Will you speak to L.A. too?' Becky asked, knowing already that he would.

'My advice will be,' Alex pronounced more firmly, 'that publicity on this thing won't look good for Ross either. The word is already out on his drinking. If he ends up closing down your movie, other producers will run scared – it could be the end of his career.'

Deep in the numbness of her heart, Becky was beginning to feel a little warm ray of hope.

'Anyway, let's not jump the gun,' Alex continued. 'If he went on a real bender last night, for all we know he'll wake up not remembering a thing that happened.'

For a moment Becky allowed herself to clutch at this straw, to believe in the possibility of an undeserved reprieve. But life wasn't really like that. There were always consequences.

'I'm going to see him after I leave you,' she said. 'I'll let you know if you have to come charging to the rescue.'

He gave her a comical grin of sympathy. She wanted to smile back, to say exactly the right thing to convey her gratitude, but she didn't have the words.

The Hyde Park Hotel was a grand English establishment in the old style, with high ceilings and heavy antique furniture. As Becky made her way through the lofty foyer towards the lifts, she began to pray that amnesia had struck Ross Piper after all.

She had rung Sandra before visiting Alex, to be told that Mr Piper was still sleeping and could not be disturbed. Sandra had sounded overwhelmed by the turn events had taken. Becky had made her promise to empty the mini-bar and hold the fort till she could get there, though she had little faith in the girl's ability to control her strong-willed employer.

Now, when she knocked, the door to the suite swung open and Sandra stood there, wide-eyed at the possibility of another confrontation. 'He's awake,' she confirmed in an awed whisper.

Becky forced her feet not to respond to the message of flight from her brain. Instead she propelled herself forward into the lavishly furnished sitting room, where her eye came to rest on the untouched breakfast trolley. Only the coffee cup had been used, its dregs a sludgy black. Next to it was a half-drunk glass of water and the discarded wrappers of some Panadol Extra Strong. The signs, she conceded, did not augur well.

The bedroom door burst open and Ross Piper strode through in a white hotel towelling robe, rubbing his salt and pepper hair with a towel. He stopped when he saw Becky, and his clear blue eyes seemed to bore right through her.

'I came,' she said, before her courage deserted her completely, 'to apologise.'

He didn't reply straightaway. If she looked hard, she could see the faint discolouration where her knuckles had connected with the corner of his mouth.

'What I did was quite unforgivable,' she continued bravely.

'Bull!' The blue eyes were twinkling. 'I asked for it – been asking for it for years, only no one had the guts to give it to me before.'

'You're not angry?' Her voice was faint with hope. Sandra's eyes bulged in disbelief.

Ross Piper threw back his head and roared with gusty laughter. He dabbed at the corners of his eyes with the towel. 'Young lady, I haven't enjoyed myself so much in years. If you could've seen what you looked like, all five foot nothing of you, swinging that punch – like an itty bitty terrier going for a prize bull. Lord, I wish the cameras had been rolling!' He shook again with mirth.

Becky found herself smiling too. 'I suppose it *was* a bit ridiculous—'

'Fantastic! I thought they didn't make 'em like you any more. Will you marry me?'

'No – but I'll make a great movie with you. Deal?'

He subsided onto a chair and took a pack of cigarettes from the pocket of his robe. When he had lit one, he puffed on it for a few moments, his expression more sombre now, and guarded. 'I haven't done any good work in years,' he said at last. 'Got a bit too fond of the old juice. Do you think I can still hack it?'

Becky was touched beyond words that he, with his great fame and achievements, should ask her this. 'It's all still in there somewhere,' she assured him, 'like never forgetting how to ride a bicycle. You just have to get in touch with it again.'

He flashed her a bitter-sweet smile, full of self-knowledge. 'I'll need a doctor.'

'You'll have one,' she promised. 'And if I can be any help, you'll have me too.'

'That,' he said, meeting her level green gaze, 'might be quite something.'

CHAPTER THREE

'You're always locked in his trailer,' Jeremy complained. 'Ross Piper isn't the only one with problems, you know. I can never find you when I need you.'

'What do you need me for?' Becky asked patiently.

He grasped her hand. His fingers were long and cool to the touch. Artist's hands . . . Yet he was dressed more like a soldier, in leather aviator jacket and thick army boots – a brave young warrior inspiring his troops, taking them over the rim of the trench and on to glory.

'You know what I need,' he said fervently. 'I need *you*.'

She tried to pull away, but he tightened his grip. His hands were surprisingly strong. They were standing some way off from the crew, who were busy setting up for the last shot of the day, but she was afraid someone might see.

'I just want you to give me some support. I feel like you're leaving me to sink or swim.'

He was so young, Becky reminded herself, to have these responsibilities thrust onto him. Although he had already made quite a name for himself in television when she first became aware of his work, directing his first feature film had catapulted him into a different league. And it was she who had insisted on having him, sweet-talking Ross Piper's agent, bulldozing Stanley Shiplake.

But now Becky questioned her wisdom in taking Jeremy on. It wasn't his work – that was as good as she'd known it would be – but he was so needy, so insistent on having his hand held. Since the incident in Ross Piper's trailer, he had also developed an endearing but inconvenient tendency to put her on a pedestal.

'I *am* here for you,' Becky sighed, 'but I have to distribute my time between a lot of other people. You know that.'

'They all want a share of you because you have so much to give, so much strength and courage. But I want more . . .'

He was gazing at her intently with puppy-brown eyes. Even his spiky hair seemed to droop a little, as though less sure of itself. His pierced right earlobe held a slim gold hoop, inspiring in her the slightly disapproving feelings of a mother towards a rebellious teenage son. He was almost ten years younger than she and yes, she was flattered by his adoration, but she didn't really want it, did she?

She let her hand lie in his just a moment longer.

'Ready for you, Jeremy!' the first assistant director bellowed.

Becky jumped. Reluctantly Jeremy released her hand. Then, just as she thought he was going, he turned back and opened his mouth as if to say something more. She waited long seconds but he only shook his head and stamped away, kicking furiously at the odd stone in his path.

'You're very thick with the American these days,' Sir Humphrey grumbled, fiddling crossly with his seatbelt which wouldn't sit right over his bulky overcoat. He was in Becky's passenger seat after grudgingly accepting a lift home, though he'd assured her he wasn't so old yet that he couldn't find his own way.

'You're the second person who's complained about me and Ross Piper. What nobody seems to mention is that he's giving his best performance in years.'

Sir Humphrey gave her a lewd grin. 'So what's he like in bed, then?'

'You're a dirty old man,' Becky said mildly, 'and you know perfectly well I'm not sleeping with him.'

'Aha – so it's young Jeremy you're encouraging, is it?'

With mock primness Becky said, 'Let me remind you that I'm a happily married woman.' She paused, then added, 'Well, married anyway.'

Sir Humphrey wrapped his scarf tighter round his stringy throat. Subtly, while he was fussing with its fringes, Becky turned up the heating.

'I don't know what's wrong with you youngsters,' he barked. 'In my day on a film set, everyone was at it. Now the only relationships people seem to have are with personal fitness trainers and fellow members of Alcoholics Anonymous. It's all such a dead bore!'

'You keep the old traditions alive, though,' Becky remarked, scanning the warren of streets around Victoria for the name Humphrey had given her. 'Helena from wardrobe was complaining to me today about how she suddenly found your hand up her skirt when she was fitting your wig.'

'Bah – she loved every minute of it!'

It was no use, Becky knew, trying to teach an old dog new tricks. He would simply never understand about sexual harassment in the workplace. His life had spanned over three generations, most of his contemporaries were dead, and he was stubbornly trying to hold on to some habits from the bad old days. Helena had been more amused than offended.

Or so she said. When Becky had walked into the production office earlier on, to find Letitia in the thick of a small group, they had all suddenly gone quiet, and Becky was struck with the absolute conviction that they had been talking about her. Letitia's nose had been out of joint ever since Becky had emerged so unscathed from her indiscretion over Ross Piper. But then Helena had chirped up that they'd just been talking about Sir Humphrey, such a naughty old man, sticking his hands where they had no business, and at his age too, and the awkward moment had passed.

Becky nosed her car into a space outside Sir Humphrey's building. He seemed reluctant to get out. 'I hope you're going to offer the chauffeur a drink,' she teased.

'Got nothing to give you,' he grumbled, but he looked pleased.

His flat was on the first floor and, as he climbed the stairs, Becky listened with concern to his laboured breathing. He fumbled with the keys and made a great show of complaining about the poor lighting when he tried the wrong one first.

When he finally flung the door open, he announced in theatrical tones that would have carried right up to the gods, 'Welcome to my humble abode.'

It was, Becky noted, humble indeed, with the temporary look of rented accommodation, the furniture of an anonymous traditional style bordering on shabby. The only personal touches were the shelves full of well-thumbed books and the memorabilia of Sir Humphrey's glory days in the theatre – golden statuettes, framed reviews, photographs with a young Queen, with Vivien Leigh, with Sir Peter Hall.

Sir Humphrey looked tired. He had done three scenes today, with his usual wit and flair. He sank into a wing chair without even taking off his coat. 'See if there's some white wine in the fridge, there's a good girl.'

Becky switched on the electric fire in the grate, then headed for the kitchen. She was glad of the few moments alone – she would not for the world have him see the pity on her face. But it was infinitely sad to her that this great man, who had brought so much pleasure into the lives of so many, had so little to go home to himself.

The fridge contained only a carton of eggs, some butter, a brie that was wilting, and a half full bottle of wine. She hooked out the bottle and took it back to the sitting room.

Sir Humphrey accepted a glass and waved it at his surroundings. 'I know what you're thinking. It's not much, is it? But it's the life, you see. You choose the life and it takes you over. Always on tour, or on some film set, or working late nights. No time to make a home, no one to come home to. Your marriages break up, your children get used to living without you. Take heed, my girl, you're on the same path. This could be your own future you're looking at.'

Tears swam in Becky's eyes. This was it, she thought. This was the nameless fear against which she had struck out in mindless rage. This was the fate she dreaded.

'You're not very good at this, are you, Mummy?' Adam looked faintly condescending as he added two more cards to his growing pile.

They were sitting cross-legged on her bedroom floor playing the Memory Game, about forty small cards with animal pictures laid out face down in a square between them. The object of the exercise was to turn up two cards per go, and try to remember the position of an animal so that when you found its mate, you could claim both. Becky, so far, had only a single pair.

'The mind's going,' Becky grimaced. 'I'm getting old, that's what.'

'You don't look all that bad. But you should go to the gym, like Princess Di.'

'Which shirt do you think I should wear?' Rupert held two up for her inspection: a crisply ironed plain white one and another with a thick dark blue stripe. As she sized them up, Adam rugby tackled a *bergère* nursing chair – one of Rupert's triumphant discoveries from their country auction days – bringing the whole thing toppling down on top of him.

'Stop that!' Becky scolded, casting a nervous eye at Rupert, whose nostrils had flared in fury.

'I'm bored,' Adam shouted, trying to use the upside down chair as a slide. 'You're not playing properly.'

'Will you control that bloody kid!'

'Daddy said a rude word,' Adam whooped triumphantly. 'Say "Sorry, God." '

Becky held Adam to her with one arm and carefully righted the chair with the other. 'You should wear the one with the stripe,' she said soothingly to Rupert. It would bring out the blue of his eyes. He was going to an audition for a new play, a piece by an unknown writer which would start life as an out-of-town run at the Royal Theatre in Bath, and transfer to the West End if the audiences and critical reaction were good enough. She could tell from his irritation level that he was nervous.

'It's your turn, Mummy,' Adam nagged, looking ominously ready for another tackle. Quickly Becky turned over the tiger. Now where had she seen the other one . . . ?

'There, silly.' Adam flashed her a cross look that said she wasn't trying hard enough. She was adding the tigers to her meagre pile when her mobile phone began to ring. She frowned. Most calls to her mobile were business and today there was no scheduled shoot. Today she was home, like everyone else, enjoying some time with her child.

'Don't answer it,' Adam begged, trying to kick it away.

She looked up at Rupert. He shrugged. She stared at the phone. It continued to ring. She knew, with a sinking of her heart, that she would not have the courage to ignore it.

'I'll be quick – I promise.' Avoiding her son's accusing look, she snatched it up.

'I want to see you in my office *right away*,' Stanley Shiplake's voice boomed across the ether. It wasn't a request, it was an order. She wouldn't have the courage to ignore that either, not when it was Stanley's money footing the bills. It's the life, Sir Humphrey had said, it takes you over . . .

Rupert had put on a navy blue jacket with gold buttons. He was almost ready to go. This job, if he got it, would barely bring in enough to pay Lolly's salary.

'Rupert, would you mind terribly . . .'

His eyes held a dangerous glitter. 'Yes?'

'Would you mind asking Lolly if she can babysit again – just for a few hours?'

A little of the tension eased out of his shoulders. 'Fine,' he said curtly, and headed for the door.

Rupert took the stairs two at a time, down to the basement level. His thoughts were not pleasant companions. He knew what Becky had been about to ask him. Fortunately for her she'd thought better of it.

He peered into the sitting room of the self-contained nanny flat. There was no one about. If Lolly was out, he decided, it was Becky's problem, not his. He shouldn't even be here, he should be cocooned in the quiet of his car, running through his lines.

Peering through the half open door to the bedroom, Rupert saw a pair of slim bare legs sprawled across the bed. Discreetly he knocked, and the legs moved. He pushed the door wider.

Lolly was just stirring from sleep, her eyes fluttering open, her brown curls tumbling chaotically across the pillows. She was dressed in a T-shirt that barely covered the tops of her legs. She looked, he thought, exposed and vulnerable and adorably young.

As she gazed up at Rupert, her eyes half-focused, he knew she was in that state between sleep and wakefulness when the inhibitions haven't yet come back into play. A gentle smile lifted the corners of her mouth, and she stretched out her arms as though to welcome him into them. She looked as if she were still dreaming, as if her dream had finally come true.

He stared down at her, and the sheer temptation of her was almost overwhelming. How easily he could lose himself in her longing, wrap himself in those coltish limbs and forget what she hadn't yet learned – the disillusion of youthful expectations, the disappointment with oneself and one's life.

But he still had a life, and he wasn't ready to give it up yet. This was his home, his castle, and a wise man didn't open the door and invite trouble to come in and shake its very foundations.

She saw his hesitation and suddenly she was fully awake, a flush spreading over her cheeks. She pulled herself into a sitting position, tucking her legs inside the baggy T-shirt in a sudden fluster of modesty.

The only way to spare her, Rupert knew, was to pretend that he had seen nothing. He pushed down the regret. 'I'm frightfully sorry,' he said, 'but I've come here to take advantage of your good nature yet again.' She looked momentarily confused, and he added, 'Becky's got another urgent meeting, and I have to go to this audition . . .'

She was too unsophisticated to hide the flash of disappointment, but she said quickly, 'It's OK, I'll look after Adam.'

'You're an angel. We'll pay you overtime again, of course.'

He had done his duty and now the tactful thing would be to leave her to get dressed, to get over the embarrassment of her disclosure. That was what Rupert fully intended, but before he realised what he was doing, he found himself bending over her and brushing her damp flushed cheek with his lips.

Upstairs, Adam scuffed his shoes against the chair leg – which made Mummy cross because she said it ruined them – and watched her getting her work clothes out of the cupboard. He didn't like her horrid suits. He liked her soft trousers and woolly jumpers that he could bury his face in. She smelled of all the lovely things in the bottles he wasn't supposed to touch.

She said she wouldn't be gone long, but when she went to work she was always long. Lolly didn't like playing the Memory Game because she never won. Mummy didn't mind not winning.

He would stay up till she came home; he didn't care how long he waited. She'd promised to read him a dinosaur story. Lolly was an OK reader but tonight was supposed to be Mummy's turn.

He glared at the mobile phone, still lying next to her pile of cards. It shouldn't keep calling her away, it shouldn't, it shouldn't . . .

Daddy came in and went straight to Mummy. 'Lolly says it's OK. Wish me luck.' He gave her a hug, the kind Adam sometimes gave her when he'd done something naughty she didn't know about and was feeling a little bit sorry. Then he kissed her on the mouth, and Adam put his hands over his eyes so he wouldn't see, it was so yucky.

They both turned when they heard the crash. Adam stared back at them, and this time he wasn't sorry at all. They came over to the window where he stood, and looked down into the garden two floors below, to where Mummy's mobile phone lay shattered on the paving stones.

As her feet propelled Becky forward into Stanley's office building, her thoughts dragged her back to World's End where she had left Adam snivelling in Lolly's lap, wiping his runny nose with the back of his hand. She hadn't had the heart to scold him.

In the open plan reception, Jeremy and Letitia were waiting in shocking pink armchairs, half-strangled by the plants which Stanley ordered by the square metre and which were instantly replaced by the contractor as soon as a single leaf showed signs of age. Stanley had a fondness for very young secretaries and metaphors about the business jungle.

Becky pictured her pocket handkerchief garden – the rioting rose bushes that were seldom pruned, the ceanothus that thrived and produced their pretty blue flowers even without much watering, and grew to awesome heights if Anthea didn't come over to cut them back. Stanley would not approve of letting things get so out of control.

His secretary Bryony, in tight leather miniskirt, was, like the plants, twined around Jeremy. 'You'd love it down there,' she drawled. 'Two quid a drink, and all the latest sounds . . .'

'Yeah, but who's got the time, know what I mean?' He shrugged, his manner faintly superior. Today he had dressed the part of the arty film director, all in black with oval mirrored sunglasses which he had refused to remove indoors and which gave him the appearance of a giant bug.

'You'd be such a hit,' Bryony persisted. 'They don't let just anyone in, you know, but *you* wouldn't have any trouble . . .'

'I'll have a coffee, thank you, when you can spare the time,' Letitia snapped.

Grudgingly Bryony removed herself from the arm of Jeremy's chair, and instantly he was at Becky's side.

'What's this all about? Why the summons from the great man?'

Letitia, flicking through the latest issue of *Screen International*, raised her head long enough to remark, 'Who knows? There's a very devious brain beneath that follicly challenged scalp.'

It would, Becky was inclined to agree, be a great mistake to underestimate Stanley Shiplake. He had made his now considerable fortune in exploitation movies – low-budget genre films like action and martial arts. He had also made several lucrative forays into the soft-porn market. But that was all in the past, and now he was Mr Respectable, only putting his company's backing behind prestigious A-grade pictures and distributing top American product in the UK. In a notoriously risky business, Stanley was a master at playing the odds. He was as famous for only using other people's money as for waging a mortal vendetta against any journalist foolish enough to ask him about his past.

'Don't worry.' Becky tweaked playfully at Jeremy's ear. 'I'll protect you.'

He scowled, a suspicion in his eye that she was making fun of him. As Bryony came back with Letitia's coffee, rattling the tray with resentment, Jeremy whispered under cover of the clattering china, 'I've missed you.'

'Don't be silly,' Becky said, with a little of the condescension that her power over him allowed. 'You only saw me yesterday.'

'We should count time by heart-throbs.' He grinned. 'I read that somewhere.'

He had caught her unawares. She knew Jeremy's gifts for film – their very familiarity even allowing her to take them for granted – but she had never thought of him as much of a reader. She was still considering him in this new light when Bryony inserted herself between them. 'Mr Shiplake will see you now.' She winked at Jeremy. 'Good luck.'

Stanley had long ago earned the industry nickname of Napoleon, whether for his high-handed dealings or his low stature, no one could now remember. Stanley knew what they called him, and was equally aware that no one would dare say it to his face. Whenever possible he avoided standing to greet people, which usually entailed looking up at them. Now he offered his visitors a seat from behind the vast expanse of his mahogany desk. It was a prop, a way of compensating, a tool of intimidation.

'How are things going on the shoot?' he asked blandly.

He was playing games, and they knew it, and he knew that they knew it.

'As well as can be expected,' Becky replied calmly, knowing he would come to the point when he was good and ready.

'Well, I *don't* agree.' Stanley paused for effect. Jeremy wriggled lower in his seat, the bug eyes glinting.

'I've seen some of the dailies,' Stanley continued, 'and I think things are going a lot *better* than that. To put it plainly, I think we've got ourselves a *winner*.'

Jeremy's antennae came up. Becky stuffed a fist in her mouth to stop herself from giggling. Letitia, finding herself the sole spokesperson, replied, 'How sweet of you, Stanley. Is it safe to say, then, that you like it?'

'I *love* it!' As a light flashed on his desk, Stanley snatched up one of the phones that formed a half-circle around him like a first line of defence. At once he was spouting off about net profit participations and bottom lines, leaving the others to wait patiently for his next prophetic pronouncement.

'Is this bloke for real?' Jeremy muttered.

'Of course not,' Letitia hissed. 'He's a salesman.'

'I just *love* it,' Stanley continued, as though he hadn't missed a beat. 'Ross Piper's *magnificent*. That's where it pays off to hire an old pro. But I believe in taking a chance on young talent too – nurturing it, so to speak. I was *right* all along about you, Jeremy – you're going to be a *star*.'

Jeremy gave a modest shrug. Becky kept a firm grip on her tongue. A matter of only months ago, she had had to fight tooth and nail to make Stanley give Jeremy this break. Time and hindsight had worked their chemistry on his brain, allowing him to take the credit himself.

'We've got the makings of a *hit* on our hands, and that's where *I* come in. I'm going to swing behind this film and market the *hell* out of it.' He zoned in on Jeremy. 'How soon can you get me a director's cut with temporary soundtrack?'

Being in the hot seat made Jeremy defiant. 'Do you want it fast or do you want it good?'

'I want it *yesterday*.' Stanley allowed another pregnant pause. 'I'm going to enter this thing for competition at Cannes. For the Palme d'Or.'

He had their attention now. Even Jeremy couldn't keep his cool in the face of the Palme d'Or. It was fame, fortune, the pot of gold.

Becky tried to keep a tight hold on her conflicting emotions. Getting their film ready for Cannes would mean even less time spent with Adam, even more overtime for Lolly. But she had been working all her life for a break like this, and now that it was within her reach, she was frightened by the intensity with which she wanted it.

Becky dipped speckled quails eggs into gently boiling water. A side of Scotch smoked salmon lay on a serving dish, decoratively presented with sprigs of parsley and lemon wedges. The choice of menu was deliberate, as if by serving Rupert his favourite food, she could somehow make more palatable the conversation she planned to accompany it.

She hummed a few lines from a Beatles' song, the one about her troubles seeming far away. She felt filled with the rich blessings of her life. After weeks of uncertainty, of feeling she had allowed herself to drift into uncharted waters, out of reach of Rupert and even her former self, she suddenly felt in control again. She had thought serious thoughts, made far-reaching plans, decided what had to be done.

When she'd returned from her meeting with Stanley, Lolly was looking alarmingly pale and she'd at once bundled her and Adam into the car and driven off to Dr Witherspoon. Lolly, he pronounced, was coming down with the flu, her resistance lowered by sheer exhaustion. It was extremely unusual for Dr Witherspoon to blame the lowering of a patient's resistance on anything but the polluted air of London, and the unhealthy lifestyle of Londoners in general. Dr Witherspoon was making plans to retire to a country practice, and disapproved of anyone who was not intending a similar escape – particularly anyone with small children to consider.

Lolly, he predicted, would be in bed for a week at least. There was no way Becky could afford to take a week away from the shoot. Rupert would have to step into the breach.

Rupert! Becky sipped her champagne to prevent the angry thoughts from returning. She hadn't meant to open the bottle till her husband came home and they could drink together to her bright future. But on the way back from Dr Witherspoon she had stopped off at a cash dispenser, and the machine had swallowed her card, refusing her request for money and instructing her to contact her branch. The young accountant type in the queue behind her had sniggered.

She knew where the blame lay. For her, a joint account was what you put your money into, for Rupert, what you took it out of. His reckless forebears had passed on to him their free-spending habits while depriving him of the fortune that would have sustained them. She would have to put a stop to it. She would have to be firm.

As a teenager, she had drowned herself in historical romances, conjuring up tantalising visions of 'profligate rakes'. But living with a real one had a lot less appeal. You could not raise children and pay mortgages while cohabiting with a profligate rake. No more fantasies for her, no more uncertainties. She would make Rupert see the light. And she would tell young Jeremy to stop pursuing her – that her marriage was sound, that he must forget all his hopes.

Smiling, because having made the decision she almost felt she had implemented it, she beat the eggs with a whisk. She would put them on to scramble as soon as she heard Rupert's key in the door.

Adam was happily asleep now that peace had been restored between them. It had cost her another round of the dreaded Memory Game, followed by two Dilly the Dinosaur stories. He was particularly fond of Dilly's supersonic scream. ('I can do one too, Mummy, do you want to hear?' 'Yes, darling, but let's wait till we're under a railway bridge with a train going over.') Lolly, he said, never let him have two stories.

Lolly knew how to be firm, but so did Becky. She also knew how to plan ahead. She and Rupert would sit down and make a coherent strategy, as they had neglected to do, for his career, starting off with roles in provincial theatre like the one for which he was auditioning, and moving on in calculated stages to the screen stardom he dreamed of. But that was for the future. Now, while she faced the pressure of finishing her film for Cannes, now he must support her in the home, take charge of the running of their daily lives, take care of Adam while Lolly was sick, shoulder his share of the babysitting when she recovered. Now it was Becky's turn to shine, but later, when it was Rupert's, when there was enough money in the bank, maybe she could pick and choose which films to make, spend more time with Adam, have another child.

They would talk quietly over champagne and smoked salmon and she would make him see what had to be done. He would understand.

When the phone rang she answered dreamily.

'It's me,' Rupert slurred. 'I stopped off at Todd's for a quick one.'

Alarm bells were ringing in Becky's head. 'When will you be home?'

'Dunno. There's this new club opening on the King's Road. We thought we'd give it a try.'

She did not want to forewarn him of the planned discussion, give him time to mount his defences. She said rather weakly, 'I've already started supper—'

'I'm not hungry. Why don't you go ahead without me, then join us at the club.'

'I can't.'

'Oh!' Rupert seemed at a loss for further suggestions. 'I'll try not to be back late, then.'

Becky felt tears of helplessness prick at her eyes. In an instant, her vital sense of control had slipped away. But forcing Rupert to return would only start things off on the wrong foot – especially if he had been drinking.

Then she remembered to ask, 'How did the audition go?'

'No good. They were looking for someone younger.'

He spoke carelessly, but she knew how disappointed he must be. 'I'm sorry,' she said.

'Their loss. See you later.'

After she'd replaced the receiver, Becky stood staring blindly at it for several long minutes. The physical sensation of hurt was so strong, it almost made her reel. Rupert was not coming home to share in her triumph, or to sort out their glowing future. He was leaving her to a solitary and empty celebration, with an almost full bottle of champagne in the ice bucket, and another waiting fruitlessly in the fridge.

The phone rang again. This time Becky grabbed it with both hands. 'Rupert?'

'No. It's Alex.'

'Alex!' She hadn't spoken to him since she'd called to say she wouldn't be needing his help with Ross Piper after all. He had been generous in his happiness for her.

'I hear congratulations are in order,' he said, 'after your meeting with Stanley Shiplake.'

She did not ask how he knew. Alex was like the hub of a great wheel, all the shifting population and changing rumours of the film world being drawn sooner or later into his orbit. He was the still point of their turning world.

'Alex,' she said, 'would you like to come round and share a glass of champagne with me?'

In the brief silence, she could almost hear his smile. 'I'll be right over.'

Curled up on a sofa and sipping from her fluted glass, shoes kicked off, hair pushed back from her luminous face, Becky looked, Alex thought, all of sixteen years old.

They were in her den, from which she had banned all pretensions at interior decor. No costly antiques in here, no pale pink fabrics that might show the wine stains, no silk cushions that Adam was banned from throwing or Bogey from sitting on. This room, like the kitchen, was Becky's, stamped with her warmth, welcoming to her child – not quite up to her husband's sophisticated tastes, which reigned in the rest of the house.

'I envy you, Alex,' she said suddenly.

'Why on earth would you do that, when you have the world at your feet?'

She shifted restlessly, bringing her knees up to her chest like a schoolgirl. 'You seem so sure of yourself – so comfortable in your own skin – like you have everything you ever wanted.'

How deceptive appearances could be. The trick, he had learned, was trying not to want what you could not have. He looked into the depths of her green eyes, ageless like the sphinx, in which all mysteries were contained.

'Do I take it you don't want the fame and the fortune?' he asked.

'Of course I do, I want it badly – but not at any price. I also want to be loved.' She thought of Sir Humphrey's rented flat. 'I want a life with my child and my husband.'

'Talking of which, where is Rupert tonight?'

A shadow crossed her face. 'Who knows? Some new club on the King's Road . . .'

'How often does he desert you for the bright lights?'

'It's not his fault,' Becky said defensively. 'Rupert's wasting his life in bars because he can't get any decent work as an actor. It's so frustrating for him.'

'Does it ever occur to you that he may not be trying hard enough?'

'He *does* try. He's forever at auditions.' Alex fixed her with an unwavering gaze. 'Well, he does his best, but I'm not sure he knows what it takes. His parents gave him everything on a plate. His father used to say to him, "In the beginning God created the Carlyles, and then all the little people . . ." So I suppose he thinks he's above the struggle, but can you blame him?'

Yes, Alex thought, I can, but it wasn't what she wanted to hear. 'Is there anything I can do?'

She lowered her eyes, waging her own internal struggle. Finally she said, 'There *is* something . . .'

'Just say the word.'

'You could take Rupert on as a client and save his career and my sanity.'

He looked at her sharply but she wouldn't meet his gaze. An awkward, unaccustomed silence fell between them while Alex considered how to respond to her request. He knew what it must have cost her. She was trading on their friendship, not on her husband's appeal as a potential client. Rupert was an unknown quantity, a lightweight – possibly without gifts besides the obvious ones of his looks and charm. Alex, in the normal course of events, did not represent lightweights.

He had been lost in thought for longer than he'd intended. 'I'm sorry,' she burst out. 'I shouldn't have asked.'

'Don't be silly. I was only wondering how best to go about it . . .'

She smiled, then, for her husband's hopes as she hadn't smiled for her own. The trick, Alex reminded himself, was trying not to want what you could not have.

'You're a complete darling,' she said. 'Rupert will appreciate this more than you can imagine—'

'I'm not doing it for Rupert.'

She jumped up and planted a fervent kiss on his forehead. 'Let's get a refill.'

Alex followed her through to the kitchen. The half-prepared feast lay on the counter, a silent accusation.

'I've been stood up, as you can see,' Becky said lightly. 'How hungry are you?'

The trick is never wanting . . .

'I can't stay,' he said. 'I've already made arrangements to have dinner with one of my clients. The story of my life these days . . .'

'Another time, then.' She smiled, but before she turned away he caught a glimpse of the loneliness in her eyes.

Becky lay on her bed, fully clothed. Her head swam unpleasantly and she felt faintly sick. She should have eaten something, but she didn't feel hungry, only tired.

Tomorrow she would give Rupert the news – the good news and the bad news, the carrot and the stick. Tomorrow they would talk as she had planned.

She closed her eyes. Sleep hovered, tantalisingly close.

She heard footsteps in the passage and groaned. Adam was prone to wake in the night and not settle back down till she sang him a song. He would hold tightly onto her fingers and any attempt to withdraw them too soon could result in his eyes flying open again.

But it was Rupert who beamed at her from the doorway. 'Told you I wouldn't be late,' he said proudly. His unsteady approach to the bed proved he was no more sober than she was. He tumbled down beside her and lay very still.

'How was the club?'

'A damn bore – besides, I missed you.'

It would be so easy, she thought, to leave it at that – easy but not wise.

'Rupert,' she said, 'we have to talk.'

'I know, I know.' He buried his face in her neck. 'I've been acting like a selfish jerk and I haven't been any help to you . . . I'm sorry.'

'But if you know, then why – ?'

' 'Cause you make me feel like such a bloody failure.'

'I don't mean to,' she said, mortified. 'If that's what I've done, I'm sorry too . . .'

'Forget it.' He was fumbling with a button on her blouse. 'Let's forget all of it.'

Instinctively Becky knew this was not the moment for words. Instead she removed his hand and undid the difficult button herself and guided his head down onto her breast. She tried not to think, to let the feelings take over.

It was like before, like the days in his tiny flat when their lives were so simple and the sex was so glorious. She had forgotten, had closed herself off, and now that she was opening again like a flower, she was filled with gratitude and wonder.

When it was over, she lay contentedly in the arms of her sleeping husband, her head tucked into the hollow of his shoulder, his arm draped heavily over her breasts. It wasn't the outcome she had planned – it was infinitely, miraculously better. If they understood each other's problems, if they could still feel like this when they made love, there was no limit to what they could achieve. For the first time in many long months, her heart felt light with hope.

Now, if hope was to become fulfilment, the real work would have to begin.

CHAPTER FOUR

Adam looked hungrily at his sausages and chips, then stole a sidelong glance at Mahmoud sitting beside him, staring silently at his plate. He wouldn't touch a mouthful till Mahmoud gave the all clear. This week, Mahmoud was his very best friend.

The child raised his large chocolate-brown eyes and fixed them on Rupert. 'These are pork,' he said accusingly. 'I'm not allowed to eat pork.'

'They aren't pork – they're beef,' Rupert countered with a great effort at patience. 'Mrs Carlyle knows you aren't allowed to eat pork, so she bought these beef ones especially, and Mrs Christos has gone to a lot of trouble to cook them for you, so you must eat them all up.'

'They're sausages,' Mahmoud persisted. 'I don't eat sausages.'

'Then you will have to starve,' Rupert said through clenched teeth.

'Mahmoud's used to it,' Adam chipped in. 'He always starves at Ramadan.'

'But *you* don't. You can eat your sausages.'

'I won't if Mahmoud doesn't.'

Rupert looked at Mahmoud's stubbornly clenched jaw and for a moment imagined grabbing him by his stocky neck and throttling him. 'Mrs Christos,' he called, 'do we have any turkey dinosaurs?'

Adam gazed longingly at his sausages. 'If Mahmoud has turkey dinosaurs, I want them too.'

'Go away,' Rupert barked. 'Go and play in your room, and I will decide whether poor Mrs Christos should go to all the bother of cooking you ungrateful little wretches a *second* lunch.'

Mahmoud slipped instantly from his seat and slid away to the door. Adam gave his plate one last look of regret before following faithfully after his swiftly retreating friend. They both darted past Mrs Christos as she attempted to bar the door.

'Where you going?' she grumbled. 'You no finish your lunch—'

'This lunch,' Rupert explained, 'has been rejected, but I'm sure it will do very nicely for Bogey and Mrs Brockenhurst's dogs next door. Now I would like you please to serve mine while there's some peace and quiet in here, and when those two little monsters upstairs are so ravenous they beg for it, could you kindly make them some turkey dinosaurs.'

Without waiting for a reply, Rupert flicked the television onto CNN and contentedly lost himself in floods and hostage-takings and crises of any kind except the domestic, while Mrs Christos muttered about waste and children starving in the *barrios* and slapped steaming pasta and garlic bread onto plates. One she thumped down in front of Rupert, the other she placed on a neatly laid tray.

'Shall I take Lolly's down for her?' Rupert offered helpfully. Lolly was still convalescing from the flu, but past the most infectious stage.

Mrs Christos glared at Rupert's open-neck shirt, revealing a smooth expanse of bronzed and muscled chest. 'You no go,' she declared grimly, seizing the tray. 'I go.'

Rupert's lips twitched with amusement. Perhaps it was just as well, he reflected, remembering the last time he had seen Lolly in bed. There was no point courting temptation, not when he was making such an effort to be the model husband and father. The babysitting was something of a strain, but the sex with Becky was great again – better than it had been for years. No point rocking the boat, he decided, as he tucked into tortelloni with ricotta and spinach.

Mrs Christos had been gone some time, and he was watching a piece on European monetary union when she suddenly appeared in the doorway, her face flushed with alarm. 'Adam's door, it won't open,' she panted. 'I smell the fire.'

Rupert had bounded from the room and up the stairs before he was even conscious of the message from his brain to his legs. He wrenched at Adam's door but it wouldn't budge. From the other side came an ominous quiet and the distinctly acrid scent of something burning.

'Adam,' he yelled, 'open the bloody door.'

'I can't,' came the muffled reply. 'We've piled some things against it.'

'What the hell's going on in there? What's burning?'

'Nothing. Only Mahmoud's hair.'

'Shit!' Rupert raced next door to his own bedroom and heaved up the sash window. Sticking his head out, he looked across to Adam's window and was instantly weak with relief that it was open a good foot, though the curtains were drawn.

Praying to a God he hadn't thought about in a long time, Rupert climbed up onto the ledge and eased one foot along the wall, feeling his way across to the other sill. The tricky part, he knew, would be the transfer of weight from one ledge to the other. Spread-eagled across the bricks, clinging to either side with whitened knuckles, he didn't even want to think what a fool he must look. He had a momentary vision of Becky's mobile phone smashed on the paving stones, and almost lost his nerve.

'It's OK, Adam,' he yelled, as much to reassure himself as his son. 'I'm coming in through the window.'

He made the leap, fingers clutching helplessly at smooth glass until they found some purchase on the wooden frame, and he was able to steady his trembling legs and beating heart before sliding in through the narrow gap and onto Adam's bedroom floor.

'Wow,' Mahmoud breathed, staring at him owlishly in the gloom with a new-found respect. 'That was like Spiderman.'

Smoke, Rupert noticed, curled from the singed edges of his once-thick fringe. Rupert struggled out of his shirt and clamped it over the startled child's head.

'You little idiots!' he yelled above Mahmoud's muffled shrieks. 'You know you're not allowed to play with matches.'

In the half dark created by the drawn curtains, he could make out toy chests stacked against the door, and lighted candles placed altar-like on the bookcase. Tethered to one side, Bogey sat patiently, draped in a long black cloak.

'We were playing vampire bats,' Adam explained sheepishly. 'We wanted to make a bat cave . . .'

Given a timely reminder of his fangs, Mahmoud stopped struggling and sank his teeth into Rupert's hand. Rupert yelped, as much from shock and outrage as from pain. He snatched his shirt off the boy's head, noting with extra ire the dull brown singe marks on the white fabric. 'That does it!' he shouted. 'You two are doing Time Out – twenty minutes on your own in a corner.'

It took some time to pull down the barricade and get the door open, especially since the boys, hopeful of putting off their punishment, were more hindrance than help. When it was done, Mahmoud was banished to the bathroom while Adam remained rusticated in his bedroom, now devoid of candles and matches. Both boys drooped their heads in exaggerated sorrow.

The twenty minutes passed very slowly. It would feel a great deal longer – an eternity, in fact – Rupert reflected sourly, until six o'clock, when Mahmoud's mother would relieve him of her troublesome offspring.

Letitia waylaid Becky outside the cutting-room doors. 'I wouldn't go in there,' she said. 'He's in one of his moods.'

Becky sighed. Since she'd had her little talk with Jeremy, he'd become increasingly difficult. He was behaving, not to put too fine a point on it, like a sulky child deprived of a promised treat.

'It's the pressure,' she said evasively. 'Stanley's putting too much pressure on him.'

Letitia gave her a hard look. 'If you ask me,' she said cuttingly, 'Jeremy's problems have nothing to do with Stanley.'

'Letitia, please—'

'*You're* the reason he can't concentrate on what he's supposed to be doing in there.'

Becky looked round nervously, but there was no one else within earshot. 'I can't help his schoolboy crush,' she said. 'It's hardly my fault . . .'

'Of course it is. You should have put a stop to it long ago. You led him on in the beginning.'

'I did not!'

'Be honest.' Letitia's eyes raked over Becky, taking in, in a sweep, or so it felt, the fact that she had dressed in her usual hurry – her imperfectly brushed hair, the lack of any make-up but mascara and a little lipstick, even the small ladder in her tights just above her hemline, which she had halted with a dab of nail undercoat. 'It's very flattering for a woman your age, having a young stud like Jeremy fall in love with you.'

Becky closed her eyes, remembering the sensation of soft flesh flattening beneath her knuckles as her fist connected with Ross Piper's mouth. In the shame afterwards, she had been quite certain she would never want to hit another human being.

'Letitia,' she said, in a voice trembling with the effort of control, 'you are wrong. I did *not* want Jeremy to fall in love with me.'

'Well he did, and you didn't stop it, and the least you could have done was follow through. What's one little fuck if it keeps Jeremy happy and wins us all the Palme d'Or?'

Becky gripped her hands together. I will *not*, she told herself desperately, allow myself to lose my temper. I will never do that again.

The cutting-room door flew open and Jeremy stood there, framed like an avant-garde portrait, his white face glowing against the dark beyond. 'Come and see what I've done,' he commanded.

Becky, still wound as tight as a spring, deliberately held back to let Letitia go first. When she entered the room, Jeremy and Letitia were sitting on the only two chairs in front of the editing console, leaving her to stand behind them. Jeremy looped film through sprockets and fiddled with buttons and the face of Sir Humphrey Humes filled the screen.

'He's dead good in this scene,' Jeremy enthused. 'Wait and see.'

It was the vital confrontation between Sir Humphrey and Ross Piper, fighting for the love of the young Juliette Winters. The story of *Abstract Love* was as familiar to Becky as her own – a tale of a young girl caught between two demanding older men, her rich grandfather who exacts her devotion and care as the price of inheriting his fortune, and the talented painter who rescues her from this life of servitude, awakening her passion, only to become equally obsessed with keeping her under his control. She becomes his mistress, his model, his muse, a reminder of lost youth, an essential inspiration for his work. Slowly she comes to realise that she has exchanged one cage for another, that her lover, like her grandfather, is concerned only with his own needs. To be truly free, truly her own person, she must escape from both of them.

It was, Jeremy was fond of expounding to interviewers, about the selfishness of money and of art. The rich are isolated by their wealth, used to the gratification of their every whim. The artist is divided from lesser mortals by his talent, and demands their homage to it. Both kinds of selfishness can destroy those who come into its orbit.

Jeremy had written the screenplay with a young friend from film school days. Like his painter hero, he was a genuine talent. Was it true what Letitia said, that Becky was damaging that gift, eroding his abilities and concentration?

She watched the on-screen battle between the two men with growing dismay. True, Sir Humphrey's performance was a gem, but Ross Piper in the dailies had been equally good. It was Sir Humphrey, however, who now had the lion's share of the close-ups, the camera lingering lovingly on his every word and reaction. Ross Piper's great moments had landed on the cutting-room floor, the laurels for the scene handed to Sir Humphrey on a plate.

'Well?' Jeremy enquired with just a hint of defiance. 'What do you think?'

She would have to plan her reaction with extreme caution. There could be only two reasons for Jeremy's childish attack with the scissors: he was trying to goad her, or he was still jealous of the man he saw as his rival. Probably, Becky feared, a little of both.

Before she could couch a carefully worded reply, Letitia snapped, 'I thought Ross Piper was supposed to be the star of this picture.'

'It's not my fault if Sir Humphrey upstages him,' Jeremy scoffed.

'Yes, Jeremy, it is,' Becky said quietly. 'That was a very clever piece of work, if your sole aim is to cut Ross Piper down to size. But don't you think you're employing your talents – your considerable talents, I might add – in the wrong direction?'

'We don't have time for your bloody silly games—'

'Letitia,' Becky interrupted firmly, 'would you mind letting me have a word with Jeremy in private?'

Letitia looked from one to the other with a knowing sneer. 'Sure – as long as you *both* get your acts together. I'll be waiting outside.' With a snort of contempt, she sashayed from the room.

Jeremy stared sullenly ahead at the frozen face of Sir Humphrey on the screen. 'I like it the way it is,' he said mutinously.

'I know you do – but for all the wrong reasons.' Becky came up beside him and took his hand in hers. He let it lie there stiffly, like a wax model's. 'You like *me* for the wrong reasons too. You think I'm a hero, a rebel, someone who also cuts superstars down to size with a well-timed smack in the face. But that's not really me,

Jeremy. I was tired, not myself, I didn't know what I was doing. There's nothing heroic about me in the normal run of things. I just try to get by, like everyone else.'

'That's not true.' Jeremy's fingers gripped hers with the desperation of a drowning man's. 'You don't realise how special you are, how inspirational . . .'

He was not going to let it go, Becky realised, he was determined to keep the illusion intact, whatever the cost to them both. 'Jeremy,' she said wearily, 'you don't need my love in order to finish this film. You don't need anything. You can do it on your own.'

'I know,' he said, and his face was a picture of youthful wretchedness. 'The trouble is, I don't want to.'

When Becky emerged from the darkness of the cutting room and Jeremy's despair, blinking like a mole into the light of day, she found Letitia in intimate conversation with Juliette Winters, who had come to do some voice-overs.

Raising her head from Juliette's whispered intimacies and her cup of machine coffee, Letitia called over, 'Becky, aren't you great friends with Alex Goddard?'

'Yes,' Becky said shortly. 'Hi, Juliette.'

Even dressed in jeans and a sweatshirt, her face almost bare of make-up, the girl had a beauty that seemed to light up the room. Her eyes, the colour of liquid amber, were huge in a gamine face framed by dark curls, her smile a brilliant flash of even white teeth. Unconsciously Becky ran her tongue over her own teeth, checking for lipstick marks.

'Perhaps you can satisfy our curiosity, then,' Letitia said. 'Juliette was just wondering if Alex has someone special in his life.'

'I don't think so . . . not since his divorce.'

'What luck!' Juliette's voice was thick and dark, like chocolate. 'I fancy him like crazy. I thought he'd have women crawling all over him.'

Becky eyed her warily, feeling a little surge of protectiveness towards Alex. She was, as Letitia had pointed out, one of his greatest friends. She didn't want to see him hurt again, not by another narcissistic actress.

'It's tough finding a decent man in this business,' Letitia sympathised with Juliette.

'Don't tell me! They're all gay and off-limits, or only after one thing and disgustingly vulgar, or seeking help for some addiction problem. Alex is in a different league.' She looked Becky up and down as though assessing the competition. 'Don't tell me you haven't noticed how heavenly he is?'

'Our Rebecca tends to prefer them a little younger,' Letitia said spitefully.

Becky flushed a dull red. Juliette shrugged gracefully. 'Each to his own. Personally, I prefer a real man any time. Alex is so deliciously powerful and sure of himself. And so self-contained. It would be quite a challenge, getting a man like that to fall in love with you. Don't you agree, Becky?'

Becky was aware that Juliette was watching her closely. 'I've never really thought about it,' she said.

'Couldn't you arrange for us to go out in a foursome some time – you, Rupert, Alex and me? Sort of fix up a date?'

'My nanny's sick,' Becky said evasively. 'I can't go out at all right now. In fact, I'd better be getting home . . .'

Before Becky could make good her escape, Juliette pressed her pretty, puckered mouth to her cheek. 'I'll be merciful and let you go,' she said, 'but only this time. I'm not going to let you off the hook, Becky. I want you to set me up with Alex Goddard.'

Becky had the feeling that if she held out on her, Juliette would find another way.

Becky stared at the strange brown marks on her husband's crumpled shirt – Rupert, who wouldn't be seen dead in anything that wasn't cleaned, starched and ironed to within an inch of its life. Her eyes travelled upward to his usually sleeked down hair, now standing on end in patches, as though he had run his hands through it countless times in the past few hours.

'How was it?' she asked unnecessarily.

From the dining room came the sounds of the scouts' oath, Mahmoud following Adam in his slightly accented English: 'On my honour, I promise that I will do my best to do my duty to God and to the Queen to help other people and to keep the scout law . . .'

'They have made a tent,' Rupert said, in tones of trembling outrage, 'from the Madeira lace tablecloth.'

Becky smiled at the vision this conjured up: flower-scented

Madeira, where she and Rupert had spent a blissful holiday before Adam was born, when they still had the leisure and the freedom for such things. They had lain all day in the sun, and drunk the sweet wine in the bar of the famous Reid's hotel, and watched over Funchal harbour for the strange green flash which follows the Madeira sunset, and made love for hours in the quaint narrow bed beneath the whirring electric fan. Then they had returned to wintery London with their memories and an ornate tablecloth of handmade lace which had taken Rupert's fancy and which was too good to use for anything but the dinner parties she no longer had time to hold.

'I'll deal with the little monsters,' she promised. 'You look to me like you could do with a drink.'

Rupert turned towards the kitchen. 'A double Scotch, I think.'

'No,' she said, catching his arm and drawing him towards her. 'I mean a break, away from domestic cares. Give Todd a ring, take yourselves off somewhere for a couple of hours. You've earned it.'

They smiled into each other's eyes. It felt good, this new partnership. It was so much easier, so much less effort, to pull together, in tandem, in the same harness.

It was past eight when Alex came into his orderly Knightsbridge flat where, in an average week, the cleaning lady spent far more time than he did. During his brief journey here from the office, the messages had already piled up on his answering machine. He let Wellington off his lead and the dog padded through to the study on stiff old paws.

Beside the phone, just where it should be, was the notebook in which Alex recorded all the calls he would have to return. Mrs Bryce the cleaner, trained to it from the start, always put things back in their proper place. There was no other presence besides Wellington's familiar one to disturb the fixed routine of Alex's life. He selected a pen from the well-stocked drawer and opened the book to the proper date. His hand reached for the playback button.

'Alex, it's me, Melissa,' a girlish voice breathed. He had signed her only a week before, fresh out of RADA and full of bright talent. 'I'm sorry to call so late, but I just can't decide what to do about those two scripts you sent me, whether the Jane Austen or the E. M. Forster has the better role for me, and I wondered if you wanted to come round and talk. I'll feed you, of course, I have pasta here – far too much for one – and a bottle of wine . . .'

He noted down her number, though he knew he would not accept the invitation. There had been a time, after Lara left, after Becky married Rupert, when his guard had been down and he had allowed himself to respond to the advances of a succession of young actresses. He was young still, a man of flesh and blood, he needed their company and what passed for their love. And he had tried to live up to their expectations that being with him would transform their lives, burdened as he was with guilt at Lara's reproaches that marriage to him had done nothing for her career. But in the end what he could offer them was never enough, and what they gave him wasn't what he was looking for, and he came away feeling even emptier than before. So that now, he preferred his solitary life to another of these unsatisfactory encounters.

Precisely, efficiently, he noted down the names of the other callers, all business – problems with contracts and overdue payments, tickets to ceremonies where his clients were expected to pick up awards, his travel agent asking about his flight and hotel requirements for the Cannes film festival. There was nothing urgent, nothing that couldn't be dealt with in the morning.

Briefly he wondered whether to phone Becky and ask if she could use some company on the plane to Cannes. But she would be travelling in an entourage, her whole team along for the ride, their hopes pinned on the big prize. It would be better if he made his own arrangements.

He went through to the bright, white-tiled kitchen that looked almost untouched, like something out of a showroom, and peered inside the large American fridge. There was a loaf of bread and some cheese that would do for a sandwich. It didn't seem worth the effort to cook for one, and besides, he didn't mind something simple after all the business lunches and dinners that were a way of life. He went to look in the cupboard for a tin of Wellington's dog food.

Alex ate his sandwich on his lap in the sitting room while he watched a half-hour television sitcom written by one of his clients. At nine o'clock he switched it off and headed for his study.

It was the only room in the flat that looked as though someone actually lived there. His well-thumbed collection of history books lined the walls. Wellington's basket was in one corner, the dog curled up and snoring lightly. It was starting to be an effort for him to get up for his night-time walk.

Alex thumbed through a pile of scripts on his desk and pulled out the two most urgent ones. He riffled through the pages with a thumb, weighing the weight of words. If he read very quickly, he might just get through both of them before he would have to switch the light out and snatch a few hours' sleep. Tomorrow morning, as usual, he would be at his desk by six.

At the end of Lolly's bed, Hugo Brockenhurst shuffled awkwardly from foot to foot. At seventeen, he had the skinny gangliness of a boy whose height has increased too rapidly to allow his body time to fill out proportionately. He also had a shock of dark hair whose fringe dangled constantly into his eyes and had to be flicked away when he actually wanted to see what he was looking at.

At the moment he was looking at Lolly, demurely tucked under the sheets, her rich brown hair spread over the pillows like a Pre-Raphaelite painting. He cleared his throat and tried to speak. 'I – I brought you something.'

'Thanks. Like what?'

'Not a present or anything. I just thought . . . you must be so bored and all that . . . I thought you'd like to borrow my CD Walkman.'

Lolly sat up a little, revealing a nightgown with a scooped neckline and a tantalising glimpse of something underneath. Hugo hung his head and let the fringe fall into his eyes.

'Great! But don't you want it yourself?'

'Too busy. I'm supposed to be studying.'

He would be writing A-levels before the summer, Lolly realised. The aura of it, the burden, hung over him palpably, like a cloud.

He was digging in his jacket pocket from which he produced the promised Walkman and a handful of discs. Shoving them at Lolly, he muttered, 'I didn't know what kind of music you like. I don't really have any mainstream pop like Madonna or anything.'

'I can't stand Madonna,' Lolly declared, watching his tentative grin of relief. 'She's so gross about sex.'

Hugo blushed to the roots of his hair. Of course, Lolly realised, he was still at an all boys' boarding school; he probably wasn't used to talking about sex with a girl.

'I bet we like the same sounds,' Lolly said quickly, to put him at his ease again. 'What have you got there?'

'Some Seal . . . and k d lang . . .'

'Great. I love her voice – and her style.'

Hugo looked alarmed, as though Lolly might start up on sex again, something about k d lang coming out of the closet. She decided to change the subject.

'Isn't it weird going to boarding school?'

Hugo peered at her uncomprehendingly through his fringe. 'It's OK. I've been going since I was eight. Everyone does.'

No, Lolly thought, everyone does not, but this had obviously never occurred to Hugo. The Brockenhursts moved in a narrow set in which boarding school was the inevitable destiny of their offspring. Strange, Lolly mused, how different people were, how varied their views on what was good for their children.

'At least it gets me away from Mum and Dad and their rows.'

'Is it a real bummer for you?' Lolly asked sympathetically. 'The divorce?'

'Pretty awful. Mostly it's a pain not being able to stay put in one place – having to go backwards and forwards between them. There's no peace to study.'

It wasn't fair, Lolly reflected, the problems of the parents being visited on the children. She saw it in her job all the time. Her thoughts strayed back to her own childhood in Kent where her mother ran the village shop and post office, working long hours to supplement her father's modest income as a furniture salesman in a Canterbury store. They had thought it best for the children that they both work, preferable to have a little more to spend on them, but they'd never asked *them* how they felt about it. So Lolly and her sister Hayley became latch-key kids, their parents comforting themselves that since their cottage was in the same street as the shop, the children could just nip over if they wanted anything. But the fact remained that they had to take care of themselves because there was no one else to do it – or rather Lolly, as the older one, took care of them both, cooking meals, supervising homework, growing up before her time. She had lost her childhood and even her adolescence – never taking A-levels as Hugo was doing, moving quite naturally, because she'd had so much practice, into child care as a profession, with all its adult responsibilities. She gave her charges the devotion she had missed out on, the attention their own parents couldn't because they were too busy working. Children like Adam, mothers like Becky.

Why have a child if you didn't want to bring it up yourself? Lolly just didn't get it, would never have dreamed of doing such a thing herself. Why leave your own child in someone else's care – or worse still, to fend for itself? Why pack it off to boarding school to sink or swim amongst strangers?

In the silence between them Hugo fidgeted awkwardly, as though he felt he had outstayed his welcome. 'I should be getting back,' he muttered. 'Maths paper . . .'

'Thanks a million for the Walkman. And good luck with the exams.'

He slumped gloomily, his mind already back with his books. 'I just wish it was all over.'

'I just wish Hugo's A-levels were over!' Anthea declared as she attacked Becky's rosebushes with the vigour of a zealot, hacking away at the dead branches with a saw. 'Even when he's up for half-term, he has simply piles of wretched homework to get through. It's inhuman – they expect those poor kids to be absolute *Einsteins*.'

Becky's gardening talents were confined to watching. 'I know,' she commiserated. 'Adam's already started on his times tables.' He had told her with some indignation that Lolly made him do his twos and fives in the bath.

Anthea snorted. 'Just wait. It gets worse and worse. I stopped being able to understand the boys' maths in their first year of prep school. 'Course I'm as thick as a plank, but luckily in my day you could get through anything if you knew which knife and fork to use and said "napkin" instead of "serviette".'

She was tearing the suckers now from the roots of a parent plant. 'You should never cut these, you know – they only grow back more vigorously.' At Becky's blank expression, she said with exasperation, 'I don't know why I waste my pearls of wisdom on you. I'm the only one who ever wields the knife in this garden anyway.'

'How's Hugo coping with the divorce on top of everything else?'

Becky said calmly, knowing perfectly well that Anthea liked to feel she was coming charging to the rescue.

'I haven't a clue. He just sticks his nose in his books and doesn't utter a word. Joshua's the one who lets all his feelings hang out. There's absolute hell to pay when it's his turn to go to Daddy and he doesn't want to. And I feel like such a *beast* trying to make him.'

How, Becky wondered, would she cope with trying to divide Adam in two, sending him off against his will to spend time away from her? As it was she didn't see enough of him, but what if she couldn't even go into his room when she returned late from work and gaze at him, lying angelic in sleep, safe beneath his dinosaur duvet? She shuddered. It didn't even bear thinking about.

'And it doesn't stop there,' Anthea was saying. 'There's the endless battle to keep them in the style to which they were accustomed when Daddy was around. God knows what's going to happen about Hugo's university fees. Now the new baby's about to pop out, I'm sure Miss Credit Management will be putting the squeeze on Simon, trying to cut down the expenditure on the first family. They all do it, so I'm told.'

She was, Becky perceived, quite powerless in the situation, dependent on the largesse of a man who no longer loved her, unable to direct her own destiny or that of her children without his continued indulgence.

'Perhaps,' Becky said, 'that's why I work so hard. Maybe I'm terrified of having to rely on someone else for money.'

'*You'll* be all right,' Anthea said airily as she set about pruning the nearest bush, cutting away ruthlessly at the middle to allow the air to circulate. 'You're off to Cannes to become an overnight sensation.'

'There's nothing overnight about it,' Becky retorted indignantly. 'I've worked for years for this – I've *earned* it. And I can't bear the thought of anything spoiling it.'

'Or anyone?'

'If you mean Rupert, he wouldn't do that.'

Anthea gave her a sceptical look. 'Perhaps not – at least, not consciously. I suppose that would be cutting off his nose to spite his face.' She gave a particularly vicious hack at an offendingly drooping branch.

'Give him a break, Ant. He's really trying.'

'That's what worries me.'

Hugo poked his pale face out of the door. 'I'm going back,' he muttered and vanished almost as soon as he had appeared, like a dim hallucination.

'He looks so peaky,' Anthea moaned. 'I expect it's just the unbalanced boarding school diet. And of course, he has a simply hopeless crush on that pretty little nanny of yours.'

'You can bring the boys over for some pot luck here, if you like.'

'Not tonight, thanks.' Anthea gave the bush a last satisfied snip. 'I'm making a stab at a roast chicken. If it's burnt to a crisp, I'll let you know... And do tell Rupert the hounds absolutely *adored* the beef sausages. They've been letting off in the house all afternoon, which is their way of showing appreciation.'

CHAPTER FIVE

The Croisette was crawling with paparazzi, posers and onlookers, an influx of foreigners who had forced the natives of Cannes from their famous beachfront promenade where they liked to stroll amidst stately palms and manicured flowerbeds tended all year round by a small army of gardeners.

From their vantage point on the terrace of the Carlton Hotel, relic of a more gracious age when the English aristocracy flocked to holiday on the Riviera, Becky and Jeremy sipped Perrier and watched the tide of humanity sweep past them, rolling ever onwards towards the next screening or publicity party or photo opportunity. Stanley had insisted that they all stay at the Carlton, in the centre of the action, where, like those streaming by on the Croisette, they could both see and be seen.

It was Jeremy's first time in Cannes. Shielded as he was behind sunglasses that reflected back the swirl of activity around him, it was possible for Becky to gauge his excitement only by the speed with which his head jerked from side to side, taking it all in.

And through his eyes, she saw it all again as though for the first time – the terrace swarming with the famous and the wannabe's, the producers with ponytails and Hawaiian shirts the colour of flaming sunsets, the distributors wining and wooing smooth-talking agents with flashing white teeth and all-year-round tans, the starlets with pneumatic breasts taking coiffed pet poodles to the Doggies' Bar. It was a collective madness in which everybody, participant and onlooker alike, was irresistibly caught up.

'Yo, Jeremy!' A producer of low-budget horror films detached himself from the crowd, his T-shirt advertising his latest gruesome offering: *Nazi Grannies Fight Back*. He gave Becky a curt nod before grabbing Jeremy's arm and pumping it like a soda syphon.

'Hear your movie's a hot tip to take the old golden statuette. Way to go, bro'!'

'We haven't won yet,' Jeremy said cagily.

'What's that gotta do with it? With the kinda word of mouth you've got going for you, you don't even *need* to win. You're on your way, bro! Fancy knocking together a little video nasty for me some time?'

'Well, I . . . er . . . s'pose I could think about it . . .'

Becky turned away to hide her amusement. A hovering German distributor took instant advantage, sidling into the vacant seat beside her. He seemed vaguely familiar, though she could not have put a name to the face. 'I bought some foreign rights on your first film, remember?' He beamed with the pride of an indulgent benefactor. 'A brave little effort. But the latest one – *Abstract Love* – this is the fulfilment of your promise. I hope you have kept the German rights for me?'

It was ironic, Becky reflected, how so many strangers suddenly seemed to want a piece of her, a stake in her soul, when she was exactly the same person who'd had to fight for every penny of her budget a matter of mere months ago. Just one little whiff of success and they all came crawling, like bees to a honey pot, even though she herself had no control over the selling of her dreams. That was Stanley Shiplake's department, and this beaming man with the faint fragrance of beer on his breath must have known it.

In the awkward pause, they could hear Jeremy quizzing his new buddy on the best parties to go to. 'The Japanese give great gifts,' the producer confided, 'but if it's pussy you're after, you gotta go to the Australian beach barbecue.'

Becky grinned apologetically at the German, who seemed to be making a mental note of the advice, but she was saved from comment by the welcome buzz of her mobile phone. Instantly everyone round the table reached for theirs.

'*Mea culpa*!' Becky said, holding it up for proof. 'Excuse me.' She turned slightly away and the German took his cue and moved off in search of further victims.

'Howz life in the fast lane?' the voice crackled, and Becky's face relaxed into a smile as she recognised the teasing tones of Ross Piper.

'You're missing all the fun,' she said, picturing him in his hotel hideaway. Ross had refused all Stanley's entreaties to stay in the Carlton, opting instead for the Hotel du Cap, secluded in gardens of tall pines and separated from the madness of Cannes by the bay of Golfe Juan.

'What fun?' Ross laughed. 'I been around the block a few times – and back again. Not even Stanley Shiplake's gonna sell me some fairy story about how great it is to have a camera goin' off in your face every time you step out for some air.'

'It'll be a whole lot worse if you win Best Actor,' Becky threatened.

'You don't know what "worse" is. If you win that Palme d'Or, they'll be chasing your tail all the way down the Croisette.'

'I hate to admit it, but as a first-timer I might just enjoy that.'

'You go right ahead and wallow in it. You've earned it.' His laughter filled her ear. She caught Jeremy giving her a sideways scowl before he was approached by yet another ardent fan who only a week ago had never even heard his name.

'I'm so nervous,' Becky said into the phone, 'about the awards tonight, I can hardly sit still for two minutes at a time.'

'Tell you what – if I win, I'll take you to lunch tomorrow at the Eden Roc. If you win, you choose the restaurant and you pay the bill.'

'Deal,' she agreed, hanging up just as Jeremy rid himself of the aspiring actress whose breathless compliments had taken up only half his attention, his other ear visibly tuned in to Becky's conversation.

'Fancy a walk down to the Palais?' Becky enquired lightly, refusing to take any notice of his suspicious stare. 'I think we should check up on what Stanley's doing with our movie.'

'All work and no play, huh?' Jeremy sulked. 'Even when we're together on the Riviera. This place is supposed to be steeped in romance, in case you hadn't noticed. I mean, this is the town where Isadora Duncan died!'

Becky pictured the long floating scarf, the dancer's trademark, suddenly entangled in the axle of the open car, pulling tighter and tighter round the slender white neck until the larynx was crushed, the breath choked off forever. She shivered, as though a cloud had crossed the sun. 'Thank you, Jeremy,' she said, 'for sharing that cheerful thought.'

* * *

'Here's looking at you, kid!' Ross Piper raised a glass of mineral water and clinked it against Becky's champagne flute.

'If we're going to toast,' Stanley boomed from the other end of the table, 'let's toast the *winner*! Here's to *you*, Ross.'

Everyone raised their glasses. Becky glanced uncertainly across the table at Jeremy, whose face was pale but impassive, and at Letitia, sipping champagne serenely at Stanley's right hand.

'The rest of you,' Stanley rolled on, 'better luck *next* time.'

'Hey, now,' Ross objected, 'this time was good enough. They deserved this win more than I did. Hell, I owe it all to them anyway.'

'Sure,' Stanley said, 'but you know what they say. A miss is as good as a mile.'

A dull red flush rose in Jeremy's cheeks. Becky caught her breath, anger tightening her chest. What had it mattered to Stanley, in that crowded auditorium the night before, whether the Palme d'Or was awarded to them or not? What did it mean to him apart from a few more zeros in his profit column? But for her – and Jeremy, clutching her hand in the dark – it had for a few seconds seemed a matter of life and death, the hope gripping her stomach like a clenched fist, and then the rush of angry disappointment when the coveted prize went to a Swedish rival . . . and the relieved aftermath in which she realised that it wasn't terminal after all, that at least there would be no more waiting, and that the throng waiting to congratulate and commiserate were proof, if proof were needed, that to have been so close to winning was success in itself.

'What are you saying, Stanley?' Jeremy asked with ominous calm. 'You think I screwed up?'

'Of course you didn't!' Becky almost shouted. She felt a fierce, overwhelming protectiveness towards Jeremy; she wanted to take him in her arms and cradle his head to her breast. She also longed to shake Stanley till he lost all power of speech.

'Perhaps you'd like to rephrase that, Stanley.' Alex Goddard, till now an objective onlooker, gave Becky's hand a quick squeeze. 'I'm sure you didn't mean it to come out quite the way it sounded.'

'Hey, I love these guys.' Stanley looked from one to the other, affecting a wounded air. 'You're a great team – I'm *proud* of you.'

A waiter made a timely approach with a mountain of profiteroles glistening darkly with chocolate sauce. Stanley eyed them beadily, flicking a tongue lizard-like over thin lips. He had already consumed garlic snails and a chateaubriand so rare that, in his own instruction to the waiter, a good vet could have saved it.

Looking at him, Becky felt a rising nausea, wishing now that she had refused to cancel her lunch with Ross so that Stanley could take them all to the optimistically named Palme d'Or restaurant in the Hotel Martinez, where they could be seen celebrating Ross's triumph. Her head was swimming from the champagne and the anger, and she had a sudden impulse to lay her head on Alex's shoulder and rest.

'Great food,' Stanley enthused, as the waiter spooned a pyramid of profiteroles onto his plate. 'Even better than the Carlton. Where are you holed up, Alex?'

'In Picasso country.'

'Oh yeah – where's that?'

'Mougins,' Jeremy chipped in derisively. 'I thought everyone knew that. That's where Picasso spent the last years of his life and where he died. In the final five years alone, he created a thousand works of art.'

'A *thousand*, eh?' Stanley's eyes danced up and down like figures on a cash register as he appeared to tot up the total worth. 'Isn't there a great restaurant in Mougins?'

'One of the Riviera's finest,' Alex confirmed. 'I'd be delighted to invite you all.'

If she thought about food again, Becky feared, she really would be sick. Ross, who'd stuck to the Caesar salad, caught her eye and winked.

'So what are your plans for the afternoon, Alex?' Stanley beamed expansively, conscious of his generous offer that his team should take the rest of the day off.

'I'm hoping to take a boat out to the islands, if anyone else is up for that?'

'What's the big deal about the islands?' Stanley demanded through a mouthful of choux pastry.

'They have an interesting history. The mysterious Man in the Iron Mask was held prisoner on Ste-Marguerite at the end of the seventeenth century. To this day, his identity remains a mystery.'

'Is that a fact?' Stanley stared at Alex with disbelief. 'There are fifty thousand people who come to this film festival every year, and only you would know this.' He shook his head. 'What else you gonna see?'

'There's a wonderful old monastery on St-Honorat.'

'Alex,' Stanley protested, 'am I right in saying you're a single man? This is the goddamn Côte d'Azur. There are beaches out there full of women with naked breasts. And you wanna go look at a bunch of *monks*?'

Alex threw him a mischievous look. 'You should come with me, Stanley.'

'Hey, no offence, but count me *out*. I think I'll hit the casino.'

'You can't,' Letitia interrupted indignantly, 'You promised you'd go shopping with me on the Rue d'Antibes.'

Alex glanced down at her hand, clamped insistently on Stanley's arm. On one finger she wore a serpent ring with ruby eyes that he thought he remembered seeing in one of the jewellery stores on the Croisette.

'We'll do both, OK? The more we *win*, the more we'll have to *spend*. Anyone else wanna try their luck?'

Jeremy lit a menthol cigarette, a new experiment since Cannes. Like Bill Clinton, he didn't seem to inhale. 'I'm going to take a look at one of the movies in Director's Fortnight,' he drawled in a tone that implied he preferred this offbeat fare to the attractions of the main festival. 'How about you, Becky?'

His look was an appeal, and her first impulse was to go with him, to soothe his wounded pride and reaffirm his belief in himself. But her brain was still thick from the champagne and suddenly the prospect of open water and a stiff sea breeze was irresistible. 'I'm voting for the monks,' she pronounced, averting her gaze from his.

Ross smiled at the look of comic dismay that came over Jeremy's face. 'I guess that just leaves you and me,' he said. 'So what's this piece of high-falutin' crap you're gonna drag me off to?'

'I don't think you and I like the same things,' Jeremy said stiffly.

'Relax,' Ross teased. 'I ain't plannin' on pickin' out drapes with you. I'm just offerin' to take you to the movies.'

As the boat pulled away from the Old Port, Becky stared up at the looming Palais des Festivals – purpose-built to house the multiple festivals and conferences to which Cannes was now an eager host – its architecture so hideous as to earn it the nickname '*Le Bunker*' from the irreverent French. As the boat gathered speed and the pink concrete bulk began to diminish in size, she felt at the same time guilty and free, like a child playing truant from school.

A few tourists leaned over the sides, pointing out landmarks in a clatter of colliding tongues, but the boat seemed mainly filled with *Cannois* determined to escape the invasion of their town for a few hours of peaceful picnicking, an assortment of wicker baskets and plastic cooler bags wedged between sandalled feet.

As Alex struck up a conversation with a local in passable French, Becky was content to lean over the bows and let the wind whip cooling spray into her face, emptying her mind of all thought. The sky was a perfect cornflower blue, the sea an only slightly deeper reflection so that the horizon seemed almost seamless. The coastline behind them was a pretty vista of pink-roofed villas climbing wooded hills, with the larger hotels like a string of pearly teeth along the shore. Becky lifted her face to the sun and let its warmth flow through her like wine.

She didn't know how long she had been basking in her contented trance when the first of the islands loomed up to one side, and Alex's cotton shirt was brushing against her bare shoulder as he leaned forward to point it out to her.

'Ste-Marguerite,' he said, 'with the old Fort Royal Prison. It's a youth centre now.'

'How appropriate!' Becky thought of Adam's fascination with the macabre and the way he nagged her and Lolly to take him to the forbidden delights of the London Dungeon, where he longed to pore over instruments of medieval torture.

'There are still some gruesome relics there, if your taste runs to that kind of thing. You can see where they kept the Man in the Iron Mask, or the unfortunate Huguenot pastors locked up by Louis XIV for thirty years in solitary confinement. All of them but one went mad.'

'No one can say you don't take me to all the best places!' Becky joked.

'We're not stopping there. This boat goes straight on to St-Honorat – a much more salubrious spot. The man it's named after founded a monastery there in the fifth century, and parts of the eleventh-century building are still standing. His sister founded the nunnery on Ste-Marguerite.'

'Before the prison, I assume.'

'St-Honorat is the smaller of the two islands, only about four hundred metres wide, but for centuries it was the centre of religious life for the whole of Southern Europe, and so powerful it owned most of the land along the Mediterranean coast, Cannes included.'

It was hard to imagine, Becky reflected, as she gazed back at the sprawling conference town and tourist attraction that Cannes had become. 'In the days when God still came before Mammon,' she murmured.

'The monks weren't short of the good things in life, make no mistake. In fact, that was their downfall. They had so much wealth they were a constant target for raiding pirates and corrupt popes.'

The island was coming into view now, the honey-coloured outline of the old keep rising above its own reflection in the water, and from a certain angle it looked almost intact, restored to its former glory, as though its worldly fame and fortune had not long since passed into the history books.

As the boat approached its moorings, Alex drew her to one side, away from impatient picnickers jostling for position, as though the two of them had all the time in the world, and the present could not be measured against the perspective of the centuries he was about to reveal to her. They waited till the boat had disgorged its other passengers before stepping onto the rocky shore.

They strolled contentedly beneath pines and eucalyptus trees as the daytrippers melted away in search of sandy coves and shallow pools, the cadence of their chatter fading away on the breeze and returning the island to silence and to the monks, grave Cistercians tending rows of vines and orange trees, or going about the daily ritual of their worship.

'This is blissful,' Becky said. 'How could you have dreamt of inviting Stanley here?'

'I was thinking more along the lines of Ste-Marguerite for him,' Alex replied wryly.

'Perfect! Thirty years in solitary confinement is just what Stanley needs!'

'Quite,' he agreed. As she half stumbled over a gnarled tree root, he gently took her arm. 'But given that Stanley has the sensitivities of a pre-Neanderthal, why do you let him get to you?'

'You mean at lunch?' Becky frowned. 'He was upsetting Jeremy and I won't allow it. Jeremy doesn't deserve that, not after the wonderful job he's done. And if our film isn't quite as good as it could be, that's Stanley's fault for putting so much pressure on Jeremy to finish it quickly.'

'Becky,' Alex said wearily, 'the film is great but that isn't the point. Why are you only drawn to men you feel you have to protect?'

'I'm not aware that I—'

'Now don't go getting on your high horse. Even you must admit how you mother the men in your life, and maybe – just maybe – it isn't good for them. Jeremy may be young but he *is* a grown-up. I'm sure he can stand up for himself.'

And Rupert, he wanted to say but didn't dare, Rupert has taken advantage of your protective instincts, the generosity of your impulses, since the day he met you. And as a result, he's still sucking you dry.

'I don't see myself as Jeremy's mother,' Becky said defensively, 'but I *am* his producer and he has a right to expect my support . . .'

From the prickliness of her tone and the stubborn set of her jaw, Alex knew he could say no more. But it broke his heart to see her allowing her life-giving energies to be used up again and again by these needy men – holding herself back from the fulfilment of her own potential, the blossoming of self that could not be achieved in the shadow of others' dependency – learning nothing from past mistakes, just as his readings had taught him how the errors of history, of the human race, were destined to be repeated over and over. She would keep on propping up the same weak types, as Alex would always seek to replace the mother who had abandoned him.

They skirted the ruins left by the old inhabitants, passing the comparatively modern nineteenth-century monastery built as a replacement, drawn ever on towards the old keep, symbol of this place and all it had once stood for.

Alex said lightly, 'Have you noticed if anything's going on between Stanley and Letitia?'

'Come off it!' Becky giggled. 'She's at least a foot taller than him.'

'That doesn't make it logistically impossible.'

'Only wildly improbable. I don't think Letitia would be turned on by the gleam of his bald spot.'

'But perhaps by the shine of his gold card.' Alex's grin faded. 'If Letitia's hooked up with Stanley, God help you.'

'Don't you mean,' Becky said mischievously, 'God help her!'

They were both smiling as the keep loomed up before them and Becky grasped his hand as they began the long climb, allowing the silence to engulf them again, a total stillness broken only by their breathing and the song of the cicadas.

When they reached the top, Becky gripped his hand tighter in sheer delight at this dizzying view he had brought her to. From up here, she could see how this tower had once served not just to repel invading pirates but to allow the monks of old to survey the great sweep of land over which they held sway. Far across the waters, Cannes shimmered like a distant mirage, a flicker on a silver screen. The extravagant wedding cake façade of the Carlton Hotel with its twin cupolas modelled, so the story went, on the breasts of the *Belle Otero*, a famous courtesan of the day, was a mere white dot on the horizon. The false beaches with their imported sand raked over each morning by minions from the grand hotels were a thin line of paint on a vast canvas. From here the whole town could have been a trick of the light, as insubstantial as a dream. Only this rock on which her feet were rooted seemed real, and this man beside her, this friend, solid as the honey stone of the tower on which they were standing. But no sooner had this revelation come to her than it was drawn away again and merged, inevitably, inescapably, into the past that was all around them.

'Alex,' she said, 'how is it that you know so much?'

'You mean all those dry old facts from the history books?'

'Not just that. I mean about living, striking a balance. Like how to work in the film industry and not sell your soul.'

'Most of the people who work in it don't have a soul to sell,' he laughed.

'And you?'

'I try not to live it all the time. I do other things, read other things. I have another life.'

So did she, Becky reflected, and she wondered why the thought of it at this moment hit her with the chilling force of a cold shower,

washing away the revelation she had been groping towards from
this higher, clearer perspective. Suddenly her hand in Alex's felt
awkward, wrong, and she drew it away and lowered her eyes and
found herself by the stairs, the way back down.

As if of one accord they began to descend, Alex a step behind
her. 'When do you leave Cannes?' she asked over her shoulder.

'Tomorrow. I'm flying straight to L.A.' It was a twice yearly
pilgrimage to head office, a familiar event in his calendar, and yet
this time there was more to the trip than habit. Alex was worried
about his father – nothing he could put his finger on, just something
in the way Frank spoke to him, a loss of edge, a slackening of
concentration. He would be glad to get to L.A. and see for himself
if the unease he was feeling had any real foundation.

'How about you?' Alex said to Becky. 'When are you going
back?'

'Another two days before I relieve Rupert on the home front.'

'How's he been coping?'

'Fine, I think. He's really making an effort with Adam . . . and
everything.'

'That's great. When I get back, I'll set up some auditions for
him.'

'Good.' She paused, conscious of the awkward need to make
Alex understand, to have his blessing for what she was attempting
to do. 'I have to try and make this marriage work, Alex. There's so
much riding on it. Adam's security, for starters.'

'I know – I've been there too, remember.'

'But you gave up on yours in the end, when you realised she
wasn't right for you. You don't think Rupert's right for me either,
do you?'

'Becky,' Alex said quietly, 'don't do this.'

'What?'

'Ask me to tell you what to do about Rupert, when you've already
made up your mind.'

He was right, Becky knew, to reserve his opinion, but that didn't
make her any less anxious for his approval.

'Spoken just like a man,' she said tartly.

'Becky – I *am* a man. Not one of the boys you usually play your
games with.'

She glared at him but he was smiling, and he reached out and gently brushed back a strand of hair from her eyes. 'Let's go and take a look at the church.'

It was wonderfully cool inside and she lit a candle and sat quietly in a pew beneath vaulted arches, glad of the silence of stone-enclosed spaces. Alex sat beside her, saying nothing, asking nothing, and peace was restored between them.

They decided not to do a tour of the museum, opting only to buy the honey and sweet Lerina liqueur which the monks produced themselves, a bottle of each for Becky to take home to Rupert. As they emerged back into the sunshine, Becky asked the smiling-faced Cistercian, 'What's that wonderful smell?'

He was Spanish, he had told them, but spoke English without an accent. 'We grow lavender here,' he explained.

'No, something else,' Becky insisted.

'Ah, the almond blossom.' The monk pointed out the tree. 'Legend has it that when St-Honorat founded this monastery, he agreed to see his sister only when a particular almond tree was in flower, which happened once a year. But she prayed so hard that the tree began to flower every month.'

Beside her Alex listened attentively, storing away the tale in the treasure-house of his knowledge. Looking at his tall, rangy figure in the slanting rays of the late afternoon sunshine, the thick brown hair curling at the collar, the eyes that were windows to the kindness of his soul, Becky marvelled at the depth of human longing and at the simplicity of a faith that could bring forth a flower.

Deep within the bowels of the Palais, amidst the endless glass maze of exhibitors' stands, Becky, Jeremy and Letitia, obedient to Stanley's summons, had presented themselves at the temporary headquarters of the sleek selling machine that was Independent Films.

Stanley was bursting with bonhomie. 'Kids, I want you to meet Harry Widmark, CEO of Pantheon Pictures.'

'I'm your biggest fan.' A smooth-faced, silver-haired man in his fifties extended a manicured hand. Jeremy took it tentatively, as though handling dangerous explosives, and gave it an experimental shake.

'This is Janet Jarvis, my Vice President in charge of Production.' Harry indicated a neatly packaged brunette in her late thirties, her mouth set permanently into a thin line of determination.

As soon as the various introductions were over, Stanley steered the conversation to the business at hand. 'Harry and Janet have a proposition for you I think you're gonna *love.*'

Nerves fluttered in Becky's stomach like butterflies against glass. They'd had a lot of offers since coming to Cannes, but none so far from such a big American studio.

'Harry has a screenplay he thinks is *perfect* for you,' Stanley enthused. 'He wants to run it by you. Just hear him out, OK?'

Harry smiled, revealing perfectly capped teeth. 'It's set in London, right? It's about this female detective and the serial killer she's tracking down – turns out it's a woman, and they sort of relate to each other in a weird way. Like *Thelma and Louise* meets *Seven.* A British chick flick, but with lots of big bangs.'

'You mean violence?' Jeremy looked mutinous. 'I don't believe in gratuitous violence.'

'Did I say gratuitous?' Harry looked round with an air of injured innocence. 'Did anyone hear me mention the word "gratuitous"?'

'That's not what you said,' Stanley confirmed.

'I deal with real human relationships,' Jeremy insisted stubbornly.

'That's why I like you,' Harry went on undeterred. 'That's why you're so right for this picture. This picture's about relationships.'

Letitia was beginning to look edgy. 'I think it sounds great!' she asserted. 'I'm sure Jeremy will too – once he's actually *read* it.'

'It may need a little work,' Janet admitted.

'I think what Jeremy means,' Becky intervened smoothly, 'is that we'd want script approval.'

'I usually write my own stuff,' Jeremy asserted boldly, forgetting that one film didn't give him veteran status.

'We'd love you to do a rewrite,' Janet assured him. 'We want your input.'

'*Sure* we do,' Stanley cajoled. 'Harry and Janet and I are betting on the talent of this team. I want you to know I'll be putting up *half* the budget myself in exchange for foreign rights.'

Becky could well believe it, and not out of selfless loyalty. Before this meeting, Stanley had boasted to them that he'd sold all rights to *Abstract Love* for a tidy profit. But this time she knew he'd be risking more than small pennies and big talk. The budget of an

American studio picture would be many times larger than anything they'd handled before.

'We're talking major expenditure here,' Harry said persuasively. 'Enough to get you A-list stars – Emma Thompson, whoever you want.'

Jeremy had a gleam in his eye, but he didn't surrender without a final fight. 'I hope it's not too mainstream,' he grumbled.

'What's wrong with mainstream?' Stanley reasoned. 'Mainstream means more tails on seats to see *your* work.'

'Look, kid,' Harry argued, 'you do a nice little picture for the art circuit, win yourself a few prizes, that's great, you make a name for yourself. But sooner or later you gotta cross over into that middle-American market or you'll never make the grade in Hollywood. I assume that's what you want?'

Jeremy fidgeted under his scrutiny, as though unwilling to confirm these vulgar ambitions, yet not quite able to deny them.

' '*Course* it's what you want,' Stanley pushed. 'You'll do it, right?'

'I'll read it,' Jeremy confirmed. 'And I'll do it *if* I like it and Becky wants to be my producer . . . and Letitia, of course.'

Letitia flashed him a furious look. Harry gave him an avuncular pat on the back. Becky expelled a breath of relief and felt the butterflies fly free. It would come, the success she had worked so hard for, and when it was finally hers she might just be able to afford a little time off, a pause to take stock of her life, to decide what really mattered.

'How are you, my baby?'

'Not fine.' Adam's voice sounded so close he could have been in the next room, and Becky cradled the phone to her as though it were the child she longed to cuddle.

'What's the problem?' she asked in a voice that wasn't quite steady.

'I hate school. Nobody played with me in break time today.'

Becky knew, from constant swapping of stories with other mothers, that remarks like this couldn't always be taken at face value. Children knew which buttons to press, how to inflict maximum guilt, and their tales of woe were often exaggerated to the point of absurdity. A friend of hers, dismayed by her child's constant assertions that no one at school ever played with her, had

at last, feeling desperate and not a little foolish, hidden up a tree
in the playground and watched with a mixture of anger and relief
as her daughter skipped happily out for break, surrounded by a
veritable army of chums.

But these cautionary tales were little comfort when you were
hundreds of miles away, cut off from the truth, unable to ascertain
if your child was truly suffering or just dramatising to get attention.
'What about Mahmoud?' she asked.

'Mahmoud only plays with Freddie Foley now,' Adam said
tragically. 'They won't let me join in. What shall I do, Mummy?'

'Ignore them,' Becky counselled, knowing it wasn't what he
wanted to hear. 'Play with someone else. They'll soon start missing
you and then *they'll* ask *you* to play.'

Adam stifled a little sob, and the mental picture of him shedding
tears alone in her bedroom was almost more than Becky could
bear. 'What do you want me to bring back for you from France?'
she asked brightly.

He cleared his throat and considered. 'A Captain Comet action
figure,' he said at last.

'That's American. I'll buy you one of those on my next trip to
L.A.'

Adam burst into floods of tears. 'I don't want it – I don't want
you to go away again.'

Becky felt tears of helplessness prick her own eyes. Her son
needed her, and she wasn't there. 'Darling, I didn't mean that. I'm
not going away again, not for a long time.'

'You can't. Bogey needs you. He has a sore foot – you have to
take him to the vet.'

'Daddy or Lolly can do that. Let me speak to one of them.'

'No!' Adam wailed. 'Bogey and I want *you*!'

'I'm coming, baby. I'm coming in just two days.'

Becky knew it was hollow comfort. At Adam's age, two days
must seem an eternity.

Becky and Jeremy stood at the window of her hotel room and
looked down at the pageant that was Cannes spread out at their
feet, the crowds still streaming along the darkened Croisette, the
lights winking on hundreds of yachts in the harbour, from which
the distant music and laughter of a dozen private parties was carried

across to them on the breeze. They were no longer on the outside of it all, craning to get a peep in. Now they were on the inside looking out.

'What did you think of Pantheon's offer?' Jeremy asked.

'I think we should be opening that bottle,' Becky said, pointing to the complimentary hotel champagne, 'and giving ourselves an enormous pat on the back.'

'We showed this town, didn't we?' Jeremy grinned, moving over to pop the cork.

They clinked glasses, the excitement and disbelief in both their eyes, like children at the beginning of a roller coaster ride, knowing the thrills and spills to come, fearing them and wanting them at the same time.

Jeremy lit a menthol cigarette, his hands trembling slightly. 'I just hope it's the right move to make,' he said. 'If you shoot a small art film and it doesn't make money, no one cares because of the prestige value. But if you do some big American-style picture and it flops, overnight you're box office poison, no one wants to know.'

'You're right, that's the risk,' Becky agreed. 'But if you don't try it, you'll never know if you can do it.'

Jeremy blew out a cloud of mint-scented smoke. 'But I've seen so many Brits go wrong that way. Talented blokes who make great little pictures for the home market. Then they get seduced by the Hollywood big time, they forget their roots and stop making films about the things they know, and it just doesn't work. Before they know it, they're history.'

'That's true, but it doesn't mean the same thing will happen to you. You have to assess your chances for yourself. I can give you my opinion but you're the director. At the end of the day, it's your call.'

Jeremy played nervously with his cigarette. It seemed more of a prop than a necessity, and Becky hoped he would give it up before it became an addiction. 'I want your opinion,' he said earnestly. 'Tell me what I should do.'

What shall I do? Adam had asked her, but she was too far away, she couldn't really help, she was in a strange town dealing with the insecurities of a man who still acted like a boy, though he had passed his quarter century. *Why do you always choose men you have to mother?* Alex had enquired, and he was right to hold that mirror up to her and make her take a long hard look at herself.

She went over to her cupboard and pulled out a suitcase.

'What are you doing?' Jeremy asked, his voice almost panic-stricken.

'We've sold all the rights to our last film and we've been offered a lot of money for the next one,' Becky said firmly. 'I'd say we're in pretty good shape. There's nothing more to be done here, no more to be achieved by staying another two days.' She snapped the suitcase open and when she spoke again, her voice was light with happiness. 'I'm booking myself out on the first plane tomorrow. I'm going home.'

CHAPTER SIX

Becky stared out of the window at lowering grey skies and monotonous rows of terraced houses backing onto the motorway, the dull tableau at a standstill as the taxi's motor idled behind a long line of stationary vehicles stretching ahead as far as the eye could see. The traffic was not one of the things she had missed about London. And she so much wanted to be home before Adam came back from school, to see the surprise and joy spread over his little face.

She was, she supposed, returning a conquering hero, the spoils – in the form of Pantheon's screenplay, neatly bound with their logo on the front – in the briefcase at her feet. She would lay it before Rupert, a victorious general submitting the enemy's tribute, and wait for his words of praise. And he would give her her due, now that they had cemented this new partnership, this easy friendship, now that his jealousy was appeased by Alex's pledge to guide his career to new and sunnier heights.

She laid her head contentedly back against the seat and looked out at the rows of houses, inching slowly past her now as the taxi crawled forward. She had begun to read the screenplay on the plane, and though she found it a little obvious, heavy handed, there was potential there, especially in the relationship between the two women. The detective, theoretically on the side of the angels, was in reality too obsessed, too work driven, so that the line between her and the killer could become blurred, morally ambiguous, if it were delicately handled in the rewrite, portrayed more subtly through the skill of Jeremy's pen. Jeremy would be reading it now in Cannes, and she felt sure he would see its potential, whatever his former fears – whatever his annoyance with her at abandoning him in the romantic Riviera to fly back to the bosom of her family.

The frantic schedule of the last week was beginning to catch up with her, and as she let her head loll back, she drifted into a gentle slumber, her eyes flickering open again only when the taxi ground to a final halt in front of her door. She cast around in her purse for English money, finding barely enough and sending the driver off with back stiffened in protest at the inadequate size of his tip.

Becky lugged her suitcase into the entrance hall. A heavy silence hung over the house. Her watch told her that Lolly would even now be fetching Adam, and the lack of movement elsewhere suggested Rupert was probably out and Bogey locked in the back garden where Rupert would have preferred he remain at all times. There was no sound even of the banging of Mrs Christos's brooms, this not being one of her days.

Leaving her suitcase in the hall to be dealt with later, Becky climbed the stairs. She would just have time to slip into a comfortable tracksuit before Adam came barrelling through the door, starving for cake and biscuits.

As she trod silently along the thick pile of the passage carpet, a slow awareness came to her, a consciousness that she was not alone after all, that noise was coming from behind her closed bedroom door, a sound as old as time itself, unmistakable and yet unthinkable. She was drawn on, ever on, towards the source of the sound, as a passerby cranes for a glimpse of a gruesome accident even while longing to flee, knowing already what she would find, not quite believing it while always at some level suspecting it.

She opened the door and the sight that met her was already fully etched into her nightmares. In the large four-poster in which Rupert had first taken Becky to bed all those years ago, which had witnessed most of their joyful couplings and was to her almost a symbol of their marriage, Rupert moved to that ancient primal rhythm, flesh pounding against flesh, breath coming in ragged gasps, a pair of endlessly long legs wrapped around him, drawing him even closer, a riot of soft brown curls spread across Becky's pillows.

Lolly was the first to become aware of another presence, head swivelling towards the door, eyes widening with the horror of discovery. Rupert turned his head more slowly, his face still flushed with pleasure, his eyes dull with incomprehension. Becky stared evenly back at them, her face a mask, her mind empty of all emotion, all thought, except the one that suddenly, incongruously seemed the most pressing. 'Isn't someone,' she said clearly in the silence, 'supposed to be fetching Adam?'

Becky sped towards Launceton Hall, heedless of screeching tyres and the whiff of burning rubber. She was becoming quite an abandoned driver, she thought inconsequentially, a fitting sparring partner for that boy she had seen behind the wheel of the Porsche on the King's Road – was it only a few months ago?

In the awful seconds after her discovery, she had flung herself into a frenzy of activity, searching for car keys, driving off to fetch Adam. That was what women did in a crisis. They concentrated on the practical things, on what had to be done.

She pulled up in front of the school and left the car defiantly on the yellow line, almost daring a traffic warden to challenge her. As her heels rang out in the empty hallway, she saw that Miss Hungerford's door was reproachfully shut, and headed instead for the stairs to the secretary's office.

Adam was waiting in the chair by Hermione's desk, a small figure with watchful eyes and a slightly abandoned expression. He looked puzzled when he saw her, even a little put out. 'Why are you late?' he demanded crossly and she thought of how she had hoped to surprise him, to see his face light up. 'Where's Lolly?'

Hermione hadn't even looked up from her work, her stubby fingers flying over the keyboard of her computer, her bespectacled eyes fixed firmly on the screen. But Becky felt she had to direct her explanation at least in part to this representative of school authority.

'Lolly was . . . busy with something else.' She mustn't think about it, that way lay madness. 'That's why I came. That's why I'm late.'

Hermione looked up at last, and her pleasant round face broke into a frown of concern. 'Are you all right, Mrs Carlyle? You look ever so flushed.'

'I expect I caught the sun in Cannes.' She wanted to sound like a jet-setting businesswoman, a person who made enviable trips to exotic locations, not a poor cheated wife, an object of pity.

'Aren't you the lucky one!' Hermione's hands were already

hovering over her keyboard again, and Adam was pulling at Becky's sleeve, anxious no doubt about all the children's TV he was missing. She allowed herself to be dragged towards the door.

'Thank you for looking after him,' she said weakly over her shoulder.

'Don't give it a thought – he was no trouble. He *was* a little worried about being left, though. Best not to go making a habit of it.'

No, Becky thought, as she made her way blindly back to the car, it wouldn't do to make a habit of leaving her husband alone with the nanny, expecting them to remember, when they had other plans entirely, a small child abandoned at school after hours.

She drove down the Fulham Road on automatic pilot, past the expensive conversions that were once workmen's cottages, full now, no doubt, of thirty-something wives burdened with two point five children and too many responsibilities and husbands who looked for their entertainment elsewhere. She drove past the discreet beige façade of the restaurant where she and Rupert had held their wedding dinner, the menu printed in black on stiff white card: mushroom risotto and poached salmon hollandaise and a cake that was a silly optimistic fantasy of white meringue and cream. The obscure French wines had been selected by Rupert, who shared his absent father's adventurous and expensive palette. Her own father, very much present and seated at her side, had planted a laughing kiss on her nose and said, 'Just the right amount of food and drunkenness and fuss for a wedding. If you keep on this way, I can't see why you shouldn't make a roaring success of it.'

'Mummy,' a little voice came from the back, 'why are you crying?'

She had almost overshot her turning, and she swung the wheel sharply. 'It's nothing, darling. I think I'm just missing granny and grandpa.'

'I miss them too. You can use this if you like.'

He pushed between the seats the scrunched up blue square of one of his school handkerchiefs which no one would imagine were always neatly ironed by Lolly. The sight of it caused the tears to flow more freely, and Becky dabbed at them impotently with the small scrap of cloth.

For once there was a parking space right outside her front door and for once she didn't want it. The primrose house seemed alien, violated, a setting for dramas in which she played no part, for lives that took no account of her own.

She edged the car reluctantly into the space and sat there stupidly for a few moments, not knowing what to do. She thought of Alex, so many miles away in Cannes, and the yearning she felt to confide in him, to fall into the comfort of his arms, was a physical ache.

'Come on, Mummy,' Adam said impatiently. 'Let's go inside.'

'We can't.' She cast about for an alternative plan. 'We're going first to Anthea's house for tea.'

'What about my cartoons?'

'Anthea does have a TV, you know. She also has very good pancakes.'

Adam looked uncertainly at his mother's tear-stained face. 'I expect,' he said, 'you want one of those yourself.'

Anthea watched Becky push pancakes pointlessly round her plate, though she had made them hot and buttered, just the way she liked them. Adam had already escaped with his and was blissfully ensconced in front of Joshua's TV.

'I feel just awful,' Anthea said. 'As though I made it happen by predicting it.'

'Perhaps I made it happen by ignoring it,' Becky replied glumly.

Anthea wasn't having any of that. She gave Becky's hand an admonishing pat. 'The fault lies squarely with Rupert, not with you.'

'I don't know,' Becky protested weakly. 'Somehow I have the feeling I started it all when I lost my temper with Ross Piper. You were probably right – it *was* Rupert I wanted to hit. I wanted to say no, stop, we can't go on like this, I can't accept it any more.'

'And so you couldn't. He was taking advantage.'

'But I thought we'd sorted it all out. I thought he was really trying . . .'

The tears were coursing hotly down her cheeks, and Anthea enfolded her in a fierce and protective embrace. 'He's not worth crying over. He's a rat – they all are.'

'I know, but I'd sort of got used to thinking of him as *my* rat.'

It hurt, Anthea knew, when you actually saw betrayal with your own eyes. Not that she had surprised Simon and Daphne in bed, but in its way it had been just as painful. She had been coming out of Marks & Spencer with some bits and pieces for dinner when she saw Simon going into Mothercare with a young woman she didn't know, an unmistakably pregnant woman with stylishly cropped black hair and an air of calm competence. Almost without planning it Anthea followed them inside, watching the woman prowl the aisles with methodical efficiency, selecting little vests and babygros and a navy blue carrycot that could double as a crib. At one point Simon put his hand almost absentmindedly on her stomach so that Anthea knew, even before he paid the bill with his Mastercard, that the baby was his.

The effort of speaking had left Becky looking pinched and exhausted. Anthea tossed the pancakes decisively into the bin, producing instead a bottle of brandy. 'Drink up,' she said, placing two full glasses firmly in front of them. 'Doctor's orders.'

Becky took a sip and was glad to feel the burning in her throat, relieved to experience any sensation that wasn't numb misery. She took another sip and this time swirled the liquid round her mouth, feeling in its heat the righteous anger she knew she must draw on to exorcise the pain.

'What are you going to do?' Anthea wanted to know.

Becky had been asking herself that since she had turned blindly away from her bedroom and stumbled off in search of the car keys. What *did* you do when you caught the father of your child making love to the woman you had trusted to act as a mother to your child? Where did you all go from there?

'I am going to drink this brandy,' Becky decided, 'one mouthful at a time. And when I get to the bottom of the glass, maybe this whole horrible mess will have gone away.'

Rupert stared into his tumbler of Scotch and wondered for the umpteenth time what folly had led him to give in to temptation under his own roof.

'A man's got to do what a man's got to do,' his father had counselled him all those years ago, before he had felt what he had to do was leave Rupert's mother. 'But don't get caught doing it on your own doorstep.' It was sound advice – if there was one thing the old devil knew about, it was how to handle a bit on the side – and Rupert had followed it to the letter until now, he'd kept his

little dalliances safely away from hearth and home, and what Becky
didn't know hadn't hurt her. And then he'd gone and blown it all in
one moment of madness.

But then he was only human, and a man at that, and Lolly was
so deliciously young, so flatteringly besotted, so in awe of him at
a time when the rest of the world had flocked to Cannes to fawn
all over his more successful wife. And if Becky hadn't taken it
into her head to come back early, she would have been none the
wiser.

Now that she was, it made things rather awkward. He would
have to find a way of convincing her that a minor infidelity didn't
change anything: she was still his wife, the centre of his home
life, the mother of his child. He didn't want to lose her over a
momentary indulgence.

Cursing himself, Rupert let his eyes travel down the chrome
length of the bar. There was the usual scattering of lone drinkers
among the groups and couples – hopeful-looking girls with short
skirts and too much make-up trying to catch his eye, weary-looking
men with loosened ties and sweat-stained shirts trying to drown
their sorrows. He wondered how many of them had just been caught
cheating on their wives.

It wasn't that he didn't believe she would eventually forgive
him. Lolly would have to go, of course, and that was a shame, she
had provided a welcome boost to his damaged pride, and a bit
more besides. But it wouldn't be an impossible sacrifice if it helped
restore the peace.

The problem was, he knew women. Before the peace there would
be tears and scenes, and Rupert hated scenes.

The best tactic would be to plead guilty at once and cast himself
on her mercy. He had, over the years, grown to rely on his wife's
infinite capacity for sympathy and forgiveness. And he *was* guilty,
he cursed himself again – guilty of the cardinal sin of getting
caught.

It was no use putting off the inevitable, he decided gloomily.
Sooner or later he would have to go back and face the music. But
not before he'd fortified himself with another double Scotch.

Filled with brandy and sympathetic advice, Becky at last
summoned up the will to return to her own house. She had mixed

feelings when she discovered Lolly waiting for her in the kitchen. The girl was a picture of nervous misery, her face unnaturally white, her eyes a tell-tale red. She looked like a schoolgirl caught in an act for which she expected the ultimate punishment of expulsion, and Becky had to resist an absurd impulse to put her arms round her and comfort her.

She was dressed in a baggy shirt and knee-length skirt that was unusually demure for her, but Becky didn't need to see her long coltish legs to remember exactly what they looked like wrapped round the naked body of her husband.

'Where's Rupert?' she enquired coldly.

'He went out. He didn't say where.' Lolly's voice was a barely audible whisper.

'I'm going to take Adam upstairs to draw on the computer and then you and I will have a talk.'

'Why?' Adam demanded as she dragged him to his bedroom. 'Why do I have to draw on the computer?'

'Because you like it.'

'Why do you have to talk to Lolly?' he persisted with a child's intuitive sensitivity to trouble.

Becky tried to sound casual enough to put him off the scent. 'Lolly works for me. There are lots of times when I have to talk to her and tell her what I would like her to do.'

'But why can't I stay with you?'

Becky switched on the computer, hoping to distract him. He was always begging to be allowed to draw, knowing off by heart the series of steps he had to take: double click on 'Accessories' and then on 'Paintbrush' . . . But now he sat down stubbornly on the floor. 'I don't want to.'

Why, why, Becky wondered, did children always pick the worst possible moment to play up? She knew too that an angry response would only make matters worse. But it was hard, too hard in the circumstances, to summon up the energy to reason with him.

She took a deep breath and reminded herself of one of the great unacknowledged rules of parenthood: when all else fails, resort to bribery. 'If you draw me a very nice picture,' she cajoled, 'I'll give you a prize.'

Adam perked up a little, smelling an opportunity to drive a hard bargain. 'I want a Dilly the Dinosaur book – the one about the horror film.'

'Then that's what you'll get.'

'All right, then.' Adam acted as if he were doing her a big favour, but he was smiling secretively as his hand reached for the mouse.

Becky left him engrossed in choice of brush shape and took herself back down to the kitchen, her kitchen, the place where all the important family decisions were made.

She found Lolly looking almost eager for her return, as though she had been rehearsing a speech. 'I really want to tell you how sorry I am—'

'I'm sure you do, but it doesn't help.'

They sat down awkwardly at the table, beneath the bunches of dried flowers which Lolly had helped her to hang, like business associates about to discuss a failed venture. Becky reached for the Worcester butter dish and absently stroked the fat calf.

'I feel just awful,' Lolly stumbled on. 'You've been so good to me . . . like a mother.'

Yes, Becky thought, I do feel like your mother. Even now I want to reach over and stroke your hair and tell you it's going to be all right.

The girl began to cry, broken little sobs, and Becky felt she couldn't bear it, couldn't cope with any more tears. 'The trouble is, I sort of fell in love with him. I didn't mean to, but I did.'

It was easy, Becky remembered, falling in love with Rupert. The tricky part was trying to live with him happily ever after. She picked up the scimitar-bladed butter knife and began to dig with it in the soft grain of the table.

'Still, I never meant to do anything about it,' Lolly sniffed wretchedly. 'Not after I've been so happy here, the way you've treated me like one of the family. I don't know what got into me . . .'

Rupert, Becky wanted to quip, Rupert got into you, and she felt a crazy, almost hysterical urge to giggle.

'. . . Not that I'm trying to put the blame on Rupert. I'm sure he never meant to do anything like that. I think he's just been alone so much lately, and maybe he was missing you . . .'

What, Becky wondered, was she trying to imply? That all this was actually Becky's fault? That Becky had deserted her husband and this was the outcome? Anger began to stiffen her resolve.

'This is what I would like you to do,' she said quietly. 'Please give Adam a bath and change him into something comfortable. Then pack a suitcase for him. I am taking him to stay for a week or so with his grandparents in Tuscany. The weather's quite warm in May . . . he'll need shorts, T-shirts, swimming trunks, sandals . . .'

She knew she was avoiding the difficult part, taking refuge in harmless lists as though this were a package holiday she had booked months ago. She also knew that Lolly wasn't fooled, that she was watching her anxiously like a condemned man waiting for the axe to fall.

'While we are away,' Becky said, coming at last to the point, 'you will have only that week to find another job and pack up your things. I don't want to find you here when I get back.'

Lolly nodded, swallowing down a lump in her throat. 'Are you going to tell my agency?'

'No, but you will have to do without references, I'm afraid. If I had to recommend you to another family, I would feel obliged to tell the truth.'

The girl's relief was a momentary flash amidst the pain, but Becky no longer felt any desire to touch her, to comfort her.

'One last thing,' she cautioned. 'Please don't tell Adam that you're leaving. He's very attached to you and I want to let him know in my own time and my own way.'

Lolly nodded eagerly, as though it were the least she could do.

Rupert paused in the hallway and listened to the unaccustomed silence. There were none of the familiar domestic sounds which should now be issuing from the kitchen indicating that the family supper was being prepared. For a moment the alarming thought came to him that Becky had already left him.

The stairs were a little tricky to negotiate, the effect of the third fortifying double Scotch he had consumed – Dutch courage, he knew, but in the circumstances badly needed. His father had offered no useful tips on how to deal with getting caught.

As he passed Adam's doorway, Rupert was relieved to hear splashing noises coming from the bathroom. Becky, that meant, was still in residence. Becky must be bathing Adam, taking over the chores from the nanny who must by now have left in disgrace.

He was about to put his head sheepishly round the door when

he heard Lolly's voice, raised in gentle protest against Adam's refusal to wash behind his ears. Lolly, that meant, was also still in residence – a fact against which Rupert would have been prepared to wager his last penny. Perhaps, he speculated optimistically, Becky had decided against making an awful fuss and rocking the boat of their marriage. Perhaps she had accepted Lolly's apologies, as she would his, and everything could go on almost as before.

With a more confident swing to his step, he covered the distance to their bedroom. And there was Becky, which would have been his greatest comfort had she not been neatly packing fresh summer clothes into the suitcase she had just brought back from Cannes, its previous contents dumped unceremoniously in a heap on the floor.

He slumped despondently into the *bergère* nursing chair and watched her. She was casually dressed in a pair of linen trousers and a silk shirt, and her freshly washed hair was neatly styled into its bob. She didn't even look at him.

'I don't suppose it would change your mind,' he said in his smallest and most pathetic voice, 'if I told you how sorry I am?'

'You're right,' she replied without turning, 'it wouldn't.'

He had dreaded tears and scenes but now he thought that would be preferable. This calm, controlled Becky was somehow much more worrying.

'Please don't move out,' he begged.

This time she did turn, and the look she gave him was frank and direct. 'I assure you, Rupert, I have no intention of moving out. I'm going away to give you time to sort out somewhere else to live. By the end of this week, I want *you* out.'

This wasn't going to be quite as easy as he had thought. She was actually threatening to turn him into the street, and the shock of it couldn't quite penetrate Rupert's well-fortified ego. 'Where am I supposed to go?' he enquired in a voice that he hoped sounded pitiful.

'I'm afraid that's your problem.'

He still couldn't quite believe she would actually go through with it. Whatever he'd done, she loved him, didn't she? Or was she just looking for reassurance that he still loved her?

He got up to go to her, to take her in his arms and feel her resistance melt . . . but something about the look in her eyes made him stop in his tracks.

'How long are you going to make me stay away?' he asked instead.

'I don't know. That's the other reason I'm going. I can't make any long-term decisions about our future till I've thought this thing through.'

Looking at her standing there with her suitcase, about to embark on a journey that would decide the fate of them all, Rupert felt suddenly lost, rudderless, cast adrift. 'You can't give up on me, Becky,' he said, playing on the sympathy he had always been able to arouse in her. 'I need you.'

She looked at him almost kindly. 'I know,' she said, 'but the question I have to ask myself now is – do I still need you?'

Strapped into her seat, looking out of her window at the concrete maze of Heathrow disappearing beneath her, Becky felt disoriented, as if her life no longer had a centre, a fixed point to which she could return. Only six hours ago she had watched these same buildings grow closer as her flight from Cannes came in to land, and her heart had been filled with the joy of coming home.

On the way back to the airport, passing those same rows of terraced houses she had never expected to see again so soon, she had once more fielded Adam's suspicious questions.

'Why are we going to visit granny and grandpa if it isn't the holidays?'

'I told you – I'm missing them.'

'Won't I get into trouble for skipping school?'

She had managed to appease his fears regarding the wrath of Miss Hungerford, but his other doubts were not so easy to overcome.

'Why did we leave Daddy behind?'

'He didn't want to come.'

'Then why did he look sad when we left?'

But all Adam's reservations were forgotten in the excitement of being on a plane. As soon as the seatbelt light was switched off, he went in search of adventure, settling on the many gadgets in the lavatory as a suitable subject for initial investigation. A red-faced businessman holding his legs tightly together waited agitatedly for him to emerge, obviously having consumed rather too much in the airport bar before take-off. After a full three minutes Becky took pity on him and pounded on the door to summon her son out.

'They'll be serving dinner soon,' she said to discourage Adam from farther wanderings.

'You never let me eat plane food. You told me it's poisonous rubbish.'

'We'll have to eat it this time. It'll be far too late for dinner by the time we get to Pisa.'

'You said I could have spaghetti and ice cream.'

'And so you can – for lunch tomorrow.'

Adam began to fiddle rebelliously with the gadgets in his arm-rest, switching lights on and off until Becky began to feel a headache coming on. She was almost ready to kiss a passing steward who offered to take him up to the flight deck to meet the captain.

Leaning her head against the window, she pressed a finger to her aching temple. Darkness had fallen swiftly, and far below the lights of some unknown European city winked in the black void. She felt suspended above the world, far outside her own life, co-ordinates and destination unknown.

Long before the plane landed Adam was fast asleep, his head in Becky's lap. When she woke him to disembark, he grizzled all the way through the seemingly endless process of passport control and baggage collection. Finally, while she was filling in forms at the car rental counter, he curled up on top of the luggage and went back to sleep.

Becky studied the street map of Pisa provided by her rental agent, whose badge pinned to her blazer identified her as Violetta. She wanted Violetta's advice, never having stayed overnight in Pisa before, always driving straight down to her parents' farmhouse in Chianti. Violetta admitted rather mournfully that her home city was favoured more by daytrippers and couldn't boast hotels as fine as those in Florence or Siena. But she could recommend a very comfortable one, moderately priced, with pretty views over the River Arno and a garage that Becky would find a godsend, parking being such a problem in Pisa.

Her route conscientiously worked out in advance, Becky drove slowly but with few wrong turns, and found herself without undue delay at the promised comfortable hotel with garage. While she

carried the sleeping Adam up to their room, a bellboy followed
with their luggage.

The room was functional and modern with none of the
sumptuousness of the Carlton. She laid Adam gently on the bed
and pressed some recently changed lire into the smiling young
bellboy's palm. When he had left, she crossed the room and drew
aside the curtain. The view over the Arno gave her a sudden
unbidden rush of nostalgia for the Mediterranean and Alex and
the mad frenzy of Cannes and the impossibility of being left alone
with only a sleeping child and her own thoughts for company.

Over the remains of breakfast – a simple affair of *briosce* and
orange juice and coffee – Becky eyed the telephone and wondered
if she should call her parents to forewarn them of her arrival. But
wouldn't they wonder why, in the middle of a school term, she
was descending on them without explanation? Wouldn't they ask
questions that she didn't feel ready to answer – not yet, not in
front of Adam?

Deciding firmly against it, she instructed Adam to brush his
teeth and get ready for their sightseeing trip to the Campo dei
Miracoli. Once they had stopped off in Pisa, she reasoned, they
might as well visit its most famous landmark.

Seen from up close, the leaning tower conceived by Pisano and
built over two centuries by him and successive architects was indeed
a strange and wonderful sight. To Becky it seemed the perfect
symbol of her own crazily tilting world. Adam stared at it with a
frown of puzzlement.

'Did they make it like that on purpose?' he asked.

'Some of the experts think they did, but the people who live
here get very cross when you say so.'

'It looks like my Lego when I get it wrong.'

That, Becky thought, was as apt a description as any. Adam
grinned at her with evident self-satisfaction. 'Poor Mahmoud and
Freddie Foley are at school now, aren't they?'

'You're learning something too. Travel broadens the mind, that's
what they say. Do you want to know another interesting thing about
that tower?'

Adam looked uncertain, as though he might be in for one of
Miss Hungerford's more boring discourses. 'OK, then.'

'The story goes that a very important man from Pisa called Galileo—'

'That's the airport, silly—'

'Well, the airport was named after him because he was so famous. Anyway, he did some experiments on that tower. He dropped a whole lot of objects from the top to prove some of his ideas about gravity.'

'Can I do that too?' Adam begged. '*Please*!'

'Not in the middle of the tourist season, darling.'

Adam kicked angrily at the grass. 'Why do only grown-ups get to do whatever they want?'

Unbidden, the image of Rupert and Lolly flashed back into her mind. Rupert had indeed done exactly what he wanted, as heedless of the consequences as if Galileo had dropped his cannon ball into the midst of a crowd of onlookers. Had Rupert once thought of the pain he would cause her, or only of the pleasure of the moment? Had there been others besides Lolly? How often? How many?

Hand in hand with Adam, she wandered miserably towards the souvenir shops crowded around the Campo, forcing herself to focus on their tacky offerings: light-up leaning towers in shades of pink and yellow, kitsch plastic kittens and naked ladies which reminded her of Anthea's Roman nudes and made her wonder if she too should take some home to castrate in a fit of pique. Somehow she had the feeling that she wouldn't experience the same cathartic release, but would only feel foolish.

Adam was absorbed in an irresistible array of medieval weapons – cudgels, crossbows, maces and whips – all cunningly designed to appeal to the child with a taste for the macabre. She had no chance, Becky realised, of escaping without some grisly purchase.

Armed with a crossbow, the least Adam would settle for, they picked a restaurant with yet another flashing neon leaning tower on the front window, and went in to order Adam's promised spaghetti and ice cream. Becky, mindful of the drive ahead, tried to stimulate her non-existent appetite with a plate of *polenta* and mushrooms.

With luck, if they left by mid-afternoon, they would arrive at her parents in time for cocktails round the pool. The image of it filled her with longing to escape from tourist-friendly Pisa to the remote enchantments of the Tuscan countryside, the sensible advice of her parents, and a glass of the delicious red Chianti that never tasted quite the same outside the small designated region from which it drew its name.

CHAPTER SEVEN

The breeze lifted Becky's hair and the sun warmed her arm resting on the wound-down window of her rented Fiat. She imagined her skin, pale from the hibernation of an English winter, transformed to a light gold by its rays. She would lie by her parents' pool and soak up the sun and feel its purifying heat heal her wounds.

After a game of 'I Spy' which Becky had lost rather disastrously as she kept a wary lookout for road signs, Adam had fallen asleep on the back seat, still tired from the dramatic events of the day before. Becky drove silently through the landscape that had inspired the great artists of the quattrocento – a rolling vista of hills that looked as though they could have been painted by Piero or Perugino, their gentle curves hugged by geometric rows of terraced vines, their peaks crested with dark cypresses standing like sentinels against the sky, and here and there among their folds a farmhouse or splendid villa amidst olive groves and gardens brimming with flowers.

And all the time, the doubts were gnawing at her. Had there been some signs of restlessness on Rupert's part that she had failed to notice, some neglect on hers that she had failed to remedy? If she hadn't so often been tired, too tired for sex, would he still have looked for it elsewhere?

'It's Rupert's fault, not yours,' Anthea had said, but she wasn't sure. She wanted so much to be honest with herself, fair to both of them, but her mind kept circling senselessly round these same questions without coming up with any answers, so that she felt only frustration and an aching tiredness and a longing to reach the haven of her parents' home.

Not that they had ever had a home in the sense that most parents did. Hugh Haydon, her father, had spent his entire career with the

Foreign Office, travelling from one posting to the next, his wife Alice traipsing willingly and competently in his wake. In the early years and later the holidays there were the children for her to see to, but as soon as Becky and her brother Michael were of prep-school age, they were packed off to proper English boarding schools and the sort of education that had once built the backbone required for Empire. It was this very quality, present even more con-spicuously in Hugh's wife than in himself, that had ensured his steady rise through the ranks. No matter where they were sent, whatever the challenges they were faced with, Hugh and Alice Haydon coped admirably.

So it never occurred to Becky, alone at the age of eight in a dormitory full of girls she had never set eyes on, to do otherwise. If her mother could deal with the vagaries of Delhi plumbing, the deviousness of juvenile pickpockets in the Rio streets, the conundrum of starting a motor car in temperatures of minus-twenty in Toronto, then she, Rebecca Haydon, would show that she was made of the same stern stuff. When it came to the small matter of being sent thousands of miles from her parents to a country she hardly remembered, she too would cope admirably.

There were many in her dormitory who did not, who spent the first weeks shedding copious and lonely tears into their pillows, wondering why the girl with the straight blond hair and solemn green eyes, who was the smallest and youngest of them, never showed any outward sign of distress. And so they gravitated to her, to confide in her their problems and draw comfort from her quiet strength, to discover her secret.

And Becky, while she took on a mothering role unsuited to her years, could never explain that it was no secret at all – that she simply drew her strength from the bottomless well that was in her parents. It wasn't that she didn't miss her mother and father, it was that they had built her character to make her whole and so able to survive without them.

So the young Haydons were sent off on their journey through life with the sense of purpose that came from knowing they were loved and what was expected of them. Returning to their parents for school holidays in a variety of exotic capitals, the world quite naturally became their backyard, so that when Becky made her home in London, she still ventured off to whatever distant location her filming took her to build her career. Michael was now an investment banker in Hong Kong, married to a high-flying Chinese trader, and every so often they would descend on London or Tuscany with their adorable twin girls, sleek-haired and almond-eyed, and a suitcase full of inexpensive cameras and watches and toys for Adam, who would turn them over solemnly to look for the 'Made in Hong Kong' imprint. Then the whole family would talk non-stop for days, to make up for separations both past and to come, the conversation ranging over topics and regions as diverse as the Chinese takeover in Hong Kong, the latest craze in children's action toys and water shortages in the Tuscan hills.

Yet, although she loved them all, it was her father who had a special place in Becky's heart. His brand of competence was somehow a little less intimidating than her mother's, his standards a little less uncompromising, his personality more inviting of confidences. And despite his absolute fairness to the claims of all his family, Becky suspected he had a secret soft spot for her too. Her mother, she felt, though undoubtedly equally fond of her children, had brought the same rigorous efficiency to breeding as to everything else she undertook, being safely delivered of two perfectly healthy children, one of each sex, the 'heir and spare' as she referred to them so that Hugh would enquire in a gently chiding voice: 'And who is the "spare", my dear – not our Rebecca, surely?'

It was Hugh Haydon who decided, when his retirement loomed, not to go back to his native England where he retained many contacts but, after years abroad, no social circle close enough to make up for the uninviting climate and the absence of the strong colours he had become accustomed to under harsher, sunnier skies. So he bought an old converted farmhouse in the countryside outside Castellina known as 'Chiantishire', and Alice at once adapted, with Darwinian efficiency, to life among the locals and the large and well-heeled expatriate community. She took up contract bridge, perfected the Italian she had picked up during Hugh's first posting to Rome, enrolled for a course on quattrocento art, and uncovered essential supply lines of Cooper's Oxford Marmalade, Gordon's gin and the *Daily Telegraph*. Hugh joined in those of her activities for which he felt inclined, and withdrew to his study and his books to escape from those for which he did not. And so he passed his retirement with his wife, as he had his active service, in an atmosphere of companionable independence.

Becky smiled. She would sit in her father's study and drink brandy from a great balloon glass and confide to him her troubles, and although he would not tell her, as he never had, how to resolve her current crisis, she would draw from his goodness and wisdom, as she always had, the strength to make her own decision.

The car swung up the dirt track between solid gateposts, through olive trees and the riot of foreign flowers her mother had learned to coax from unfamiliar soil. When Becky pulled up in front of the solid, two-storey farmhouse structured from local stone, Adam stirred on the back seat as though instinctively aware that they had arrived at their destination.

Becky climbed stiffly from the car, stretching luxuriously. Adam leaped out as nimbly as a mountain goat. 'Where are granny and grandpa?' he demanded, his voice squeaky with excitement.

From the other side of the house, where she knew the pool to be, she could hear voices raised in desultory chatter. Parked next to her own dusty Fiat was a sleek black Aston Martin that belonged to neither of her parents. 'Quietly, darling,' she cautioned Adam. 'They have visitors.'

They circled the house, following the voices, and came upon a scene that could have been played out at any poolside across Tuscany: two elderly couples sitting round a table, drinking from glasses that rattled with ice cubes, reaching occasionally for a slice of *prosciutto* or salami, an olive or a piece of *bruschetta* covered with tomato and mozzarella.

Hugh Haydon's hand stopped halfway to his mouth and he stared in the gathering dusk at his daughter and grandson, his face registering in quick succession surprise, delight and concern. Alice followed his look and, almost without missing a beat, took the situation in her stride.

'Darlings, what a lovely surprise. Don't hover, come and give us a hug.'

Adam barrelled into his grandmother's open arms. Hugh rose more slowly and enfolded his daughter in an embrace that was both quieter and more intense.

'You've been growing while my back was turned,' Alice chided

Adam. 'You're quite up to my waist. Now you must both meet Roger and Bunny.'

Squeezing Becky's shoulder, she turned her towards a red-faced man with a receding hairline and his buxom, buck-toothed wife.

'We've heard so much about you—'

'—It's a real thrill meeting you at last,' Roger and Bunny chanted in chorus, one finishing the other's sentence as though married life had turned them into two halves of a person which only together made up a whole.

Without awaiting the request, her father handed Becky a glass of the red Chianti she had been dreaming of all through the drive, and moments later produced a grape juice for Adam, who fell on it like a Bedouin at a well. When Hugh raised his gin and tonic to Becky in a welcoming toast, she read the questions he couldn't yet voice in his eyes.

'If you want us to go, we quite understand—'

'—So you can catch up on family gossip,' Roger and Bunny offered helpfully.

'Don't be silly, there'll be time enough for that when you've finished your drinks,' Alice insisted, ignoring the doubtful look on her husband's face.

Adam was already tugging at his grandfather's hand, wanting him to help catch fireflies, and reluctantly Hugh allowed himself to be dragged off for this customary game. Alice at once took command of the others.

'Eat some more of these snacks, for heaven's sake, or Francesca will be in a terrible sulk and never prepare any more. You must be hungry, Rebecca. Did you drive straight down?'

Becky launched into a light-hearted account of their morning tour of Pisa, and Roger and Bunny nodded in unison.

'Of course, you have to see the tower once—'

'—But once is more than enough!' They brayed with the distinctive laughter so jarring in the English abroad.

'For my part,' Alice said firmly, 'I haven't seen it at all, and consider myself none the worse off.'

'Adam wanted to throw cannon balls off it,' Becky recalled, 'like Galileo.'

'I doubt there's a word of truth in that story,' Alice observed with her irrefutable logic. 'Can you imagine him trying to drop objects of different weights at the same time, and then running all the way to the bottom of the tower to see how quickly they fell?' She tossed her head, dismissing the subject. 'Roger,' she informed Becky as she filled her glass, 'is in wine.'

Roger smiled modestly. 'I was once very active in the trade—'

'—But now he's retired, he just keeps his hand in,' Bunny explained.

'Is there perhaps a bottle or two of something special I could find for you to take back?'

'I do love this Chianti,' Becky confessed.

'I think it's a tragedy,' Roger observed, managing a whole speech without assistance, 'what they've done to that simple, spontaneous glass of wine that inspired Elizabeth Barrett Browning to write her greatest verses. Now it's all *appellation contrôlée*'s and limited edition numbered bottles – stuff and nonsense, if you ask me.'

Becky swirled the wine around her tongue. The distant hills were as purple as the grapes on the vines, and the fireflies hung in the bushes like the shimmering lights of a miniature city. Once in a while, a bat swooped from the shadows to skim insects from the surface of the pool. 'It still tastes pretty good to me,' she said.

'Ah – that's because what you're drinking isn't pumped full of chemicals to travel to the London wine shops. Just a simple brew for local consumption—'

'—From our son-in-law's cellar,' Bunny joined the duet again. 'Our eldest, Clarissa, married a wonderful man from these parts – Stephano Fresconori, from quite a noble family – Roger introduced them, you know, and they have such a wonderful home, a castle really, with its own vineyard.'

'Your father and I always buy from them,' Alice confirmed. 'Their wine is really quite wonderful and totally unpretentious. Becky, have another piece of that *prosciutto* before the insects get it.'

'They'd love you to visit while you're here,' Bunny chirped. 'They have children close to your son's age – Lorenzo's five and little Lucia is three. Quite bilingual—'

'—From going to the local village school. Happy as larks there too.' Roger beamed as though he too were as content here as the proverbial songbird.

'Won't do them any harm at their age,' Alice said firmly. 'We did the same with ours. But your daughter will have to think again when they turn eight. Nothing like a good English boarding school education at that age.'

'I suppose so.' Bunny took another slug of gin and her eyes filled with sentimental tears, as though the departure of her clever bilingual grandchildren were just around the corner.

Hugh returned with Adam in tow and the net with which he pretended to assist in the capture of the elusive fireflies. 'We nearly got one this time,' Adam told Becky, his eyes shining with the closeness of victory.

All around them night was falling, thick as velvet. Regretfully Roger and Bunny drained their glasses, and wove back to the Aston Martin and the precarious drive home through the Tuscan hills.

She had yearned to be alone with her father, to pour out the confession she had thought could not wait, but now that the moment had come Becky was inexplicably tongue-tied, almost ashamed of what she had to tell him.

Francesca had prepared an excellent dinner, expanded to accommodate the extra mouths under the beady eye of Becky's mother, who reminded them all that she had dealt with many a more complicated catering crisis in her time. They had eaten delicious *fritto misto* – lamb chops and sweetbreads and *zucchini* fried in a crisp batter – followed by the spicy *panforte* that was Adam's favourite, filled with nuts and candied fruits. Heavy with food, he had been taken up to bed by his grandmother, leaving the coast clear for Becky and her father.

She could see the battle he was waging with himself, anxiety to know what was undoubtedly wrong warring against respect for her need to tell him in her own time. She must put him out of his misery.

'I caught Rupert,' she said bluntly, 'in our bed with the nanny.'

Her father did not reply at once. They had brought their brandies not to his study but to the cool of the sitting room, its French doors open to the night breezes, and as she took in the familiar setting she was struck by how unmistakably it had the look of an English country house, with its chintzes and good antiques and fresh flowers and candles, though it contained just as many exotic objects from around the globe: bronze elephants, a statue of the four-armed god Shiva, a brightly coloured Mexican rug, a Roman urn for the flowers. And her father too, straight-backed, silver-haired, shirt buttoned right up to the collar despite the warmth of the evening, had never looked to her, even with his light Mediterranean tan, so endearingly the fair-minded and reticent Englishman.

He said at last, 'Knowing you as I do, I would say you may not be able to live with such a betrayal.'

'And if I can't,' Becky cried, 'what then? Divorce?'

The word hung between them, like a dirty secret at last brought out into the open.

'You know,' Hugh said, 'that I can't advise you on such a drastic course. It's a terrible decision, and one you'll have to make for yourself. The life of a single woman with a child isn't an enviable one.'

'What about the life of a married woman with an unfaithful husband?'

She cradled her brandy, her head spinning not from the drink but from the awesomeness of the decision confronting her.

Her father looked at her as though his heart would break. 'He's destroyed your trust and when trust is gone, there's often nothing left to build on. But we mustn't forget that we're all human, we all make mistakes, and we have to try and forgive one another. Has he asked for your forgiveness?'

'He's said he's sorry but it doesn't seem enough.'

There was a sharp click of heels on tiles and Alice appeared with a glass of *vinsanto* and took her place on the sofa beside her husband.

'He went to sleep like a lamb,' she said. Alice had a firm touch with children, who knew instinctively that they would get away with no nonsense while she was in charge. 'Now you'd better fill me in on what this is all about.'

'It appears,' Hugh said quickly, to spare Becky further pain, 'that Rupert has been unfaithful and Rebecca is trying to decide whether she wants to end the marriage.'

'I see.' Alice took a delicate sip of her dessert wine. 'Of course, you would be quite within your rights to do so, but what would be your reasons?'

Becky, jolted with indignation, leaned forward in her chair.

'Isn't cheating on me with the nanny reason enough?'

'It may be,' Alice said calmly, 'and it may not. Have you perhaps been neglecting Rupert, darling? Working too hard?'

'No doubt, but that's because he hasn't been working at all and someone has to keep him in the style he's accustomed to!'

Hugh looked anxiously from his daughter's hurt and angry face to his wife's composed one. 'Perhaps Rebecca's thought about it enough for one night.'

'Don't baby her, Hugh,' Alice said impatiently. 'Men are always so frightened of feelings but you have to face them, even when they're painful.'

'Daddy's right,' Becky almost shouted, 'I don't want to talk any more—'

'Allow me to say just this.' Alice looked squarely at her daughter. 'As I recall, you made no move to marry Rupert until you were pregnant with Adam. So I'm assuming you married him for the sake of the child.'

Becky stared at her blankly. In her mind, familiar events were shifting like the multicoloured pieces in a kaleidoscope.

'If that is the case,' Alice continued, 'you may have to face the fact that you should *stay* married to him for the sake of the child, whatever he's done.'

The kaleidoscope stopped moving, the pieces fell into place, and suddenly Becky was looking at the results of what her mother had created – an entirely new picture of her past.

'Spread out your arms and legs like a starfish, take a deep breath, and float,' Hugh instructed patiently, standing up to his waist in the lukewarm water of the shallow end, ready to fish his grandson out of the pool if he got into any trouble.

Adam filled his lungs and belly-flopped onto his stomach. He would have to get this part right, Hugh knew, if he were ever to stay waterborne long enough to swim a width of doggy paddle. As things stood, despite weekly lessons at the Fulham Pools, he could manage only a couple of yards before he had to put his foot down.

'What do they teach him there?' Hugh had asked in bafflement.

'I don't know,' Becky replied truthfully, since it was always Lolly who took him.

Adam emerged, spluttering. 'How was that?'

'Ever so good. You're a clever little chap. Now try again . . .'

They had been trying for five days now while Becky, distant and dream-like, lay on a pool recliner and soaked up the sun. The wan pallor of her skin when she first arrived had been overlaid by a coating of bronze like a fine pottery glaze. She looked healthy and well but what, Hugh wondered, was going on beneath the gilded surface?

Since that first night in the sitting room she had not spoken of her troubles. She had not done much of anything, apart from lie by the pool. To give her the peace she so obviously needed, Hugh and Alice had cancelled their usual round of drinks and bridge afternoons and dinner parties – no great penance, given their constant opportunity to see the same faces – and Hugh had begged Becky to stay with them for as long as it took her to think things through, but what was actually going on in her head he had no way of knowing. If she spoke at all, it was only about the wine or the weather or the news from Michael in Hong Kong or the plans for Adam's entertainment.

Both she and Adam had been invited, as promised by Roger and Bunny, to visit the Fresconoris, but Becky had politely declined, remaining in her recliner while Alice drove off with her grandson. Adam had returned filled with awe and chatter about the real castle they lived in with real weapons on the walls, and how Lorenzo and Lucia didn't even realise how wicked it was because they were still too babyish to understand anything. He had made them play soldiers and they had, to his disgust, been very unsatisfactory troops.

But even alone with her father, Becky had made no attempt to talk about Rupert. She seemed almost in a kind of trance – avoiding the issue, Alice would no doubt have said. But Hugh felt it was her right to avoid it, if it would help her get through the initial shock. It was a subject he now tried not to discuss with Alice, after the tense rows it had caused behind their closed bedroom doors. He knew Alice's philosophy – that it was better to face unpleasant truths and deal with them right away – just as she had been far more philosophical about the children's departure for boarding school, observing that they would have to stand on their own feet one day and they might as well start sooner rather than later. But Hugh had lived too long and seen too many different cultures to believe there was any one way of doing things, and he felt now that he would have defended to the death his daughter's right to choose her own.

Through the French doors to the sitting room he heard the telephone ring and his wife answer it. Then her heels clicked to the doorway and she glanced quickly at Adam, still absorbed in practising his tummy float, then mouthed to Becky, 'It's Rupert.'

Hugh's eyes swivelled to his daughter. She sat up very slowly, as though struggling to surface from beneath deep water, and stared blankly at her mother. Then she simply shook her head.

Alice's clipped footsteps returned to the phone. 'I'm sorry,' she said in a voice quite audible on the terrace, 'she doesn't want to speak to you.'

Becky had returned to her reclining position but now she seemed to be not resting but coiled for any action that might be required, gathering herself for a defensive strike. She remained in this state of prepared stillness as Alice's voice continued.

'I think it's so much better to be honest, don't you? As long as Becky hasn't made up her mind what she wants to do, she really has nothing to say to you. So I suggest you wait until you hear from her. If you call again you will simply put Hugh and me in the position of having to make excuses to you, which we don't want to do. Of course if you wish to speak to Adam, that's another matter . . .'

In the silence that followed, Becky seemed to be holding her breath.

'That's probably the wisest course,' Alice said. 'There's really nothing for you to worry about – he's having a wonderful time here. And missing a little school is hardly serious at his age . . . Of course, I'll give them both your love. Goodbye, then.'

As her mother hung up a little of the tension seemed to flow out of Becky, and Hugh waited for her to sink back into her somnambulant state. But suddenly she sat up and squinted at the midday sun. 'I think,' she said, 'I'd like to do a little sightseeing this afternoon.'

Becky and her mother decided to drive to San Gimignano. Once there they would go their separate ways, Becky to look at the art collection of Florentine and Sienese masters in the Museo Civico, and Alice to initiate Adam into the joys of the torture museum.

'What instruments do they have?' he asked, in a fever of excitement that after months of forbidding him entrance to the London Dungeon, his mother had so suddenly and unexpectedly caved in over this current ghoulish expedition.

'The usual horrors,' his grandmother replied. 'The rack, the Iron Maiden . . .'

Adam had never seen an Iron Maiden, not even in pictures, and asked to have it described to him in minute detail as they drove westwards past Poggibonsi towards what the guidebooks called 'Italy's best preserved medieval city'.

Becky said nothing but she seemed more alert, Alice noted with relief, more interested in her surroundings. Alice had been distressed by the emotional void into which Becky had descended in the past five days, and had been dissuaded from shaking her out of it only by Hugh's quite implacable opposition.

It was unusual for Alice to argue with her husband. They had lived through forty-two years of marriage with very little in the way of raised voices or resentful silences, muddling along on a largely successful mixture of compromise on joint matters and independence on individual ones, an unspoken accommodation to the needs of one another and their children. But now, quite suddenly, Alice found herself totally indignant with the stand Hugh had taken on Becky – in fact, quite furious with his refusal to see what had to be done.

She had felt that way only once before, and the memory of it was still with her, but faint, like a scar that has mostly healed with the knitting over of new tissue, the overlay of happier experiences, the long march of time. She had been only twenty-three at the time, married for just a year, when she miscarried at six months and gave birth to a hopelessly premature baby. It had been a proper labour, but one with no reward at the end, and it was she who saw the perfectly formed little boy and knew exactly what they had lost. Hugh had not been present, it wasn't the custom of the time, and she felt she would never be able to make him understand the raw pain that made her cry for days in a rage of non-acceptance.

Not knowing what to do with her, he turned to the doctors for something to 'calm her nerves', to 'help her sleep'. Alice knew these were just euphemisms for oblivion, but she didn't want forgetfulness, she wanted to remember this outrage, to protest it to the heavens. But the doctors were of Hugh's opinion, they believed in their magic pills which for her only delayed to some indefinite future date the inevitable process of grieving. What none of them would understand was that Alice hated her suffering as much as they did, but she knew, unlike them, that if she didn't face it now it would just grow into something bigger, something even more unmanageable. And so she pretended to take the pills and threw them away when no one was looking and learned, slowly and painfully, to live with her loss.

'Are we nearly there yet?' Adam demanded, bouncing impatiently on the back seat.

'We'll get there in the end.' One always did, whether the short way or the long way, and Alice had forced herself right there and then to learn that lesson, she had sworn she would never shrink from pain. That didn't mean she relished it, any more than Hugh did – it simply meant that she had taught herself to cope.

And her reward had been two healthy children and the healing of the rift that had threatened so early on to destroy her marriage. She knew overall how fortunate she was, that Hugh was basically a good man, that his fear of strong feelings had not prevented him from being a loving husband and father. So why did she feel this rage against him again, after all these years? Why was she so fearful that, because he was able to reach Becky where she so often could not, he would somehow set her off in the wrong direction, one that would cause her a great deal more suffering in the long run?

Tense with suppressed frustration, Alice swung the car into the parking ground outside the Porta San Giovanni, where they would have to leave it and continue on foot through this ancient town closed to all but essential traffic. Adam scrambled for his door, Becky climbing out in the unhurried, leisurely way that Alice had come to find so much more irritating than the frenetic pace at which her daughter normally lived her life.

They all looked up at the outlandish sight of the town's famous Belle Torri, great towers looming above them to a height of over fifty metres. Once there had been seventy, built as strongholds in the days of the region's bitter family feuds. Now fifteen remained, packed together within the confining walls, pointing like warning fingers to the heavens.

'Wow!' Adam breathed.

'Shall we climb the tallest one together?' Becky asked in a sudden burst of enthusiasm that Alice found vaguely reassuring.

With difficulty, Adam was persuaded to postpone the promised visit to the torture museum, bribed by a strawberry *gelato*. As he curled his tongue luxuriously round the ice cream, they made their way steadily and breathlessly up the awesome tower of the Palazzo del Popolo.

The views from the top were an extraordinary vista across the hill country of western Tuscany. Becky and Alice stood side by side, quietly, companionably, looking out to the cypress-studded horizon.

'Can I drop my ice cream from here?' Adam asked, remembering his Galileo lesson. '*Please* – it's soft, it won't hurt anyone?'

Alice turned her level gaze on him, and at once he retracted the hand holding out the cone. 'I want to go and see the Iron Maiden, then,' he said rather sulkily.

'And so we shall – when you have finished your ice cream.'

Alice took a last look at her daughter's profile, remote against the splendid backdrop. She did not expect her to share her thoughts – she knew Becky would not have believed that the mother she considered so stoical understood her sense of loss, probably better than her father did. She and Hugh had never told their surviving children about that first miscarriage. It would have served no purpose. But Alice was glad to observe that Becky was looking out now, beyond herself, forward to the future that had to be faced. She left her leaning on the parapet with her eyes fixed on the horizon.

Though she was looking out at the view, Becky realised, her eyes were unseeing, her mind taking in nothing, her fingers gripping the parapet so that the knuckles were white. She unclenched them and turned quickly away, back to the descent of the hundreds of stairs she had so painfully climbed with her mother and Adam just so she could stare blindly inwards at the landscape of her own mind.

She had come to this countryside with one purpose: to make a decision about her future. But over the past days her mind had remained a stubborn blank, the painful choices on hold, the decision-making process quite blocked until finally a mild panic had set in, even more paralysing than the inertia which had preceded it.

She descended slowly, putting one foot in front of the other. There had been only one thought that had recurred constantly over these last hazy days, the memory of her mother's startling words . . . *You made no move to marry Rupert until you were pregnant with Adam. So I'm assuming you married him for the sake of the child . . .*

It seemed incredible to Becky now, after hours of turning it over in her mind, that she had never confronted this possibility before. Her actions at the time had been so instinctive, so little subject to any sort of reasoning process. Was it then true that she had never actually made a conscious choice of Rupert as a husband? Had she allowed that crucial decision to be made for her by the simple fact of her physical condition?

Her feet had finally reached solid ground and in a daze she walked through an archway into a courtyard that still looked much as it must have done in the days when Dante came here as the ambassador from Florence to persuade the citizens to take sides in the struggles and join the Guelph League. She passed, without seeing them, the frescoes and the painted coats of arms of the Florentine governors, and climbed the stairway to the museum.

If she had not married Rupert for his own qualities, but for his child that was in her womb, should she then have married him at all? Would she have done so, all other things being equal? Or had she always known subconsciously what he had now proved beyond doubt – that he lacked those attributes that would make him the kind of husband and father she wanted, the kind her own father had been?

Then, if she had been without the blinkers of that biological constraint, was there some other choice she could have made, some other path that could have been taken, some chance of happiness she had missed?

The question brought her dizzily close to the abyss and, shrinking back from it, she fumbled in her purse for the money to pay her entrance. She wandered aimlessly through the first rooms, past paintings that had made westerners see the world with new eyes, that had changed their perceptions and their civilisation forever. She heard an English tour guide giving a well-rehearsed patter on the pictures by Taddeo di Bartolo depicting the story of San Gimignano, the saint from whom the town took its name, a man who could apparently calm seas and exorcise devils.

Hers were not so easy to cast out. If she had entered a marriage for the wrong reasons, then could she risk compounding the error by leaving it for equally bad ones? Her mother had also said, *you may have to face the fact that you should* stay *married to him for the sake of the child, whatever he's done.*

One of the paintings suddenly caught her eye and she came to a stop in front of it. It was, the plaque said, the *Crucified Christ* of Coppo di Marcovaldo (*c.* 1270). Becky looked at the rather awkward figure hanging on the cross, at the almost tangible anguish that radiated from it, and suddenly she realised that the decision she thought she couldn't make had actually been forming within her all along, that it had crystallised and taken shape into something inevitable, fully formed, almost tangible.

With lighter steps she made her way outside to the Piazza del Duomo and her rendezvous with her mother and son. They were waiting for her, watching a trio of classical street buskers. She almost skipped in her haste to join them, and while Adam was absorbed in the virtuosities of the flautist (she had recently given him a recorder from which he produced an assortment of discordant sounds), she drew Alice aside and told her softly, but with just a hint of defiance, 'I've decided to ask Rupert for a divorce.'

This time she was ready for her mother, ready to counter her cool logic with reasoned arguments of her own. She could not undo the mistakes of the past but neither did she have to pay for them forever. She would not be a sacrificial lamb. For years Rupert had been wearing her away, but imperceptibly, like water dripping on stone. Now the drip had become a flood, the damage almost irreparable. If she let it go on, she had the feeling she would slowly crumble, disappear, cease to be the person she wanted to be, the wife she ought to be, the mother Adam needed. She was doing this for her son as much as for herself. Her mind was made up.

She opened her mouth to say so, but before she could speak her mother grasped her in a sudden, fervent embrace. 'Good for you, darling,' she said into Becky's hair, and her voice sounded almost choked with pride.

And then, quite without meaning to, Becky burst into tears.

CHAPTER EIGHT

'Why won't Daddy be there when we get home?'

They were on the plane again, heading back the way they had come to the unfamiliar life that now awaited them, half a family that would never be whole again, and it was Adam's turn to look tearful.

Becky cast about for the words, like a traveller in an unknown land who has not yet mastered the language. 'I'm afraid Daddy and I are having problems – grown-up sort of problems – and we're going to try living apart for a while—'

'You mean get divorced?'

She couldn't quite bring herself to match her son's directness. 'Do you know what that word means?'

' 'Course I do. Princess Diana's divorced. So are lots of the Queen's children. Even Andrew Mackenzie's parents are divorced.'

'Daddy and I are going to be too, I'm afraid.'

Adam poked a finger into the ice cubes in his drink. 'Why?'

She tried to remember what the experts told you to say in these situations, the conventional wisdom of the textbooks and the TV chat shows. 'Well, sometimes grown-ups fight a lot, just like you do with your friends. You know how you've been fighting with Freddie Foley?'

'Yes . . . ?' he said cautiously.

'And then it's better if they don't live together any more, but that doesn't mean they can't still be friends. And whatever happens, Daddy and I will always love you. This isn't your fault—'

'Is it Daddy's fault?'

'Perhaps it's nobody's fault.'

'When we fight at school, Miss Hungerford always says it's someone's fault.'

Becky sighed. She hadn't meant to leave all the explaining till the last minute, but Adam had seemed so happy, so contented in Tuscany, she hadn't had the heart to spoil those last few days of carefree childhood.

'There's something else,' she said. 'It's Lolly . . . Lolly can't look after you any more.'

This time Adam just stared at her with huge round eyes.

'I know you'll miss her and she'll miss you, but it's time for her to have a change—'

'It's not *fair*!' Adam kicked the back of the seat in front of him, and a woman with a tight grey perm turned round and gave them a pointed look.

'Don't do that, darling,' Becky begged. 'You're disturbing the lady.'

'I don't *care*. I don't want Lolly to go as well.'

'Nannies can't stay with you forever, you know, not like mummies—'

'That's not why. She's going because she doesn't want the divorce. I don't want it either.'

'I'm sorry, darling, I know it's hard—'

'It's *your* fault,' Adam shouted and he burst into inconsolable tears.

A solicitous cabin attendant appeared at his side. 'Can I get you anything?' she enquired.

'Yes,' Adam gulped between sobs. 'I want Lolly!'

It seemed to Becky that an entire roll of fax paper had been disgorged onto her study floor: sales figures from Stanley Shiplake's office, and repeated misspelled notes from the miniskirted Bryony asking her to contact Mr Shiplake 'imediately'. The red message light on the phone flashed insistently.

Ignoring it, she started to dial Alex's number, only remembering midway through that he would still be away in Los Angeles. A feeling of the most complete desolation came over her.

She must pull herself together, she thought weakly, she must remember her determination to make a go of things alone. Firmly she reached for a pad and pencil and pressed the playback button.

Letitia's angry voice filled the room. 'I don't know what you

thought you were playing at, running off like that from Cannes . . .'
And then: 'You seem to have disappeared without trace. If you're
there can you kindly pick up the phone . . .' And finally: 'What on
earth do you mean by never returning a single message, let alone
showing your face at the office? Perhaps one of these days you'll
remember you have a business to run . . .'

In between the tirades were several clicks – a receiver being
hastily replaced. Who, she wondered, had not wanted to leave a
message? Jeremy? . . . Rupert?

And then she heard her husband's voice, and her heart gave an
involuntary leap. 'Becky, I know you're probably still angry, but
please, *please* phone me as soon as you get back. We have to talk . . .
I'm staying at Todd's place, the number is . . .'

She knew the number only too well. For months Rupert had
used Todd's flat almost as a second home, a base for his excursions
into London's nightlife. How often, she wondered bitterly, had he
returned there from some bar and with whom?

Briskly she rose from her chair and began to file away the faxes.
She had more important things to deal with than Rupert's needs –
starting with what to do about their son. As soon as she had opened
the front door he had rushed off to check Lolly's bedroom, and
then his father's, and finding their clothes gone he had run to his
own room and slammed the door, refusing to be enticed out by
Becky's offer of milk and chocolate biscuits.

She put the fax file on top of the pile awaiting her attention –
unopened bills, unread scripts she had brought from the office in
the vain hope of having more time at home to read them. She
could not imagine a future in which she would feel strong enough
to tackle it all.

And yet, she thought, I could cope with almost anything if I
could just spare Adam the pain, if I could somehow take it all on
myself. But I can't, and that's what I don't know how to live with.

She went to the foot of the stairs that led up to Adam's closed
door and listened. The house seemed huge, echoing, empty, and
she dreaded the long lonely days ahead so that the sound of a key
in the lock made her turn with the sudden foolish hope that Rupert
had ignored her wishes and returned after all.

'Knock, knock.' Anthea stuck a head round the door, waving
the spare set of keys Becky had left for her so she could look in on

the animals. 'I've come to drag you away for supper – on no account will I allow you to stay here and mope.'

Becky's face must have registered her quite illogical disappointment because Anthea quickly assured her, 'Don't worry – I'm not attempting to cook. I've bought something pre-prepared from dear old Marks & Spencer.'

'I'd be grateful for anything I didn't have to make myself,' Becky said, smiling wanly, 'but I don't know if I'll be able to convince Adam. I'm afraid he's cutting up a bit rough.'

'You leave him to me,' Anthea said firmly. 'I've rented him a video which the nice young man in the shop promised faithfully was dinosaurs from start to finish.'

'Oh, Ant!' Becky felt the tears that were never far from the surface these days springing to her eyes. 'What would we do without you?'

Becky was struggling to do justice to the de-boned and ready-stuffed Chicken Kiev which Anthea had merely popped in the oven for twenty minutes ('Even I would have trouble ruining that!'). Adam, rather subdued despite Anthea's successful choice of video and his joy at being reunited with Bogey, was having his hot dog in front of the TV.

'I don't know how to help him,' Becky said in a small, tight voice.

'You can't. The first few weeks are simply ghastly. You just have to get through them, that's all you can do.'

Becky traced a doodle with her knife in the little pool of garlic butter on her plate. 'How long did it take your boys to get used to the divorce?'

'I'm not sure they have yet. But each week gets easier than the one before.'

'Oh God,' Becky wailed, 'where did we go wrong?'

Anthea relieved her of her plate and the necessity of pretending that she was eating. 'You know perfectly well,' she said. 'We married very attractive and hopelessly unsuitable men, and we've got no one to blame but ourselves.'

'Yes,' Becky sighed, 'Adam seems to think it's all my fault.'

Anthea optimistically produced two meringue nests filled with raspberries and whipped cream. 'Simon's new piece gave birth while you were away. A girl . . .' She tucked a strand of greying hair behind her ear and she looked, Becky thought, suddenly defeated and every year of her age. 'Simon always wanted a girl.'

'But he adores the boys—'

'Not enough to keep paying up for them. I'm feeling the pinch so badly I've advertised for a lodger.'

'You're joking!' Becky was intrigued. 'Any replies?'

'Dozens, and you wouldn't believe how frightfully unsuitable they all were. First there was this very unattractive little man with a gold front tooth, said he was in retail – a salesman, darling – and he asked if he would have his own toilet. I said if he didn't know the proper word for it, he wouldn't be using one in my home!'

Becky giggled and picked up her spoon. The raspberries suddenly looked mouthwateringly delicious.

'Then there was this gawky boy who was studying at the Catholic seminary. He took one look at my castrated nudes and fled. Funny, I thought an aspiring priest would approve of that sort of thing . . . Oh, and you wouldn't have believed this dreary little librarian type in a polyester frock – I knew at once she'd be drip-drying things all over the spare bathroom – and she asked me would I mind if she brought her cat, so I said by all means, my whippets are very partial to a bit of cat . . . Oh good, you're eating your meringue.'

Becky was, in fact, almost choking on it. 'Honestly, Ant, you're hopeless. You'll never get anyone at this rate.'

'I suppose not, but then subconsciously I probably don't want to. It's ridiculous having to share with strangers at my age. But needs must . . . Are you going to be all right for money?'

'I doubt it,' Becky said grimly. 'Rupert spent it as fast as I earned it.'

'I suppose he'll qualify for legal aid. You'll have to dig into your own pocket, though. I must introduce you to my lawyer, Shirley Fossey, she's a complete darling. Not that she's beating Simon into submission, but I don't think there's a silk in the land who could do that. And she's always good for a sympathetic ear and a decent cup of tea.'

Becky pushed her plate away, her appetite quite gone again. It was, of course, the next logical step. Once she had spoken to Rupert, it would be time to bring in the lawyers.

* * *

On the twenty-fourth floor of the downtown L.A. office block where IAM had its headquarters, Alex stared out over the flat, sprawling city of his birth. He felt slightly winded, the stuffing knocked out of him by the bombshell his father had just dropped.

'Why is Ross Piper leaving the agency?' he asked.

Frank spread his hands in a gesture of defeat. His fingernails, Alex noticed, were freshly manicured, his thick silver hair newly cut. He seemed, from outward appearances, as much on top of things as ever.

'This'll look very bad for us,' Alex said. 'He's a big star, and his career's on the up again after his Best Actor award at Cannes . . . Is there nothing we can do to change his mind?'

'He says he wants to go with one of the big agencies, the top three,' Frank said. 'So let him – let him see if the grass is greener on the other side.'

Alex watched his father closely. He had never known him give in without a fight. 'But it might make other clients restless, start a trickle of other defections . . .'

He had been studying the books over the past week, and the trickle he predicted had in fact already begun, a small haemorrhaging of talent away from IAM to its main competitors. He wondered if Frank would have come clean and told him about it if he hadn't checked up for himself.

'Dad,' he said, 'what's the real reason Ross is going? Wasn't he satisfied with the service he got here? He must have given you some explanation, after all the years you've looked after him, the bad times as well as the good . . .'

Frank sighed. 'Perhaps I haven't got what it takes any more – and perhaps I don't care. Do you know how old I'll be next birthday?'

Alex stared at his father. He had always thought of Frank as ageless, above and beyond the march of time.

'Seventy. I'll be seventy. And most of it has been all work and no play, and now I'm tired. There are things I want to do before I get tireder still. For myself, not for my clients.'

Alex voiced the unthinkable. 'You can't mean you want to retire?'

'No, just take a bit more of a back seat. There's this woman I've met . . .'

A woman! Alex tried to take it in but it made no sense. His father had never allowed women to get in the way of business – never, in his memory, seemed susceptible to that or any other form of human weakness.

'Now I know what you're thinking,' Frank wagged a cautionary finger, 'and it's not like that. She's fifty-six, nothing much to look at, not in the business – a property dealer's widow, as it happens. But she makes me laugh, and I don't do enough of that.'

Alex thought of childhood holidays spent with Frank in the big house in Beverly Hills. There had been no laughter in those days.

'I'm glad, if she makes you happy,' he told his father.

'What about you?' Frank leaned over and touched him lightly. 'Do you have someone? Is that what keeps you in London?'

Alex looked down at his father's hand, manicured for the widow's pleasure. He shook his head.

'You should have someone,' Frank said. 'You deserve a little love. I was so sorry about Lara . . . and your mother . . . I've been thinking lately, about all those years after your mother left, when I was working so hard I never got round to finding another woman, someone who could have taken care of you . . . It must have been lonely for you. I'm so sorry, my boy.'

Alex was alarmed to discover tears pricking at his eyes. He looked down at a fixed point by his shoes.

His father patted his arm and removed his hand. 'Enough said. I know I've made mistakes and I don't want to see you repeating them, that's all. You've done wonders with the business in London, but just promise me you'll live a little too. Just promise me that.'

Alex swallowed. He didn't know what to say. He had been trying not to feel, not to miss that other part of life for so long now, how could he let his guard down just like that? Where would he even begin?

'And who'll help you run things here?' he asked when he could trust himself to speak.

'We got some good people, Alex. If you don't want to come back, we'll choose someone else to take charge for the time being. I'll be looking over his shoulder all the time, don't you worry. I haven't gone that soft.'

Then Frank did something Alex couldn't remember him ever doing before, not even when Alex was a child and had learned to

do without such things. He put his arms around his son and held
him tightly, as though to make up for all the lost years.

The fish restaurant had been Becky's suggestion, because it was
possible to have a totally private conversation by sitting in a booth.
But the minute she came in she regretted her choice when a whiff
of frying fish combined with the butterflies in her stomach to make
her feel quite nauseous.

Rupert was already waiting for her in one of the booths. He
stood while she took a seat opposite him, like someone on a first
date. Beneath the artificial tan he looked unusually pale, unwell,
and her first instinct was to fuss over him, enquire if he was eating
properly. But she knew she must avoid that trap, force herself to
remember why she was here.

They took their time over the ordering. Becky suspected Rupert
was no hungrier than she was, and that both of them were grateful
to put off for as long as possible the reason for this meeting. A
waiter with a long white apron brought white wine in an ice bucket.

Then they were alone, avoidance no longer possible.

'Rupert, I thought very hard about everything while I was away,
and I've decided—'

'Are you sure you've had enough time to decide anything?' he
said with an edge of desperation.

'I want a divorce.' Though her voice was scarcely above a
whisper, the words seemed to her to echo round the whole room.

For long moments he sat staring into his wine glass. It was the
first time she could remember him being at a complete loss for
words.

'I'm sorry,' she said awkwardly. 'I wish I could feel differently,
but I can't.'

'You mustn't do this, Becky,' he said at last. 'It's not right for
you to make this decision for all of us. There are three people's
lives to consider here.'

The waiter came back with two impossibly large Dover soles.
Becky was glad he had stopped her from saying it was Rupert
who had forgotten to consider the other lives he was hurting. She
wanted to keep this as painless as possible, for both of them.

When the waiter left them, she pushed her plate to one side. 'I
have considered how this divorce will affect us all, and I think it

will be worse if we remain in what has become an impossible marriage.'

'Why impossible?' Rupert demanded, banging his fish fork down on the table. 'Why because of one little mistake—'

'It isn't the one mistake. We both know that.'

'And what about Adam? Have you thought what a divorce will do to him?'

Becky looked haunted. 'I have thought of almost nothing else,' she said.

'I still love you, Becky,' Rupert said miserably. 'Whatever I've done, that never changed.'

'And I,' she said, close to tears, 'have not entirely got over my love for you.'

He raised to her eyes that were suddenly full of hope. 'Then you mustn't rush into this divorce. You must give yourself time to be absolutely sure you're not doing the wrong thing. I've got my pride, you know that, but I'm prepared to wait . . .'

Becky was beginning to feel quite irrationally sorry for him, as though she were the guilty one and he the injured party. 'All right, Rupert,' she said weakly. 'I'll give it a few more weeks – but I doubt very much I'll change my mind.'

He flashed her a smile, a little of the old Rupert breaking through. 'I can't promise not to do my best to change it for you.'

Becky looked down at the wedding band that still circled her finger, and prayed he would not do this, wouldn't stop her making a clean break. If he did, if things were allowed to linger on, then she couldn't vouch for having the strength to carry through her resolution.

'You should at least have phoned,' Letitia accused.

'The whole point about being in pain,' Becky said patiently, 'is that you don't necessarily do what you *should* do.'

' 'Course you don't,' Jeremy chipped in protectively. 'Stop giving her a hard time.'

Becky had at last made the trip to Covent Garden, to the offices she had rented on her first production and kept on as the work continued to roll in – a maze of interconnecting rooms faced in raw brick and hung with film posters, some her own and some favourite golden oldies. She was looking now at a black-and-white

James Dean lighting a cigarette on a kerb in the rain. He must have been even younger than Jeremy, she supposed, when that car mowed him down.

'Naturally you have all my sympathy,' Letitia said, managing for a moment to sound as though she meant it. 'But we were worried . . . not to mention having to cover for you with Pantheon.'

'As I would have done for you,' Becky pointed out.

'Can I get you anything?' Jeremy asked solicitously. 'A coffee? A stiff drink?'

Becky shook her head. She had drunk more wine than she had intended at her lunchtime meeting with Rupert, and she felt a gnawing anxiety in the pit of her stomach at the concession she had allowed him to force from her, when she had meant to be so firm. She must write to him, she decided, after a few days, and tell him she was serious about wanting the divorce. If she could just avoid seeing him face to face, she was sure she would have a better chance of standing firm.

'We can't afford to let personal matters affect the business at hand,' Letitia was saying now. 'This offer from Pantheon is too important to us—'

'She looks tired,' Jeremy said anxiously. 'Do you want to lie down for a few minutes?'

'I'm fine.' Becky felt, on the contrary, exhausted, having been unable to face sleeping in the four poster the night before, so that she had been forced to settle for the unfamiliar bed in the spare room, where she had been woken by the dawn light breaking through curtains that she hadn't realised till that moment needed a good heavy lining.

'Why don't you give me an update?' she forced herself to say. 'Have you read the script, Jeremy?'

'Three or four times.'

'And?' Letitia asked impatiently.

'I think,' Jeremy replied teasingly, stretching it out just to annoy her, 'I think there's some potential there. In fact, I might just be able to do something with it after all.'

Rupert sat with his head in his hands on Todd's Swedish leather sofa and fought against a feeling of almost total abandonment. His surroundings, so familiar from the countless hours he had spent here with his friend, seemed somehow a great deal less congenial now that he no longer had his own space, his own lovingly accumulated treasures, to go home to. He was, in fact, a fish out of water amidst this department store furniture which looked as though it had been purchased in bulk from a catalogue.

He put his coffee mug down on the glass-topped table which was covered with dirty wine glasses and empty bottles left there by half a dozen of Todd's mates who had popped in looking for some action the night before. A cute little redhead with Cupid's-bow lips had made it quite obvious to Rupert what kind of action she was after, but he'd found the mere thought of it totally un-appealing.

Todd's dainty little Filipino cleaner, with tiny hands and feet and only a nodding acquaintance with the English language, came once a week and scarcely had time to make a dent in the constant chaos. In between her visits Todd did the bare minimum in maintenance, and was perfectly good humoured and philosophical about the resultant mess, so that it was left to Rupert to do the lion's share of the tidying up. Only today, he hadn't felt up to it.

'Can you believe,' he said to Todd, who was knocking back an American bottled beer with a slice of lime in the neck, 'that Becky actually seems serious about this divorce?'

'Heavy!' Todd commiserated. 'She never got this worked up before.'

'It must be her parents. They've talked her into it. She'd never have come to a decision like this on her own.'

'Shouldn't interfere,' Todd pronounced. 'None of their business.'

'I persuaded her to take a bit of time, think it over, but I know she only agreed to humour me. I can tell – not just from what she says, but the way she looks at me – like I'm already a stranger – she's not really going to change her mind. '

Todd considered this for a moment. 'Sure you want her to, old pal? I mean, you're free as a bird now. Party time! It's not like you can't pull the chicks.'

'That's not the point. She's my *wife*.'

'Hey, is this Rupe the Raver talking? You gotta pull yourself together, my man – don't let her get to you. Who needs her anyway?'

'I think,' Rupert said irritably, '*I* do.'

More than that, he needed the life they had together, the structure of it, the house they shared with each carefully collected piece of furniture in its proper place, the orderly flow of domestic routine. Without it he felt lost, directionless, though he couldn't bring himself to confide this to Todd. Looking at him slouched on the opposite sofa, feet up on the table, beer bottle in hand, he was amazed at how much his best friend was getting on his nerves these days. He found himself wishing fervently that Todd would remember some errand he had to run, leaving Rupert alone with his dark thoughts.

Memories kept coming back to him of the cruel suddenness with which he had been forced to leave his family home, Heath Park, when he was a child and the money ran out. He saw images of the huge menacing furniture vans, the empty rooms, his nanny crying in the abandoned nursery, comforted by the housekeeper. But no one had been able to comfort Rupert, reeling with the shock of it, the inability to understand why it was all happening, why they were having to leave and his father was not coming with them. He had felt as though his whole life had been taken away from him, that he had been sucked into a great black hole with nothing at its centre.

The intercom buzzed and Rupert suppressed a groan. Far from being relieved of Todd's company, it seemed he would now have to put up with that of another gaggle of his friends – even before they had got rid of the mayhem inflicted by the last lot.

Todd perked up at once and jogged off to buzz the caller in. Rupert picked up his instant coffee in its 'I love NY' mug and was hit with an unbearable wave of longing for his Brazilian blend and his Clarice Cliff china and the smell of furniture polish on old wood and the sound of Mrs Christos busily working with her brooms and brushes. Suddenly his heart was gripped with a terrible anger against Becky for depriving him of all this that was so dear to him, for taking away his whole world for the second time in his life.

He looked up through the fog of his fury and at first could hardly focus on the figure standing in the doorway, her face brimming with tender concern.

'I hope you don't mind me coming here,' Lolly said. 'I just had to know how you were.'

'As you see,' Rupert gestured bitterly at the debris around him. 'I've been cast to the swine. Becky asked me today for a divorce.'

Lolly sank down, mortified, beside him. 'Oh Rupert, I'm so sorry. I never meant to cause so much trouble.'

'No, nor did I.' She was wearing a simple tunic dress, her cloud of hair loose on her shoulders, and he looked at her long legs and remembered how he had ached to know what they would feel like wrapped around him and what a price he had paid for the undoubted pleasure of finding out. 'So what are you doing with yourself these days? Found another job?'

She shook her head. 'I can't face looking. I have a few savings, and I'm staying with an aunt in Kilburn till I can . . . well, I'm not ready to live with another family yet.'

She was a picture of wretchedness and Rupert was faintly touched that she seemed to yearn for her former life as much as he did. Her trembling lips, tilted towards him, were lusciously full.

'Did you miss me?' he whispered.

She nodded helplessly, and her face was filled with blind adoration. He felt an involuntary stirring in his groin.

'Come here,' he said gruffly, pulling her against him. She melted unresistingly into his arms, and the taste of her was mildly intoxicating, like a glass of well-remembered wine.

He took her by the hand and led her almost roughly towards the spare bedroom that was now filled with his neatly stacked pullovers and the shirts he had to iron himself, though painfully out of practice. He felt powerfully masculine again, the decision-maker, the one who was in control.

As he turned to close his bedroom door, he saw Todd in the hallway giving him a lewd grin and a thumbs-up sign.

Becky lay, alone and lonely, in the giant four-poster and felt dwarfed, almost crushed by the sheer size of it, the weight of the memories it contained. She must, she decided, get rid of the monstrosity – send it to Rupert, if necessary, since he seemed so attached to it – and buy something else quite unconnected with the past.

And yet the memories it stirred were not all bad, the longing at times for Rupert to be there beside her an almost physical ache. At this treacherous hour when sleep would not come, she couldn't help thinking that maybe Rupert was right, that she had no business turning her back on a marriage that had worked in its way and possibly still could.

The rectangle of light in her doorway was suddenly blocked by a small silhouette. Adam too, it seemed, had his midnight demons to confront.

'It's all right, you didn't wake me – come over here,' Becky coaxed.

He hesitated. 'I had a nightmare and I was scared and I . . . couldn't really help it but I wet my bed.'

Becky went to him at once and gave him a reassuring hug. Taking his small hand in hers, she led him back to his bedroom to wash him and find some clean pyjamas. And all the time the guilt was descending on her, like a great immovable stone. Adam had been potty trained by Lolly, with very few setbacks, by the age of three. Why was he now, two years later, wetting his bed again?

He allowed her to see to him without making any fuss. Dressed in fresh Mickey Mouse pyjamas, he opened his mouth in a giant yawn. It was after one in the morning. Becky eyed the damp patch in the middle of his bed, thought of rummaging through the linen cupboard for clean sheets, and decided against it. She picked Adam up, and his head rested heavily on her shoulder.

'You can come and sleep with me,' she said, 'just for tonight.'

She laid him down on the side of the bed that used to be Rupert's, and tucked the covers up to his chin. He seemed almost to disappear, drowned in a sea of bedclothes. She climbed in beside him and he took her hand and held it against his cheek. Within seconds he was breathing evenly.

Becky gently released her hand and rolled away. Adam's breathing remained steady and comforting, like a heartbeat. At last, with this other presence beside her to keep the loneliness at bay, she felt herself begin to relax into sleep.

White-faced and trembling, Becky held out the document she had received in the post that morning, still too choked to utter a word.

'For God's sake,' Anthea said, 'sit down before you fall down – and let me take a look at that.'

Becky sank into a chair and with unnecessary force shoved across the kitchen table the papers bearing the logo of Musgrove, Fisher & Moss – names she had never heard before and now would never forget.

Anthea took out her reading glasses and began to peruse with great care and, it seemed to Becky, unbearable attention to detail, each and every page. The words she was now seeing for the first time were still turning over and over in Becky's head, a mad jumble of unthinkable threats, impossible disasters.

Halfway through, Anthea looked up with a puzzled frown. 'I don't quite get what's going on here. I thought Rupert was giving you time to think things over. I thought he said he didn't mind waiting . . .'

'That's the last thing he told me,' Becky said wretchedly.

'Then what on earth can have happened to make him do a thing like this?'

What had happened was that Rupert had paid a visit to Messrs Musgrove, Fisher & Moss, solicitors specialising in family law, who had agreed to represent him in matters pertaining to his divorce from his wife and contact with his minor child, their new client having been recommended to them by Mr Carlyle Senior, whom the firm had represented in a similar matter some fifteen years previously.

Bernard Fisher, senior partner, was taking cryptic notes on a yellow legal pad. In his late fifties, he had a full head of dark curly hair, a florid complexion, and an abundance of impatient energy which compensated in part for Rupert's distinct lack of it.

'All I want is my old life back,' Rupert said listlessly. 'And I want to know what my rights are if my wife won't let me have it.'

'You say you left the marital home without taking any advice from a solicitor?' Bernard Fisher enquired almost accusingly.

'It wasn't a question of wanting to leave,' Rupert pointed out rather petulantly. 'My wife threw me out when she caught me with—'

'You told me about that part. But you do realise, don't you, that she can't actually force you to leave the marital home? Is it in her name?'

'It's in both our names but I always thought . . . I mean, she pays the mortgage . . .'

'Aha!' Mr Fisher looked quietly triumphant. 'So she's been supporting you?'

'I suppose so. I mean, it's a tricky profession, acting, there are times when you can't—'

'She'll have to go on supporting you then, won't she? You must apply for maintenance.'

Rupert rather dazedly turned this unfamiliar proposition over in his mind. He had never liked to think of himself as being bank-rolled by Becky, had preferred not to dwell too deeply on who contributed what percentage of their income. The idea of being supported by her even after a divorce was something he didn't want to examine too closely either.

'I'm not sure I could go in for—'

'Who's paying your bills where you are now, then?' Mr Fisher demanded.

Rupert looked momentarily stunned. He had been staying at Todd's place for only two weeks, had not even expected to be there that long until Becky dropped the bombshell about the divorce. The question of bills had not yet come up.

'You have to think ahead, Mr Carlyle,' his new mentor said smugly. 'If you've been obliged to run the household, keeping the home fires burning, so to speak, you might not find it so easy to slip back into the workforce – not in your profession, not in the current economic climate. Then how are you going to keep the wolf from the door?'

Rupert was trying very hard not to be swamped by a growing sense of panic. 'I hadn't really thought—'

'Most of my clients don't, till they come to see me. My job is to think for them. Now if the child's mother has been in fulltime employment, and you've been at home, I assume you're the one who's been looking after the little chap?'

'Not exactly. We employed a nanny for that.'

'Ah, yes. The one you were caught with *in flagrante delicto* . . .'

'That's right.' Rupert shifted uncomfortably. 'Naturally she isn't looking after Adam any longer.'

'And is she still looking after you?'

'I don't see,' Rupert said, flushing crimson, 'that that's any of your bloody business!'

'It might be,' Mr Fisher responded without the slightest

embarrassment, 'if it were to tip the scales in your favour. Suppose a judge were to be told that you and this nanny were living together.'

'We're *not* living together,' Rupert said a touch too forcefully. In fact, it was a couple of days since that first afternoon when he had taken Lolly to bed in Todd's flat, and somehow she had ended up staying the night, and then she hadn't quite got round to leaving the next day either . . .

'Just humour me, Mr Carlyle. Suppose the two of you were getting along quite well, and you decided on cohabitation.'

Rupert didn't know where this was leading but he was prepared to go along with it in theory. Not that he had any plans to get tied down to Lolly, but she was undeniably lovely, a balm to his bruised ego, and he wasn't in that much of a hurry to get rid of her just yet either.

'Now then,' Mr Fisher continued, 'don't you think a judge might look rather favourably on an application for the child to reside with the two people he was used to having at home with him, taking care of him, rather than the mother who was always out at work?'

Matters were taking a rather alarming turn. Certainly Rupert was angry with Becky, very angry, but that didn't mean he planned on taking over responsibility for Adam just for the sake of revenge. 'I don't think you understand, Mr Fisher. I didn't say I wanted to take Adam away from his mother—'

'Child support, Mr Carlyle,' the solicitor smirked. 'If the child were to reside with you, your ex-wife would have to pay maintenance *and* child support. I would think that might include providing you all with somewhere to live, something similar to what you have been accustomed to . . .'

He had said the magic words, and they opened for Rupert a Pandora's box of images: the house at World's End, his four-poster bed, his beloved antiques and porcelain and silverware. Granted, he had been the one at fault, but why should his punishment be the loss of all he held dear? Why should it go to Becky because of one stupid mistake on his part that she wasn't generous enough to forgive?

'Explain to me,' he said to Mr Fisher, 'exactly what you had in mind.'

* * *

Anthea looked up, when she had finished reading the papers, with a face almost as white as Becky's own. 'Tell me I'm crazy,' she said, 'but my understanding of all this legal mumbo jumbo is that if you don't take Rupert back, he wants to live with Lolly *and* Adam in one big happy family, and he also wants you to move out of *your* house so they can all stay there in style while you foot the bill.'

'That's about what it boils down to,' Becky said in a voice that trembled on the verge of disbelieving hysteria.

'I always knew he didn't play by the rules,' Anthea growled, 'but this goes far beyond what could be termed as "not cricket".' She marched purposefully to the telephone. 'I'll get Shirley Fossey onto this right away.'

As Anthea went again through the horrible details for the benefit of the woman Becky supposed would now be her sole defence against this monstrous attack, she was still struggling to believe it was actually happening. How could Rupert, her Rupert, the man she had loved and married and lived with for ten long years, be doing this to her? She had thought, when she saw his naked body entwined with Lolly's, that he could never hurt her more than he had already – and now this. Not just the one betrayal, but actually planning to live with the girl he had betrayed her for. And then, compounding the treachery, to threaten her with taking Adam. The house, to leave that would be a wrench – but the loss of her child was unthinkable. She could not bear it, would not believe it, had no idea how to turn the helpless panic boiling within her into some constructive form of action, some plan for self-preservation.

When she had asked Rupert for a divorce, she had dreaded his hurt, his anger, his recriminations. She had even braced herself for his entreaties. What she had never bargained on was that he would go for all-out war.

CHAPTER NINE

As promised, Shirley Fossey was all tea and sympathy. 'What a business, eh?' she said as she showed Becky into her office. 'Hope you're keeping your chin up.' And she patted her on the back with the heartiness of a school hockey mistress. She was a large, smiling-faced woman who seemed not at all self-conscious about the extra weight she was carrying or the rather startling effect of the brightly coloured summer dress she wore. She looked to an already nervous Becky more like an astrologer or exotic agony aunt than a member of the legal profession.

'I'm rather sorry we're dealing with Bernard Fisher on this one,' Shirley said as she moved a stack of files from a chair so Becky could sit down. 'Not that I can't handle him, but I'd rather not have to. He tends to go all out to win for his client at any cost – and the cost is usually the welfare of the family as a whole.'

'What he's proposing,' Becky said bitterly, 'is certainly not my idea of what's good for the family as a whole – Adam in particular.'

'I suspect,' Shirley replied with a sigh, 'that the motive behind it all is to get the largest possible financial settlement for his client, a sizeable percentage of which will end up in Mr Fisher's already comfortably lined pocket. Although I wouldn't like you to quote me on that.'

The tea arrived in a white china pot with wafer-thin cups, and Shirley poured it out, her large fingers surprisingly nimble. She passed Becky the delicate milk jug and sugar bowl.

'What's she like, this girlfriend who used to be the nanny?' she enquired. 'If Bernard puts her on the stand, is she in a position to do you a lot of damage?'

Becky thought back anxiously to the long days when Lolly had taken care of Adam single-handed while his mother was stuck on some film set, the long nights when she had babysat for the same reason, the implied accusation on that last day that Becky had neglected her family – and her heart sank. 'I suspect she could damage me quite a bit,' she said frankly.

Shirley took out a cheap ballpoint pen, chewed at one end. 'All right, you'd better give me all the gory details, and please make it the whole truth and nothing but the truth or I won't be able to help you as much as I could.'

So Becky recounted the story of her marriage, of the relentless work that had kept her so often from home and her child but produced a career that paid the bills, of Rupert's failure to find his own success, of the accidental pregnancy, the necessity for her to carry on working after Adam's birth, the treadmill she found herself on with the house, the nanny, the school fees all having to be paid for from her earnings alone.

'It's true that I saw a great deal less of Adam than I would have liked, but I had no choice. How can the law punish me for being a hard-working mother and reward Rupert for being an out-of-work father? It simply isn't fair.'

Shirley gave a loud snort. 'Whoever told you life was fair, Mrs Carlyle? Look what happened to Marcia Clarke in America, when she was prosecuting the O. J. Simpson case, the murder trial of the century, with the whole world watching her courtesy of the television cameras. Can you imagine the pressure she must have been under, the hours she had to work? And in the middle of it all her husband took her to court demanding custody of the children because he said she was working too hard to look after them properly. So you see, women have been told they ought to pursue successful careers, like men do, but no one's warned them of the risks.'

'I may work hard,' Becky said, 'but I still do a lot more childcare than Rupert. If the court makes Adam live with Rupert, he'll just palm him off on Lolly like he did before.'

'Maybe, but will Lolly admit that? I presume she's in love with your husband?'

Becky fiddled irritably with her teacup. How was she supposed to judge Lolly's adolescent emotions?

'What worries me more than the past,' Shirley said kindly, 'is your future plans. Are you going to be able to look after Adam if he stays with you?'

Becky gave a helpless shrug. 'I'm not rich enough to give up work. I'll have to hire another nanny for Adam.'

Shirley put down her chewed ballpoint and looked at Becky over the top of her reading glasses. 'To be frank with you, Mrs Carlyle, that may be a problem. Let me explain what usually happens in disputes over children. We haven't gone crazy in this country yet, like in some states in America where the courts try to split the children down the middle along with the rest of the couple's assets. The golden rule here is that the interests of the child come first. More often than not, the court will find that it is in the child's interests to live with the mother and have reasonable contact with the father. A mother has to be proven a bad influence to lose her child – a drug addict, a prostitute, something along those lines. But what makes your case tricky is that a judge will also look at which parent can provide the best care. Now if your husband can show that he and his girlfriend, who has been the child's principal carer in the past, will be there when Adam gets home from school, to supervise homework, to take the child to piano and swimming lessons and so forth – while you will not – then the judge may conclude that Adam will get better care with them. Unless you can show that the father is a bad influence.'

'What do you mean?' Becky asked warily.

'Well, the same sort of thing that would prove a mother unfit – a drug or alcohol problem, for example. Is your husband a heavy drinker?'

Becky remembered the double Scotches, the nights spent in bars, the morning hangovers – and knew that she was being offered a reprieve, a means of keeping Adam with her, a straw to clutch at. 'Rupert sometimes drinks to excess,' she admitted, 'but I wouldn't be prepared to make any formal accusations. Whatever's happened, he's still the father of my child. I don't want Adam to find out one day that I stood up in court and accused his father of being a virtual alcoholic.'

Shirley nodded with grudging approval. 'Somehow I thought you'd say that. If only Mr Fisher had the same scruples.' She glanced down at her notes. 'We'll have to think of another tactic to keep you from losing your son and your house. Not to mention a large share of your income. Tell me, do you stand to make a great deal from your next project?'

'It's a very big film – I suppose so.'

'Oh dear, then Mr Carlyle will certainly have a claim.' She looked
despondently into her empty cup. 'More tea, perhaps?'

Fortified by her strong brew, she seemed to revive a little. 'There
are other matters to consider,' she said, 'like what type of divorce
you want. A no-fault one where both of you agree will take two
years and you might be in more of a hurry—'

'I'm not in a hurry,' Becky assured her. She would have felt
foolish admitting that, on the contrary, the whole subject filled
her with an inexplicable reluctance and dread.

'Then there's the question of Adam's contact with his father.
When were you thinking of arranging the first weekend visit?'

Becky braced herself to face this most difficult of subjects. How
could she know when the best time would be to start Adam on this
seesaw, this journeying back and forth between parents that would
be the pattern for the rest of his life?

'I'm sure he wants to see his father . . . but how long would he
be expected to stay?'

'That depends on the child. Your son is still very young . . .'

Becky thought of Todd's flat, of the confined space and the
spare room where Rupert must be sharing a bed with Lolly. 'If
Adam stays overnight, I'll want to know what the sleeping
arrangements will be,' she said firmly.

'We'll make that plain, then.' Becky was grateful that her lawyer
seemed to require no further explanation. 'And I will point out at
the same time that we contest all your husband's other claims. Then
it will be up to him to apply to the court. All we can do is wait, and
formulate our defence. In the meantime, please try not to worry.'

The interview, it seemed, was over. Becky stood to leave, feeling
anything but reassured, and wondered how she would possibly
manage to do anything except worry a great deal.

Adam lay on the sofa, his favourite blanket clutched to his cheek,
his thumb plugged firmly into his mouth. Every so often he
removed it to take a wheezy breath that rattled in his chest where
his cold had now moved, or to howl in protest if Becky shifted
away from him by so much as an inch. Bogey lay faithfully at his
feet, content, unlike Becky, with this stationary vigil.

They had come to the sitting room for a change of scene, and because Becky hoped to coax Adam into watching the television artfully concealed in a Chinese lacquered cabinet, because Rupert had banned modern gadgets from this room which was his holiest of holies, housing his most valuable treasures. As a result, in the normal course of things, no one except Rupert – and of course, Mrs Christos – had ever come in here.

But Adam refused to watch television or indeed to do anything except hold onto Becky and grizzle. She couldn't take much more of it, she thought guiltily, she was exhausted from sitting up with him for half the night and she would have killed for a cup of coffee to soothe her parched throat. But there seemed no chance of getting away even to boil a kettle while Adam was in this state.

She thought she had never sat in one place for so long in all her life, and after hours of patiently putting up with it, she now had to force herself not to snap at Adam or push him away when his hands clutched possessively at her. She was, she reminded herself, the only familiar face left in his dramatically changed world, and she knew he was clinging to her as much from insecurity as from illness. She wondered if he was missing Lolly, how Lolly would have coped with the problem. It seemed, and the irony was not lost on her, that she was a lot less competent at handling her own child than the teenage nanny she had just fired.

Even when Adam wasn't ill, when she had only his everyday life to cope with, the routine of it was still something of a mystery to her. She couldn't discover any timetable of extra lessons, which Lolly must have kept in her head, and rather than admit her ignorance to the girl she now thought of as her rival, she had phoned around swimming pools and karate clubs and finally built up a picture. But she was amazed by the sheer amount of time that Adam's daily needs consumed, the enormous chunk it took out of her working day.

She could not, she knew, carry on like this forever, not with all the unfinished business piling up at the office, not with Pantheon and Stanley Shiplake chasing them for the rewrite. Today she was supposed to be going through the screenplay with Jeremy, but when the babysitter from the agency had arrived – a good-natured German-Swiss girl, eager to please – Adam had hidden under his bunk bed, right in the corner where he couldn't be reached, and cried so hard that Becky had feared he would make himself even more ill, and she had been forced to send the bemused girl away with her bus fare paid and a little extra for her trouble. An emergency call to Anthea had produced no better results. Adam took one look at her and bellowed in protest, prompting Anthea to agree that she *was* looking an awful fright but she *had* just dragged herself out of bed to come to the rescue.

Becky's efforts to find a full-time nanny had met with the same barriers. At the mere sight of a strange face, Adam would retreat behind his mother and announce in a quavering voice, 'I want Lolly!'

He would be seeing her, Lolly, and his father at the weekend. Once the thorny issue of sleeping arrangements had been negotiated between lawyers (round one to Shirley, Adam and not Lolly would be sharing his father's bedroom), the first 'contact visit', as she must now refer to them, had been arranged. She had explained it to Adam and he had said it was all right, but he wouldn't talk about it. And she certainly couldn't voice her own fears: what if he hated it and wanted to come home straightaway? Even worse, what if he was so pleased to see Lolly he didn't want to come back at all? He might even feel a wrench at leaving Rupert, un-accustomed though he was to expecting his attention. A negligent father was still a father, and Becky was aware of a child's natural tendency to defend the underdog.

But there was no sense, she told herself, in worrying about things over which she had no control. Instead she reached cautiously for the phone, one eye on Adam, and dialed the office.

'So we're to be deprived of your company yet again,' Letitia said frostily. 'No doubt we'll manage without you – heaven knows, we should be used to it.' But the phone was quickly grabbed by Jeremy, offering to come charging to the rescue – he would, he declared, simply pop himself and the screenplay into a taxi so they could work on it at Becky's place.

He arrived in record time with a huge bunch of bright yellow sunflowers, bringing the first cheer of many days into the house. Adam glowered at him from his corner of the sofa, not sure whether this intrusion called for another powerful lung exercise.

'They're lovely,' Becky said of the flowers. 'Like sunshine indoors. Would you mind finding some water for them in the kitchen? If I move, we'll all be in for an ear-bashing.'

'No problemo.'

'And while you're at it, I'd be eternally grateful for a cup of coffee.'

Jeremy bounded out on his mission, full of self-importance, and returned in record time with a wide grin, a mug from which steam curled promisingly, and the flowers poking their glorious heads from a pretty pottery urn she had bought on a long-ago visit to her parents in Italy.

'You're an angel of mercy,' Becky said. 'And how clever of you to find that urn – I've been looking for it everywhere.'

'I am very resourceful in a crisis,' Jeremy said smugly.

'You'll have to be, if you're going to solve our little problem.' She cast a rueful glance at Adam. 'He won't watch a cartoon or do anything at all on his own. I don't see how we're going to get any work done.'

As if to prove the point, Adam climbed onto his mother's lap, gripping her tightly and trying to block her from Jeremy's view. Becky felt again guiltily claustrophobic.

'That looks like a dead good game,' Jeremy said enviously. 'Sitting on Mummy . . . Can I play too?'

Adam rolled a suspicious eye at him.

'Go on, move up, then – I want a turn.' Jeremy made a great show of shifting Adam forwards, then planted himself behind him on Becky's knees, making sure not to burden her with his full weight.

Adam began to giggle. Jeremy tickled his sides and the giggle became a delighted laugh. Then he tickled Becky too, unfairly, while her arms were pinned, and she shrieked indignantly and Bogey barked furiously and jumped onto the sofa, toppling them all.

'That was fun,' Jeremy said, poking his head out of the tangle of limbs. 'Shall we take pity on Mummy now and give her a break?'

Adam nodded, still smiling, and climbed back into his corner. Bogey lay down protectively on the cushion beside him, one eye on the crazy intruder. Becky thought how furious Rupert would be to see the dog on his precious sofa and decided to leave him where he was.

Within minutes Adam was asleep, his blond hair resting on Bogey's wheaten curls. Becky felt light with release as she sat for

the first time on her very own chair and sipped coffee which had
never tasted so good, though it was now half cold.

'You're a genius,' she said to Jeremy.

'Not really. The little guy just needs to know he's not going to
lose you . . . and that life's going to be fun again one day.'

'I don't suppose he's had a barrel of laughs with me lately,' Becky
admitted.

'Now don't go beating up on yourself. Anyone can see how
much he loves you. You must be doing something right.'

'I just can't cope with doing it all. I have to find him another
nanny, but the thought of it fills me with dread. Unless . . .' she
grinned '. . . I can talk *you* into taking the job.'

'Do I get to look after you as well?'

She thought how, all through these months of change, he had
remained constant in his idea of her, his belief that she contained
within her the essence of something essential to him, something
he could get from no one but her.

'We'd better do some work,' she said, 'while the going's
good.'

He bent his head obediently over the page, but it didn't dispel
the feeling she had that the balance of power had somehow shifted,
and she was no longer the one in control.

It was two endless, work-filled hours before Adam stirred again
and announced he was starving hungry. Becky, feeling generous
and loving, offered to make him whatever he wanted.

'Mothers never make the best food, do they?' Jeremy scoffed.
'What do you say to a takeaway double cheeseburger with fries
and milkshake.'

'That is *exac-ly* what I want,' Adam said firmly.

'You're spoiling him,' Becky warned.

'I'm spoiling *you*. No need to slave over a hot stove as long as
there are fast-food outlets.'

'Except that I loathe fast food.'

'You,' Jeremy promised, 'are in for an entirely different sort of
treat.'

He returned with a sandwich almost a foot long from the Italian
deli, filled with roasted peppers and aubergines and sundried
tomatoes, and a bottle of Merlot from the off-licence, and they

brought plates and glasses to the sitting room and picnicked around the coffee table. Bogey became instantly devoted to Jeremy when he discovered he had a hamburger all to himself.

They had never before, Becky realised, as she sat on the floor and sipped wine and laughed with Adam at Jeremy's silly jokes, brought food into this hallowed room. She couldn't even remember ever being in here with Adam, let alone the dog that had been the bane of Rupert's life. She allowed Bogey to eat his burger off the carpet.

'And now,' said Jeremy, when he had helped her clear away the plates, 'what do you suppose I brought you for pudding?'

'What, what?' Adam's voice was shrill with excitement.

With a great flourish, Jeremy produced from behind his back a video of *The Lion King*.

'That's my favourite film,' Adam shrieked.

'Mine too,' Jeremy said solemnly. 'Can I watch it with you?'

While Adam proudly showed how he could work the video recorder all by himself, Jeremy took Becky firmly by the hands. 'Time for an afternoon nap,' he said.

She did feel, suddenly, quite exhausted. 'Thank you,' she said simply.

He leaned forward and brushed the top of her head with his lips. 'Sweet dreams.'

She left her son and Jeremy on the sofa fast-forwarding through the previews and blowing bubbles in their milkshakes with their straws. Bogey sat happily between them, eyes glued to the screen.

Becky hardly had time to put her head down on the pillow before she fell into a deep, dreamless sleep.

Letitia flicked a duster over her twin-seat leather sofa – hand-crafted, according to the man who had sold it to her – and wondered, not for the first time, whether it was worth the price she had paid.

The trouble was, she simply couldn't tell. Brought up in Muswell Hill by parents who had no aspirations beyond the culture of suburban north London, she had suffered throughout her childhood from her father's passion for 'home improvements', which seemed to mean only that their semi-detached was in a permanent state of change. Even Letitia could see that what resulted was seldom better than what had been there before. But while she knew instinctively that the fitted towelling toilet seat covers favoured by her mother and the mock-Tudor dovecote constructed in the garden by her father were vulgar, she did not see how she was to develop any taste of her own with no example to follow. So at seventeen she left Muswell Hill forever and answered an advertisement to share a flat off Sloane Square with two girls from the home counties. She copied their plummy accents and their understated clothes, but looked on their dinner-party catering jobs with ill-disguised contempt. Letitia was determined to move up the ladder of success, and move up fast.

Rebecca Carlyle was her third experiment in flat-sharing, and it was she who revealed to Letitia the possibilities in the film industry. With the right choices, a canny woman could win herself a fortune and a reputation. But Letitia did not trust herself to make those choices, not without some guidance. So she hitched her wagon to Becky's star and watched in wonder as it rose ever higher with Letitia in its wake. Even when Becky moved on to live with Rupert, Letitia did not dare to let go.

She had come a long way since then, with her own two-bedroom flat in West Kensington filled with reproduction furniture, good imitations of pieces so classic they could never be considered in poor taste. She took the pine polish and gave the low wooden coffee table a good spray. She was always catching her shins on it when she moved around the room, but at least it was solid mahogany and gave the place an air of substance – or so she hoped. She rubbed furiously at the polish with the duster. She had come a long way all right, but not far enough.

Through sheer dogged determination, through being there whenever she was needed and sacrificing any personal life of her own, she had worked her way up through the ranks and finally earned her own producer credit and a partnership in Becky's business. But by then the resentment had set in – the anger that it all came so easily to Becky, that her instincts were so sound, her taste so unerring. But that was hardly to be wondered at, with the start she had had in life – the private boarding schools, the ambassadorial residences in foreign capitals, the exposure to a dozen different cultures – while Letitia had walked daily to the local state school and taken holidays with her parents in Brighton or Broadstairs. And then, of course, came Rupert, a man bred to the appreciation of the finer things in life, able to add the final touch to Becky's innate good taste.

Letitia looked for a moment at her reflection in the gilt-framed mirror over the fireplace. She was unlikely to attract a man like Rupert, but her slim, boyish figure had its attractions and she made the most of them, always showing off her pencil-slim legs – her best feature – in tight jeans or short skirts, like the one she was wearing tonight. Stanley preferred her in skirts. They wasted less time, he said, when he was ready to get down to the nitty gritty – and *time*, as he kept telling her, was *money*.

She understood Stanley, though she wasn't always sure she even liked him. She knew he was driven by the same urgent need to succeed, to put behind him his humble boyhood in Croydon and take his place by force among the great and the good. She understood why he covered up his homegrown accent with an indistinguishable mid-Atlantic drawl, and why no amount of money was ever enough to make him feel secure. They were quite a pair, she and Stanley, a pair of strays who recognised the need in one another.

The doorbell rang and quickly she put away the duster and checked her hair in the mirror. If her luck held, it would only be the delivery service, bringing a preordered dinner from a local French restaurant, and she would have enough time to throw away the incriminating cartons and transfer the food into her own dishes, waiting in the warming drawer of the oven. The way to the heart of a man like Stanley, she knew, was pretending you could cook a decent meal even when you couldn't.

The delivery man tried to keep his eyes above Letitia's hemline and didn't quite succeed. She gave him an unusually generous tip in acknowledgement of his appreciation, and whisked her booty away into the kitchen.

She needn't have worried. Stanley, as always, was late. 'That smells *great*!' were his first words on coming through the door. 'What're we eating – I'm *starving*.'

She was glad he hadn't asked what she had cooked, so she wouldn't have to tell an outright lie. 'Provençal fish soup followed by poached salmon steak in a lobster sauce . . .'

'*Two* fish courses, eh?' He looked childishly disappointed.

'Darling, you told me you wanted something light. You're on a diet, remember.'

She was not foolish enough to confuse Stanley's diets with other people's. Stanley was far too devoted to his food to attempt more in the way of reduced calorie intake than replacing the meat he loved with fish. After weighing himself for a couple of days and losing no more than a kilo or two, he would give up on the whole charade.

'I hope I'm allowed *something* for dessert,' he grumbled, and she prayed the night's menu would not put him in a bad mood.

'Of course,' she said soothingly. 'Lemon sorbet.'

He wrinkled his nose and she wondered if he realised how badly he needed to lose some real weight. She tried not to think of his rotund white belly studded with coarse black hairs, and his fingers ballooning like sausages from the confines of his rings.

Letitia was, above all things, a realist. It was a terrible thing, she knew, to be born with such a hunger for success and without the talent to feed it. The people she was surrounded with at work, people like Becky and Jeremy, could not possibly know how that felt, or how much at times she hated them for their gifts which they took for granted. But she would get what she wanted, even if she had to use other means. In her closet was a double string of pearls with diamond clasp and matching drop earrings, and on her finger was a ruby serpent ring. She had not been able to afford real stones before Stanley.

'Let's eat,' she said, knowing his priorities, knowing too that she dare not leave the food to stand much longer. Stanley moved to the table with alacrity.

She waited until he had gobbled down his soup, lifting up the bowl to drink straight from it, before she mentioned casually, while serving the salmon steaks in a nest of mashed potato, 'I wanted to ask you something about the movie with Pantheon.'

He began to protest, with his mouth full, his dislike of discussing business at meal times, but she was ready for him. 'Sorry, darling, I shouldn't have . . . I'm just so stupid about these things and I thought you might be able to help.'

He mellowed a little. He even paused between mouthfuls. 'Sure, toots, if it's *help* you need, fire away.'

She gave him a melting smile of gratitude, a promise of things to come. 'I just wondered – is it a priority for Pantheon who the producers are?'

'Don't you worry – they're very impressed with you girls, they *want* you. But OK, sure, at the end of the day it's the *director* and the *stars* who really count.'

'And the producer's fee is a fixed amount, isn't it? They wouldn't really be interested how we divide it up?'

'Now, toots, I hope you're not thinking of taking anyone else on board 'cause we're stretched to the *limit* here, we can't give you any more—'

'But you wouldn't make it less if there was, say, just one producer?'

'No – it's a fixed fee. Now what's this all about?'

She looked at him with wide, soul-searching eyes. 'I didn't want to tell you this, but I don't think I can take the responsibility alone any more, perhaps it'll help if I share it with someone . . .'

Stanley took the bait. 'Come on, toots,' he said, actually laying down his fish knife and fork. 'Whatever it is, you *know* you can tell your Uncle Stanley.'

All the way on the bus, Adam kept his eyes cast downwards and his mouth firmly closed. He was wearing his new trainers, and shorts from which his legs protruded, thin and vulnerable, and the baseball cap Becky had bought him on a trip to L.A., and his Chelsea football club T-shirt. On his lap was a small overnight bag which he clasped to him like a lifebelt.

Becky had decided it would be easier for them all if she met Rupert on neutral ground. So they had arranged a rendezvous outside the South Kensington tube station, near Todd's garden square flat, and she had come with Adam on the bus so she wouldn't have to circle round looking for parking on a Saturday morning.

Although she had had days to prepare for it, she still did not know how she would face Rupert, how she would manage to look him in the eye and talk to him politely when she knew what he was planning against her. But she would have to do it – she must for Adam's sake – this was hard enough on him already.

They reached their stop and for a moment she thought she saw pure panic in Adam's eyes. But then he took her hand and picked up his suitcase and followed her quietly off the bus.

Rupert was waiting for them by the exit to Pelham Street. She looked at him standing there in his jeans and navy blazer and striped shirt, at his striking profile and the heads turning in admiration, and was forced to acknowledge objectively how handsome he really was, how charming he must seem to the passers-by, how little the dangerous foe.

'Hello,' she said and her voice came out squeaky and strange.

He gave a quick acknowledgement of the greeting, and then he was bending down to make a fuss of Adam. 'A Chelsea shirt, how smart – when did you get it?'

Adam swallowed and looked up at his mother and his eyes were bright with unshed tears.

'You're going to have such a lovely time,' Becky said quickly, squeezing his hand. 'Daddy's going to take you to a film and to the park to play football . . .'

Rupert tried to take his bag, but Adam held onto it as though his life depended on it. Inside it was a single change of clothing and his toothbrush in a Mickey Mouse sponge bag and his favourite cuddly toy, a rather mangy dog that reminded him of Bogey.

Becky tried to disentangle his little hand from hers. 'Go on, now, darling. You'll be fine . . .'

But he stood, immobilised between them, and Becky knew that Rupert couldn't very well drag him off physically, though he looked as though he would like to, and neither could she force Adam to let go of her hand, and she wondered with growing helplessness how it was all to be resolved without resorting to farce.

Then Rupert knelt down beside Adam and pointed off down the road, towards Onslow Square. 'Look,' he said, 'Lolly's waiting for you.'

It was his trump card. Adam followed the direction of his father's pointing finger, down the block to the corner, where a slender figure with a cloud of hair was poised, watching tensely. Becky looked too and felt herself stiffen with anger that Lolly had dared to come, that she was waiting there, at a safe distance, to take her son, and at the same time she felt Adam begin to slide his hand out of hers.

Rupert's mouth curved in a triumphant smirk and it was only then that Becky came close to striking him. Quickly she bent to give Adam a parting hug, and he clung briefly to her neck, kissing her hair. 'I'll miss you, Mummy.'

'Me too.' And now, as she watched her son go, it was Becky's eyes that were bright with tears, and ever after she would not be able to pass the road to Onslow Square without remembering the sight of a small figure clutching a tiny suitcase and walking resolutely on to an unknown future.

Though she had thought before that the house at World's End felt empty, she had not realised until she returned to it without Adam what emptiness truly was. Sitting alone in the silent kitchen that had always been filled with noise and laughter, Becky thought she might go quite mad.

She could not think of Adam without dissolving into tears, and yet she could think of nothing else. The office in Covent Garden, the pile of work in her study, were not to be faced while she felt so desolate.

She made herself a cup of warm milk with cocoa, as she did for Adam when he was in need of comfort, and drank it on the small sofa where she read his stories to him, and wondered where to go from here, how to find the new life that would have to replace the old. There had to be a way forward, for she would not believe this misery could last forever.

The phone rang and she resolutely ignored it, but when it started up again straightaway she was afraid it might be Adam and quickly snatched it up.

'I'm in the phone box round the corner,' Jeremy said. 'I'll be with you in two minutes and I don't want you pretending not to be in.'

When she opened the door and found him standing there with his aviator jacket and his spiky hair and his tense hopefulness, she thought she had never been so glad to see anyone in her life. He was like the answer to a prayer she had not dared to utter out loud. It was the way he knew how she was feeling without a word needing to be said that was her undoing. She fell into his arms and let the tears flow while he covered her wet face with kisses.

He took her hand and led her, following like an obedient child, to the sitting-room sofa – not to the four-poster, somehow he seemed to know she couldn't have borne that – and she realised then how rejected she had been feeling, how second-hand, cast off, and what a wonderful thing it was to be wanted again.

'You're beautiful,' he said into her hair, and the way he said it made her believe it without question, know it to be true. His eagerness filled her with relief, and as he unbuttoned her blouse and buried his face inside it, she breathed in the smell of leather and tobacco and menthol, the male otherness of him, and almost laughed out loud for sheer joy at the discovery that there might be a new life after all.

There were things she could face now, tasks that had once seemed impossible but could finally be contemplated, even executed. The pain was still there, the fear of what would happen with the divorce and with Adam, but underneath it, like a counterpoint to the dominant theme, was something else – the echo, faint at first but growing stronger, of a different tune to which she might some day dance.

Stanley had summoned her and she had calmly agreed to a meeting and now here she was, hacking her way through his office jungle, feeling none of the dread at seeing him that had dogged her for weeks.

'He's on the phone,' Bryony informed her, 'with calls holding.' And Becky, who had never known Stanley to be anything else, calmly took the expected seat.

Bryony busied herself with some typing and in the middle of it, without looking up, asked offhandedly, 'How's Jeremy?'

Becky considered this very seriously, as though it were a matter of great importance. 'I think,' she finally announced, 'that he is happy.' At least, he had told her he was – the happiest man alive – and when she searched his face, tracing its contours with her fingers, it seemed to her that yes, there was a radiance that hadn't been there before.

Bryony looked at her rather oddly. 'Mr Shiplake's off the phone now. You can go in.'

She trod lightly into the vast office with its oversized desk and smiled almost fondly at the familiar, tubby little figure sitting behind it. 'How are you, Stanley?'

'I'm *winning* – I always win,' he assured her. 'But it's not *me* I'm worried about.'

She felt warmed, comforted. All around her people were rallying to her, helping her to get through this nightmare. 'You mustn't

worry about me either,' she said. 'I have a lawyer, I have friends.
I'll pull through.'

'Good, 'cause it's as a *friend* that I wanna talk to you.'

She smiled again, inviting further confidences.

'You and I go back a bit,' Stanley said. 'I think it's fair to say *I*
was the one who gave you your start. Wouldn't you say that was
fair?'

Becky was in a mood to be generous. 'I would.'

'Then you *know* I have your best interests at heart when I tell
you what I think here. And what I think is you're *biting* off more
than you can *chew*. Are you with me?'

Becky had to admit that no, she wasn't quite sure she knew
what she had bitten off that Stanley felt she couldn't chew.

'It's the *kid* that counts, isn't it?' Stanley insisted. 'You gotta be
there for your kid.'

'What are you saying? I should work from home?'

'I'm saying maybe you shouldn't work *at all*.'

She was even less sure she was following him now. 'You know
I have to work, Stanley. I have bills to pay.'

'I'm just talking some temporary *time out*, that's all.'

'That's not possible. Have you forgotten I'm about to make a
major film for you and Pantheon?'

'That's just the point,' he said, all sweetness and reason. 'It's a
major movie, and with your current problems, I don't think you
can give it the *commitment* it needs.'

Too late, she saw the trap that had been sprung. 'Stanley,' she
appealed, 'I've worked for this all my life, so hard . . .'

'*Too* hard. When you do that, you *fall apart* sometimes – your
marriage, your kids, even *you*. You start doing crazy things, like
disappearing without telling anyone where you're going – like
punching out the star of your picture.'

Who, Becky wondered numbly, had told him, and why had he
waited till now to let slip that he knew? She began to see the full
precariousness of her position.

'I thought you really wanted to do this film,' she said, trying to
claw back the ground she had lost. 'And if I don't produce it, then
who—?'

'*Letitia*,' Stanley pronounced, and suddenly the pieces fell into
place and Becky saw whose hand was behind it all. 'Letitia has

the experience now, she could take over on this one while you have a bit of a *break*, get your house in order, get yourself ready for the *next* one.'

But there would be no next one for her, Becky knew, not if Letitia were determined to oust her. *If Letitia's teamed up with Stanley, God help you,* Alex had said, and he had been right, as he always was, and she had refused to heed his warning.

'Of course, you deserve to get *something* out of it – say a co-producer credit, a smaller share of the fee . . .'

Crumbs, she thought, he was offering her crumbs and expecting her to take them in desperation because she had other battles to fight, lawyers' bills to pay.

'Stanley, can you give me some time to think this over?' she said, praying that she did not sound as if she were begging.

'Sure – take *all* the time you need.'

Letitia looked into Becky's office, at the warm brick walls hung with film posters, at the bright rugs and scatter cushions and witty ornaments purchased from the Covent Garden market, and resisted the temptation to try out the swivel chair behind the desk. Instead she passed on to Jeremy's adjacent room and poked her head round the door.

'Can I buy you a coffee?' she asked brightly, proffering two china mugs decorated with red London buses.

'Huh?' Jeremy peered up at her through a fog of broken concentration and suspicion.

Before he could gather his thoughts, she stepped in and pushed the door closed with her foot. Jeremy watched her warily, as though believing her quite capable of some act of bodily harm.

'I know,' she said, placing his mug before him, 'that we haven't always been friends. But I want to change all that – I really do.'

'Why?' he asked baldly.

'Because I'm worried about Becky – and I know you are too.'

He looked at her narrowly, and lit one of those dreadful menthol cigarettes he had been affecting since Cannes. She bit back a cutting remark about the effects of passive smoking.

'Why all the sudden concern about Becky?' he asked rudely.

'Look, Jeremy, I may not always show it but I'm also fond of

her, you know. We go back a long way . . . And now she's in trouble
and I want to help.'

'Like how?'

He wasn't going to make it easy for her, he was all prickles and
angles, but she knew how to get beneath his crude defences.

'If she carries on pushing herself like this, she won't be able to
cope. I think she's heading for a breakdown.'

A dark shadow crossed Jeremy's eyes. He unfolded his gangly
limbs from the chair and began to pace up and down, puffing
furiously.

'I know I can help her, if she'll only let me,' Letitia continued,
watching him closely. 'I can take most of the burden of this film
off her shoulders, leave her free to fight the court case, to win
back her child . . .'

'It's so unfair, what that husband of hers is doing to her,' Jeremy
burst out. 'If she cracks, it'll be his fault.' He clenched his fists.

'That's why she needs us. You and me. If you back me up, I'm
sure you can convince her to stay at home, take all the time she
needs to sort out this horrible mess. She can't run a film while
she's got that on her plate. But *we* can – together, for all of us.'

He came and stood next to her, menacingly close. 'You're not
trying to muscle her out, are you?'

She stood her ground, looking him full in the eye. 'Of course
not. She'll still get a credit and a fee.'

He took a step backwards and she saw a little of the fight go out
of him. 'OK. I'll talk to her.'

'Thanks.' Letitia clasped his hand to cement the pact. 'I need
your help on this one, Jeremy. But more important, so does Becky.'

It was six o'clock exactly when the doorbell rang. Becky stared at
the pile of unironed clothes in the wash basket and the half-
dismantled Hoover she had been trying to fix and wondered where
the time had gone.

Casting a glance at the exposed innards of the Hoover, Becky
suppressed an impulse to ask Rupert to have a look at it, since he
was here. He was, she reminded herself, the enemy now, and besides
she couldn't really face him, she was punch drunk, like a boxer
who has taken too many blows to the head. If she was dealt another,
just one more, she was sure it would be the finish of her.

And yet she could not surrender either, not to Rupert, not to Stanley and Letitia. From somewhere, some as yet unknown reserve, she would have to draw the strength to carry on the fight.

Reluctantly she went to open the door, and the sight of Adam standing there in his baseball cap hugging his suitcase, the sheer joy of his homecoming, was almost enough to wipe out the rest. She bent to give him a hug but he just stood, oddly stiff, in her arms.

'Did you have a nice time?'

'Yup.' He disengaged himself and walked on past her, throwing a casual goodbye to his father over his shoulder, his back ramrod straight, his bag in his hand – off to the kitchen to find Bogey.

The transition times are the worst, she had read in some book from the library about divorce and children. The most traumatic moment is the handover from one parent to the other. She must not be hurt by Adam's seeming rejection. She must try to understand.

'Thank you for bringing him back,' she said to Rupert, who still stood awkwardly on the doorstep. But unfriendly or not, she could not bring herself to invite him in.

'My lawyer will be in touch,' he replied stiffly, and she tried not to take it as a threat.

In the kitchen Adam was silently watching television, cuddled up to Bogey.

'Are you hungry?' she asked brightly.

His eyes did not move from the screen. 'Don't know.'

'Did you eat supper with Daddy?'

'No.'

'Would you like some scrambled eggs and toast soldiers?'

'OK.'

She got out the eggs and a bowl and the whisk and set about the business of making his supper, the routine that would bring him back to some sense of normality. When he took the plate from her without saying thank you and ate from it with his eyes still glued to the television, she did not remark on it. Nor did she give in to the urge to sit down beside him, to ask how his weekend visit had gone, what it had been like for him with his father and Lolly, and without her.

But later, when she tried to put him to bed in his bunk, the crying started. He clung round her neck like a monkey and refused to let go while the sobs racked his small body. Becky carried him through to her room and laid him down gently in her bed. Only there, with her arms around him and his head buried in her neck, did the crying finally give way to a deep and exhausted sleep.

Jeremy came later with wine and a video and Becky hunkered down with him on the sofa, laying her head in the curve of his shoulder as Adam had sought refuge in hers.

'Rotten day?' Jeremy asked.

'The worst.' She wondered what he would say when she told him of Letitia's betrayal, Stanley's complicity.

'Don't you think you're doing too much?' he burst out before she could speak. 'Like biting off more than you can chew?'

They were Stanley's words, the ones he had used to draw her into the trap. Slowly she sat up and looked at Jeremy. 'What did you say?'

'I'm worried about you.' Stanley's words too. 'So is Letitia.'

'Have you spoken to Letitia about me?'

'Yeah . . .' He squirmed a little. 'I mean, she thinks you should let her run things for a while so you can straighten out this mess with Rupert.'

'And what do you think?' Becky asked in a voice that was ominously quiet.

'I don't know. It might be a good idea.'

He was in it too. He was with them, and that meant he was against her. She had opened herself to him, allowed him into her most secret places, when all the time he was plotting with her enemies. It was the final blow, the one she had feared would be the end of her.

'Get out!' she screamed in a voice she could hardly recognise as her own. 'Get out of my house!'

CHAPTER TEN

There were far too many people crowded onto the Italian-tiled pool terrace overlooking the Pacific Ocean, but in this town, Alex thought wryly, numbers were supposed to equal success. By that standard, Jared Harmon's party could be considered a very big success indeed.

Jared, a martial arts cum action star with more fans than intelligence, was actually Frank's client, not Alex's, and it was he who should have put in a compulsory appearance at the actor's home after the première of his new film. But he had wanted to take the widow away for a weekend in Palm Springs, and Alex had offered to go in his place.

On the other side of the patio a space was somehow cleared in the throng, and two compact Japanese men in *gis* bowed to each other, and commenced a dazzling display of kick-boxing for the entertainment of the guests. Alex watched as one performer's foot, which he presumed could be classed as a lethal weapon, whistled dangerously close to the surgically sculpted nose of a girl in a micro-skirted red sheath dress. She gave a little gasp of admiration.

Alex turned away. He had seen, somewhere in this direction, large trays covered with colourful strips of sushi and sashimi and California rolls, and he hadn't eaten since the baguette filled with lemon grilled chicken that he had grabbed in the office at lunchtime.

'Hey Alex, how's your father?' a vice-president of production called over.

'Fine,' he said automatically, 'fine.' In fact, Frank was more than fine. Pushing seventy or not, Alex hadn't seen him looking this young in years.

He wedged his way into a gap in the food line, and took a fistful of cocktail sticks to spear the little raw pieces of fatty tuna and salmon and dip them in green mustard and soy sauce.

'Hungry?' a voice behind him asked.

He looked round into huge amber eyes framed by dark curls. 'I bet you don't remember me,' the girl challenged.

'You underestimate your fame, Juliette,' he said without missing a beat.

'I'm flattered,' she laughed, 'no really – I am.'

He offered her a tuna piece and she accepted it, sucking it daintily off the stick, her eyes never leaving his face.

'Don't tell me we're going to start seeing Juliette Winters in martial arts pictures?' he asked in mock alarm.

'No – I'm doing a film for Warners, but we seem to get invited to all the parties.'

She was on a winning streak, Alex thought, as he nibbled a concoction of squid and rice, the green mustard bringing a little sharp shock to his sinuses. She had youth and beauty and talent, all on her side. Her reviews in Becky's film had described her as radiant, like a young Audrey Hepburn.

'What's it like doing your first big studio picture?'

'Wonderful,' she said. 'They keep telling me what a big star I'm going to be, so of course I'm lapping it up. Which is not the same as taking it seriously.'

'Sacrilege!' Alex said, pretending to look shocked. 'Taking yourself seriously is a religion in this town.'

'I don't believe in religion.' She came a little closer, and her amber eyes were twinkling. 'But I do believe in sin.'

'And what counts as sin in your eyes?'

'Not doing what you want when you want to do it.'

'What is it exactly,' he said, and his voice was hoarse, 'that you want to do?'

'Show you how much I've always admired you.'

He smiled but she put a finger up to his lips and suddenly her pretty features were flushed with something close to anger. 'You must take me seriously, Alex. I'm not another silly little actress looking for a career boost. I'm doing very nicely without you, thank you all the same. And you don't represent me, do you?'

'No,' he conceded.

'So I'm not asking you for anything, except what you're willing to give.'

She was close enough so he could see the perfect olive tones of her skin, and smell the musk of her perfume. In that moment, he thought he might have been willing to give her anything. She put a hand up to touch the hair where it curled on his collar.

'I don't think there have been enough women in your life who haven't wanted something from you,' she said. 'I think you've forgotten what it's like to be wanted just for yourself.'

Gently he reached up and touched her fingers. He found his own were shaking.

'There's no reason why we shouldn't go somewhere else now,' Juliette said, 'is there?'

'No,' he said, 'no . . . but Jared's a good client. I should wait just another ten minutes.'

Juliette made a little impatient *moue* with her mouth. 'Ten minutes – and not a second longer.' She stepped back reluctantly and picked a piece of sashimi from the tray. He watched, mesmerised, as she nibbled it between pearly teeth. 'So tell me,' she said, 'what do you think about this business of Becky Carlyle getting divorced?'

It took a moment for his mind to come into focus again. 'What?' he said stupidly.

'I gathered you were such a particular friend of hers, I was sure you'd know all about it. It's gone around London like wildfire . . .'

'I've been in L.A. for a while—'

'Well, she's thrown her husband out. Caught him in the act, cheating on her – or so the story goes.'

'My God – poor Becky.'

Juliette saw how the blood had drained from his face behind his two-week tan, and was furious with herself for the change of subject. 'Only five minutes to go,' she said in a voice full of warm, dark promise.

Alex was still looking at her, but she could tell he no longer really saw her. 'Juliette,' he said, 'I'll have to take a rain check. I just remembered I have to pass by the office on the way home – all sorts of loose ends to tie up before I fly back to London. But I'll see you there when your picture's finished shooting . . .'

Don't call me, I'll call you, Juliette thought angrily as she watched him threading his way through the partygoers, heading for the nearest exit. She cursed herself for ever mentioning the name Rebecca Carlyle.

The tea was stronger today and Becky feared the worst. Rupert's lawyer had, as threatened, been in touch, and now Shirley Fossey wanted to 'talk turkey' to her client. She was dressed in a large multi-coloured kaftan which Becky could only hope was not scheduled to make an appearance before some sober and disapproving judge.

'A court date has been set,' she announced like a brightly robed prophetess of doom.

Becky had almost allowed herself to believe, up till this moment, that it was all some huge misunderstanding, a practical joke, a bad dream from which she would awake to laugh at the foolishness of her fears. But there was no laughter in her now as she said, 'Is there nothing we can do to stop all this?'

'Your husband's not going to back down, if that's what you mean,' Shirley said firmly, putting false hope finally beyond her reach. 'We've tried the negotiating route, without success. Mr Carlyle wants everything that was once yours, and Mr Fisher has led him to believe that he can have it, and if you do not give it to him he will try and take it from you in court.'

The future was becoming very clear to Becky, though no Cassandra herself. The future was a battleground on which she stood alone, facing attack from all sides. Victory, survival even, would depend purely on where she concentrated her resources.

She felt a little stirring of her old energy. 'What is it going to take,' she asked Shirley simply, 'for me to win?'

'That's the spirit!' Shirley gave her a hearty beam of approval. 'Onward and upward . . . Now the next thing that will happen is a visit from the court welfare officer. He – or probably she – will be the court's eyes and ears, assessing how Adam gets on with both parents and what his own wishes are in respect of where he should live – as far as a child so young can express them.'

So Adam would be interrogated, analysed, subjected to the scrutiny of a stranger who would decide his fate, because the parents who were supposed to protect him could not come to their own accommodation. Becky had never hated Rupert so much as in that moment.

'If your relationship with your child is good, let it speak for itself,' Shirley advised. 'I wouldn't try to influence the outcome by coaching Adam in advance if I were you.'

'No,' Becky said quietly, 'that wouldn't be right.' It wasn't just a question of ethics, she had always believed – perhaps foolishly, but no less strongly for that – that you couldn't gain anything worth having unless you could live with the tactics you used to get it.

'The court welfare officer will speak to Adam first with you, and then alone. She will also visit Rupert's current place of residence and interview him there with your son. Then she will reach her decision, which will carry a lot of weight with the court.'

'Is there anything that we can do that would actually help?' Becky asked.

'Absolutely!' Shirley cried, her bosom heaving alarmingly beneath the concentric circle print of her kaftan. 'We must formulate a strategy that proves you are the best person to have care of Adam. We must show that satisfactory arrangements are in place for him to be looked after when you are at work – by family members, a new nanny, whatever. We must bring in character witnesses to demonstrate your fitness as a mother.'

'My family all live abroad,' Becky confessed. 'I haven't taken on a new nanny yet because Adam won't accept one.'

'In that case,' Shirley said, rattling the wooden bangles on her arms, 'there is a great deal of work to be done.'

'Darling, don't say another word,' Alice insisted. 'Your father and I will be over just as soon as we can.'

'Are you sure?' Becky wound the phone cord tightly round her finger. 'It's just until after the court case – till I have time to break in a new nanny.'

'It might take longer than you think,' her mother cautioned, 'to find the right person, and we're perfectly prepared to hold the fort till then.'

Mrs Christos appeared laden down with the newly fixed Hoover and its various extensions which she deposited with a clatter in the broom cupboard. Since Rupert's departure her spirits had visibly risen and she seemed to work twice as hard, as though by diligent cleaning she might expunge all traces of him. Becky waited till she went off with the beeswax polish, humming tunelessly.

'I wouldn't have asked,' she said to her mother, 'except that Adam won't seem to take to anyone new right now . . .'

'I should think not – poor pet.'

'And I won't have to worry so much, if I know he's got you and Daddy.'

'It's not just Adam who's a worry,' Alice said sternly. 'You must be feeling terribly low. We want to be there for you too, darling. There's no need for you to go through this alone.'

'Thank you,' Becky said with feeling.

'Don't be silly. Besides, it'll be such a treat to spend some of the summer in London. Your father wants measuring for some new trousers – he seems to have lost a bit of weight. I suppose I've missed the Chelsea Flower Show, but I can still do Ascot . . .'

They could make the necessary arrangements, Alice said, by the end of the week, and be with her at the weekend. Becky put the phone down feeling that she had made her start on the work Shirley said had to be done.

When Michael phoned half an hour later from Hong Kong, wanting to know how he could help, Becky felt that the Haydon ranks were closing around her, that the battle lines were truly being drawn.

Adam was playing David Attenborough in the bathtub. He had on his swimming goggles, the ones that protected his eyes from public pool chlorine, and he was diving deep beneath the ocean surface to discover its underwater wonders. His fingers were corals, his toes wriggling fish, and his perfect little bottom poked above the water like a smooth white island.

'Get out, now,' Becky said as he surfaced for air. 'Supper's nearly ready.'

'I haven't finished washing yet.'

'Well do it. You've got five minutes.'

He grabbed the soap in his fingers and dived again. Beneath the water it became a great sea turtle, slipping through the coral.

Of all the chores she now had to tackle, it was bath times Becky loved the most – the contours of Adam's solid little limbs beneath the water, the clean soapy smell of him when she wrapped him in his towel.

The whole routine of her day with him had become easier, now that she had grown accustomed to its rhythm, now that she knew each afternoon's schedule. She had discovered why he wasn't progressing in swimming lessons – a teacher with over-full classes – and swapped him to another at the Chelsea Pools; which days he came back from school too tired to do anything except watch television; what inducements would get him into bed on time. It seemed incredible to her now that these were things she had not known before.

'You're wasting that soap,' Becky said sternly when he emerged again. 'Out!'

'Can I have a big towel all the way down to my feet?'

Becky gave him Rupert's enormous bath sheet. Later he would sleep on Rupert's side of the bed. She hadn't been able to coax him back into his bunk yet, and she worried what effect that was having on him, what the court welfare officer would say.

'You'll never guess who's coming to stay,' she said as she rubbed him briskly dry. 'Granny and Grandpa.'

'Good. I want to show them how fast I can go on my new rollerblades.'

She had been buying him rather a lot of presents lately. The guilt factor, Anthea called it, promising that common sense would set in again with the arrival of her next bank statement. Becky didn't want to think about her next bank statement, or the dent being made in it by Shirley Fossey's fees.

'Granny and Grandpa are going to look after you so I can get some things done. And after that we're going to find the perfect person to take care of you.'

'Mummy,' Adam said kindly, 'I think *you're* the perfect person.'

Afterwards, she was to remember it as the moment when life became simple again.

'If Stanley is on the phone,' Becky said firmly, 'I'll hold.'

'He has another call waiting,' Bryony warned.

'I'll still hold.'

Balancing the phone between her shoulder and her chin, she began to make a list of Things to Do. 'Get hamster food, fetch Adam's name tapes, buy Gordon's gin, make up spare-room beds . . .'

'Becky,' Stanley's voice barked. 'It's *good* to hear from you.'

He was hearing from her sooner than he had no doubt expected, but whether or not that was good was something on which he might wish to reserve judgement. 'Stanley,' she said, 'I'm resigning from the film.'

'*Resigning*!' he yelled indignantly. 'Hold on a minute – isn't that a bit of an *over-reaction*?'

'I don't think so. Not when the alternative is being ousted from my own picture.'

'*Ousted*. That's a very strong word. Did anyone say you were being *ousted*?'

'I'm saying it.' She added to her list, 'Clear out office desk . . .'

'Becky, I urge you to think about what you're doing here. You don't want to *rock* the *boat*—'

'Surely it's better than *biting* off more than I can *chew*?'

'You got no call to take that tone with *me*,' he said with a wounded air. 'I was speaking as a *friend*—'

'Baloney, Stanley.' Suddenly she was weary with it all, impatient for this conversation to be over. 'We both know what's going on here. You're sleeping with Letitia and she wants to run the show and she's using you to get her way.'

'Now *wait* a minute—'

'I haven't got a minute, Stanley. I have to get on with my life. You're wasting time trying to blow smoke in my eyes. I know Letitia – I gave her her first job, remember – and she's worked her way up through sheer hard slog and determination and I admire that. That's why I took her on as a partner – because she deserved it, and because I needed someone to share the load. But you're going to find out something about Letitia, Stanley. She's not as good at this job as I am.'

'Hey, I know that *already*,' Stanley cajoled.

'Then you shouldn't be letting her lead you around by the balls. She's got greedy, she doesn't want to share, she wants it all. She wants to leapfrog over me and grab the lion's share – the money, her name up in lights – "Produced by Letitia Harker", while I get co-producer, which everyone knows is not the credit that counts, when I was the one who used to run the show. Well, it's not going to wash, Stanley. I won't settle for that.'

It was amazing, she thought, what a release it was to say it all at last. She was filled with a great lightness, like a helium balloon.

'OK, so Letitia's *ambitious*,' Stanley wheedled, 'but I'm sure we can work *something* out here.'

'I've already worked it out. You were right about one thing, Stanley – it's Adam who counts. I'm giving up work for a while so I can fight this court case and win it.'

The words had been spoken now, they were out there in the ether, and that gave them a reality, an existence outside her own thoughts which they hadn't had before. She wrote on the list, 'Rollerblades, size 5' and imagined herself gliding with Adam after school down the tree-lined walks of Battersea Park.

'All right, all right,' Stanley conceded, a harder edge creeping into his voice. 'Do what you have to do. But what about *Jeremy*? Why are you trying to *ruin* that poor boy's career before it's even *started*?'

'What do you mean? This has nothing to do with Jeremy—'

'You're telling me it's a *co-incidence* he walks off the picture the same day you do?'

'He's resigned too?' she repeated stupidly.

'Now who's blowing smoke in whose eyes? You're in this *together*, it's plain as the nose on my face! You're trying to *destroy* this picture—'

'What exactly did Jeremy say?'

Stanley sounded aggrieved, wounded. 'He accused me and Letitia of *setting* you *up*. He said he was quitting in *protest*.'

Becky closed her eyes and saw Jeremy delivering his verdict, fists bunched angrily, blue eyes crackling defiance. She smiled indulgently. 'You have my word, I had nothing to do with this.'

'Then you gotta talk him *out* of it,' Stanley demanded. 'Convince him he's committing career *suicide*.'

'You convince him, Stanley. I am no longer involved with this film.'

The image of Stanley gaping impotently as she put the phone down gave her a feeling of quiet elation. In large, careful letters she wrote 'Phone Jeremy!' on the bottom of her list.

They met in a pavement café on the King's Road, and drank white wine in the afternoon sunshine and watched the tourists and the shoppers and the students go by.

'We're like them, now,' Becky said to Jeremy. 'No desks to go back to.'

'Better that,' he said darkly, 'than a desk next to Letitia.'

'Jeremy.' She twiddled the stem of her wine glass between tense fingers. 'You're the only one who's stood by me through this. I don't know how to thank you . . . for your loyalty.'

He closed a hand over hers, forcing her fingers to relax, raising them to his lips. 'There was no other choice,' he said simply.

'Yes, there was. You could have thought of yourself, your own career. Stanley isn't the sort of man you want as an enemy. And it was such a big chance for you . . .'

He looked at her with a complete calm, an inner radiance. 'There'll be other chances, better ones, films I can work on with you.'

It didn't seem the moment to point out that maybe it wouldn't be good for them always to work together, that they might both need to broaden their horizons.

She glanced at the watch on the wrist he had imprisoned. 'I have to go and fetch Adam soon.'

'Can I come round later?'

'Yes, of course – after he's gone to bed.'

Jeremy bent his head to her lips, and kissed her right there on the pavement in full view of the passing crowds, and she felt absurdly young and irresponsible and just a tiny bit embarrassed.

Adam stood upside down on his head and looked backwards through his legs at Mrs Gummer, the court welfare officer. She was thin with a lot of coarse sticking-up hair and seen from this angle she looked just like a very long broom.

'Please sit down,' Becky said.

Mrs Gummer folded herself into a chair, which made her look less like a broom and more like one of those funny toothbrushes with a bend in the middle so you can reach all the tricky places where the food gets stuck.

'Adam, will you get up off the floor . . . I'm sorry about this,' Becky said weakly.

'It's quite all right, just let him settle down in his own time.' Mrs Gummer sat smiling at the room in general. She seemed to Becky kind and patient and in a position of almost unimaginable power. 'This is a lovely home you have, Adam.'

Adam's legs were getting tired. He did a somersault onto his back.

'I'm not allowed to play in here in case I break Daddy's things.'

'Does Daddy get very angry with you when you break things?'

Adam looked at her the right way up. He didn't think she was very pretty, her eyes bulged like the grouper's he had seen in the aquarium at London Zoo. 'I have two goldfish,' he said. 'Would you like to see them?'

'Yes, I would very much like to see your room, and the rest of the house, but first I want to ask you a few questions.'

Becky poured out the tea with hands that shook slightly. Adam helped himself to two chocolate biscuits.

'Darling, offer the biscuits to Mrs Gummer as well.'

'No thank you,' she said firmly. 'And no sugar in my tea, if you wouldn't mind.'

'The court welfare officers are very good and very experienced,' Shirley had said to Becky before this dreaded visit, adding her favourite admonishment: 'Try not to worry.'

'Now, Adam,' Mrs Gummer proceeded. 'Tell me what it's like, living here with Mummy.'

'Mummy and I have made a very good environment to live in,' Adam explained, 'for my mini-beasts. We've put a lot of soil in, and some leaves, and we caught some ants and a ladybird. I think ladybirds eat greenfly, do you?'

'I think they do,' Mrs Gummer confirmed.

'We don't want any worms in case the ants eat them.'

'That wouldn't be very nice. But you – you like living here with Mummy, do you?'

'Of course!' Adam said impatiently.

'And Daddy – how about living with Daddy?'

'Daddy says Manchester United are going to win the Cup Final, but I want Chelsea to win. What team do you support?'

'I don't follow club football,' Mrs Gummer admitted, making her a person of much less consequence in Adam's eyes. 'Does Daddy take you to matches?'

'I'm not allowed to play with matches.'

'I mean . . . football games?'

'Daddy played football in the park with me last weekend,' Adam said proudly. Becky stifled the desire to add that it was one of the few times Rupert had been near a park with his son. 'Mummy and I are going to go rollerblading.'

'Ah, so you also go to the park with Mummy,' Mrs Gummer said approvingly.

Adam ran round in a circle with his arms spread like aeroplane wings. Why don't you say it, Becky prayed, say what you told me in the bathroom, that I am the perfect person to take care of you. But she knew he would not come out with it on cue. Instead he stuck his finger up his nose, and Becky pulled a tissue from her pocket. 'He had a cold not so long ago,' she said apologetically.

'Who usually looks after you when you're sick, Adam?' Mrs Gummer enquired.

'Lolly. She takes my temp-rature.'

'And who is Lolly?'

'She used to be his nanny,' Becky explained quickly. 'Now she's . . .' But she couldn't think what to call Lolly now, not in front of Adam, and in any event, she thought crossly, it wasn't up to her to explain these things to Mrs Gummer. She would no doubt find out for herself during the next phase of her investigations.

'Mummy,' Adam said insistently, 'I'm *des*prate for a pee.'

'Perhaps,' Mrs Gummer suggested, 'we can all go upstairs and then we can talk some more while you show me your room.'

While Adam dealt with his little emergency, Becky pointed out to Mrs Gummer how his room was just next to hers, so she could hear him if he woke in the night, and how she'd bought the bunk beds so he could have friends to stay, and how nice it was for him to have space for all his pets because he was animal mad, and all the time she thought how much like a salesman she sounded, or an estate agent closing in on a prospective buyer.

'Yes,' Mrs Gummer said, 'you've made it very nice for him, I can see that. Now would you mind leaving us for a while, Mrs Carlyle. I would like to speak to Adam alone.'

Becky smiled and said 'Of course' and went back downstairs where she sat amongst the teacups and the half-eaten biscuits and felt sick to her very soul.

She didn't see how anything of monumental importance could be decided from what Adam had said so far. But still to come was Mrs Gummer's visit to his father and Lolly, when Becky would not be present and would know nothing of what took place. Only then would Mrs Gummer draw her conclusions, reading, no doubt, between the lines – and what she would divine there, Becky was powerless to predict.

Alex came to Becky's house almost straight from Heathrow, laden down with flowers, ready to step into the breach and offer the shoulder to cry on she must so desperately need. But he found her sitting calmly at the kitchen table, painstakingly sewing name tapes into Adam's grey school socks. At the other end, Adam's head was bent next to Jeremy's over a complicated jigsaw puzzle, a map of Africa showing the habitats of the various indigenous animals – a recent present, it appeared, from Jeremy.

'It's so sweet of you to bring all these – half the florist shop, from the look of them.' Becky paused, rather distractedly, to put the flowers in a vase and pour them all a glass of wine, but returned almost immediately to her name tapes. 'I bet you never expected to see me with a needle and thread,' she said, raising impish green eyes to Alex. 'And do you know, I'm rather good at it!'

'I've always thought you'd be good at anything you turned your hand to,' Alex said gallantly, and though he meant it he was also aware of talking almost for the sake of it, while he tried to assess what great changes had taken place in her life in the brief time he had been away, what new set of circumstances she – and he – was dealing with.

'The colobus monkey doesn't belong in that pink country,' Adam objected from the other end of the table.

'Zaire – yes it does,' Jeremy countered.

'Doesn't!'

'Does too!'

'It should be in that green one,' Adam insisted.

'It comes from the Congo *and* Zaire.'

'OK, so we're both right, then.' They gave each other a high five and bent back over the puzzle, a team again. Becky smiled indulgently over her sewing.

'Would you like to talk?' Alex asked.

'In a minute. It's nearly Adam's bed time.'

'*No*, Mummy, it's *not*,' Adam wailed.

'Oh, yes it is – and I'm going to take you up.' Jeremy hoisted him easily onto his back, and brought him over to Becky for a good night kiss, and the three of them stood there for a moment,

in their own charmed circle, Becky's cheek pressed to Adam's,
Jeremy's arm resting lightly on her shoulder, and Alex realised
with a wrench of his heart exactly what the new circumstances
were that he was dealing with.

Jeremy's footsteps and Adam's shrieks of laughter faded up the
stairs. Becky at last put her sewing aside.

'I'm sorry,' she said, 'I never seem to get a moment to myself
these days. Jeremy will hear Adam's reading and settle him down,
but I still have to iron his sports kit for tomorrow.'

'Go ahead,' Alex said, feeling horribly in the way. 'I'll keep
you company for a bit – if you don't mind?'

' 'Course not. Anyway, we can talk while I do it.' She filled the
iron with water from the kettle. 'Not that I can bear to talk much,
it's all such a nightmare. . . .'

'Then don't. Just tell me if there's anything I can do.'

She smiled at him with pure affection, the way she might look
at her son. 'There's going to be a big court case,' she said, 'to
decide who Adam should live with, and it seems I'm going to
need some character witnesses and I wondered if you . . .'

'Sure,' he said. 'I'll make you sound like a cross between the
Queen Mum and Mother Theresa.'

'Mother Theresa,' Becky pointed out severely, 'does not have
any children of her own.'

'That's why she keeps borrowing other people's.'

Becky laughed, as he'd known she would. It was better to keep
things light, avoid the topics that were painful to them both.

'I see you've acquired another child yourself,' he said without
meaning to.

Her face went white. 'Don't you dare,' she said furiously, 'go
judging me. You don't know what it's been like for me . . . the
loneliness, the fear . . . and Jeremy was there, he was there for
me . . .'

Yes, Alex thought, he was there and I wasn't. Fate has cheated
me yet again. By a simple accident of timing I wasn't there, and in
her need Becky has turned to someone else.

'I'm sorry,' he said. 'You're right, it's none of my business.'

'I don't need a bloody lecture right now. I need help – help with
the ironing and the sewing and the child care – help to feel OK
about myself again, that I haven't made a complete mess of my

life – but most of all, help to win this court case, not to lose my child and everything I've worked so hard for.'

'I promise I'll do everything I can,' Alex said.

'Good.' Her lip was still trembling. 'Good. And don't go criticising Jeremy either. You don't know how far he's gone out on a limb for me, how much I owe him . . .'

Did he dare, Alex wondered, put his arms round her and tell her again how sorry he was, how he had never meant to add to her burdens – but he was only human too, and he had suppressed his hopes for so long, accepted loneliness without even knowing he was lonely, and it was a cruel blow, just when he had allowed himself to hope again, to find himself empty-handed once more . . .

'Adam's read three pages of *The House at Pooh Corner,*' Jeremy said from behind him, 'with only five mistakes, and he's expecting you up in ten minutes to check on how beautifully he's gone to sleep all by himself.'

'Thanks a million.' Becky lowered her eyes from Alex's. She spread out little navy tracksuit bottoms on the board.

Jeremy went to fold the pieces of kit that she had finished ironing. 'Has she told you about how we've both walked off the Pantheon film?' he asked Alex.

'No, we haven't had much time—'

So Jeremy told him instead, and Alex saw all too clearly the chance Jeremy had been given to make a grand gesture, to bind Becky to him with ties of obligation.

'I'm sorry,' Becky said to Alex, 'that I didn't listen to you about Stanley and Letitia.'

Alex also had his regrets but he couldn't voice them, not with Jeremy standing there packing Adam's kit into his sports bag. 'You don't need Stanley and Letitia,' he said instead, 'or even Pantheon. You have a solid track record now, a hit film – there'll be plenty of other takers for the next one.'

'We're going to do the next one together,' Jeremy declared proprietorially.

'He had this wonderful idea for an original screenplay when he was in Cannes – set in France, maybe a European co-production . . .'

Alex listened to them outlining their plans for the future, for the intertwining of their lives, while Jeremy helped Becky fold

away the ironing board, and he wondered when it would be polite
for him to say he had to leave. There was no place for him here,
not now, not until Becky was strong enough again to make choices
that were not based on vulnerability and need.

Letitia sat in the bare brick offices in Covent Garden and was
terrified by the emptiness she had created.

She had caught Lydia the receptionist, in her lunch hour, going
through the Situations Vacant in the classifieds, and had shouted,
positively bellowed, so that everyone within earshot had stopped
talking and stared, that *nothing* had changed, nothing at all, they
were still in business and no one had to go looking for another
job. Lydia had burst into tears and fled to the Ladies'.

None of them thought she could hold it together like Becky
had, none of them believed she had the ability – she knew it from
the way they looked at her as she walked down the corridor to
Becky's office.

'Tell me what to do,' she had said to Stanley, but it wasn't her
problems he was worried about.

'You realise,' he'd said, and two bright spots of anger shone in
his cheeks, 'that without the *director*, we got nothing to sell. You've
made me look like an *idiot*.'

'But I didn't know Becky and Jeremy—'

'You knew he was *screwing* her.'

But she hadn't, she'd wanted to protest, the last she was aware
Jeremy was rejected and resentful. But that was before Becky's
marriage broke down, before Letitia got so wrapped up in planning
the achievement of her own most secret desires that she forgot, for
a fatal moment, to keep her eye on other people's.

She had to find a way, Letitia thought now, staring at posters of
films Becky had made before she even met her, she had to work
out how to placate Stanley and save her own skin, now that it was
her job on the line. Even without Jeremy, she must somehow
convince Pantheon to let her produce this film. She had come this
far from Muswell Hill, and she wasn't going back.

And then it came to her, in a flash, the person who could save
her, the bait that would keep Pantheon on the hook. If she could
offer them a female star big enough to attract another good director,
then Letitia would still be in business.

She looked at Becky's posters again and thought it really was time she took them off the walls. She opened her Filofax on Becky's desk and began to dial a Los Angeles number.

Since her success in *Abstract Love*, Juliette Winters had gone on to even bigger things at Warner Brothers. Juliette had always hit it off with Letitia, but she had never really liked Becky, never warmed to her as most other people did. Juliette would not be averse to coming on board a film from which Rebecca Carlyle had just made a forced exit, especially one with such a strong part for a woman.

In the final analysis, and Letitia's fingers trembled as she dialed the multi-digit number, Juliette Winters was a much bigger draw card than Jeremy Dunne.

Becky's parents had brought with them an entire suitcase full of delicacies from Tuscany which her mother was now busily unpacking into Becky's kitchen cupboards.

'Do you want to find room for these in the fridge?' Alice asked, laying packets of *prosciutto* and salami and pecorino cheese out on the table.

'There isn't room,' Becky said rather grumpily. 'There's enough here to feed the Household Cavalry!'

Alice cast a beady glance in her direction. 'Mothers always say at times like this that you have to eat, to keep your strength up, but you're far too sensible not to know that, so I'm just providing the wherewithal and you can get on with it in your own way.'

'I know,' Becky said, 'and I'm grateful, honestly.'

She was trying to clean out the rotting stash at the bottom of Bogey's basket. To prevent him making a nuisance of himself while she did it, Hugh and Adam had taken him for a long walk.

Wearily, Becky removed cushion covers caked with weeks'-old grime. It had been a mammoth task getting the house into shape for visitors, with Mrs Christos away on a week's holiday in Portugal. And then she had had to tell Jeremy that he couldn't stay for a while, that it wasn't a question of her parents being old-fashioned, it just wouldn't be right.

'Why?' he had demanded sulkily. 'Why don't you want your parents to meet me? Are you ashamed of me?'

'You know I'm not.'

'Is it the age difference, then? Are you embarrassed because I'm younger than you?'

'It doesn't make things any easier – but no, it's not that either.'

'You hardly ever go out with me, I never meet your friends. And now you don't want to acknowledge me to your parents, like I'm some dirty secret—'

'Don't be so bloody childish!' she had shouted then. 'If you can't see why it's not a good idea – not now, not with the court case coming up – then I'm damned if I'm going to explain.'

He had backed off then, but grudgingly, still with an air of wounded rejection, and she had relented a little and promised to have him over to dinner one night when her parents were settled in.

'But you have to understand,' she said firmly, 'that you still can't stay.'

'How long, then – how long till I can be with you? I won't be able to stand it if it's too long . . . I don't see how you can either . . .'

But it wasn't like that for her, not at the moment. As the court date loomed closer, she found that it filled her vision, occupied all her thoughts so there was room for nothing else.

Alice was placing bottles of fat green olives in the cupboard. 'Are you all right for money?' she asked.

Becky shook the last of the chewed bone and biscuit fragments from the bottom of the basket. 'I don't want to think about money just yet.'

'But you'll have to, dear, sooner or later.'

'Then I'd rather do it later!' she snapped.

Alice gave her a level look, then continued arranging the bottles in little symmetrical rows on the shelf. Becky looked at her stiff back and busy hands and thought she really should apologise. But somehow she couldn't bring herself to care enough, to believe that anything mattered, except the outcome of tomorrow's hearing.

She stared into the empty bottom of Bogey's basket and wondered if there would be a future for her when it was all over.

CHAPTER ELEVEN

Becky stood rooted to the pavement of the Strand and looked up at the vast Gothic cathedral-like structure of the Royal Courts of Justice towering above her. With every fibre of her being, she longed not to have to go inside. Gently, her father took her arm and propelled her forward towards the arched double doors.

In the huge central hall, Becky allowed Hugh to remove her bag from her shoulder and put it through the security check, following him like a sleepwalker through the frame of the metal detector. Jeremy brought up the rear, in a baggy black jacket that was his token gesture to court dress code. When he had arrived at her house bright and early that morning, Hugh had looked rather pointedly at the open neck of his shirt where his tie ought to have been.

Flanked by her two male supporters, Becky was almost frog-marched down the maze of corridors to the Queen's Building, a Sixties addition to the vast, sprawling complex of the High Court. They were to meet Shirley Fossey on the second floor, where a judge from the Family Division would decide the future course of all their lives.

Shirley had retained the services of a barrister named Lionel Keegan – a solid chap, she assured Becky – to represent her in court. Over the past weeks they had sat closeted in consultation with him, running through the testimony of Becky and her witnesses until the words were a mad jumble inside her head.

The lift disgorged them into the second floor corridor, where anxious groups of clients huddled round tables with their black-robed and bewigged counsel, chain-smoking and talking in hushed, tense voices over thick files full of paperwork. Becky prayed silently that, among these strangers, she would not suddenly come face to face with Rupert.

'There you are!' Shirley gestured them over to a table piled with her own files and a copy of Stone's Justices' Manual. She was dressed, quite soberly for her, in an emerald green two-piece suit. 'Lionel's just robing. We're on shortly in Court 48, with Mr Justice William Blakelock. Now try not to—'

'I know,' Becky said. 'You don't have to say it.'

Her voice was hoarse with fear. Jeremy brought out a packet of humbugs and gave her one to suck. An usher put his head round the door and nodded to Shirley just as Lionel appeared in his gown and wig.

'That's us,' she said, and Becky gripped the table. Shirley gave her hand an admonishing pat.

'You will get through this in the only way possible,' she said. 'By taking it one step at a time. But I promise, you *will* get through it. Now chin up and follow me.'

She picked up her files and led her group towards the right-hand door through which Lionel had disappeared. At the same time Rupert's team emerged from the throng and headed for the left. Everyone stared straight ahead, avoiding eye contact.

Becky stepped into a small courtroom as solemn and quiet as a church. There was no public gallery, Lionel having reassured her earlier that family matters were always heard in chambers, being of such a personal nature. It had been one slight comfort amidst the swirling anxieties.

Justice Blakelock sat high above looking down on them from beneath his wig, less a man to Becky than a figure of awesome authority. Ranged in front of him in a row were the associate, the usher and the court stenographer. Lionel and Shirley gave a quick bow to the bench and slid into the front seat. Hugh and Jeremy followed with Becky, taking up their now accustomed positions on either side of her.

Anthea had said she would make her own way. There was a banging of doors behind them as she now came breathlessly in, followed by Alex in a conservatively cut suit, both slipping into seats directly behind Becky's. On Rupert's side there was similar flutter of movement as the opposition arranged its ranks.

Becky did not dare allow her gaze to wander to the left, where Rupert must be sitting with Lolly at his side. Instead she stared at a fixed point in front of her. 'Please note,' she read dully, 'the consuming of soft drinks and the chewing of gum is prohibited in court.' Quickly she swallowed down the last of her humbug.

Rupert, being the plaintiff, would go first. His barrister, a Ms Anne Logan, stood up to present his case, and Becky allowed her eyes to shift just slightly in that direction.

'. . . It is our contention,' she was saying, 'that our client is in a position to provide better care for the child, given his more flexible work schedule . . .'

What work schedule? Becky wanted to shout. I thought it was your contention that I should do all the work so I can support him and his girlfriend and our son.

Anne Logan was calling her first witness. Becky forced herself to concentrate. It was Jilly Dickson, the swimming instructor who had never actually taught Adam to swim.

'Adam Carlyle has been coming to lessons with you for the past year and a half – is that right?' Anne Logan began.

'Yeah, that's right.'

'Who was it who usually brought him to these lessons?'

'It was always the nanny, Lolly.'

'Did Mrs Carlyle ever bring her son?'

Jilly flicked back her curly red hair. She was dressed, rather inappropriately Becky thought, in a well-used grey tracksuit, perhaps intended to convey her professionalism. 'She came with 'im once – about a month ago – and that's the last I saw of the pair of 'em.'

'In other words, since the nanny left, Adam has stopped coming to swimming lessons.'

'It's a shame an' all. 'E was getting on ever so well.'

'Thank you. No further questions.'

Lionel consulted his notes and rose to his feet. Jilly gave him an insolent look.

'Miss Dickson, can you tell us if Mr Carlyle ever brought his son to swimming lessons?'

'I couldn't say off the top of me 'ead . . .'

'Let me put it this way. Have you ever seen Mr Carlyle before today?'

Jilly looked Rupert up and down, appreciation in her eye. 'No, I reckon I would've remembered 'im.'

'So Mrs Carlyle isn't the only parent who did not bring her son to swimming . . . Now, then, is it not also true that Adam was not progressing very well in his lessons with you?'

'Now 'ang on a minute,' Jilly said indignantly. 'It takes time to get a kid that age used to the water, you know.'

'I'm sure it does. But isn't it a fact that you tend to accept a large number of children into your class at one time?'

'Nothink so strange about that,' Jilly said defensively. 'There's lots of kids in the area, we got to give 'em all a chance . . .'

'But the fact remains that, after a year and a half with you, Adam still couldn't swim, could he?'

' 'E could an' all – 'e could swim across the width with 'is boards under 'is arms.'

'But not without aids?'

'Gimme a break. It takes time to get a kid waterborne—'

'So you said. So wasn't Adam's lack of progress the reason Mrs Carlyle did not bring him back?'

'I dunno. She never said.'

'Perhaps she wished to spare your feelings.' Lionel looked dismissively down his rather long nose. 'No more questions.'

Shirley leaned round Hugh and winked at Becky. So far, she seemed to say, so good.

Next up was Adam's piano teacher, a man whose existence had entirely slipped Becky's mind. If she had been able to swallow her pride and ask Lolly – after she had moved in with Rupert – what Adam's afternoon schedule was, she would have been reminded of Wednesdays with Mr Chubb.

Rupert's barrister went through the same process of establishing that it was Lolly who had taken Adam to piano lessons, not Becky. She then extracted Mr Chubb's confession that in the last weeks, subsequent to Lolly's departure, Adam had ceased to attend at all.

'Did you ever,' Lionel enquired, when it was his turn to cross examine, 'phone Mrs Carlyle to ask why Adam had stopped coming?'

'No,' Mr Chubb admitted.

'And why was that?'

'I didn't wish to appear too pushy, if she'd changed her mind about sending her son to me.'

'But did it not occur to you that Mrs Carlyle might have a lot on her plate? That she might simply have forgotten the lessons?'

'I would not have assumed her son's musical instruction was something she would forget.' Mr Chubb looked terminally offended at the suggestion. Lionel, cutting his losses, allowed him to stand down.

This time Shirley did not wink. Becky felt a little sinking of despair in the pit of her stomach as Mr Chubb walked past her in his badly pressed trousers and ill-fitting jacket.

Rupert's character witness was a Sir Wilfred Ashcroft, an illuminary of Gloucestershire society, who had known the family, according to his testimony, for some thirty years – without once making an appearance in Rupert's life, to Becky's knowledge, in all the time he had been married to her. But Sir Wilfred claimed an intimate acquaintance with the plaintiff, and a great admiration for Rupert's many sound qualities, which he proceeded to list for the court, and which seemed to have little to do with the Rupert Becky knew and had once loved. When he had finished his rambling eulogy, Lionel declined to ask him any questions.

'We call Miss Lorraine Matthews.'

It took a moment for Becky to register that it was Lolly who was being summoned to the stand. She stiffened. Her father put a protective hand on her shoulder. On her other side, Jeremy clasped her arm.

In high heels that seemed alien to her, Lolly approached the witness box with very small steps. It took an interminable time for her to get there. She had to pass within inches of Becky but she would not look at her. Her cloud of hair was held neatly back at the sides with two combs, her long legs hidden beneath a calf-length navy skirt with matching jacket. She looked, Becky thought, far older than her years, scarcely the teenager she had hired two years ago at the tender age of seventeen.

'I swear to tell the whole truth . . .' Lolly intoned in a small frightened voice. If she had known, Becky thought, all that time ago when she hired her, that it would come to this, what would she not have done to spare them all?

'You'll have to speak up a bit,' Anne Logan said kindly, pointing to the microphone. Lolly, pale and terrified, moved closer to it. Becky feared that her obvious distress might be swaying the sympathies of Justice Blakelock.

'Now, what were your hours supposed to be when you started

working for Mrs Carlyle?' the interrogation began.

'Seven a.m. to seven p.m., with two hours off after lunch, and every Sunday and every second weekend free,' Lolly said in a voice that grew more audible.

'And how did that work out?'

'It didn't, really. Mrs Carlyle was always working late – nights, weekends . . .'

'And what happened on those occasions?'

'She asked me to do overtime . . . I nearly always said yes.'

'We've established from other witnesses that you always took Adam to his extra lessons. Did you also supervise his school homework?'

'Yes.'

'So, in fact, Mrs Carlyle has had almost nothing to do with the upbringing of her son for the past two years. That has been left entirely up to you.'

Lolly paused for only a moment. 'I suppose so . . .'

'And was Mr Carlyle around during this time?'

'He was at home far more often than Mrs Carlyle was.'

'So Adam has always been more used to spending time with his father than his mother?'

Lolly looked anxiously in Rupert's direction. Becky held her breath, and for the first time allowed her eyes to dart to the left. Rupert was steadily returning Lolly's gaze, his face as hard as granite.

'The witness should answer the question,' Justice Blakelock intervened rather severely.

'I – I'm sorry,' Lolly stumbled. 'Yes, I suppose that's true . . . Adam was more used to being with his father . . .'

Becky expelled her breath and slumped a little. Anne Logan smiled encouragingly at her witness.

'Would you go so far as to say that Mrs Carlyle actually neglected Adam?'

'Yes,' Lolly said, more conviction in her voice. 'No mother who works as hard as Mrs Carlyle can give the proper time and attention to a child.'

'Thank you. No more questions.'

Lionel Keegan rose ponderously to his feet. He could not afford, Becky suspected, to be seen to bully this witness. She came across as too vulnerable, and any attempt to come down hard on her might alienate the judge.

'Miss Matthews, you speak of neglect by my client, but is it not also the case that Mr Carlyle never showed the slightest interest in looking after his son, even though, being often out of work, he had far more opportunity to do so than my client?'

Lolly would have been coached by Bernard Fisher and Anne Logan to expect questions like these. She would know what answers would inflict the minimum damage on Rupert.

'It was my understanding,' she said, 'that as an actor, Mr Carlyle had to be available to attend auditions and chase after jobs. I wasn't led to think, by him or Mrs Carlyle, that his work was any less important than hers.'

'But it was Mrs Carlyle who paid your salary?'

'Yes – but it seemed to be from a joint account.'

'So you're saying Mr Carlyle was also tied up with work, or trying to get work, and so he must also have neglected Adam?'

'His work was more flexible, so he could pop in to see Adam more often.'

'And how often,' Lionel enquired, 'was that?'

'It varied, depending on his commitments. A couple of times a day, I suppose.'

Who, Becky wondered, had Rupert 'popped in' to see? His son? Or Lolly?

'Is it not also true,' Lionel persisted, 'that Mrs Carlyle, not her husband, always drove Adam to school in the mornings?'

'Nearly always – if she was around.'

'And that she was the one who looked after him on your days off?'

'I don't know what happened on my days off,' Lolly said rather cockily.

'I find it hard to believe Adam never mentioned anything to you.'

'He talked about things he did with both his parents.'

She wasn't coming across as quite so vulnerable now. Becky fervently prayed the judge had noticed.

'Tell me, Miss Matthews, was your employment with Mrs Carlyle terminated by her when she found out that you had been sleeping with her husband?'

Lolly hung her head, a picture of shame. 'Yes,' she said.

'So that, in fact, your testimony here today in favour of Mr Carlyle is not entirely unbiased?'

'I have tried,' Lolly said in a voice filled with sincerity, 'to tell the truth . . . not influenced by my own feelings . . .'

'I'm sure you have, Miss Matthews . . . but I wonder if it's possible not to be influenced by one's own feelings . . . No more questions.'

As Lionel sat down, Becky caught his eye. He gave a little half-encouraging shrug.

Lolly left the witness box far more speedily than she had entered it, her heels clicking on the wooden floor, passing Rupert on his way up. Becky saw him reach out to give her a brief, reassuring touch, and she had a childish urge to put out her foot and trip him.

On the stand, Rupert gave what Becky had to acknowledge was one of the better performances of his career. Cool and unflustered, led expertly by Anne Logan, he admitted that yes, he hadn't always spent enough time with his son, but that was because Becky had taken authority over the child's upbringing, had arranged with the nanny a schedule of activities for Adam, and he hadn't wished to show disloyalty to his wife by contradicting her instructions. All that would change, however, if he had residence and care of Adam. Then *he* would make the decisions, he would take the child to extra lessons and supervise his homework, assisted by Miss Matthews, the person Adam was most used to. Rupert told the court how much he regretted the circumstances that had led to his infidelity with Miss Matthews, implying that Becky had neglected him as much as she had Adam, but that unfortunate incident was not relevant to Rupert's qualities as a father. From now on, he intended to devote his life to his son.

'Are you claiming,' Lionel enquired, 'that you, an able-bodied and presumably intelligent young man, are intending to give up work so that you can go into childcare full-time?'

'Of course not. I can do both.'

'How is that?'

'When I'm working, Miss Matthews will take care of Adam, as she has in the past.'

'And will your earnings from this work be able to support you, Miss Matthews and the child?'

'I am applying in a separate action for my wife, as the higher earner, to continue funding Adam's living expenses.'

'And your own?'

'It is not unusual,' Rupert said coolly, 'for the higher earner to pay both child support and maintenance.'

'Yes, well, that is for another court to decide,' Lionel said. 'Our business today is to evaluate your relative merits as parents. What makes you think you can give Adam better care than his mother?'

'I'll be around more.'

'So you're accusing Mrs Carlyle only of being a diligent worker and the supporter of her family. You're not suggesting she is an unfit mother in any other way?'

'I'm saying she doesn't have time to be a mother at all.'

'Just answer the question, please, Mr Carlyle. Is your wife unfit to be a mother by virtue of, say, a drug or alcohol problem?'

'No.'

'When Adam is with her, is she to be trusted with his welfare?'

'Yes, sure – when she's around.'

'Thank you, Mr Carlyle. No more questions.'

Both sides shuffled papers and stretched legs. The plaintiff's case was concluded and now the defence would have its say. Becky looked up at the witness box and her mouth was dry with fear.

First Lionel called Trevor Roper, Adam's new swimming instructor, to refute the extra lesson testimony. For the past few weeks, Trevor stated, Adam had been attending lessons with him at the Chelsea Pools and making good progress. In each case, it was Mrs Carlyle who had brought him. She seemed to him an interested and involved mother. Anne Logan let Trevor go with no cross-questioning.

'We call Mrs Anthea Brockenhurst,' Lionel announced.

Anthea marched up to take the oath. Her confident plummy tones rang out around the tiny courtroom.

'Mrs Brockenhurst,' Lionel said, 'you're the Carlyle's next door neighbour and a close friend, is that right?'

'One of their closest,' Anthea assured him.

'And what do you think about the claim that Rebecca Carlyle is a negligent mother?'

'Stuff and nonsense! I never heard such drivel, and frankly, it makes my blood boil. Becky is a wonderful mother, and what's more, Rupert knows it.'

'Would you agree that she didn't spend enough time with her child?'

'What choice did she have? That husband of hers wasn't exactly bringing in the bacon . . . it's only because Becky went out to make a living that that back-stabbing little nanny got paid at all. And what thanks did Becky get? The girl steals her husband!'

'Just answer the questions, please,' Justice Blakelock admonished.

'But my dear Honour, that's precisely what I'm doing.'

'How much time,' Lionel intervened hastily, 'would you say Mrs Carlyle did spend with her son?'

'A lot more than plenty of women I know who have no job and nothing better to do with their lives than paint their nails and go to lunch.'

'Could you be a bit more specific . . . ?' Lionel said faintly. It had clearly been a complete waste of time rehearsing Mrs Brockenhurst.

'Oh heavens, do you want a list? She always drove Adam to school in the mornings, and put him to bed at night when she could, and spent her weekends off with him . . . And now that the horrid little nanny has gone, she's doing simply everything for him, and a much better job she's making of it, in my opinion.'

Lionel decided to quit while he was still, marginally, ahead. Anne Logan rose with relish.

'Mrs Brockenhurst, is it true that you have recently separated from your husband on the grounds of his infidelity?'

'Yes, that and his snoring.'

'This hearing is a serious matter, Mrs Brockenhurst, and I would ask you to be equally so.'

'I'm just as serious as you are,' Anthea said indignantly.

'Isn't it true that you are prejudiced against men like Mr Carlyle because of your own husband's infidelity?'

'My dear Ms Logan, if you are married, which I am beginning to doubt, then you will know that infidelity is only one of the many reasons why women are prejudiced against men.'

Anne Logan gleefully allowed Anthea to stand down, and Lionel gave a little despairing shake of his head. 'Sorry,' Anthea whispered as she passed Becky's row.

It would be Alex to the rescue. As he took the stand his eyes met Becky's for only a moment, but it was enough for him to convey that he would not let her down. Lionel looked at him with visible relief.

'Mr Goddard, your position as head of the biggest talent agency in London makes you an important and well-respected figure in the film industry, isn't that right?'

Alex smiled self-deprecatingly. 'I guess so.'

'And you are both a business associate and a close friend of Rebecca Carlyle. In fact, you are the godfather of her son Adam, are you not?'

'That's right.'

'Please tell the court a little bit about Mrs Carlyle.'

'She's very hard-working, very good at what she does, but that doesn't mean she puts business before her family. I happen to know, because we've discussed it several times, that Adam's welfare – and before this divorce, her husband's – is far more important to her than success in her career.'

'And do you think her work as a film producer makes it impossible for her to spend enough time with her son?'

'No. It makes things more difficult, sure, but not impossible, not to someone like her. The thing about Becky is, she puts her whole heart and soul into everything she does, and that includes being a mother.'

'So you, as Adam's godfather, would regard her as a good mother?'

'If I had kids,' Alex said, emphasising every word, 'I could think of no better mother for them than Rebecca Carlyle.'

Becky looked up at Alex, her eyes misted with tears. She heard again Adam's voice, telling her she was the perfect person to look after him. As Anne Logan allowed Alex to stand down and Lionel rose to call Becky to the stand, her heart knocked painfully against her ribs but she knew what she would have to say.

Carefully she stood, brushing off the helping hands offered by Hugh and Jeremy, and walked as steadily as she could to the witness box, her head held high. She had rehearsed, with Lionel, a carefully planned series of questions and answers. Lionel wouldn't like it if she threw away the script, but that was exactly what she was going to do.

Before he could ask his first question, Becky raised her eyes to the judge. 'Your Honour, is it all right if I say a few words . . . ?'

'That's perfectly in order, Mrs Carlyle,' the great man pronounced.

Lionel was frantically signalling caution with his bushy eyebrows, while Shirley clasped an anxious hand to her emerald bosom. Becky ignored them both.

'I remember,' she said with quiet determination, 'the first time I discussed this case with my solicitor. She told me that women have been encouraged to seek the same career opportunities as men, but nobody told them about the risks. If the risk is that they lose their children, then it's too high a price to pay.

'Today I'm being accused of being too successful in my career and spending too little time with my son, and no one regrets that more than I do. But there are no allowances made out there in the business world for a mother who might want to take time off when her child is sick or has extra lessons or homework to do. Male executives don't miss work for those reasons, and women who want the same job opportunities aren't expected to either. That's why I had to hire a nanny to take care of Adam, to see to the things I couldn't do myself.

'And now, because of that, I'm being accused of neglecting my child, and threatened with having him taken away from me. Well, I wish someone *had* warned me a long time ago that this could happen. Maybe I would have made some different choices.

'All I can do now is choose better for the future. The time I've spent with Adam over these past weeks, since this terrible mess started, has shown me exactly what it is I've been missing. It's also taught me that my son is far and away the most important thing in my life. I can't afford to give up work because without my income we wouldn't survive, but I can fit my work around Adam if I don't set my sights quite so high.

'So I'm going to do less work than in the past. I've given up the Hollywood film I was going to produce, which means a drop in living standards, but at least I can set up my office at home so I'm available for Adam when he needs me. And I'm going to work flexible hours so I *can* be with him when he comes home from school, to supervise his homework and take him to extra lessons, and just to be with him because, at the end of the day, that's what being a mother is all about.

'Of course Adam has to spend time with both parents, and I will co-operate with his father to make sure he does. But a child that age belongs with his mother, and I think he should be left where he is, to live with me.'

The silence, after she had finished speaking, seemed to last a long time. Then Lionel rose and said, 'No questions, Your Honour.' She thought she detected a faint gleam of approval in his eye.

Anne Logan, however, was not going to let her off the hook. 'Mrs Carlyle, you are a film producer, are you not?'

'Yes.'

'You're not thinking, as part of your brave new plans, of changing your profession?'

'No – I wouldn't really know what else to do.'

'Don't film producers have to go away on location for weeks at a time when they're shooting a picture?'

'The shooting of a film is only one small part of the process. There are months of putting the deal together, and then pre-production, and post-production after the shoot . . . The time spent away on location is actually a very small percentage of the whole.'

'I appreciate that,' Anne Logan said wryly. 'But nonetheless, you do have to go away for long periods when you're shooting?'

'That's right.'

'And what were you planning to do with Adam on those occasions? Surely you're not suggesting it's a good idea to have him with you on a film set, to take him out of school for all that time . . .'

'He wouldn't have to be on set as such,' Becky explained. 'Nor would he have to miss schoolwork. It's customary for a private tutor to be paid for out of the film's budget for the children of stars or key personnel who are accompanying their parents on location.'

'Don't you think it would be very disruptive for Adam to be moved around like that?'

'Not necessarily. My father was with the Foreign Office and we were constantly moving when I was a child. I don't think it made me insecure – on the contrary, it broadened my horizons and taught me a lot about life that I wouldn't have learned in school.'

'And what happens if you and my client are not in agreement on these matters?'

'Then I expect we'll end up back here, which is totally wrong, in my opinion. We are Adam's parents. We shouldn't hand over responsibility to a court to decide what should happen to him. We should make those decisions ourselves.'

'An admirable sentiment, Mrs Carlyle. But it is your inability to do so that has brought you here today . . . No more questions.'

Becky stepped away from the microphone and looked down at her hands. She had not realised till that moment that they were shaking. Clasping them together, she walked back down to her seat, and was rewarded with a proud smile from her father.

Both sides now rustled papers and turned to the report submitted by Mrs Gummer, the court welfare officer. It had been sent to them prior to the hearing and they had all had time to study its contents. The child, Mrs Gummer said, appeared confused and had been evasive in her questioning of him as to which parent he wanted to live with. Possibly, at his age, he had not understood the concept. Observing his interactions with the parents, she had concluded that he seemed perfectly at ease with both, and also very attached to his former nanny Miss Matthews, currently resident with the father. Mrs Gummer could not make a firm recommendation for or against either party.

Lionel had told Becky that he would not be calling Mrs Gummer to the stand, since he felt it unlikely that he could sway her into saying anything more favourable to their case. As he had predicted, Anne Logan also declined to cross-examine her.

'There will now be a short adjournment,' Mr Justice Blakelock announced.

They all rose as he withdrew to his chambers to mull over the testimony he had heard and reach his decision. There would be no further opportunity to influence the outcome, and Becky couldn't help wondering if she had done enough.

Back in the corridor, her team found an empty table as far away from Rupert's as possible, and huddled around it. Hugh cleared his throat and frowned at a woman at the next table hunched into a C shape and blowing clouds of smoke in their direction.

'How short,' he asked Lionel rather crossly, 'is a short adjournment?'

'It can be only fifteen minutes, but who knows?'

Hugh bent tenderly over Becky. 'How are you bearing up, my dear?'

'I'm OK – I'll make it.' But she wasn't at all sure she would. It would be, she thought, the longest fifteen minutes of her life.

'I'm positively wracked with guilt,' Anthea said. 'Have I wrecked the case?'

'Let's just say,' Lionel replied heavily, 'that you cast some doubt on your objectivity as a witness.'

Becky reached up and kissed Alex's cheek. 'Thanks – you were wonderful.'

'What about you?' Jeremy intervened. 'Your speech was brilliant – like a scene from a movie.'

If only, she thought, it were just another of their movies. If only it mattered as little as that.

'You nearly gave Lionel and me an instant coronary,' Shirley said. 'But I think you pulled it off.'

'Only think?'

'You and Rupert are both saying the same thing – that you'll put the child first and he'll be better off with you. We won't know who Justice Blakelock believes till we hear from him.'

They heard from him twenty minutes later. In sombre silence they filed back into the courtroom.

Shirley had warned Becky that the judge's summing up of the evidence might be rather long-winded, and that it was often not possible to tell which way he was inclining until the very last minute. Hugh had changed places with Becky so Shirley could interpret for her, if necessary, what was going on. Jeremy and Hugh sat side by side in their dark jackets, like undertakers at a wake.

' . . . Whereas the plaintiff said that the defendant had spent insufficient time caring for the child,' Justice Blakelock intoned, 'it was also the contention of the defendant that the plaintiff had not . . .'

Becky found herself, almost deliberately, not paying attention, not wanting to escalate her fears with amateur attempts at deduction. She fixed her eyes at a point somewhere just above Justice Blakelock's wig.

He seemed to slow down, his words becoming more pronounced. Shirley gripped her arm. '. . . So that I find for the defendant and order that the child should reside with the defendant, with contact with the plaintiff as per . . .'

'Did we win?' Becky whispered, quite unable to make sense of it all.

Grinning broadly, Shirley nodded.

Becky, awash with relief, found herself trembling from head to foot. Now, for the first time, she turned fully to face the other side of the courtroom and look directly at Rupert, sitting silent and white-faced amidst his advisers. I have won, she told herself, and victory is sweet . . . but in her mind, the person she saw on the opposite side of the court was not the man who had betrayed her, but the father of her child – and she knew that when husband turned against wife there were no real winners, only casualties.

CHAPTER TWELVE

Alice surveyed with some satisfaction the kitchen table groaning with food – Tuscan titbits courtesy of her and Hugh (someone had to eat them, Becky hadn't made much progress), and some good old favourites from the neighbourhood delicatessen, like taramasalata and smoked salmon and French bread. She and Adam had made the trip there while the others were in court, and Adam had helped her carry the bags home. It was good practice, he said, for when he was older and started training with weights.

Alice was glad to see Becky laughing again, sharing some joke with Anthea and Jeremy. She had missed her daughter's laugh. There had been times in these last weeks when she had feared she would never hear it again.

But now, she hoped, the worst was over. Whatever the future held for Becky, at least she would face it with Adam. Together they would find a way forward.

Hugh brought round a tray with glasses of champagne provided by Alex, who was sitting in a corner teaching Adam to play chess. He was a good man, that, and solid. Becky, in Alice's book, could count herself lucky having a friend like that.

She was less sure what she thought of the younger one, Jeremy, who seemed to follow her daughter's every move with an expression of dog-like devotion. Alice wasn't a great believer in that sort of adulation. In her experience, it always ended in disillusionment and then tears.

Still, it was Becky's life, and she would make her own mistakes regardless of Alice's opinion. Only Alice hoped, for her own sake, she would not be making too many more.

'To victory,' Hugh toasted, 'and the future.'

Everyone raised their glasses. Adam, not understanding but

entering into the spirit, asked Alex if he could try just the teensiest, weensiest sip.

'Sure, as long as you earn it. Next piece you take off me, I'll give you a taste.'

'Coo-ool!' Adam bent back over the board, a study in concentration.

'You'll have to wrap it up quickly, you two,' Alice called over. 'We're ready to eat.'

Becky, she saw, was already piling a plate with an assortment of cold cuts and bread and cheeses. She would not, Alice promised herself, make any predictable maternal remarks about how good it was to see her eating properly again.

They all helped themselves, buffet-style, and found a seat round the huge kitchen table. Becky's face was shining as she looked from face to face, as though revelling in the contentment of seeing her house full again, of entertaining and enjoying herself like any normal human being.

'More champagne anyone?' Hugh asked.

'Don't trouble yourself to get up again, Mr Carlyle,' Alex said at once. 'I'll see to it.'

Alice watched the way he moved easily round the table, bending over Becky and lightly touching her shoulder. There was a history there, she thought, there might even be a future, but it wasn't her place to wish things for her daughter that she might not want herself.

'I was having a drink with some mates in Wardour Street yesterday,' Jeremy was saying, 'and the word is Stanley Shiplake and Pantheon are still going ahead with the movie, even though we've walked off. You know why?'

They all stopped eating and looked at him, tension at once in the air. Why, Alice thought, could the young fool not have the tact to steer away from talking shop, and let Becky forget her problems just for this brief moment?

'Letitia's pulled a rabbit out of the hat,' Jeremy said. 'She's got Juliette Winters to agree to do the lead role.'

'Really?' Alex frowned. 'That must be a recent development. I saw Juliette in L.A. a couple of weeks ago, and she didn't mention it.'

Becky seemed to be studying Alex closely. She was probably

worried about this film business, Alice thought, but she could have sworn she saw something close to jealousy in her daughter's expression.

'It doesn't seem right that they can get rid of you without any compensation,' Hugh said. 'Don't you have a claim against them?'

'The last thing I need,' Becky said firmly, 'is another court case. As it is, Shirley and Bernard Fisher haven't even started wrangling over the financial settlement, so I still have another battle on that front.'

Hugh and Alice exchanged looks. They had been trying to pin Becky down on the state of her finances for at least two weeks, but she always evaded the issue. They were, of course, only too happy to help in any way they could, but how could they help if she wouldn't even speak to them?

'Oh, you'll never guess,' Anthea said. 'I might just have solved some of my own little money worries. I interviewed a woman the other day who might do for renting my spare room. A qualified accountant – too clever for me by half, I expect.'

'If she takes it, she won't last,' Becky laughed.

'As it happens, she's frightfully keen. Knows her own mind and likes what she saw. She particularly approved of the castrated nudes.'

'Help!' Alex said. 'Another man hater.'

'All the better. I won't have to put up with visits from the boyfriends.'

'Anthea,' Adam said, 'what is a castrated nude?'

'It's the sort of chap I might marry if I'm ever stupid enough to do it again.'

Becky peeped over her sunglasses at Shirley's scarlet and gold embroidered jacket worn, mercifully, over a plain black skirt. She folded the glasses – rather expensive ones, if she remembered rightly – and put them carefully away in their case.

'The bottom line,' she said, 'is that most of the cash is gone.'

'Are we talking a lot of cash?'

Becky took a gulp of tea, the hot liquid almost scalding her tongue. 'I earned a reasonable fee on the last film but our expenses have always been so . . . unreasonable.'

Shirley nodded wisely. 'You've lived from hand to mouth,

haven't put enough by for a rainy day . . . Was that Rupert's doing, or yours?'

'Rupert doesn't really understand the concept of living within one's means.' Becky said obliquely.

'Well, he'll have to learn now,' Shirley said with some satisfaction. 'If there's no money left, and no big film on the horizon, he won't be getting any cash handouts from you.'

'What will he get?'

Shirley stuck her feet out and surveyed, with a gleam of appreciation, her black and gold military style boots, bought for a song at Camden Lock market. 'He is entitled to half the house and also half the contents. It doesn't sound like there's much else left to argue over. At least we may avoid another costly court case.'

'I've put something aside,' Becky said quickly, 'to pay legal expenses.'

'Rupert will have to pay the last court costs – or rather, the legal aid will pay them for him – because he brought the action. But you, of course, will have to settle Lionel and I'm afraid he didn't come cheap. As for my own fees, I'm perfectly happy to make some arrangement for you to pay them off over time—'

'Thank you,' Becky said, 'but I prefer to settle my debts straight-away.'

'As you wish.' Shirley fiddled for a moment with her epaulettes. 'Now, is there any way you can pay Rupert out in cash for his share of the house?'

'I can't get my hands on that sort of money, not now . . .'

'Then you'd better think about putting the house on the market right away.'

'The fellow's a damn scoundrel,' Hugh barked, 'to leave you and Adam in this position.'

'Hush, Hugh,' Alice remonstrated. 'You're talking about the man Rebecca married. No need to make her feel more of a fool for it than she does already.'

'Sorry, my dear.' Hugh reached out and touched his daughter's hand. 'No offence meant to you . . . Well, it looks like your mother and I will have to see you right.'

He seemed, lately, both tired and irritable, quite unlike his even-tempered self, and Becky couldn't bear to think she had been the cause of so much worry for him. 'I don't want to take money from you.'

'Be sensible, darling,' Alice said calmly. 'There's nothing wrong with accepting a little help from your parents.'

But if she did, Becky thought, she would be guilty in her own eyes, in some way she couldn't explain to her mother, of exactly what she had found so reprehensible in Rupert.

'Let's wait and see what happens,' she said, 'when I sell the house. Maybe I can buy something smaller with my half and still have a bit of cash left over.'

'You might not be able to sell it right away, you know,' her father warned.

'Let's just wait and see.'

'I should never have listened to you,' Rupert said furiously. 'Your so-called brilliant strategy has blown up in my face!'

'Now then, Mr Carlyle, I never said I could guarantee success.' Bernard Fisher gave a shrug of his broad shoulders that seemed to absolve him from any blame.

'You realise what you've done?' Rupert rose and began to pace up and down the length of the Turkish rug. 'By making me go for residence of Adam, you forced Becky into a corner – you made her give up this big film deal of hers to prove she has time to look after him. So now she won't be able to pay me maintenance, will she?'

'Calm yourself, Mr Carlyle . . . that's a very expensive carp—'

'Don't talk to me about expense.' Rupert leaned menacingly over Bernard Fisher's desk, and Bernard withdrew fractionally into his leather upholstered chair. 'Who's going to pay those bills you kept telling me I had to think about?'

'You are still entitled,' Bernard said huffily, 'to half the house and its contents.'

'Great!' Rupert collapsed back into his chair. 'Once we've sold it, and paid off the rather large mortgage, there'll be just about enough left over for me to get a small two-bedroom flat – and then where will I put the half-share of the furniture I'm entitled to?'

Bernard Fisher looked at him with an expression of great

disappointment. 'I had imagined there would be more cash, more assets . . .'

'Well, there aren't. What's more, with Becky playing mummy at home, there aren't going to be.'

'Then it looks, Mr Carlyle, very much as though you will have to get a job.'

The man from the estate agency was here, and Adam had gone under his bunk bed, right to the very corner, and he wasn't going to come out until Mummy made the man go away again.

She had told him they had to sell the house, something about the money, but he knew they couldn't do that. If they sold the house, there wouldn't be anywhere for them all to live when Daddy and Lolly came home.

He hated the way things were for him since Daddy and Lolly left. He hated having two homes instead of one, two places he was supposed to sleep, and nowhere he could be with both his parents together. He didn't want it to be like that. He wanted things the way they were before.

But they couldn't be if Mummy sold the house. Then there would be another new place for him to sleep, and when he thought about that, he was absolutely certain he wouldn't be able to bear it.

So he burrowed down under his bunk and waited, waited for the man to go and for Mummy to realise that she was making a big mistake. There wasn't any way for him to explain it to her. Grown-ups never understood when you tried to explain. He would just have to wait until she worked it out for herself.

In the meantime, he wasn't coming out. It was dark under here, but he could just make out the outline of his laser gun. He eased a finger forward and pulled it closer towards him. If that man came in here, he might just have to shoot. It was only a toy gun, Adam knew that, but at least it made a good noise, and with any luck it might frighten the stupid man right away.

'I know it's usually your father you speak to about these things,' Alice said, 'but he's feeling a little worn out by it all, so I've sent him upstairs to take a nap.'

She reached up and took some dried flowers from Becky, perched up on the stepladder and disengaging bunches of them from their ceiling hooks. She wanted the flowers gone, Becky had told her mother, even before the move. They were part of the old life she no longer had any use for.

'Are you sure – they're quite pretty,' Alice had said, but Becky insisted she didn't want pretty. The trouble was, Alice wasn't quite sure what it was that her daughter did want.

She had no such doubts about Adam. Adam, she knew, didn't want the house – the only childhood home he had known – to be sold. He had said so quite definitely to Alice and Hugh and Becky, and when they had tried to explain to him the unavoidable necessity of it, he had disappeared beneath his bed. The man from the estate agency had been rather alarmed when he suddenly stuck an arm out from under it, firing a laser gun.

'The market is sluggish,' Mr Egglestone the agent had said, recovering from his little shock over a cup of tea in the kitchen. 'You may have to drop your price.'

'I can't do that,' Becky had said firmly. 'If I don't get what I'm asking, I won't be able to buy a flat big enough for me and my son, and pay out the other half to my husband.'

Mr Egglestone had looked sceptically at the ceiling, and then at Bogey curled in his basket. 'Will you be taking the dog with you to this flat?'

Becky had said of course, and Mr Egglestone had shaken his head thoughtfully and said there weren't any flats in the area with gardens big enough for a dog that size.

'But I have to be in this area – my son goes to school here.'

'In that case, Mrs Carlyle, you've got yourself a problem.'

No one mentioned the problem to Adam. Instead Becky wondered to her parents whether she might have to move further afield, and face a longer drive to and from school.

But Adam didn't want to move anywhere. He also, he told his grandmother, '*des*prately' wished she and grandpa would stay longer, so the house wouldn't be so empty, at least till Daddy and Lolly came home. And that was when the plan began to formulate in Alice's mind, the solution she was careful to discuss first with Hugh and win his approval. But her husband, she suspected, would endorse any proposal that relieved him of some of the growing concern he felt for Becky and Adam.

'Your father and I,' Alice said, packing some of the dried flowers neatly into a cardboard box, 'have a suggestion to make.'

Becky stopped unhooking bunches and looked narrowly at her. 'About what?'

'We thought if you moved out of the house for a little while, instead of selling it, then it might not be quite so traumatic for Adam. You could get quite a lot for this if you rented it out, and then you'd be able to pay half to Rupert, and keep the other half yourself – just until you're back on your feet again.'

'And where would Adam and I stay for this short period?'

'We thought,' Alice said carefully, keeping her eyes on her task, 'that you might want to come to us in Tuscany. Adam would have his family around him, and he could go to that nice local school with Lorenzo and Lucia Fresconori. It wouldn't do him any harm just for a term – on the contrary, he'd get to learn a new language and experience new things . . .'

'And what would I do while he's at school?'

'You said yourself, dear, that you can't work on this new film of yours until Jeremy has written the screenplay. If you come and stay with us, it'll give him a chance to do that with no distractions.'

Alice was conscious of Becky's eyes boring into the back of her head, but she carried on neatly arranging the flowers between layers of tissue paper. 'I think it would do both Adam and you the world of good,' she said, 'to get away for a bit, from everything . . . and everyone.'

'I see,' Becky said. 'And what does Daddy think?'

'He thinks it's an absolutely wonderful idea.'

Becky reached up and began to unhook a bunch of white and yellow daisies. 'I'll give it some thought,' was all she said.

At least, Alice thought, it was not an outright rejection. She and Hugh were at their wits' end to know how else to help their daughter without wounding her delicate pride.

It was so quiet in Todd's flat, Lolly thought, as she paced from room to room – so quiet and so empty.

She strained again for the sound of voices in the street below, a key in the lock, but there was only the distant roar of traffic and the silence. Nothing for her to do, she told herself, except wait. Rupert hadn't rung, hadn't told her where he was going, and she didn't have a clue, really, where to find him. Worse, she wasn't sure he wanted her to.

She fetched herself a glass of Coke and a packet of crisps and went and sat, hunched with misery, in front of the telly. There was nothing she particularly wanted to watch, but anything was better than the silence.

It's not like this is the first time, she thought wretchedly as she flicked from channel to channel. In fact, it's starting to become a pattern, this going off with Todd and not coming home till after midnight. Just like he used to do when he was with Becky . . .

No, she mustn't think like that, she told herself crossly. It wasn't like she neglected Rupert, the way Becky had. If anything, she waited on him hand and foot. It couldn't be something she was doing wrong, it must be all the worry about money.

Lolly hadn't wanted to take another live-in nanny job, not now she was with Rupert, so she'd put her name up in the local news-agent for babysitting, and got quite a few bookings. The trouble was, every time she did night work Rupert went out with Todd, and it made her uneasy, wondering what they got up to. And now he'd started doing it even when she was home.

The money from the babysitting was OK but it wasn't really enough. Todd had introduced Rupert to some modelling contacts, and he'd got a few jobs from it, but there weren't enough of those either. It made him really irritable, having to cut corners. Lolly didn't mind so much – how could she be unhappy as long as she had Rupert? – but she couldn't blame him for feeling low, he was used to better things than she was.

She wished she could give him the kind of life that Becky had, make it up to him for everything he'd lost because of her. If he'd just won the court case things would have been different, he'd have had his home back and all the bits and pieces that meant so much to him. But since he lost he'd been slipping into a deeper and deeper depression, going out more and more often to drown his sorrows. It wasn't as though he was deliberately unkind to her, but sometimes he acted as though she just wasn't there. And then she would get this awful feeling, which she quickly tried to suppress because it seemed so disloyal, that he'd only let her move in with him to win the court case, and now that he'd lost he might decide he didn't need her any more. She loved him so much, if he didn't love her back she thought she might not be able to bear it.

She gave up at last on the channel-hopping, settling for a new hospital drama. Amazing, she thought, how many of them there were – viewers getting vicarious thrills from other people's suffering. With any luck, and enough gore, maybe she'd also be able to focus for a few forgetful moments on someone else's pain.

She wasn't sure when she drifted off, but the screen was showing the test pattern when she finally woke, stiff-necked and cold, to realise that Rupert still hadn't come home.

Rupert's mind drifted somewhere above the dance floor, in a haze of wellbeing permeated only by the thud of the rhythm to which his body moved almost of its own accord. He felt pleasantly light-headed and numb after the two magnums of champagne bought for their table by an Arab friend of Todd's, and the joint he and Todd had shared afterwards in the men's loo.

'Let's sit the next one out – I need a drink.'

Rupert peered vaguely at the pretty black girl he'd almost forgotten he was dancing with. She took him by the hand and he followed her unsteadily back to their table. Todd's friend, fortunately, was still running a tab. Rupert ordered two double Scotches.

The girl – Lisa, he thought she'd said her name was – had her hand on his thigh. He felt soothed by the steady beat of the music and the stroking movements of her fingers. Here, at least, he didn't feel like a loser. Nobody here knew he no longer had a wife or a home or any of the things he cared about. Here women found him desirable and men looked at him with envy, and he could walk tall again.

'You're not married, are you?' Lisa cooed, nibbling his earlobe.

Her ill-timed words made the anger flash through him again, the feeling of rejection he had come here to escape, the burning need to get back at Becky for causing him so much pain.

'Hey, sorry I asked,' the girl said, backing off from the thunderous expression on his face.

He pulled her roughly back against him, and ran his fingers down her spine. She shivered with delight, ripe for the taking.

He wanted Becky to know how much other women longed for him. He wanted her to regret casting him off like old clothing. He wanted her on her knees, begging his forgiveness.

*   *   *

'Bit of bad news, I'm afraid,' Shirley said apologetically down the line.

At once Becky's heart began to pound in her chest. 'What is it?'

She had asked Shirley to approach Bernard Fisher for Rupert's permission to take Adam to Tuscany for one school term, during which time they could rent out the house and split the proceeds. Mr Egglestone had assured her that a short-term let would bring in a very tidy weekly sum, which Becky suspected Rupert needed as much as she did.

Shirley's proposal included the suggestion that Adam could fly back regularly to spend weekends with his father. She sent it off in an optimistic frame of mind.

'Rupert,' she now said heavily, 'has gone to court and taken out an *ex parte* judgement against you – a Prohibited Steps Order, it's called.'

'I don't understand . . .'

'He's persuaded a judge there is a danger, because of your film producing career and your parents living abroad, that you will take the child out of the country against his will. So the court has now effectively stopped you from doing so.'

'But *why*?' Becky cried. 'I wasn't going to do anything without consulting him . . .'

'Whatever you were or weren't going to do,' Shirley said grimly, 'the bottom line is that you now *cannot* leave England with Adam unless you have Rupert's permission. If he refuses it, and you still want to go, you have to ask the court.'

'Is he refusing to allow me to take Adam to Tuscany?'

'I'm afraid so. Insists the child should remain here where he can see him too. He also doesn't want strangers renting your house and ruining his antiques – about which, judging from the tone of the letter, he seems to be considerably more concerned than he is about Adam.'

Becky dropped her head into her hand and tried to bring her mind into focus. 'Don't I have a say in what happens to us? Do I just have to take this lying down?'

'When someone gets an *ex parte* judgement, another hearing is arranged, usually within a week, at which both sides get a chance to argue their case. That's when a final judgement will be made.'

It seemed to Becky an almost unbearable prospect. Back to court again – and so soon. 'How good are my chances of getting this Prohibited Steps Order thing lifted?'

Shirley sighed heavily. 'Not very good, I'm afraid. Judges are always cautious when it comes to the possibility of a child being abducted. They'd rather be safe than sorry – don't want any comeback on themselves if they were wrong and a parent does skip the country with the kid.'

'So is there any point in fighting it?'

'Not really – but obviously we will if that's what you want.'

What she wanted, Becky thought, was an end to this senseless warfare. 'I thought I was suggesting something that was good for both of us. I just don't understand why Rupert's done this.'

'Pride, perhaps. He lost the last battle, but this is one he'll probably win and I'm sure he knows it.'

Becky replaced the receiver and stared at it blankly. It sounded less like pride to her than sheer bloody-minded revenge. Even now, she could scarcely take it in. Without having committed any crime, simply because she had a child with someone who had once loved her and no longer did, she was now trapped, a virtual prisoner in her own country.

She had never felt more like leaving England in her life.

Hugh and Alice had taken Adam to feed the ducks at the round pond by Kensington Palace, and Becky was sitting alone in the garden in the long summer twilight, gazing at the tangle of growth, when Anthea waved at her over the fence.

'Yoo-hoo,' she called. 'I was just going to pop over.'

Becky, unwilling or unable to move, threw her house keys over the garden fence.

Soon there were footsteps through her kitchen and not one face but two peered out at her through the door.

'You simply must meet my new lodger, Henrietta.'

A woman of about forty with cropped black hair stepped forward, hand outstretched. 'Henri,' she said. 'I'd much prefer it if you'd call me Henri.'

Becky took the proffered hand and winced a little at the firmness of its grip. 'Nice to meet you,' she said. 'I'm afraid you've caught me on a bad day.'

'Never mind, darling, we'll cheer you up. I've brought the wine . . .' Anthea plonked a bottle of Chardonnay down on the wooden garden table, '. . . and I'll just fetch some glasses.'

She disappeared back into the kitchen, and Becky and Henri stood for a few moments in awkward silence.

'Please,' Becky said, 'sit down.'

'You're sure you don't mind?'

'Anthea doesn't allow me to mind about things. It's one of her missions in life. You're very brave,' Becky warned, 'to take her on.'

'Nonsense,' Anthea said, returning with the glasses and filling them almost to the top. 'I'm terribly easy to live with – ask my dogs. Now, Becky, what's this latest blow to your spirits?'

Mindful of Henri's keen attentiveness, Becky explained rather awkwardly about the Prohibited Steps Order.

'Honestly,' Anthea said, 'I can't imagine what that man will get up to next!'

Becky took a quick, angry gulp of wine. 'Now I know why women are called the fair sex. It's because men are the *un*fair sex.'

'They're also the *af*fair sex,' Anthea said, nodding in vigorous agreement. 'There's not one of them can keep their trousers up.'

'Hear, hear!' Henri raised her glass in a toast. Becky wondered what secret disillusionment Henri harboured in her breast, and whether she would shortly reveal it in the general atmosphere of confession.

'Frankly,' Henri said, 'I think women should be able to select men for their probable genetic potential and then get on with rearing the children on their own – like they do in the animal kingdom. Women simply don't need men for anything except their sperm – and hopefully, in the future, we'll be able to dispense with them even for that.'

'Oh, I don't know.' Anthea plucked one of her favourite cream 'seagull' roses from the wildly climbing strands of bush behind her and placed it behind her ear, looking a little nostalgic. 'Even I can remember some other uses for—'

'Women bear the children, don't they?' Henri said aggressively. 'They give birth to them, which is no picnic, they give up all sorts of things to look after them properly . . . and then along come the men claiming rights over them, just because they provided some of the genes.'

'Well, I'm not sure that's all there is to it,' Becky protested gently.

'Then do you believe,' Henri demanded, 'this soon to be ex-husband of yours has the right to stop you going where you want to?'

'I think,' Becky said, 'he should be talking to me rather than a judge.'

'He's just using the child as a hold over you.'

'I'm afraid that's probably what it comes down to . . .' Becky looked curiously at Henri. 'Do you have children?'

'Can't stand the little brutes – but that doesn't mean I can't sympathise with your problem.'

'I suppose not,' Becky said doubtfully, and then, with polite interest, 'Anthea tells me you're an accountant.'

'That's right. Anything men can do, we can do better.'

'And how are you liking it so far in our little neck of the woods?'

'Marvellous wine,' Anthea said dreamily, swilling it round her tongue. 'Amazing what they come up with these days in Chile . . .'

'I like it here,' Henri said, 'very much indeed.' She looked from one to the other of them with something like satisfaction. 'I feel that I am going to be among soul mates.'

Alice stood in the hallway amidst her neatly labelled brown leather suitcases. 'I wish there were more we could do here,' she said to Becky, 'but there isn't and we have to get back.'

'I know.' Becky looked at the bags and felt childishly desolate. Adam, who was spending this weekend with Rupert, had already said his goodbyes. He had sat for a long time afterwards in Bogey's basket and refused to speak to anyone.

'It's not just a question of the young man who's been house-sitting for us not being able to do it any longer,' Alice said. 'It's your father – he's not as young as he used to be, and he simply can't take all this pressure. It wears him out.'

'Is there anything else the matter with him?' Becky asked anxiously.

'Nothing that won't be cured by some peace and quiet and sleeping in his own bed again.'

'But have you – ?'

'Shh.' Alice put a finger to her lips. Becky turned and saw her father slowly descending the stairs.

He came to Becky and put his arms round her and held her close. His breathing was slightly laboured. It was several moments before he could speak.

'I hate leaving you like this,' he said into her hair, 'knowing you can't just pop on a plane and come over to see us.'

'You never know,' Alice said brightly. 'Perhaps when Rupert calms down he'll change his mind and lift the order.'

Hugging her father tightly, Becky found she couldn't trust herself to speak. But she doubted Rupert would do any such thing. In court a few days ago, when another judge had confirmed the Prohibited Steps Order despite Lionel's arguments against it, Rupert had looked quietly triumphant.

Hugh released Becky and stared at her intently. 'You will let us know what's going on, won't you?'

She forced a little smile. 'Don't worry about me, Daddy. You've seen me through the worst of it – things can only get better.'

'Of course they will,' Alice said.

'But you'll let us know if you need any money?'

The doorbell jangled harshly, announcing the arrival of the taxi. They all looked at each other for a moment before Becky went to open the door.

She was glad of the distraction of loading suitcases into the car. By the time it was done, she felt reasonably in control of her emotions.

But she was not prepared for the sight of her father's face as the taxi moved off, staring at her fixedly through the window, as though he were quite convinced he would never see her again.

'I'm glad you're not going to Tuscany,' Jeremy said, tracing the contours of her face with his finger. 'I want you here with me.'

She settled her head against the bare skin of his shoulder and allowed him to hold her close.

'I wouldn't have been able to write anyway, if you'd gone,' he said. 'You're the one I get all my inspiration from.'

Becky sighed, and saw how her breath ruffled the little dark hairs on his chest. 'Do you understand what's happened to me? What it means for my future?'

'You're free now, to have a future with me.'

'No,' she said, 'I'm not. I'm trapped here, in England. I'm not free to do anything.'

Jeremy stroked her hair. 'That's OK. We're both here.'

She raised herself on one elbow and looked at him. 'You really don't get it, do you? What about this screenplay you're writing? It's set in France, Jeremy – *France*. That's where you'll have to go to shoot it. And I can't come with you.'

'Can't you leave Adam behind with his father while we're filming?'

'No. I would have to spend too long away from him. He'd miss me too much. He needs me with him right now.'

Jeremy pulled her back into his arms. 'I'll just have to write something else, then, set in England.'

'You can't do that. You can't limit yourself just because of me. It'll start damaging your work—'

'Being without you will also damage my work.'

Becky pulled away again, and took his face in her hands. 'Listen to me. I told you once before, and I'm going to tell you again. You're a great talent – you don't need anybody. You can succeed on your own.'

'But I *want* to do it with you.'

'Jeremy,' she said patiently, 'have you ever heard of a film producer who can only produce films in England, who isn't allowed to travel?'

'There's got to be some way round it . . .'

'There isn't. Not without constant trips to court and I can't deal with any more of those.' She took his hand and held it gently against her cheek. 'I have to face it, Jeremy. Unless Rupert changes his mind, my film producing days are over. And I don't know what on earth I'm going to do.'

CHAPTER THIRTEEN

'Sorry to come barging in on you at the office like this,' Becky said. 'I just suddenly felt I had to get out of the house.'

Alex looked at her pacing restlessly along his bookshelves and picked up Wellington's lead. 'Why don't we go for a walk?'

Wellington eyed the lead and thumped his tail, but it was a few moments before he pulled himself to his feet. Becky glanced uncertainly at the pile of papers on Alex's desk. 'Are you sure you've got time?'

'I'm sure,' Alex said firmly. 'Come on, old boy.'

They went out into the foyer and pressed for the lift. Becky was fiddling constantly with the strap of her handbag, and Alex noticed that her fingernails were cut very short, and wondered whether it was for convenience on the keyboard or to stop herself from biting them.

'What's at home that you want to get away from?' he asked.

'Nothing,' she said defensively. 'Just Jeremy writing his screenplay.'

'Are you still going to try and produce it?'

'I can't. I can't leave the country. I've told him he has to get on with it without me, but he isn't exactly being . . . oh, never mind!'

Though he would dearly have liked to hear more, Alex didn't press her. He held the lift door open and stood aside for her to pass.

They strolled down towards the Victoria Embankment Gardens, Wellington limping slightly on his right back foot. He'd better let the vet take a look at it, Alex thought, though it was probably his old trouble with the arthritis. 'Are you still trying to sell the house?' he asked.

'Not at the moment. Rupert has finally accepted an alternative proposal. Since I'm not likely to need a nanny in the near future, I'm going to rent out the basement floor where Lolly used to stay as a self-contained flat. Rupert will get the money from it, minus his share of the mortgage. The selling point, as far as Rupert's concerned, is that there are none of his precious antiques down there for a tenant to ruin.'

'Why doesn't Rupert just take his blessed antiques so you can stop being responsible for them?'

'I'm sure he's dying to, but he hasn't got the space. He's decided to carry on sharing with Todd and just pay rent on one room, instead of a whole flat. Even then, he won't have much left over to live on. The only thing I've insisted he take is the four-poster, but he's had to put it in storage for the time being.'

'What about you? Are you happy with the arrangement?'

Becky shrugged. 'It beats forcing another move on Adam. I don't think he could take it right now. It also means I have the space to work from home – which will be great when I finally figure out what kind of work I can possibly do.'

Wellington seemed to be tiring. Alex steered them all towards a bench looking out over the river.

'You could write,' he said. 'You could write your own screenplay.'

'*Me*?' Becky collapsed onto the bench and looked at him as though he'd finally taken leave of his senses. 'I've never written a thing in my life.'

Alex detached the lead and let Wellington sink down, weary and relieved, at his feet. 'You've always contributed ideas to the films you've produced, haven't you? And you've read hundreds of screenplays. You must have some idea how to write one yourself.'

'Jeremy's the writer, not me.'

'What makes you so sure he has the monopoly on that particular talent?'

'I can't . . . I wouldn't even know where to begin!'

Alex looked up at the thin monolithic structure of Cleopatra's needle, pointing up at the clear blue sky. 'Yes, you would,' he said. 'There are no limits to what people can achieve, if they only have the will.'

She followed the direction of his gaze, and her voice sounded small and far away. 'I don't know if I still have enough belief in myself. I've taken so many knocks . . .'

'But I do believe in you,' Alex said. 'Enough to say I'll take you on as a client. If you just try, if you write something that's any good, I'll represent you, I'll sell it for you.'

She smiled at him uncertainly. 'You'd really do that?'

'I really would.'

'But I thought you only represented actors.'

'I've taken on quite a few writers lately, and it makes for a pleasant change. In fact, it might just become my new area of speciality.'

It was important, Alex felt, to specialise. It was a principle he had tried to impress on his father when Frank had told him he was handing over the day to day running of the L.A. office to David Wiseman, one of his Young Turks. David was a competent agent, aggressive and ambitious, but Alex wasn't sure he trusted his ideas on how to shape the company's future. David wanted to take on the big boys, compete with the top three, and Alex didn't think that would work. He believed the answer was to find a niche in which IAM could be the best and then stick to it – like he'd always done in the London office. For years it had been known in the business that Alex represented the best of the British stage actresses, and now he was developing a stable of promising writers too. But when he pointed this out to his father, he got the feeling Frank was impatient at any obstacle to his own plans. There might, Frank had hinted, be wedding bells in the air.

'Let's just give David a chance to do it his way,' Frank insisted, 'and then we'll see.'

Alex only hoped that if what they saw was disaster, it wouldn't be too late to fix it.

'Penny for your thoughts,' he said to Becky, who was staring pensively at the obelisk, as though trying to decipher its obscure hieroglyphics.

'Well, I . . . suppose you've got yourself a new client. I just hope we don't both live to regret it.'

'Good for you.' He watched a stately barge float down towards Waterloo Bridge, and remembered the great Vivien Leigh film. 'As your new agent, I have only one piece of advice. Write about what you know, something you feel strongly about.'

'I have a lot of strong feelings right now—'

'Then use them, channel them onto the page, and I promise you won't go wrong.'

She gave a bitter little shrug. 'No one wants to hear about my problems.'

'Don't be so sure. There are plenty of people out there who've been through the same sort of thing. You may strike a chord.'

She smiled weakly. 'I suppose it would cut down on the research . . .'

'What better place to do your research than in the school of life?' He reached down and fondled Wellington's ear. 'Now, are you going to be all right for money until the screenplay is written?'

'Are you asking as my agent or my friend?'

'Both.'

She looked down at her trainers, scuffing the toes against the gravel of the path. 'Money's very tight at the moment. I'm thinking about letting Mrs Christos go, though I'd hate to do it, she's been with me so long, and the house is rather big to manage on my own . . . But I have to find some way of cutting down on expenses. And I don't really know what to do about Adam's school fees. They're absurdly high, of course, but all the private schools seem to charge the same. Perhaps I'll just have to send him to a state one for a while . . .'

'You don't want to move him, Becky. He's been through too many changes to adapt to new friends as well. And you don't want to confuse him by switching back and forth between systems.'

'Of course I don't *want* to,' Becky said tartly. 'I may have no choice.'

'Yes you do. You can let me pay his school fees.'

She turned sharply and stared at him, her blond bob swinging across her face so that he was tempted to reach forward and brush it gently back.

'I can't let you do that, Alex—'

'But you must, or it negates the whole point of asking me to stand as Adam's godfather. It's a sacred responsibility, and it means I'm supposed to step in at times like this and do whatever I can. Like paying Adam's school fees when you can't afford to. You *must* let me do it, Becky, or it makes a mockery of the duty you asked me to take on.'

'When I asked you, Alex, I didn't expect you to take on that much.'

He stared out at the river, that great body of water that looked so timeless and yet was constantly changing, moving onward. 'None of us expect the blows that life is going to deal us. But now that this has happened to you, you mustn't retreat back into responses conditioned by pride and fear. You must open yourself to other possibilities, new solutions you may not have contemplated before.'

She was silent for a while. Then she said, 'Funny, isn't it, how lately I always seem to be part of the problem and you're always part of the solution.'

'Becky—'

'No,' she said. 'Not now.' And she stood and kissed him lightly on the head and began to walk away rapidly, back very straight, towards the Embankment tube station. He sat on the bench with Wellington at his feet and watched until her small upright figure disappeared into the milling crowds on the pavement, and was lost from sight.

Becky walked the streets round Victoria, seeking by memory and guesswork the address she had visited all those months ago. She turned a corner and there, in front of her, was the very building. She scanned the labels next to the bells and found the right name. A crackly voice demanded that she identify herself before the buzzer sounded.

It was the first floor she wanted, if she remembered rightly. As she headed up the stairs, a door at the top was flung open.

'An unexpected pleasure, m'dear. Looking to wheedle another drink out of me, no doubt,' Sir Humphrey cackled.

She gave him a fierce hug and felt how frail he was, all skin and bone, and he made a great show of trying to struggle from her grasp. 'Now, then, what's all this sentimental nonsense . . .'

'I've come to make you an offer you can't refuse.'

'Don't be too sure. I've turned down better than the likes of you, missy.' He winked. 'But that was twenty years ago. I'm not so fussy now . . . You'd better come in.'

She followed him into the rented flat that had haunted her dreams, and looked around at its well remembered cheerlessness. There was nothing of Sir Humphrey except his books and photographs, and those would fit into one small suitcase.

'I want you to come and live with me,' Becky said.

'Aren't you the forward one!'

'It's a basement flat, I'm afraid, but it does get plenty of light, and it opens straight onto my garden . . .'

'Hold on a minute.' Sir Humphrey put up a hand. 'Perhaps you'd better start from the beginning. A very good place to start, as Julie Andrews once sang in a well-known blockbuster.'

Becky sat in one of the hard chairs, facing Sir Humphrey's wingback. 'It can't be much fun, living here by yourself. I thought it might be company for you if you moved into this flat in my house—'

'I don't need any favours from you!' Sir Humphrey said tartly.

'Believe me, you'd be doing *me* the favour. I have to rent it out to make ends meet, and I don't want it going to a stranger.'

Sir Humphrey looked a little mollified. 'What sort of rent were you planning on stinging me with?'

'It certainly won't be more than you're paying here. It's furnished too, though not, I'm afraid, with antiques . . .'

'Listen, my dear, being an antique myself, I'd far rather be surrounded with things that are not.'

Becky giggled. 'Would you like to see it?'

'What are you waiting for?' Humphrey grumbled. 'Lead on, Macduff!'

'Mummy, I want to come home!' Adam wailed down the phone.

Becky held tightly onto the receiver and forced herself to calm the protective motherly instincts that instantly rushed to the surface. It would do no good, she reminded herself, to dash straight round to Rupert's flat and create a perhaps unnecessary drama.

There were times when Adam simply couldn't face being uprooted and going off to his father for the weekend, other times when once he was there he longed to come home. On these occasions he required very careful handling – gentle coaxing out from under his bunk bed, quiet reassurances over the phone. All children from broken homes went through this misery, Anthea confirmed gloomily – her Joshua was just the same.

'What's the matter, darling?' Becky asked soothingly.

'I miss you,' he sobbed. 'I want to come ho-o-ome.'

'Don't cry, baby. I'm sure if you're homesick and you just talk to Daddy, he'll bring you back.'

'Daddy's not here. He went out with Todd. There's only me and Lolly.'

Becky looked at her watch. It was eight o'clock, Adam's bedtime, and Rupert had gone out, leaving Lolly to deal with his parental responsibilities as though she were still just the hired help, paid to do the job. Becky couldn't help wondering how that made Lolly feel.

'In that case,' she said, 'maybe you'd better ask Lolly to read you a Dilly the Dinosaur story.'

'I don't want Lolly – I want *you*.'

Becky had to suppress a small, unworthy feeling of self-satisfaction. 'All right, my darling, I'll read you a story over the phone, but I think it's better if you try to go to sleep where you are, because it's already very late . . .'

'Who's going to sleep in the bed with me if Daddy isn't here?' Adam demanded.

'You can ask Lolly to stay with you till he comes.'

It was amazing, Becky reflected, how she was still having to rely on Lolly, the girl she had fired from the job, to look after her child – how Rupert had fought to have care of Adam and yet went out and left him with the ex-nanny – how he had betrayed Becky with Lolly but was perhaps even now betraying Lolly with someone else. The players might have changed places, but the farce was still going on. She could almost feel sympathy for the girl.

'Will I come home tomorrow, then?' Adam asked tremulously.

'Yes – and I've got a lovely surprise for you. Someone's moving into our downstairs flat, a very nice man. I think we're going to have lots of fun with him.'

'Who – Alex?'

'No, not Alex. His name is Humphrey Humes, and he's a real "Sir".'

'That's a funny name,' Adam giggled. 'OK, read me the story.'

Becky laid down the receiver and went to choose a book. She would have to speak to Rupert, she decided as she flipped through the pile by Adam's bed. There was no point in sending Adam to him for the night, with all the upheaval that entailed, if he couldn't even be bothered to stick around till bedtime.

* * *

'I have come to lighten your darkness,' Sir Humphrey intoned.

'How?' Adam asked with genuine curiosity.

They were in the kitchen, to which Humphrey had quite naturally gravitated, as did everyone else in the house. He liked his basement flat perfectly well, he said to Becky, nothing wrong with it now his photographs were up, but he wanted to be in the centre of things and that centre was the kitchen.

'For example,' he said, 'look at that good woman over there.'

Adam looked uncertainly at Mrs Christos, a person he didn't normally find very interesting, and saw that she was polishing the silver with a vigour that made the flab of her upper arms wobble like a jelly.

'See that crucifix round her neck, the mark of all her Catholic superstitions,' Humphrey said in tones of disgust. 'It will keep her chained to her brooms and mops, forever a member of the down-trodden classes.'

Mrs Christos shook a silver teapot at him, causing the flab to ripple even more alarmingly. Sir Humphrey was right, Adam thought, if he hadn't been looking he wouldn't have seen that amazing sight. Mrs Christos, he decided, would probably be very good at weights, if she ever decided to do some training.

'Madam,' he said, 'may I ask why you are dressed in that funereal black?'

'Husband die,' Mrs Christos said shortly.

'Oh dear, I'm so terribly sorry. When?'

'Fifteen year ago.'

'*Fifteen*! Heavens, woman, no one should mourn that long. You'll never get yourself another husband if you carry on dressing like that. You probably have a fine figure beneath that shapeless garment.'

Mrs Christos blushed furiously and turned her back on him.

'As for you, young man, if you stare too long at that infernal machine, it will addle your perfectly good young brain.' Humphrey waved disapprovingly at the television in the corner.

'I like it,' Adam said, 'except when it gives me nightmares.'

'There you are, you see – who wants nightmares?'

'But it's nice, sometimes, being frightened – only not in the dark.'

'Then you should read a good scary book, but not at bedtime . . . What are you watching now?'

Adam glanced over at the screen. '*The Lion King*. Jeremy bought it for me.'

'Jeremy, eh?' Sir Humphrey shook his head. 'Another product of the television era. I'll bet he's never even seen a Shakespeare play, and do you know, *The Lion King* pinched its storyline from a very famous one called *Hamlet*.'

'What's it about?'

'The very same thing, only with people. The bad uncle kills the king and takes his place. Then the son has to avenge his father's death and get rid of the uncle. No happy ending, though, because it's a tragedy.'

'Mummy says the state of my toenails is a tragedy.'

'Yes, but this one's more interesting. It's got a real ghost.'

Mrs Christos banged down the good set of fish knives, muttering about stupid old men filling children's heads with horror stories.

'Will you read it to me?' Adam begged.

'I'll do better than that,' Sir Humphrey promised. 'We'll act it out, like a real play, and we'll get Jeremy to direct it for us. Do him a world of good . . .'

'OK,' Adam said, 'as long as I can be the ghost.'

Becky looked at the new lined notebook with sharpened pencils lying beside it, and thought that she was finally ready to jot down some of the ideas for her screenplay that had been swimming round vaguely inside her head. The prospect filled her with simultaneous terror and excitement.

She had accepted, in the end, some of the new solutions which Alex had said she must embrace. She had allowed her parents to give her a temporary loan, and Alex to pay this term's school fees for Adam, and now she must settle down and write her screenplay, attempt this thing she had never done before, and make it good enough for Alex to sell so that she could pay everyone back the money she owed them.

Jeremy too had offered financial support – pressing his naked body to hers in the new bed which contained no ghosts, and in which she could make love to him with more abandon – promising in the heat of the moment to take care of her and Adam. But he was too young for such heavy responsibilities, she told herself, she didn't want such sacrifices from him or the burden of further indebtedness. He had his own battles to fight, unlike her parents and Alex whose success was long established. It was enough that she was taking so much from them.

She looked down nervously at the blank page. For reasons she wasn't quite sure of, she hadn't been able to bring herself to tell Jeremy about her new career ambitions. He was suffering from writer's block, carrying about with him an aura of frustration and depression almost visible in the cloud of cigarette smoke over his head. 'If Picasso can have a blue period,' he said with gallows humour, 'then so can I.' Becky didn't want to add to his burdens by making him feel that she was somehow competing with him. Not that she saw it that way, but she had a dark suspicion Jeremy might.

She picked up one of the pencils and jotted down a heading. It was a start, the first step towards a new beginning, and she knew that she must make a success of it, she who had been used to flying from a film set in England to a screening in Cannes to a meeting in Los Angeles, and was now confined within these four walls with only the hum of her computer for company.

But the old life had almost cost her her child. She must be content within the limitations of the new one, knowing that at least, when school ended, she could fetch Adam and bring him home with her and share in the little rituals of his life that she had missed out on for so many years.

The telephone rang, and it was she, not a secretary, who answered it, as it always would be from now on.

'Becky, darling, it's me,' came Alice's voice.

'Mummy, how are you?'

'There's no time for that. Your father has had a heart attack, he's been taken to hospital in Florence. You must come right away.'

'The terms of the court order are very clear,' Shirley said. 'If you don't get written permission from Rupert, you can't take Adam with you.'

Fighting back the tears, Becky whispered into the receiver, 'But I've just phoned his flat. Lolly says he isn't there.'

'Doesn't she know where to reach him?'

'I've told her to try.' But although Lolly had been reluctant to admit it, Becky was quite sure she had no idea of Rupert's whereabouts.

'If I don't take Adam with me,' she said to Shirley, 'he may never see his grandfather again.'

'My dear, I don't mean to be blunt, but it sounds to me as though if you wait to bring an application – even an urgent one – before the court, then *you* may never see your father again.'

'Oh God,' Becky wailed, 'what am I going to do?'

She drove to the flat off Onslow Square, with Adam and the hastily packed suitcases in the car, and no idea what would happen when she got there.

'I have to go away for just a little while,' she said to Adam, preparing him for the worst scenario, 'but you'll have a lovely time with Daddy and Lolly.'

'You said you wouldn't be going away any more,' Adam whimpered. 'You *promised.*'

'This is something different. It isn't work – it's grandpa. He isn't very well.'

Adam sat forward, straining angrily against his seatbelt. 'Then I want to come with you. I want to see my grandpa.'

Becky gripped the steering wheel and her knuckles were white as her face. 'He's in hospital, darling. They don't allow children into the hospital.'

Little rivers of tears had begun to flow from the corners of his eyes. Becky put up a hand and dashed the moisture from her own. The fear was like a great serpent coiled in the pit of her stomach, the fear that it was too late for both of them.

'You're a very good, brave boy, and I promise I will get grandpa to phone you just as soon as he's feeling better.'

She pulled up in Rupert's street and parked on a double yellow line. As she ran up to the front door, holding Adam's hand, Lolly opened it.

She tried to look Becky in the eye, but her own shifted uncomfortably to the ground. 'I'm sorry,' she said. 'I couldn't find Rupert.'

Becky's heart sank like a stone in a pond. She had not realised, till that moment, how much she had been hoping. 'I'll get Adam's suitcase,' she said dully.

They clung to each other on the doorstep. Adam's lower lip trembled. Every fibre of Becky's being protested at abandoning him like this, leaving him behind for no good reason when he so clearly wanted to come with her.

As she drove away she saw Adam in the rearview mirror, one hand in Lolly's, and the other waving frantically at Becky, as though signalling for help.

The taxi wove madly through the Florence traffic, but still the trip to the hospital seemed interminable to Becky's shattered nerves, after the eerie plane trip when she had sat suspended above the earth, drinking brandy with hands that trembled uncontrollably, not knowing whether her father was alive or dead.

The hospital staff were kind and forbearing of her broken Italian, and one of the neatly uniformed nurses took her personally up to the Intensive Care ward where Hugh Haydon was hooked to a frightening array of blinking machinery, unconscious but mercifully still breathing.

Alice sat alone by his bed, a forlorn and almost unrecognisable figure, bereft of the confident energy that normally radiated from her. Becky put her hands on her mother's shoulders and Alice clung to them as though to save herself from drowning.

'He may pull through,' she said, 'but they don't know yet. Thank God you're here.'

Becky went and stood at the head of her father's bed and bent to kiss his forehead. She had been afraid it would be cold to the touch, had been preparing herself for the worst, but what she felt beneath her lips was warm living flesh. For now there had been a reprieve, but for how long?

This is all my fault, she thought, my fault. I laid my troubles on him because his shoulders have always been so broad, his love so encompassing. But I forgot about the passage of time, forgot that he had reached an age when the roles should have been reversed and I should have been the one looking after him.

Give me a second chance, she prayed silently to the blinking lights of the machines rigged above him like some artificially intelligent deity. Let me make it up to him. Don't let him die because of me.

'It's not your fault,' Alice said behind her, 'and don't go letting yourself think it is. The doctors said this had been coming for a long time . . . a blood clot that moved round the body and then into the heart . . .'

'But I've been such a worry to him—'

'He's lived with worry all his life. It came with the job. And smoked too many duty-free cigarettes – a so-called perk that came with the job too. You can't go taking the blame for the habits of a lifetime.'

Becky sat beside her mother and let her eyes rest on her father's still face, the tubes snaking from his finely chiselled features as though he were some surrealistic piece of sculpture. 'What do we do now?'

'We wait,' Alice said, 'and we hope.'

Lolly drifted slowly up to consciousness. She stretched out her legs, and realised she still had all her clothes on, her jeans and now probably crumpled shirt. She must have fallen asleep with Adam after she'd read him his Pooh Bear story in Rupert's bed. He hadn't wanted her to leave him alone, he'd been tearful and clingy, crying for his mother, wanting to know when she was coming back. Lolly couldn't tell him that. No one could.

She felt so sorry for Adam, caught up in the middle of all these grown-up dramas and not really understanding any of it. It was so hard for a kid his age to handle, and she hated thinking part of it was her fault. Falling for Rupert was something she couldn't have stopped, no more than you can stop the path of an avalanche. But she'd never meant it to hurt Adam.

At least he was soundly asleep now, and she could leave him without guilt. Whenever Adam came to stay he shared his father's bed, and Lolly moved to the sofa bed in the sitting room. It wasn't easy, even for a night, to go to sleep without Rupert's arms around her. She felt almost sick with longing for him. But she knew it wouldn't be right for Adam to see them sharing a bed, not so soon after his parents' split-up. She hoped he'd be able to handle it some day, but not yet.

Rubbing the sleep out of her eyes, she thought she heard the low murmur of voices from the sitting room. Was that what had woken her? She couldn't see her watch in the dark but it must be after midnight. If Rupert was home then she'd make him have a talk with her, she'd tell him straight how much pain he was causing her by going off drinking without her and never even telling her when he was coming back. She knew he hated feeling tied down, but she had to make him see that she just couldn't bear the uncertainty any more. Not to mention that Becky hadn't been able to contact him when she urgently needed to. Lolly had been so embarrassed, having to admit to Becky that she didn't have a clue where Rupert was. She knew what Becky was thinking.

And now Adam was asleep in Rupert's bed and he didn't even know it. She'd start with that, and about Becky's father being so ill. Maybe then Rupert would realise that his son also needed to have him around more, at a time like this.

Summoning all her courage, Lolly padded across the hall on bare feet. She blinked in the sudden light, and saw two figures on the sofa that she would soon make up as a bed, and opened her mouth to ask Todd if she could please speak to Rupert alone. But then she saw that it wasn't Todd but a stranger, a girl with long blond hair the colour of corn, and Rupert had his hand inside her blouse and his lips nuzzled against the side of her neck.

'Rupert!' The cry was torn from Lolly before she could stop it. 'Rupert, no . . .'

He looked up and she could see he was struggling to focus through the fog of alcohol. The girl looked too, with mild curiosity.

'Oh, Lolly,' he said vaguely. 'Hi there . . .'

'Who's Lolly?' the girl asked.

'She's . . . just my son's nanny.'

Tears were flowing, thick and fast, down Lolly's cheeks. She knew how dumb she must look, how childish, but there wasn't a thing she could do. They were tears of pure grief and they came from the heart. She had loved Rupert, with all the painful intensity of first love, and now she saw that all along he hadn't really cared. She just wanted to *die*.

It had been two in the morning, the night staff said, and Becky and her mother had finally gone to sleep in their hotel room, when Hugh Haydon regained consciousness. He had slept then, again, for most of the night, and when they arrived to see him he was sitting up, propped by pillows, a nurse feeding him little drops of porridge and milk with a spoon.

'You'll soon be having your Cooper's Marmalade again,' Alice said, taking over the porridge bowl from the nurse with all her old energy. Becky knew she would never allow Hugh to see her as she had been the day before, when it had seemed he might not pull through and Alice was lost.

Becky bent over her father and gave his cheek a kiss that contained all her relief and gratitude.

'Rebecca is here, do you see?' Alice said in a loud, clear voice. 'Michael's coming too, as soon as he can get on a plane.'

Michael had, in fact, been on a business trip to mainland China when Alice had first tried to reach him. It had taken some time for Mae to get through to him with the news.

Hugh gave a feeble nod and tried to focus on his daughter. Something seemed to sparkle in the depths of his eyes. When he gave up the effort, Alice waved Becky away with the spoon.

'The doctor says he's not out of the woods yet,' she had told Becky after the early morning phone call from the hospital announcing the good news, 'but now he's got a chance.' It was this hope that had allowed the serpent of dread to uncoil a little in Becky's stomach and lightened her step down the hospital corridor to the Intensive Care ward.

'Come on, Hugh, just a little more porridge,' Alice cajoled him now and he opened his mouth obediently, like a small child. Watching him, Becky told herself that she must always remember this moment – this vulnerability of her father's – and never allow herself to burden him with her worries again.

He gestured with a shaky hand for Alice to take the spoon away. She held a glass of water to his mouth and he managed a few sips. 'Thank you, dear,' he whispered through stiff lips that seemed to be learning to speak all over again.

'We mustn't tire him,' Alice had said on the way to the hospital. 'He needs plenty of rest.'

So Becky made no attempt to draw his attention to her, to assure him she was there for him and always would be from now on. Instead she sat quietly with Alice, at the side of his bed, and began that day's vigil.

Only when Hugh was soundly asleep, hopefully for the night, did Alice and Becky return to their hotel room for a rest. The doctor had told them in rapid Italian, which her mother translated afterwards, that they must get plenty of sleep themselves or they would not have the strength they needed to look after Hugh when he was discharged from hospital.

That hope was becoming more of a reality with every hour that passed. By afternoon a little of the colour had returned to Hugh's cheeks, and he had begun to want to speak to them, though no more than a few sentences at a time.

'Sorry I gave you a fright,' he had said to Alice, and 'I should think so too,' she had replied, 'don't even think of doing it again.'

Then he had become a little agitated, wanting to convey something to Becky that he seemed to consider urgent. 'Proud of you,' he repeated a few times. 'Proud of you . . . no disgrace in divorce when you did your best . . . proud of you for making a life on your own . . .'

'I know, Daddy, you don't have to tell me, I know you love me and I love you too,' Becky had said, and 'Hush now, dear,' Alice had tried to calm him.

'I should phone Adam,' Becky said now as they walked wearily into their neatly made up hotel bedroom.

'All right, darling, but let's just order something first from room service, shall we?'

They didn't get a chance to do either. The telephone rang and they both froze, staring at it, before Becky managed to reach out her arm in what seemed like slow motion and lift the receiver.

She listened for a moment, then mouthed to her mother, 'It's Lolly,' and watched the tension drain from Alice's shoulders.

Filled with her own relief Becky sank onto the bed, and then a new fear began to wind itself round her heart. 'What is it, Lolly? Is Adam OK?'

'He's fine for the moment,' Lolly said across the miles, 'but I don't know for how much longer.'

The fear tightened. 'What do you mean?'

There were unmistakable tears trembling in Lolly's voice when she answered. 'It's Rupert. He's drinking heavily and going out a lot and . . . .well, he shouldn't be left in charge of a young child, not in the state he's in at the moment . . .'

Becky forced herself to say it, though her pride would scarcely let her. 'Please, Lolly, I'm needed here. I know it's not your job any more, but can't you look after Adam till I get back?'

'Oh Becky,' Lolly cried, 'I'm sorry – so sorry for everything. You see, I've left Rupert, and now Adam's alone with him and I'm worried for them both. If you can't get on a plane and come back, I don't know what's going to happen.'

CHAPTER FOURTEEN

Becky, Anthea and Humphrey sat like conspirators round Anthea's kitchen table. 'I don't know how to thank you,' Becky said, 'for stepping into the breach.'

'*Henry V,*' Humphrey said. ' "Once more into the breach . . ." I played him at the Old Vic, you know.'

'Humphrey was marvellous,' Anthea said. 'He really rose to the occasion.'

Becky's head was beginning to spin. 'You saw Humphrey at the Old Vic?'

'No, no, I mean he was marvellous with Adam.'

'So were you, my dear,' Humphrey said gallantly.

Becky had phoned them both in a panic from Florence to fill them in on Lolly's news and Adam's predicament. Then she had made the far more difficult call to Rupert – her first full-length conversation with him since the escalation of hostilities – to offer her sympathies on Lolly's departure, and to invite him to move back into her house with Adam while she was away, where at least he would have Mrs Christos to help with the cleaning and cooking, and where Becky knew Anthea and Humphrey could keep a firm eye on Adam's welfare.

It had been a week before Becky could return to London, a week until her father was well enough to be discharged from hospital and the crisis could properly be said to be over, a week in which she had phoned Anthea daily for progress reports, and Adam for comforting talks. But still she said now, 'Tell me all about it.'

'That wretched little nanny wasn't exaggerating,' Anthea said. 'Rupert's drinking simply gallons – Scotch, wine, anything he can lay his hands on. Luckily he didn't try and take Adam anywhere in the car – I offered to do the school run. He seemed to spend most of his time in front of the box, letting Adam watch any old thing, even if it was madly unsuitable.'

'Don't you worry – I lured the boy away from time to time,' Humphrey said with pride. 'Don't approve of him rotting his brain with that nonsense at the best of times. We read some Oscar Wilde together, and we've made a start on our *Hamlet* – minus the director, of course, since young Jeremy could hardly come round with the ex-husband in residence.'

She had almost forgotten about Jeremy, Becky realised, with everything else on her mind.

'You are a sly old thing,' Anthea said, 'finding yourself a delicious little toyboy to console you in your loneliness.'

'I knew all along you'd get round to shagging him,' Humphrey declared, pleased with his prescience.

'We were talking,' Becky reminded them rather crossly, 'about Adam.'

'He's a real little trooper,' Humphrey said fondly. 'Jolly good, too, at memorising his lines. One might even be able to hear them, if I can persuade him the ghost of Hamlet's father doesn't have to wear a sheet.'

'But did Rupert look after him properly?'

'Is the moon made of blue cheese?' Anthea scoffed. 'I don't think the man would even have noticed if Adam had spent the whole week in the same pair of underpants. But I wasn't having any of that – I did bath times and Mrs Christos, bless her, sorted out his clothes.'

'Do you mean to tell me Rupert didn't even take Adam to his extra lessons?' Becky asked incredulously, remembering his extravagant claims in court.

'Not a single one – and it was too much for me, on top of everything else, so I simply had to cancel them.'

'Where did he take him, then?'

'Only to the park, to play with that wretched football that seems to be permanently attached to one of Adam's feet – honestly, I don't know how any of your china has survived! But they did spend an awful lot of time together at home. They were thick as thieves by the end of it. You're going to find it tricky to separate father and son now it's time for Rupert to pack his bags and leave again.'

Henri poked her head suddenly round the door and raised a

disapproving eyebrow at the sight of Anthea huddled in conversation with the others. 'Sorry to interrupt,' she said rather frostily, 'but don't you think it's time, Anthea, to take the finger food out of the fridge?'

Anthea leaped guiltily to her feet. 'Oh heavens, I forgot.'

'Can I leave it to you? I'm just setting out the wine glasses. They'll be here any moment,' and the head disappeared.

'Who'll be here?' Humphrey said rather disagreeably.

'A women's discussion group.' Anthea took little trays of cucumber and tuna and cheese sandwiches out of the fridge. 'Henri likes that sort of thing, the intellectual life – a bit above my head, I'm afraid.'

'What on earth do they discuss?' Humphrey demanded.

'I think today it's something about a glass ceiling. I rather hoped it would be gardening – greenhouses, perhaps – but apparently not, it's about women trying to break into the top jobs and run things.'

'Not much help to you,' Becky said, 'since you don't have a job at all. Do you want to make your escape with us?'

'Better not. Henri thinks it will be good for me to join in,' Anthea said rather wistfully, opening a box of cheese straws. 'She says I might discover what I've been missing out on all these years . . .'

'If you fancy coming down to my basement, I'll show you what you've been missing out on,' Humphrey said, winking lewdly.

'You naughty old thing!' Anthea laughed, blushing like a schoolgirl.

The doorbell rang. Becky and Humphrey rose in unison. 'If you come to your senses,' Humphrey said, 'you know where to find me.'

Adam lay in his top bunk, holding on with one hand to Becky and with the other to Rupert. 'I don't want Mummy to go,' he chanted, 'I don't want Daddy to go.'

'It's sleep time, darling,' Becky said, gently trying to disengage her hand. Rupert made no attempt to withdraw his. When Becky had come to put Adam's light out, she had been amazed to find him sitting on his father's lap while Rupert read him a Roald Dahl story.

'Please let Daddy stay with us tonight,' Adam begged. '*Please!*'

Put uncomfortably on the spot, Becky gave Rupert an enquiring look. He answered with a little shrug, as though prepared to be as accommodating as possible.

'OK, sweetheart. He'll stay for just one more night,' Becky said firmly.

Adam gave a radiant smile and loosened his grip on their hands. 'Coo-ool!' he said, ending on a yawn and allowing his eyelids at last to flutter closed.

Becky tiptoed from the room, Rupert following, and led the way downstairs to the kitchen. 'Would you like a drink?' she asked in her polite hostess voice.

'Thanks. I'll help myself.' He moved around, quite at home, finding Scotch bottle, glass, ice, and Becky had to suppress a little shiver of irritation.

She poured herself a glass of wine. 'Thank you for moving back here to look after Adam,' she said. 'I'm sure it made things easier for him.'

'I never wanted to leave, you know. I'm not the one who wanted this marriage to end.'

Becky faced him angrily. 'Don't start that, Rupert. You know damn well you and Lolly—'

'Lolly was a mistake – a mistake that's now in the past.'

Becky sighed. How, she wondered, had she allowed herself to get into this conversation? 'There's no point discussing it, Rupert.'

'Yes, there is.' He drained his glass and poured himself a refill. There was a slight puffiness beneath his eyes that she hadn't noticed before. 'Adam wants me around. I'm his father, for Chrissakes. You should be thinking of him . . .'

'Don't you dare use Adam to get at me,' Becky shouted. '*You're* the one who should have thought about him when you did what you did.'

'OK, OK.' Rupert spread his hands in a gesture of appeasement. 'I know I was wrong, but if you can't forgive me, if you don't want me back as your husband, you could at least let me stay here, in the spare room. For Adam's sake. I wouldn't get in your way, you could live your own life. After all, we're grown-ups – I'm sure we could behave in a civilised fashion.'

Becky stared at him for long moments. He held her gaze, and it occurred to her that he was deadly serious. 'I can't believe,' she said slowly, 'you think that could possibly work.'

'I don't see why not.'

'What happens, for example, when you come home from a bar with one of your girlfriends? Were you planning on bringing her here, to my spare room?'

'*Our* spare room, Becky. This is the marital home. I didn't have to move out of it, you know. I don't have to now.'

She pressed her hands around the wine glass to stop them from shaking. 'Are you threatening to stay here whether I like it or not?'

He was cool now, sure of himself, as he'd been that day on the witness stand. 'I'd rather you didn't look at it that way. You were the one who invited me back here, when it suited you. Why should you be able to throw me out again, just because it doesn't suit you any more? Adam wants me to stay, I want to stay . . .' He looked around, his eyes caressing the symmetrical rows of brightly patterned plates on the Dutch dresser. 'I'm just suggesting you should compromise and fit in with the rest of us, instead of only considering yourself.'

Becky looked down at her hands, cupping the wine glass as though it were a vital secret she dared not allow to escape. She couldn't think of a single thing to say.

Humphrey ambled eagerly into the kitchen, sniffing in the smell of warm croissants, and stopped in his tracks when he saw Rupert sitting at the table between Becky and Adam, sipping a glass of freshy squeezed orange juice. 'Awfully sorry,' he muttered. 'Didn't mean to intrude.'

'It's quite all right.' Becky pulled out the chair on her other side. 'Come and join us.'

Rupert raised an eyebrow. 'Everything all right downstairs? Kitchen in working order?'

'Perfectly fine, thank you,' Humphrey said stiffly.

'Humphrey always has breakfast with us,' Becky explained with a huge effort at self-control.

Humphrey accepted the chair and the croissant Becky offered in offended silence.

'Are you still taking me to the zoo?' Adam asked through a mouthful of chocolate-flavoured cereal. It was Saturday morning, and Becky couldn't even remember if this was supposed to be her weekend or Rupert's, now that the lines had become so blurred.

'We'll go this afternoon,' she promised, and glanced up to see Jeremy standing in the kitchen doorway, taking in the domestic scene with a look of wild bewilderment. Don't, she prayed, let Rupert ask him how he got in. Don't let Jeremy mention the key I gave him.

Rupert looked at the newcomer with mock amazement. 'Do you have breakfast here too?'

'Do you?' Jeremy hit back.

'Daddy lives here now,' Adam chimed in cheerfully.

Humphrey darted Becky an enquiring look. Jeremy went white around the mouth.

'Croissant for anyone?' Becky said feebly. 'Coffee . . . ?'

Mrs Christos appeared from the utility room, tying on her overall. Her eyes took in the assembled group and came to rest on Rupert. She scowled, drawing her black beetle-like brows together. 'Too many,' she muttered darkly. 'How I clean for so many?'

'I'm going to the study to do some work,' Jeremy announced almost threateningly.

'Really? I'm confused,' Rupert said. 'I thought you and Becky didn't work together any more.'

'Are you coming?' Jeremy demanded of Becky, pointedly ignoring Rupert.

Becky gave up on her half eaten croissant. 'Adam, I have to work for a little while. Can you play with your toys or your computer?'

'I've got nothing on this morning,' Rupert said. 'I'll look after him.' He picked Adam up and put him possessively on his knee.

'Hang on,' Humphrey objected. 'We were going to do *The Charge of the Light Brigade* today. Don't you remember, Adam? Alfred Lord Tennyson . . . "Into the valley of Death / Rode the six hundred" . . .'

'Can't Daddy be one of the six hundred?' Adam pleaded.

Becky left the two men battling it out and followed Jeremy's stiff back to the study.

'I didn't *ask* him to move back in,' Becky reasoned. 'He just did it.'

'So where's he sleeping?' Jeremy demanded.

'In the spare room, of course.'

Jeremy kicked at the carpet. 'It's still pretty damn awkward. How am I supposed to make love to you right under his nose?'

'You can't,' Becky said flatly.

'That's great! Just great. Suddenly your ex-husband's pulling all the strings, living in the house we've been sharing, telling us what we can and can't do.'

'Not "ex" yet, unfortunately,' Becky pointed out. 'And I'm no happier about it than you are.'

'Then tell him to go.' Jeremy took her by the arms and gave her a little shake. 'He's got no right to do this.'

'I know, but what am I supposed to do? Get a court order and have him evicted? In front of Adam? I can't do that, and he knows it.'

'The bastard.' Jeremy let her go and clenched his fists. 'Maybe I should have a little word with him . . .'

'Don't talk like that. It won't solve anything.' Becky slumped into a chair. 'I may just have to wait it out, till he comes to his senses.'

Jeremy came to kneel in front of her. 'And in the meantime, what am *I* supposed to do?'

'I don't know,' she said wearily.

'But I want you. I've been dreaming about it, all the time you were away.'

He took her face in his hands and kissed her almost roughly, his tongue probing into her mouth as though he were trying to consume her. She put her hands on his chest and pushed him away. 'Not now,' she said.

'Then when?'

'I don't know. I have so much else to worry about – my father, Adam, this screenplay I'm supposed to be writing . . .'

'What screenplay?'

It was too late to bite back the words. She would have had to tell him sooner or later anyway, she reasoned. 'Alex is encouraging me to write my own screenplay, as a way of being able to work from home – change careers without changing fields. He really thinks I can do it, and he says he'll represent me.'

Jeremy sat back on his heels and stared at her. She waited, quietly hoping that he would be pleased for her, give her some word of encouragement. But the look he gave her was one of angry betrayal.

'I get it. So you say your film days are over, you refuse to work on my film, but you're going to figure out a way to do one on your own. Or rather, with faithful ol' Alex.'

'Writing, Jeremy, not producing—'

'Whatever. It still means we're not working together any more, like that asshole *ex*-husband of yours pointed out, and we sure as hell can't make love with him breathing down our necks. So where exactly do I fit into your life?'

'Maybe,' Becky said, stung to anger at last, 'maybe right now you don't.'

Becky looked around the River Room at the relaxed chatter of the other diners, at the waiters threading between tables, going about their business, and thought how calm and sane it all looked, how simple other people's lives appeared to be.

'It sounds like a French farce,' Alex said sympathetically.

'I suppose it would be funny, if it wasn't making Adam so confused. Even I feel a bit like Alice Through the Looking Glass – as though everything's been turned upside down or the wrong way round.'

Alex dipped an asparagus spear in hollandaise sauce. 'How's the writing going?'

'How do you think, in the midst of all that?'

'I may sympathise as a friend,' Alex teased, 'but as your agent I'm afraid I can't accept any excuses. May I remind you of your self-imposed deadline of six weeks?'

'I'll show you, Alex Goddard. I'll deliver that script in six weeks, and then I'll make you eat it!'

'I can't think why you're getting snippy with me,' he said with an easy grin. 'I'm not the one who's moved into your spare room. Now what's the storyline of this masterpiece in the making?'

'Well,' Becky said shyly, 'it's a sort of . . . courtroom drama. I've set it in the States, because it's so much easier to cast. It's about this attorney, working a big case for the Prosecutor's Office, who gets taken to court herself by her ex-husband because he says she's too busy and successful to look after their children properly – and then she has to decide what her priorities are . . .'

'Sounds great,' Alex said with a twinkle in his eye. 'All pure fiction, of course.'

'You were the one who told me to write what I know.'

'And how are you going to get Rupert off your back so you can get the job done? What does Shirley say?'

'That I'm between the devil and the deep blue sea.'

'And Bernard Fisher, I suppose, is the devil's advocate.'

Becky giggled. 'You're worth the ten per cent you're going to take off me just because you remind me to laugh.'

'Good.' Alex smiled too. 'So why haven't you thrown Rupert out yet?'

Becky stabbed a forkful of roquette with parmesan. 'Apart from not wanting him frogmarched out by a policeman with Adam watching from the upstairs window, I'm nervous about what'll happen when he moves back to Todd's place. He's drinking quite a lot, if the empty bottles in the kitchen every morning are anything to go by, and he's horribly irresponsible at looking after Adam by himself. I never thought I'd say this when Lolly moved in with Rupert, but it's going to be a whole lot worse sending Adam to him now that she's not there any more.'

'Be careful what you wish for,' Alex murmured. 'It might come true . . . By the way, how's your father?'

'Mummy says he's almost back to normal, except that he'll have to keep taking these blood-thinning pills, and watch his diet . . . I can't help wondering what I'll do if he has another attack. I can't go through that fiasco again, leaving Adam behind and worrying about him all the time I'm away. I wish Rupert would lift this wretched Prohibited Steps Order.'

'Can't you have a discreet go at him while he's under the same roof?'

Becky stared gloomily at the remains of her salad. 'If I ask Rupert for anything, he'll want something in return. And the sort of concessions he has in mind are not ones I can afford to make.'

'Perhaps, then,' Alex said vaguely, 'he'll come round to doing the right thing of his own accord.'

Belinda discreetly eyed the very attractive man sitting in reception. She'd given him a bit of a come-on when she offered him tea or coffee – hadn't been able to help herself – but disappointingly he hadn't responded. Now the buzzer sounded on her desk, and it was too late. 'Mr Goddard will see you now,' she said with regret.

He gave her a smile that was a brilliant flash of even white teeth, and she sat mesmerised as he disappeared with languid grace through the door.

Alex watched Rupert walk towards him, looking for signs of the alcohol abuse Becky had described. So far, apart from a little puffiness around the eyes, he seemed to be weathering its effects remarkably well. 'Thank you for coming to see me at such short notice,' he said.

'No problem.' Rupert was eyeing him warily, reminding Alex that the last time they had faced each other was across a court room. But Alex hadn't been subjected to hostile cross-examination by Rupert's barrister. He wondered now if Rupert had been leaving a door open.

'Something has come up,' Alex said casually, 'which I think may suit you very well.'

Rupert waited, venturing nothing.

'It's a good role in a new daily TV soap – a sort of rival to *Eastenders* or the *Street*, but a bit younger and more upmarket. There's a part in it that I think would be perfect for you.'

Alex had thought very carefully before selecting this particular morsel for Rupert's temptation. He had phoned round casting directors looking for a role that placed more priority on looks and less on the talent he was not yet sure Rupert possessed. He had also wanted something steady, long-term and with demanding hours.

'I hadn't realised,' Rupert said quietly, 'that you still regarded yourself as my agent.'

Alex held a pencil between the tips of fingers that were perfectly steady. 'Why not? My clients' personal lives are not my concern – unless their problems affect their work. If I put you up for this part, can you assure me there are no messy outstanding issues between you and Becky which could distract you from giving it your full commitment?'

He was aware that Rupert was watching him closely. 'Does Becky know about this?'

'It would not be ethical,' Alex said sternly, 'for me to discuss your career options with anyone but you.'

Rupert sat back in his chair, and a faint smile flickered at the corners of his lips. 'Tell me more,' he said.

'The money's very good, but the hours are punishing. You'll have to get yourself in shape. They're looking for someone young and sensational looking – they'll probably screen test – and I don't have to tell you, the camera has a tendency to magnify every flaw. If you want this part, you'll have to give up on the late nights. You don't smoke, do you?'

'No,' Rupert said with a hint of contempt.

'I wouldn't advise any heavy drinking either. Shows up round the eyes . . .'

Rupert stood up, and for a moment Alex feared he might walk out, but he only went over to Wellington's basket and stroked the dog's copper-red head.

'So you like animals, eh?'

'Sure – they're great companions.'

Rupert straightened up and smiled at him beguilingly. Standing so close to Alex's chair, he seemed to tower over him. 'You like Becky too, don't you?' he said.

Alex waited a beat. Rupert didn't move. They watched each other, like gladiators circling in a ring.

'I like Becky very much,' Alex said finally. 'She's a good friend.'

'That's right.' Rupert moved slowly round the desk and sat again in his chair. 'We're both your very good friends. Which is why you're doing this for . . . me.'

'I'm doing it,' Alex said coolly, 'because I'm your agent. Now are you interested or not?'

Rupert eyed him quizzically. 'Will I be able to afford a rather large house?'

'That's up to you. But if you make a go of it, you'll have that *and* all the trimmings.'

One eye on her computer screen, playing with the rearrangement of words in her last sentence until she could be sure she was quite satisfied with it, Becky dialled Shirley Fossey's number.

'You're not going to believe this,' she said when she finally got through.

'Try me,' Shirley challenged.

'Without a single pre-condition or argument or even any undue pressure from me, Rupert just upped and moved out again, back to Todd's place.'

'You're right,' Shirley said. 'I don't believe it.'

'I keep waiting for the catch, but so far there hasn't been one. He's pleasant and polite and . . . I don't know, sort of distracted, as though he has other things on his mind.'

'Another woman, perhaps?'

Becky tapped out a small correction. She felt a little inner glow of achievement at the 'Pg 50' sign in the bottom margin.

'I don't think there's a woman – not that I know of . . .'

'Well, well,' Shirley said. 'Can the leopard have changed its spots? . . . How's Adam taken it?'

'Of course he was upset, but I've talked him through it and he seems to have settled down. So all is quiet on the western front for the first time since I called on your services. I can scarcely believe it – I'm even getting some work done.'

'Good for you,' Shirley said. 'And long may it remain so. But if and when the catch does come, you know where to find me.'

In a sleeveless top and shorts, Becky strolled the pavements around World's End, Bogey on his leash and Jeremy at her side. The gardens and squares seemed to be bursting with wallflowers – jasmine, clematis, wysteria – in shades of yellow and purple and blue. Summer holidays were coming, and she would have to find something to do with Adam while she worked on the screenplay that was beginning to absorb her attention.

'So Rupert moved out,' Jeremy said, hands bunched into the pockets of his jeans.

'Yes.'

They strolled on in silence. The air was heavy with the scent of jasmine and the humming of bees, and Becky felt the contentment of it settle over her like a soft blanket.

'Are you managing to get on with the writing, then?' Jeremy said in a small tight voice.

'That too.'

Bogey stopped to sniff a parking meter. A French poodle, whose dandelion tail bobbed along ahead of them, had been there first to leave her calling card.

'So now that he's gone, can I start coming round again?'

She stood silently for a moment in the drowsy afternoon sunshine.

'I can't get on with anything,' Jeremy burst out, 'until you tell me what's happening with us.'

She leaned against the parking meter and looked at him. His hair stood up wildly, like a field of antennae, and she felt a great rush of tenderness towards him.

'I will never forget,' she said with feeling, 'that you were there for me when I needed someone most.'

'But now you don't need me any more?'

She took his hands. 'It's not just that. What we had together was wonderful, but it couldn't last. We're at different stages of our lives, you and I. There are things I've done already that you still have to do. There are other things I want to do now that you're not ready for. If we carried on, we'd be holding each other back.'

He pulled his hands away and clenched them angrily. 'What you really mean is you don't love me enough.'

'Oh, Jeremy.' She sighed. 'Love is necessary and wonderful but it isn't a cure for all the problems in a relationship. That's one of the things you still have to learn.'

'Don't patronise me!' he shouted angrily.

Bogey suddenly jerked on his leash, setting off in hot pursuit of the poodle, dragging Becky along behind him. Jeremy made no attempt to follow.

'I'm sorry,' she called back over her shoulder. 'Will you wait for me?'

But he only shook his head.

Becky laid the supper ingredients out on the counter: southern fried chicken breasts – a favourite of Adam's despite their spiciness – large potatoes for baking, which they loved to eat swimming with butter, corn on the cob, French green beans. She had meant to make enough for two, but now perhaps it would be three.

She was still trying to work out why Rupert had invited himself round. This was supposed to be his weekend with Adam, but he had pleaded other commitments and asked instead to visit Adam for a few hours at her house. There was also, he had said ominously, something rather important he wanted to discuss with Becky.

Pouring herself a glass of white burgundy, Becky wondered if she would now find out what the catch was. Had the sudden peace between them been simply the eye of the hurricane, the calm before the storm began again?

The doorbell rang. Steadying her nerves with a gulp of wine, Becky prepared to batten down the hatches.

Rupert stood on the doorstep in exercise shorts and trainers, his hair glistening with water from the shower. He seemed to radiate rude good health. Pecking her on the cheek, he jogged past her into the hall and through to the kitchen.

'You look well,' Becky said, following him in. 'Glass of wine?'

'No thanks. But I'd love a mineral water.'

She poured it for him in silence, popping in a slice of lime, trying to outguess him in this new game he was playing. 'Don't tell me,' she said, handing him his glass. 'You've landed a commercial for some new health product.'

'Is that all you think I'm fit for?' he asked coolly.

Adam barrelled in, half swathed in his Hamlet sheet, and grabbed his father round the legs. 'Daddy, you're here, you must come and watch our play. We're doing *Macbeth* now, and I'm the ghost of Banquo.'

Becky had told Humphrey that Jeremy would no longer be able to direct their amateur theatricals. Humphrey, suffering from a summer cold, had fixed her with a rheumy eye, but mercifully said nothing beyond, 'Bottled out, has he? I suppose I'll have to take over, then.'

Adam tried to drag Rupert away by the hand. 'Later,' Rupert said, disengaging himself. 'I want to talk to Mummy first.'

'Have just one more little practice, darling,' Becky said, watching Adam's lower lip begin to tremble. 'Then we'll both come and watch – promise.'

Adam walked slowly out, dragging his sheet behind him, down to Humphrey's flat.

'What is it that you want to talk about?' Becky said when he had gone.

Rupert sat down opposite her with a secretive smile. 'Rather good news, as it happens.'

Good news for whom? Becky wondered, hating this game of cat and mouse.

'Fortune has finally smiled on me,' Rupert said at last. 'I've landed a big role in a daily soap on prime time TV.'

'Heavens.' Becky, having steeled herself for the worst, was having trouble responding with the right degree of enthusiasm. 'Well done – I'm really pleased for you.'

'You don't sound it.'

'It's just the surprise. How did you pull it off?'

'Not without help, I have to admit.' He watched her through narrowed eyes. 'Your mate Alex arranged it all for me.'

'Alex!'

Rupert seemed to be enjoying her reaction. 'You can't have forgotten he's my agent. You're the one who talked him into it.'

From the bottom of the stairs she heard Humphrey's ringing tones: ' "Thou canst not say I did it: never shake / Thy gory locks at me." '

She kept her silence. She wasn't going to tell Rupert that she'd expected Alex to drop him when he turned against her – that helping him now felt like an act of betrayal.

But she suspected, from Rupert's expression, that he knew exactly what she was thinking. 'Jolly good of him, don't you think? Alex really pushed hard to get this part for me. The casting agent said he practically bullied her into it.'

Becky stood up and began to attack the supper ingredients with unnecessary vigour. 'I'm glad it's worked out for you both . . . Excuse me while I put the food on – you are eating with us, aren't you?'

'I'll just have a salad, if there's any going . . . .So you see, that's why I couldn't take Adam this weekend. You can imagine how busy I am.'

Becky put the potatoes onto the top shelf of the oven, and buttered the pan for the chicken pieces. While she worked Rupert chattered away, seeming hardly to notice whether she was listening or not.

'. . . Once taping begins we'll be working all day every day, and then there'll be lines to learn in the evenings, and wardrobe fittings. I don't expect I'll have a moment to myself any more . . .'

'Daddy, Mummy, we're ready,' Adam yelled up the stairs.

'Hang on a minute,' Rupert called back. 'Where was I? . . . Oh yes, then there are all the ancillary offers that come with television stardom – charity fundraisers, guest appearances on other people's shows . . .'

'Sorry to interrupt,' Becky said, 'but I really should sort out with you when you want to see Adam, now school holidays are coming up.'

'You can't expect me to take time off for that,' Rupert said almost indignantly. 'Of course I want to see Adam, but I won't be able to manage more than afternoons with him on my Sundays off.'

'That's fine, as long as I know . . .'

'I'm not in your position, Becky – working from home and accountable only to yourself. I'll be at the beck and call of other people – the director, the television company. This is a big break for me – I have to give it my full commitment.'

'I understand,' Becky assured him, stripping leaves off the cobs of corn.

'Finally I have a chance to make something of my life – to have a home of my own, which no one can throw me out of.'

There was a moment's silence. Then Becky said quietly, 'Rupert, I meant it when I said I was happy for you. I honestly wish you all the success in the world. Now supper's nearly ready. Perhaps we'd better take our seats for the banquet scene from *Macbeth*.'

'Right.' Rupert stood up, stretching his newly toned leg muscles. 'So, Adam has aspirations of stage and screen stardom. Like father, like son, eh?'

It was on nights like this, when she wanted to go out on the spur of the moment and hadn't arranged a babysitter, that Becky was so glad of having Humphrey around. It made no difference to him, he said, which part of the house he sat in to read a bit of his favourite Shakespeare or Tolstoy or T. S. Eliot.

'Damn depressing chap though, Eliot, when he starts on old age,' Humphrey said. 'I've just got to the bit about the eternal footman holding your coat and snickering. Strong stuff, when you're trying to keep one step ahead of the scoundrel yourself.'

Becky left him with his cocoa and his *Love Song of J. Alfred Prufrock*, and Adam quietly asleep upstairs, and took a taxi to Knightsbridge.

In all the years she had known him, she had never before been to Alex's flat, never intruded beyond a certain point into his private world, no matter how close their friendship. But what she had to say to him now wouldn't wait, was beyond the boundaries of polite behaviour.

He was expecting her, after her quietly insistent phone call. He opened the door to her, and his smile of welcome was a little wary.

She had prepared very carefully what she had to say to him, going over and over it in her mind. She had also chosen her clothes with particular care – a rather severe black sheath dress with a single strand of pearls and her freshly washed hair neatly styled into its bob. She wanted everything about her to convey the message that she knew what she was saying, that she meant every word, so she wouldn't lose her nerve.

He led her into a sitting room so clean, almost untouched, that she wondered if he had recently had it redecorated. 'Would you like some champagne?' he offered.

'No thank you. Something non-alcoholic.' She wanted to be perfectly sober when she told him what she had come to say.

He went out. On slightly shaky legs she wandered round the room, looking at the objects he had collected – pieces of stone tablet, pages of illuminated manuscript toiled over by long ago monks, fragments of papyrus with their odd, angular hieroglyphics.

He returned, holding a glass in which little pieces of fruit floated in amber liquid. 'A sort of Pimms Cup without the Pimms,' he explained.

'Funny,' she said, looking about her, 'how you collect words and Rupert collects things – how you're looking for truth and he only wants beauty.'

'Is it Rupert you wanted to talk to me about?'

She took the drink from him, making sure their hands did not touch. 'You went to a lot of trouble, so he tells me, to push his career and land him the role of a lifetime.'

'And do you mind?'

'I was surprised, to say the least, by the timing.'

Alex moved over to the window and stood, tall and straight, with that stiff pride she knew so well, looking out at the long shadows of the late summer evening. He was not, she saw, going to explain himself to her, but she didn't need his explanations.

'Sir Humphrey has been reading T. S. Eliot to me,' she said. 'I was struck by a verse in *The Four Quartets* where it says that after all our searching we arrive back at the place where we started, only this time we know it for what it really is. She walked slowly over to the window. 'I feel like, after all these years, I'm suddenly seeing *you* for the first time.'

She stopped in front of him, and looked steadily into his eyes, and Alex couldn't read what was in the opaque green depths of her own.

'I was angry when Rupert told me, furious, in fact . . .' She brought her face very close to his, so that he could see quite clearly the hazel flecks in the green. Then suddenly she reached up and kissed him on the mouth.

The shock of it almost made him gasp – the sudden, unexpected, delicious surprise. He searched her face for answers.

'You didn't do it for Rupert,' she said softly. 'You did it for me – to make him leave me in peace.'

Alex said nothing. He knew there was no need.

'You've done so much for me, right from the start, and I haven't always been as grateful as I should have been. But I'm grateful now . . .'

His heart, which had begun to beat wildly with hope, slowed to a steady despair. Not this, he thought, anything but this. He wanted her more than he had ever wanted anything in his life, but he could not allow her to offer herself to him out of gratitude.

He looked down at the top of her well-loved head, at the golden hair he now knew she had washed to a silky shininess for him, at last for him, and had to force himself not to run his fingers through it.

'There's another rather wise thing Eliot said.'

'What's that?' she asked, smiling, colluding with him.

'You should never do the right thing for the wrong reasons.'

Her eyes clouded with the beginnings of doubt. 'What are you trying to say?'

He made himself go on, because he would not be able to live with himself if he did not. 'I don't expect you to return the favour, Becky. Whatever you do now, it mustn't be because you feel you owe it to me.'

He saw her hurt, the way she recoiled back into herself, and wondered why it had to be so hard for both of them.

'What you need,' he said, 'is time – time to be on your own, to put the past and all its ties behind you, to think what it is you really want for your future. Then, when you know, when you're absolutely sure . . .'

'You're always so damn wise,' she said bitterly, 'and me – I just let myself be led around by my feelings.'

'I didn't mean—'

'No, you're right. As usual. And it's late. And I really should be getting home to Adam.'

When she turned away, out of reach of his arms, and walked slowly towards the door, he almost changed his mind and went after her. But then he remembered what had been done to her already by men who put their own needs first, and he stood where he was and wordlessly let her go.

CHAPTER FIFTEEN

The rest of the room was in darkness. In the middle was a little island of blue-white light cast by the daylight bulb in the anglepoise lamp beneath which Becky worked at her desk, tapping at keys and staring in fixed concentration at the gently glowing screen of her computer.

It had been like this for weeks, this losing of herself in her screenplay until she felt almost marooned, cut off from the rest of the world, alone with the words and images she was creating. But it was a voluntary isolation, a necessary retreat into herself to heal the wounds caused by Alex's rejection.

She was a fool, she told herself, for laying herself open to it. When she had finally realised all he had done for her, when she had rushed so impulsively to see him, full of warmth and gratitude and yes, even love, she had been so sure of her reception, so convinced that his actions had been motivated by the love he felt for her. She should have thought it through more carefully, she told herself angrily. Knowing Alex as she did, she should have realised that he needed no more reason to do good than the kindness of his own heart, and the friendship he had always shown her.

And now she had damaged that friendship, created a terrible awkwardness between them by throwing herself at him and forcing him to extricate himself. Her cheeks burned with shame. She felt she would never be able to look him in the face again.

And yet, in his phone calls to her afterwards, he had been as kind as ever, asking after Adam and her screenplay, pretending, to help her save face, that nothing significant had happened to change things between them. And that, she felt, was almost as unbearable as what had gone before.

She shifted her weight, loosening the tension in her back and rotating her stiff neck. She had done good work today but tiredness was finally setting in, and she doubted she could accomplish more tonight. If she set her alarm for six o'clock tomorrow morning, she should get in another hour or more before Adam woke up, demanding her attention.

She was determined to meet her deadline. More than that, she would do it with a flair and talent that would make Alex sit up and take note. She would show him that she was to be admired, not pitied. She would force him to realise what he had missed.

Becky savoured the last of her filtered coffee and cheese croissant. She had been ravenously hungry, after getting up early to write and then nipping down to the bakery to treat the household to their declared favourites. Adam and Humphrey, she had discovered, shared a joint passion for *pains au chocolat*.

Adam checked his plate for any last traces of chocolate, then carried it to the sink without being asked, and headed up the stairs to wash his face and brush his teeth. Becky busied herself clearing the rest of the table in what had become their established morning routine. She would then take Adam, with the packed lunch she had prepared before breakfast, to the Play Centre for the day, freeing her up to work and giving him the chance to mix with other children. One of them, she had been less than pleased to note, was Freddie Foley, Adam's old adversary from Launceton Hall, and she hoped there wouldn't be a renewal of hostilities between them. But so far there had been no complaints from Adam, who seemed to spend all day indulging his passion for football in the large courtyard always crowded with other eager participants.

Today, however, the Centre was taking the children on a day trip to a beach on the south coast. The sky, Becky noted, peering through the kitchen window, was an obligingly clear blue. Outings like these were the only summer holiday Adam would get this year. In the past there had often not been the time, and now there wasn't the money.

'What are you up to today?' she asked Humphrey who was slowly sipping the tea he liked to drink with two heaped spoons of sugar. It was one of the few compensations of old age and general physical ruin, he said, that an actor no longer had to watch his weight.

'Off to see that director chappy – forget his name,' Humphrey said rather grumpily. 'He wants me for Prospero in *The Tempest*. I hope the fellow doesn't go in for any of these silly avant-garde ideas, like setting it in New York in the next century.'

'Will you be in for supper?'

Since Jeremy's departure, and the newly strained relations between her and Alex, Becky had taken to inviting Humphrey to eat all his meals with her and Adam, though he insisted on paying his share. It was less lonely that way for all of them.

The only difficulty was accommodating Humphrey's contempt, anglophile though he was, for any form of English cooking. His tastes ran to more exotic Continental or Eastern fare. He was in his element with an Indian takeaway.

'Don't bother to cook for you and me,' he said predictably. 'I'll nip down to the Balti Brasserie – my treat.'

'All right,' Becky conceded, knowing it would be futile to argue with him.

'I'll also be joining you afterwards for Rupert's television debut,' Humphrey promised, 'unedifying though it will no doubt be.'

Laurel Close, as Rupert's show was called, would be screened for the first time at seven-thirty that evening. It was, he had explained, about a group of neighbouring families in the commuter belt of Surrey. All the husbands had jobs in the city, all the wives stayed behind with the children and the dogs, leading to the inevitable marital strife, steamy affairs and troublesome offspring. It should, Becky resisted the temptation to say, be right up Rupert's alley.

Most of the scenes, being interiors, were shot in a London studio, but Rupert also had to go to Surrey for a couple of days each week to shoot the exteriors. In the midst of this hectic schedule, relations between him and Becky had remained infrequent and non-confrontational – for which, she reminded herself, though with less pleasure than before, she had Alex to thank.

Adam bounded down the stairs, face washed and hair brushed askew over one eye. 'Ready, Mummy,' he said impatiently. 'I can't wait to tell everyone at the Play Centre to watch TV tonight or they'll miss my daddy.'

Sir Humphrey inhaled the intoxicating smell of fresh spices and herbs, and felt he could almost bring himself to overlook the rather brash décor of the Balti Brasserie, all tubular chrome and glass and leather. He ran his eye down the familiar menu and felt spoiled for choice.

He was in a particularly good mood this evening. The young director had been suitably respectful, deferential even, at their meeting – quite the opposite of so many of the upstarts Humphrey had to deal with these days, who seemed to regard age not as an accumulation of skill and knowledge, but as an intellectual as well as physical handicap. Not this one, though. He had assured Humphrey that he planned no unusual takes on Shakespeare's text. He had, in fact, asked Humphrey's opinion about several key passages.

'Have you made your choice?' Mr Mehta, soft-spoken and patient, waited with pen and pad poised in readiness.

Humphrey's mouth was almost watering. 'I think tonight, Mr Mehta, if you please, we'll have one Balti Chicken with Daal and one Prawns with Saag. And we must have some Onion Bhajis on the side, and some Pilau Rice.' He stopped, wondering if that was sufficient. It should be, he calculated, with the complimentary poppadums and salad and yogurt mint chutney and hot chilli sauce. He licked his rather dry lips. He mustn't get carried away and order too much, or Becky would scold him again.

She was always threatening not to let him come here alone, with the damage he did to their weekly budget, and the way he liked to argue with poor kind Mr Mehta about why his countrymen had let a race of culinary savages like the English take them over and possibly destroy their fine cuisine forever.

'No time for a political discussion tonight,' Humphrey said, looking rather more sorry than Mr Mehta. 'Have to get back and watch some ghastly trash on the television.'

'You see – even you are succumbing to progress,' Mr Mehta said triumphantly.

'Poppycock! I'm doing it out of friendship.'

In the time he had been living in her house, Becky had indeed become a friend. She had a good heart, that girl, and Humphrey was beginning to develop feelings of alarming protectiveness towards her and the boy. It wasn't wise to get too attached, he of all people knew that. The young had their own lives to lead, and when they were ready to lead them, they simply moved on.

He hoped, when Becky's time came, it would be the right move. Humphrey didn't want to be worrying himself sick over some damn fool woman and her troublesome child when the time inevitably came for him to be alone again.

The audience was ranged on the two sofas in front of the television in the Chinese lacquered cabinet – Becky next to Adam, and Humphrey with Anthea. They had been forced to sit there for ten minutes already by an over-excited Adam, anxious not to miss even a second of his father's triumph.

It had been ten minutes well spent by Humphrey, who had occupied himself by peering rather unsubtly down Anthea's cleavage. ' "Beauty too rich for use, for earth too dear," ' he sighed.

'You shameless old flatterer – keep your eyes on the screen,' Anthea scolded, trying her best to sound cross.

And then the long-awaited title appeared – *Laurel Close* – against a background of houses in a Surrey cul-de-sac. The theme music rose to a crescendo. Adam quivered with anticipation, and Becky took his hand and gave it a reassuring squeeze.

But it was another five agonising minutes before Rupert made his entrance. He was late home from the office, an implausible excuse at the ready, but his screen wife had already thrown his dinner in the bin.

'Meany,' Adam cried.

'Why didn't I ever try that?' Becky thought.

But Rupert soon sweet-talked his wife out of her temper, a last minute purchase of chocolates on the station platform finally coaxing her into a forgiving kiss.

'That's better,' Adam said.

'More than he ever did for me,' Becky thought.

She felt strange, sitting in the half dark, watching her husband's familiar face, listening to his uncomfortably recognisable lines, all of it in this totally unfamiliar setting. What was perhaps even more surprising was how good he was, how much he stood out from the rest of the cast, even apart from the almost unfair advantage of his physical beauty. Becky felt, despite herself, a stirring of pride.

'Isn't he,' she said to Adam, 'the best-looking Daddy in the world?'

'Ssh – I want to hear everything he says.'

So they all sat in a silence broken only by the occasional contented clearing of his throat by Humphrey, who had rather over-indulged himself at dinner. When even that ceased, only Anthea was aware that he had quietly fallen asleep.

'Bravo,' she said when the end credits rolled, giving Humphrey a gentle nudge.

'What, what?' he cried in alarm.

'It was over so quickly!' Adam said, and then, more anxiously, 'Humphrey, what did you think of my daddy's performance?'

'Splendid,' Humphrey said. 'Splendid work.'

'He positively stole the show,' Anthea declared.

Adam beamed with pride. 'He had so many lines to learn – just as many as in Shakespeare.'

In the midst of a long afternoon's work, Becky emerged bleary-eyed from the study to find Alex, unannounced and uninvited, bending over the chessboard in the kitchen, with Humphrey as his adversary and Adam as his questionably helpful partner.

'Why is Humphrey so upset about losing his queen?' Adam was asking.

Becky ran a hand self-consciously through her hair, scraped back into an unflattering ponytail. Her face, devoid of make-up, felt naked and vulnerable.

'Mummy,' Adam said, looking up and catching sight of her before she could make her escape. 'We're winning – come and see.'

'Cheating, more like,' grumbled Humphrey. 'Robbing me of my life's savings.'

'You're not playing for money, are you?' Becky said, coming forward reluctantly.

'We most certainly are. Where's the fun, without a modest wager?'

Alex stood up and smiled at her almost nervously. 'I would have said hello, but I didn't want to disturb the flow of the creative juices.'

'They've ground to a temporary halt,' Becky said, not quite meeting his eye. She moved off to the kettle and flicked on the switch. 'Who'd like a cuppa?'

'Anything to restore my fortunes,' Humphrey said, looking down at his woefully depleted ranks. 'Would you mind telling me, Alex, how anyone from America – never mind Los Angeles – learned to play chess as well as you do?'

'It's not all redneck country,' Alex said with a grin. 'I received most of my education in New England.'

'Ah, yes, the Ivy League.' Humphrey watched mournfully as Alex took his second knight. 'Perhaps, after all, there is some culture there.'

Becky brought their tea to the table, but withdrew to drink her own perched against one of the kitchen counters. 'Anything you wanted to talk to me about?' she asked Alex in a tone she was aware was not altogether inviting.

'I did want to have a few words,' he said, putting Humphrey into check. 'And to touch base with my godson, of course.'

'Today you'll have to make do with your godson,' Becky said briskly. 'I'm in the middle of a tricky scene and I want to get back to it.'

As she swept past with her cup, Alex reached out a hand and she thought for a moment he was going to stop her, but he only touched her arm briefly before turning back to his game.

Becky sat in her little island of light and typed 'Fade to Black' at the end of the page. She leaned back and looked at those three magic words and relished what they meant for her. She had done it – she had actually finished the task which at the outset had seemed so Herculean, and with four days to go until the deadline, days in which she could check for errors and add the final touches. Then she would deliver the completed screenplay to Alex, as promised.

She shrank a little at the thought of seeing him again, and the need to submit herself to his possibly critical judgement. But whatever his opinion, she could still take pride in the fact that she had done what she set out to do, what at first she hadn't believed herself capable of accomplishing.

She sat there sipping her half-cold coffee, filled with a sense of quiet achievement.

In the large, white-painted room, rows of Nautilus equipment gleamed beneath the vaulted ceiling. The only sound was the metallic clanging of machinery mingled with grunts of exertion as the Riverside Club's seasoned veterans went about the almost sacred business of keeping themselves in shape.

Rupert strained against the newly added weights he was using to strengthen his pectorals. A slick sheen of sweat covered his upper torso and his hair clung wetly to his scalp. But he was enjoying the effort, just as he enjoyed most things about his life these days.

As he counted in time to his painful exertions, he was aware that he was coming under the scrutiny of an extraordinarily beautiful girl with an elfin face and huge brown eyes, methodically working out her thigh muscles on the machine opposite. She must, he decided, have recognised him from *Laurel Close*. That was happening to him more and more often these days.

He flashed her an acknowledging smile. Seeming to take courage from it, she left her machine and wandered over to his. He noted with appreciation the extraordinary length and slimness of her legs.

She waited until he had lowered the weights back into place and then she said, 'Aren't you Rebecca Carlyle's husband?'

They were not the words Rupert had expected to hear and they roused in him a flash of the old anger. 'Actually,' he drawled, 'I'm not accustomed to thinking of myself as anybody's husband.'

'Sorry.' She smiled ruefully. 'It's Rupert, isn't it?'

He nodded coolly. She held out her hand. 'Juliette Winters. I worked with Becky on *Abstract Love*, but I don't think you and I ever met.'

Of course, he remembered her now. She'd changed a little – cut off all her hair – but the face should have been enough to jog his memory. He looked at her perfect upturned nose and began to thaw a little.

'I got off on the wrong foot, didn't I?' Juliette said. 'If you're finished here, why don't you let me buy you a health shake to make it up to you.'

They sat side by side on a softly upholstered sofa in the refreshment area and sipped their shakes. They had both taken a shower, and the musky scent of Juliette's perfume filled the air. 'So what are you doing with yourself these days?' Rupert asked her.

'Another film with Letitia Harker, but that's probably a touchy subject – I gather she managed to get rid of Becky in some rather devious way.'

'I don't know much about it,' Rupert said. 'You do realise Becky and I aren't living together any more?'

'I'd heard something along those lines,' Juliette confessed. 'So what are *you* up to these days?'

'Oh, keeping body and soul together,' he said with lazy satisfaction, 'thanks to the small screen and Alex Goddard.'

'You're with Alex?' She leaned a little closer. 'You must be sure to give him my love.'

'And what do I get for giving him your love?' Rupert drawled.

'No offence, Rupert, but you're too good-looking for me. Not my type – I wouldn't be able to trust you as far as I could throw you. But I'm still going to give you my phone number – so you can pass it on to Alex. He was supposed to get in touch with me.'

Becky sat, tense and watchful, across the desk from Alex. She had greeted him formally – more the client than the friend – kissing vaguely at the air beside his cheek. She had also, as he was well aware, avoided being alone with him for several weeks.

Thank God, he thought, for her screenplay – this little bridge that would keep them talking and help him win back her trust. He breathed another silent prayer of relief that his belief in her talents had been justified. 'Your script is wonderful,' he told her now.

She eyed him warily. 'You don't have to be tactful. I'd prefer the truth.'

How, he wondered, was he going to reach her, through all the barriers she had erected? 'I would never patronise you like that,' he said patiently. 'I know you can take the truth and that's what I've given you. Now I hope you'll pay me the compliment of believing me when I tell you again that the screenplay is great.'

A little of the mistrust eased from her face. 'You really think so?'

'That doesn't mean there isn't a bit of tightening up to do, and I'll give you my suggestions. But there's nothing seriously wrong with it – nothing that can't be fixed.'

At once Becky unclipped her bag and took out a notebook and pen, like a competent secretary ready to take dictation. She was hiding from him behind layers of crispness and efficiency. The week before she had delivered the screenplay to him on the exact date it had been promised.

'Tell you what,' Alex said. 'Why don't you let me take you out to lunch first? We'll work better on a full stomach.'

She hesitated only for a moment. 'I have so much to do – I'd really rather get on with it, if you don't mind.'

She was giving him no quarter, and he knew he would have to come right out and say what he had to, to break the deadlock between them. 'Becky, about the night when you came round to my place . . .'

'I really don't want to talk about that,' she said briskly.

'We have to, because you're angry – and for all the wrong reasons. I don't want you to misunderstand what I did. It's not that I don't care for you—'

He saw the flash of pain in her eyes before she closed them. 'Please,' she said in a whisper, 'don't.'

He couldn't carry on in the face of her anguish. He sat there watching her in helpless silence.

She opened her eyes again, but kept them lowered. She took the bright blue plastic top off her ballpoint pen. 'Right,' she said, 'let's hear these suggestions of yours.'

She was shutting him out and there was nothing he could do about it – nothing except wait and hope that with patience and understanding he could prove to her that he really was waiting for her, waiting until she was ready.

'Daddy says he's really sorry,' Becky told Adam, 'but he won't be able to see you this weekend. He's got so important now, people ask him to do all sorts of things, like open supermarkets and help raise money for charity . . .'

Adam was feeding Jekyll and Hyde. He kept his eyes glued to the surface of the water where the fishes' gaping mouths snatched at the floating fragments.

'He asked me to give you his love,' Becky went on in the silence, 'and to say he'll make it up to you some other time.'

Rupert had neglected to say when that other time would be. It was a fact that Adam saw more of his father on the television than in person these days. He never complained, but even at his age he had his pride.

'Anthea's invited you over to play football with Joshua,' Becky said. He was home for the school holidays, and Hugo had returned for good, having passed his A-levels in Maths, Economics and Chemistry with starred A grades. Anthea was too stunned to say anything beyond, 'Hard to believe he's my flesh and blood, isn't it?'

'Is there anything else you'd really like to do this weekend?' Becky said to Adam with forced cheerfulness.

He threw in another sprinkle of fish flakes. 'I want Freddie Foley to come and stay the night.'

'Really? I thought you didn't get on with him very well.'

'Oh, that was ages ago,' Adam said airily, poking a finger at Jekyll's gobbling mouth. 'He's always going on at me to play with him now – ever since he saw my daddy on TV.'

Every time the phone rang, it jangled Alex's nerves so that he gave an involuntary start. The waiting, he acknowledged, was becoming something of a strain.

It was about a week since he had sent out the final version of Becky's screenplay (a week in which he had experienced some difficulty in concentrating on the affairs of his other clients). This was about the time when he should start hearing back from potential buyers who wanted to put in a bid. Alex told himself firmly that the offers would be forthcoming any day now. He didn't even want to think about what would happen if no one came forward at all.

He had given Belinda a list of all the people she should put straight through to him, no matter who was in his office. She had raised an eyebrow when she saw it was all the names who'd received Becky's screenplay, and then raised both of them when he barked at her quite unnecessarily for a small typing error in a letter to a minor distributor. Even Wellington seemed to be following him with puzzled eyes, picking up on his uncharacteristic tension.

But he didn't know what he would do if he couldn't follow through on his promises to Becky. He only knew he couldn't afford to break her trust for a second time.

He jumped again when the phone rang. A glance at his watch told him that the good citizens of L.A. would have finished their early morning jogs and herb teas and would be heading into their offices.

He heard the transatlantic echo as he picked up the phone, and then, 'How are you, son?'

'Hanging in there,' he said to his father with a trace of impatience. 'How about you?'

Frank laughed with deep enjoyment. 'A helluva lot better than just "hanging in". Irene and I are at this health spa in the desert. It's doing wonders for us – you should try it next time you're over. We've just finished our seaweed wrap and now we're going for our mud bath.'

Alex resisted remarking that in his opinion mud baths were for warthogs. Frank had thought that way too, once. 'Sounds like all play and no work,' he said rather more sharply than he had intended.

'Don't worry so much. David's handling things back at the office.'

Alex thought better of reminding his father that that was precisely what he was worried about. Frank, he supposed, had earned the right, in his later years, to pass on a few of his burdens. 'You have yourselves a good time,' Alex said, meaning it.

'We will,' Frank assured him. 'We will.'

The next call was from a car manufacturer wanting to know if Rupert Carlyle would front their commercial campaign, and offering a very tidy sum for the privilege. Alex shook his head in bemusement. It wasn't that he was unhappy with the way Rupert's career was taking off – the agency, after all, got its ten percent share of the takings – but it needled him a bit that one of his least talented clients was becoming one of the most popular, though he had to hand it to Rupert, he wasn't nearly as bad a television actor as Alex had feared. Belinda was also less than impressed with the piles of fan mail she had to wade through.

He should, Alex told himself, regard this unexpected rise in Rupert's star as part of his own carefully laid plans to channel Rupert's energies into avenues more positive than persecuting Becky. It was simply a minor administrative inconvenience, as well as a major financial benefit, if those plans had succeeded far beyond his own wildest expectations.

But Alex couldn't help wondering how Becky would feel if his efforts had brought such good fortune to Rupert, but failed to gain anything for her.

CHAPTER SIXTEEN

Adam, dressed from head to toe in full Chelsea football kit, ran round and round the kitchen in breathless, excited circles. His father was taking him to see his home team play Milan in a friendly match about which all the boys in the Play Centre spoke in tones of longing, since it had been sold out for weeks.

'How did you get the tickets?' he demanded.

'It's amazing what you can do when you're a celebrity,' his father replied with a wink.

'What's that?'

'Are there any of the players you particularly want to meet?'

'*All* of them! Will they give me their autographs?'

'I'm sure that can be arranged,' Rupert grinned.

'Wow! I can't wait to tell Freddie Foley.'

Becky, ironing in the corner, watched the exchange with mixed feelings. She was as delighted as Adam that his father was giving him this chance to see his heroes in action. But she wasn't entirely sure how good it was for him to experience these swings from one extreme to the other in the way Rupert treated him – from almost total neglect to outrageous spoiling.

It was also, she admitted, a bit of a thorn in her side that Rupert could now afford to give Adam any treat he set his heart on, while Becky was struggling to provide even a few pounds of weekly pocket money. She had noticed the beginnings of a tendency on Adam's part to manipulate his father, to use Rupert's guilt at not seeing his son often enough as a means of persuading him to buy, in compensation, the latest video game or electronic toy. She would have to nip that in the bud, she decided firmly, but she couldn't do it without Rupert's co-operation.

At least that was now more than a possibility. Since the

blossoming of his career all the bitterness seemed to have gone out of Rupert, all the resentment he had once harboured against her. She found she could discuss almost anything with him, and be sure of a sympathetic hearing. In fact, she could not remember a time, since their early days together, when they had got on so well.

'We'd better love you and leave you,' Rupert said, giving her a light peck on the cheek. 'But first, I want to ask you a favour.'

'Fire away.' Becky stroked the iron swiftly and efficiently, back and forth, across a pair of Adam's jeans that needed patching at the knee.

'I've been asked to a big opening of a celebrity restaurant – a Tex Mex place called The Alamo – you know the sort of thing, owned by a couple of Hollywood stars who pull in the crowds. The press will be there, and the fans, and I really don't want to go alone . . .'

Becky stopped ironing in mid-stroke and gave him a quizzical look. 'If there's one thing you've never had a problem with, Rupert, it's getting a date.'

'I don't want to take just any old date,' Rupert said. 'I'm not seeing anyone special right now . . . I don't know about you . . .'

They stood staring at each other, and then Adam pulled at Rupert's trouser leg. 'Come *on*, Daddy, we'll miss the kick-off.'

'I'm coming.' Rupert kept his eyes locked on Becky's. 'It'll be a good evening,' he said, taking the iron gently from her rigid hand and setting it down on the board. 'When was the last time you went out on the town and had some real fun?'

Becky had just got the ironing stacked into neat piles, and the board put away in the utility room, when the doorbell rang. She strode purposefully through the hall, ready to despatch with brisk efficiency any local councillor canvassing for votes, or Jehovah's Witness clamouring for converts.

But it was Jeremy who stood on the doorstep with a huge bunch of Easter lilies. Only when he pushed them at her with a broad grin did Becky notice at his side, half-hidden behind the flowers, a slight Oriental girl with a solemn expression.

'Becky,' he said with undisguised pride, 'I want you to meet Akiko.'

Becky put out the hand that wasn't holding the lilies. The girl shook it rather awkwardly with the hand that wasn't holding Jeremy's. 'Please,' Becky said, 'come in. I was just about to put the kettle on.'

Humphrey was in the kitchen, nosing around to see if there were any chocolate biscuits Adam hadn't finished. As soon as Jeremy saw him, he propelled his companion forward for more introductions. 'Akiko,' he said reverently, 'is a student of Noh and Kabuki theatre, and now she's studying western drama at RADA.'

'Fascinating,' Humphrey said, eyes lighting up immediately. 'Of course, RADA's not what it used to be in my day. Like everything, it's been taken over by the yob culture. Not enough concentration on the classics.'

'But we study the classics all the time,' Akiko assured him.

'What are you doing now, then?'

'A production of Shakespeare's *Tempest*.'

'That's handy,' Humphrey said. 'I'm about to do it myself at the Haymarket. We can rehearse together – Adam will do for Puck – I hope you're playing Miranda . . .'

'Hang on,' Jeremy intervened. 'What if she doesn't want—'

'I would be honoured,' Akiko said seriously, 'to rehearse with an actor of Sir Humphrey's stature.'

Humphrey preened himself a little. 'You have wisdom for one so young – unlike this wretched boy. Only does films, you know – can't think what you see in him.'

Becky, who had been keeping an amused eye on the exchange while she set out the tea things, saw Jeremy flush with indignation. 'Akiko is very impressed with my work,' he said aggressively. 'In fact, she's so taken with my latest screenplay, I'm going to write a part into it, just for her.'

'Disgraceful,' Humphrey said. 'Where's your artistic integrity? Shakespeare didn't go writing in characters every time he took on a new mistress.'

Akiko laughed musically. Jeremy bunched his fists. Becky grabbed a biscuit tin and shoved it between him and Humphrey. 'No chocolate ones left, I'm afraid, but do try one of the others – they're awfully good.'

At once Humphrey was digging around for the one with the sweetest filling. Jeremy, still glaring at him, tried to push the tin in

Akiko's direction, but she shook her head. 'I have to watch my figure,' she said regretfully.

'You have a perfect figure,' Jeremy assured her.

'Tea, then?' Becky said. 'It's just plain old Indian, I'm afraid.'

'I like Indian,' Akiko said, smiling warmly at her.

'So do I.' Humphrey took his customary seat at the table, and patted the chair next to him. 'You must,' he said to Akiko, 'come and tell me all about the Noh theatre.'

'I liked her very much,' Becky told Anthea who was in her greenhouse, potting some cuttings taken from her fuchsias. 'But it was just a little strange seeing how Jeremy, almost without missing a beat, seems to have transferred all his adoration from me to her.'

'Do I detect a note of jealousy?' Anthea asked as she dipped the cuttings into hormone rooting powder.

'Surprise, mostly. I was so afraid I'd hurt him dreadfully. But he bounces back a lot faster than I gave him credit for. I'm pleased he's found someone else – I want him to be happy – but I suppose, if I'm honest, it's a bit of a blow to my pride to discover I can be replaced so easily.'

'Darling, you overestimate men in general. They'll settle for anything on two legs, as long as it has the other required bits of anatomy.'

'It's more than just sex with Jeremy,' Becky disagreed. 'He needs someone to hero worship, to give him inspiration. I can tell he's ready to see this girl as Yoko Ono to his John Lennon.'

'And if she doesn't work out, as you didn't, he'll move on to the next one,' Anthea said firmly. 'Like the way I put three of these cuttings into one pot – on the assumption I'll have at least two failures.'

Becky laughed. 'You're even more down on men than usual these days. Is it all these discussion groups Henri's dragging you along to?'

'Darling, I don't think relationships between women are any better, if Henri's ones are anything to go by. She's had some dreadful row with the latest girlfriend – all sulks and tears and late-night phone calls.'

'Poor you,' Becky sympathised. She watched as Anthea arranged her pots of cuttings in neat little rows and began to cover them with clear polythene bags. 'It can't be very peaceful, having all that going on under your roof.'

'No – but it keeps me entertained.'

'I wanted to ask you,' Becky said, 'if you would mind tearing yourself away for an evening and looking after Adam for me. I have to go out—'

'A date!' Anthea shrieked. 'You dark old horse, you. And there you were, making out it's only young Jeremy who moves on quickly. Who's the lucky fellah – anyone I know?'

Becky began to take a huge interest in some potted hydrangeas. 'Aren't these coming on well? . . . No, it's nothing like that – just a film industry function – I'm only going with Rupert . . .'

'Oh dear, how ghastly for you,' Anthea said feelingly.

'So if you could possibly look after Adam tomorrow night . . .'

'Tomorrow – that's the one time I can't do it. I've started going to this course with Henri on how to start up your own business.'

'Heavens, Ant, what sort of business were you thinking of starting up?'

'Oh, I dare say I'll never use most of it, but it's fascinating to know that books can actually balance – apart from the ones we put on our heads in posture classes. I can't wait till they show me how!'

'Perhaps,' Becky said tentatively, 'Hugo might consider looking after Adam. I haven't had much luck lately with babysitters, and Humphrey's playing every night in the West End.'

'It's brilliant, isn't it,' Anthea said, dispensing at last with her gardening gloves, 'how much energy he still has at his age. We must go and see him one night . . . Well, that's it for the fuchsias – for now at least. Let's go and treat ourselves to a cup of tea.'

Becky had laid out five evening outfits with matching accessories on the bed, and was carefully pondering which of them she should wear to the opening of *The Alamo* that night. There was a reasonable chance that whichever one she chose would end up in the pages of tomorrow's tabloids, since it was Rupert who would be by her side. Pride rather than vanity was making the decision such an agonising one. She was uncomfortably aware of how little socialising she had done in the last months, how behind she was on the latest fashion trends. She, who had never bothered much about clothes, was now afraid of feeling gauche, unsophisticated, out of date.

Adam had rejected Hugo as a babysitter, and insisted instead on spending the night with his new best friend, Freddie Foley. She had despatched him there earlier in the evening with the little packed suitcase which had been used less and less frequently for visits to Rupert.

The phone rang, and she wondered if it was Adam with a change of heart. It might be too late now, she thought rather frantically, for Hugo to take over. She was surprised to discover how much she did not want to miss this one night out of the house.

But when she picked up the phone, it was Alex who said without preamble, 'News at last.'

Her heart nearly skipped a beat. 'Good or bad?'

'You can decide that for yourself, when I've told you.'

Almost never, since they day she'd met him, had Becky heard such barely suppressed excitement in his voice.

'Harry Widmark,' he said, 'of Pantheon Pictures – who, by the way, remembers you well – has read your screenplay and says he's very impressed. He's made an initial offer.'

Becky closed her eyes and gripped the phone. 'How much?'

'It's a fair deal for a first-time writer,' Alex said. 'A hundred and fifty thousand dollars.'

She opened her eyes again and the room swam slowly back into focus. 'A hundred and fifty thousand . . .'

'I can probably talk him up a bit, but not by much.'

'Alex,' she said breathlessly, 'let's not quibble. Accept the offer.'

'There may be others still to come.'

She dared not place her faith in what might never happen. She could scarcely believe what already had. 'I don't want to wait. What if we hedge our bets and Harry withdraws the offer?'

Alex chuckled. 'I have a feeling he won't be doing that. He made it quite plain he thinks you have what it takes, and he'd like to work with you. He's none too pleased, from what I gather, that he didn't get the chance on the film Letitia bumped you off. He says the woman's a disaster – took on a seasoned Hollywood director she's far too inexperienced to control, and he's running rings around her. The picture's going wildly over budget.'

'I did warn Stanley,' Becky said, trying not to gloat.

'Harry was asking me if you're going to stick to writing now, or if you're still keeping your hand in as a producer.'

'I don't know.' She held an ivory silk dress against herself, and looked speculatively at her reflection in the mirror. 'I was so angry when I realised how difficult it would be for me to carry on producing, but now that I'm off that particular treadmill, I'm not sure I want to get back on it again.'

'Fair enough, but just give it some thought. Harry may be open to letting you get involved on the producing side as well.'

'For now I'll settle for selling it to him,' she said, deciding the ivory dress made her look too pale. 'Thank you, Alex – again – for everything you've done.'

'The credit goes to you. It's your work. Becky . . .'

'Yes?'

'Shall I bring round a bottle of champagne to celebrate?'

'I'd love to,' she said carefully, 'but I can't. I'm going out.'

There was a long silence at the other end of the phone. Then Alex said, 'Perhaps another night, then.'

As soon as she'd put the phone down, Becky swooped decisively on a red evening suit with beaded jacket. Red for confidence, she thought. She no longer minded whether the hemline was the right length for this season. It didn't seem important now what anyone else thought. She wasn't an out-of-work housewife, an ex-producer, a nobody amidst the throng of glamorous celebrities she would have to face tonight. She was now a recognised screenwriter, with a firm offer on the table for her first original work.

By the time the doorbell rang Becky's emotions had come full circle, and the nerves fluttered wildly in her stomach at the prospect of spending a whole evening in Rupert's company – effectively as his date. She could not imagine what had induced her to agree to it. It was bound, she thought now in something like panic, to end in tears.

The sight of him, tense and white-faced on the doorstep, confirmed her worst fears. He was obviously filled with the same foreboding. Then she looked beyond him, and her eyes widened in disbelief.

Parked at the kerb was an American stretch limousine with ominously tinted windows, and a uniformed chauffeur holding open the door to the cavernous interior. For long seconds Becky stared at this scenario, so out of place in her World's End street – and then she burst into peals of laughter.

'Perhaps,' Rupert said stiffly, 'you'd like to share the joke.'

'I'm sorry,' Becky said when she could finally speak. The tears of mirth had probably streaked her carefully applied make-up, and she would have to do a quick repair job in that ridiculous car. 'It's very sweet of you but it's just so . . . over the top.'

'You haven't seen the champagne in the ice bucket yet,' Rupert said, 'or the television with twelve channels.'

Then they both started giggling, while the chauffeur stood holding the door and waiting with an expression of long suffering, and Becky realised her nerves of a few moments ago had evaporated completely.

They neither drank the champagne nor watched any of the twelve channels as the car cruised across London to Leicester Square, where barriers held back the crowds of uninvited fans who had come to ogle the famous faces. When the limousine glided to a halt, Becky quickly opened her own door to avoid the embarrassment of having it opened for her by the chauffeur. Rupert slid out after her.

There were squeaks from the crowd as some of them recognised him, a few teenage girls even calling out his name. Rupert tried to look nonchalant, but Becky could see how he was revelling in all the attention. She hung back a little, letting him enjoy his moment. Then the paparazzi descended, flashbulbs popping, and Rupert's charm was directed at the cameras.

He still, she found, had plenty left over for her, as he guided her in through the doors, making room for her to walk through the crush and promising to go off at once in search of liquid refreshment. It was true, she thought, sudden success did change people – but in Rupert's case it had made him easier to deal with, rather than more difficult. As she watched him crossing the room to the bar, stopping for no more than a few words with the people who eagerly greeted him, she thought she had never seen him so happy, so relaxed, so comfortable with himself.

'If it isn't Rebecca Carlyle!' Several pairs of hands grabbed at her from behind, and she spun round to see a little knot of film people she hadn't come across in a while.

'Darling, we thought you'd dropped off the face of the planet,' said a gangly director called Tony. 'Wherever have you been?'

'I've hung up my producer's hat,' Becky told him, 'and taken to writing instead.'

'But we simply won't let you. Things are far too dull without you.'

'Love the outfit,' said an art director whose name escaped her. 'Good colour for you.'

'Oh, you'll never guess who I saw the other day with a rather famous actress whose name I will shortly mention,' his actor boyfriend chipped in, and Becky found herself, almost without taking breath, drawn back into the gossipy world she had left such a short time before, though it felt like half a lifetime.

When Rupert came back to her side with two frozen Margaritas, the actor at once broke off in the middle of his story and began to drill Rupert on how he got his break. As Becky half listened to Rupert answering the barrage of questions with remarkable patience, her eye wandered around the crowded room, picking out stars and socialites: Tom Cruise glued to the side of his wife Nicole Kidman, Elton John in a sequined straw boater, Sir Andrew Lloyd Webber fraternising with the horse racing community, Imran and Jemima Khan in traditional flowing trouser suits. Her pulse began to quicken again to the pace of the life she had once known and taken for granted.

'Enjoying yourself?' Rupert said in her ear, and she jumped almost guiltily.

They ate delicious tortillas dripping with melted cheese and spicy chicken tacos with guacamole and sour cream, washed down with more of the frozen Margaritas, and Rupert introduced her to some of the other actors on his show who seemed not the least surprised to see him there with his estranged wife. She wondered briefly what, if anything, Rupert had told them about his personal life.

'Frankly, my dear, you're welcome to him,' his screen wife – real name Meredith Browne – joked to Becky. 'As husbands go, he's a real shit!'

'He used to be,' Becky said, her eyes meeting Rupert's, 'but I think he's mellowing out a little.'

When the dancing began, Rupert circled his arms around her and guided her onto the floor. She found herself suddenly shy of him, not wanting to meet his eye. Instead she drew him closer, and allowed him to rest his cheek against her.

'I like your hair longer,' he said, nuzzling it with his lips. 'It's softer, more natural – it suits you.'

She smiled a little, and a man across the dance floor smiled back, and then he moved purposefully towards her and she recognised the beaming face of Stanley Shiplake.

'It's *great* to see you,' he boomed above the music. 'You're looking *good*. Hey, Rupert, mind if I *cut in*?'

Rupert swung round to face him. 'Sorry Stanley, but no one's going to come between me and my wife.'

Stanley shrugged philosophically. 'Can't blame me for *trying*.' He swooped forward to plant a kiss on Becky's cheek. 'You stay in *touch* now, do you hear?'

'Where's the lovely Letitia?' Becky said sweetly, but Stanley was already moving off through the crowds that were beginning to hem them in to only a few inches of floor space.

Rupert, sensing instantly the beginnings of her claustrophobia, bent to her and whispered, 'Shall we get the hell out of here?'

Cruising home in the air-conditioned quiet of the limousine, Becky thought it would not be stealing Rupert's thunder if she told him now about Pantheon's offer to buy her screenplay.

'Well, well,' he drawled, raising an eyebrow. 'So good old Alex has pulled it off again.'

'We both have a lot to thank him for,' she said a little sharply.

'Don't be too grateful,' Rupert warned. 'Keep some of the credit for yourself.'

'Alex isn't trying to take any credit from me—' she began defensively, but Rupert put a finger to her lips.

'I'm only saying you have a tendency to undervalue your own achievements. And when we were living together, I didn't help – I never gave you your due. I suppose it was just resentment, but I couldn't bring myself to tell you how proud I was of you. I want to tell you now.'

Becky looked down at her neat shell-shaped evening bag, no bigger than a fist, and could still feel the intensity of Rupert's gaze burning into her.

'All our problems,' he said softly, 'stemmed from the fact that you were so successful and I wasn't. I had to use alcohol – and even other women – to prove to myself that I wasn't inferior. But it wasn't your fault – none of it was – and now that I realise that, I want to find a way to make it up to you.'

He reached into his pocket and drew out a small blue velvet-covered box. Becky stared at it, mesmerised, as though it might contain some poisonous snake. Slowly Rupert raised the lid, and she gazed into the interior, at the small and exquisite diamond and sapphire eternity ring nestling in the artfully folded satin.

'In compensation,' Rupert said earnestly, 'for the engagement ring I could never afford to buy you.'

Still she couldn't speak, and taking her silence as assent, Rupert lifted the ring out of the satin and reverently slipped it onto the fourth finger of her left hand, where the tan mark from her wedding ring had not yet entirely faded.

'To new beginnings,' he said.

Becky looked down at the ring, and the gemstones winked back at her in the dim light. 'You know I can't take this,' she said hoarsely, 'because I have no idea whether—'

'Then don't make any decisions now,' Rupert insisted. 'Keep the ring, and think about the future. Our divorce hasn't come through yet, and we don't have to go through with it if we find we've changed our minds . . .'

Becky turned away, but she could see nothing, through the thickly tinted windows, of the world beyond this slowly moving car in which she suddenly felt a captive.

'Things are different now,' Rupert said insistently at her side. 'We're both successful, we can both hold our own. There's no reason why this marriage shouldn't work.'

He leaned towards her, and Becky stared at his mouth and remembered how in the long evening shadows she had reached up to kiss Alex's lips, and unconsciously tightened her own, waiting for what would inevitably follow.

But Rupert only gave her a gentle smile of reassurance.

'I don't know how you did it,' Shirley said down the phone, 'but you've certainly got that husband of yours towing the line.'

'What do you mean?' Becky asked.

There was a pause, as she listened to the sound of Shirley gulping a mouthful of tea. 'I've just had Bernard Fisher on the phone,' she explained. 'Apparently Rupert's instructed him to drop the Prohibited Steps Order.'

Silently, Becky slotted this new piece of the puzzle into the growing picture.

'Not only that, Rupert's prepared to shoulder all the costs. How on earth did you bring about this minor miracle?'

'I didn't,' Becky admitted. 'This has come entirely from his side.'

'Well, let's not look a gift horse in the mouth. And talking of gifts, Rupert's also offering to pay you child support and maintenance.'

'I don't need maintenance,' Becky said firmly. 'I'll be earning my own money soon.'

'Well, it's up to you, but you're certainly entitled to it. And as for Adam, his living expenses are not your sole responsibility. I would strongly advise that you take the child support.'

'Well, perhaps that . . .'

'I don't know what you're sounding so gloomy about,' Shirley said with some exasperation. 'This is all incredibly good news.'

'I know.'

'Then cheer up. Perhaps you should take Adam off somewhere for a summer holiday – you'll soon be a free woman.'

Becky looked around the walls of her kitchen and felt rather as though they were closing in on her, blocking all escape.

Later she was making the beds, her mind a flurry of dark thoughts, when the doorbell rang.

An apparition in biker's leathers and helmet thrust a clipboard and pen at her, asking her to sign in the space provided. She made a dutiful scrawl, and accepted the buff envelope with her name and address printed on it in block capitals.

Back inside she ripped it open and pulled out the contents. She stared down at her hand and saw that it was holding two air tickets, in her name and Adam's, destination Pisa. She unfolded the single sheet of paper.

'You deserve a break,' the message read, 'after everything I've put you through. Please accept my apologies and these tickets, with all my love, Rupert. P.S. I thought you might want to visit your father. Please give him my best wishes for a full recovery.'

Right at the bottom, as though just an afterthought, he had added: 'All I ask in return is that you think, while you're away, about what I said to you the other night.'

Becky looked at the confident, flourishing strokes of her husband's handwriting and said out loud, 'I'll soon be a free woman,' and then a little louder, 'I'll soon be a free woman, I'll soon be a free woman . . .'

They sat beneath an enormous white sunshade on a wooden pole stained to match the garden furniture, and protecting them from the fierce heat of a cloudless late summer day.

'Jolly decent of Rupert,' Hugh said – not for the first time – 'to treat you to this trip.'

Adam, brown as a nut, shrieked with laughter as his cousins Lily and Lee, with blunt little fringes and long black ponytails, chased him round the pool. It was over a year since he had seen them and Becky really was grateful, she kept telling herself, that Rupert had enabled her to time her visit here to coincide with theirs.

'I told you,' Alice said, dabbing at the beads of sweat on her brow with a handkerchief, 'that Rupert would drop the court order when he'd had time to calm down a bit.'

Michael winked at Becky with eyes that were as green as hers beneath darker blond hair. 'Maybe you'd better think seriously about whether to let him go, now that he's become such a big catch.'

'Michael – that's a disgusting thing to say!' objected Mae, his Chinese wife.

'Why? I'm sure you married me for my money.'

'Watch out – any day now I'll be making more than you.'

'That's just reverse discrimination.'

Becky let her mind drift as they squabbled good-naturedly, in their usual way. The heat was making her sleepy. It was too intense, by this time of day, for her to stretch out on the recliner, soaking up the sun's rays, as she had on that previous trip to her parents when she had lain there asking herself all the same questions that were now revolving endlessly through her mind. Should she go through with the divorce? Should she give her marriage to Rupert a second chance? It seemed absurd to be going over it all again, when she thought she had resolved it conclusively the last time.

'Are you feeling all right, Rebecca?' her father said suddenly, and she realised that, in an unguarded moment, she had allowed the worry to show.

She smiled brightly at him. He was looking completely well again, a light tan covering the hospital pallor, but she had not forgotten the sight of him with tubes snaking from his nose and mouth. 'I think the heat has fried my brains,' she said lightly. 'I'm going to rescue Adam from his cousins and take him for a dip.'

'No need,' Hugh said proudly. 'He seems at last to have learned to swim by himself.'

Long after the others had gone to bed, Becky and Michael sat up with huge balloon glasses of brandy and idly watched, through the French windows, the shadowy bats dive-bombing the pool for their nightly feast of insects.

'When I was a kid,' Michael said, 'I would have tried to get them with a slingshot.'

'When you were a kid,' Becky said, 'you got up to any number of beastly things.'

'Rubbish. I don't remember anything worse than cheating at Pooh sticks on the Pont Neuf in Paris.'

'What about that time in Delhi, when you tricked me into drinking the chilli milkshake you'd concocted in Mummy's blender?'

'Oh, yes – that,' Michael said sheepishly. 'Bloody awful of me – but worth it for the look on your face! It must've taken the roof off your mouth, but you refused to cry. Didn't tell on me either.'

'Of course not.' Becky looked out at thin wisps of cloud trailing across a huge Tuscan moon, hanging low on the horizon. 'We Haydons weren't always together, but we were a real family. You and Mae and the twins, you're a family too . . .'

'Come now,' Michael said, reaching over to take her hand. 'That doesn't make you and Adam second class citizens.'

'No.' She bit her lip. 'But it does make us lonely . . . I never meant him to be an only child, you know.'

'There's still time,' Michael said gently. 'Perhaps you've already met someone . . . ?'

Becky took a deep swallow of brandy and shook her head. 'There was this young director I got involved with, but he's moved on to someone else. And then there's a man I've known for a long time, a man I've always cared about . . . but he only wants friendship from me. It seems, after all, that the only one who's still in the picture is Rupert.'

She shivered a little at a sudden breeze through the open doors, and Michael put an arm round her shoulders. 'There are worse things than being alone – as long as you find your own contentment. You've always had such inner strength, I know you'll come through this and find fulfilment on the other side.'

She looked up the hill at the gnarled olives, ghostly in the light of the moon, and felt a little tingle of fear at the courage that solitary path would require.

'You can't really believe,' Michael said, 'that even happy families are all roses round the door.' He grinned. 'Have you forgotten the chilli milkshake?'

'I know what you're saying, Michael. But it's still better to be a family – even if it sometimes takes the roof off your mouth.'

Rupert fetched them from the airport in the gleaming black four-wheel drive he'd bought on hire purchase. Adam, duly impressed, investigated all the gadgets, and talked non-stop about his cousins' many exploits, and then fell into an exhausted sleep on the back seat.

'Sounds like you all had a good time,' Rupert said, smiling.

'We did.' Becky leaned back against the soft leather headrest. 'Thanks again for making it all possible.'

Rupert glanced across at her, and could see there was weariness beneath the tan. 'How's your father?'

'Better, but still a worry. I'm very grateful to you for dropping the court order – it's such a relief to know I can leave at a moment's notice if there's ever another problem.'

They drove on for a while in silence. Becky looked out of the tinted windows at the scudding clouds and rain-splattered streets. There was a feeling, already, of autumn in the air.

Then Rupert said, 'Did you do any thinking about us?'

He was staring at the road ahead, and she glanced sideways at his classic profile, and wondered how it was ever possible to tell what was beneath the surface.

'Rupert, I know you've changed,' she said. 'I just don't know how much.'

'There's only one way to find out. Give me a chance to prove it to you.'

She sighed. 'If we do this, we have to take it one day at a time.'

'Whatever works for you,' Rupert said, smiling serenely.

Becky bent over the papers spread out across Alex's desk – the complex and lengthy contract from Pantheon Pictures for the purchase of her screenplay. Alex had already negotiated all the points to his satisfaction, and they had both gone through the final version with a tooth comb. Signing now was just a formality – and yet, when he held out his black fountain pen, she hesitated for a moment.

'Everything all right?' he asked.

No, she wanted to shout, it isn't. But the problem had nothing to do with the business which seemed to have become the sole focus of their relationship. Every time she had seen Alex lately, he had been so absorbed in dotting every 'i' and crossing every 't' of the contract, he never seemed to notice that there might be other things on her mind. Nor, since the night she had refused his offer of champagne because she was going out with Rupert, had he suggested coming round to her house again.

She was aware of him watching her with that quiet patience she usually found so reassuring. 'I am doing the right thing, aren't I?' she said.

'You know your options. The final decision is yours.'

Was it deliberate, she wondered, this refusal to understand what she couldn't bring herself to put into words? She almost snatched the pen from him, and signed the last page with a flourish.

He looked down at the wet ink. 'So you're using your maiden name again?'

'What's wrong with that?' She had favoured Rebecca Carlyle for her producer credits, but now that she had developed this second career, she found herself wanting to return to Haydon, the name she had been born with.

'It's a good idea,' Alex said. 'Just as well to make the change now, before the divorce goes through.'

Becky looked at his familiar face and felt a sudden surge of unfamiliar anger – anger at all the assumptions he made because he thought he knew her so well.

'Actually,' she said defiantly, 'there may not be a divorce. Rupert and I are thinking of getting back together again.'

CHAPTER SEVENTEEN

Alex sat at his desk in the study of his Knightsbridge flat and turned the postcard over and over in his hand. It had obviously been bought in haste in some hotel lobby. On the front was a tourist photograph of two almost caricature *banditos* with moustaches and sombreros against a background of desert and *saguaro* cacti. On the back was a brief message from Frank. 'Married Irene in San Reno. Spending a few days in Mexico. Happiest man alive – longing for you two to meet.'

Alex sat back in his chair and closed his eyes and imagined his father in open-neck shirt, sitting at a beach bar with the sun setting over the ocean, a tequila in one hand and the woman he loved by his side. Then he tried the exercise again, substituting his own image for his father's. But the sheer impossibility of it defeated him.

He opened his eyes and looked at the neat stacks of scripts on his desks and the dog lying silently in the basket beside him. 'It's not enough any more, old boy,' Alex said out loud to his faithful companion. 'It's just not enough.'

He had gambled everything on Becky's ability to stand firm, stand alone, see her problems through to the finish before she decided her future. He had gambled because he thought it was a risk worth taking – and he had lost.

Instead of discovering her own inner strength, instead of building herself up so that no man would have the power to drag her down again, she had panicked, fallen back on old certainties, put her trust in the devil she knew though she knew he was not to be trusted.

Alex reached over and absently stroked Wellington's ear. What he'd asked of Becky was no more than he'd been prepared to do himself. He had stood alone, stood firm, waiting as long as it took for Becky to be free of the entanglements of her past. Now suddenly he felt all the anger of his disappointed hopes. There was no point in waiting any longer. She had shown him quite clearly that she never would be free.

He reached into his desk drawer and took out the piece of paper Rupert had given him, the one with Juliette Winter's phone number. In his mind he heard the words she had spoken on the pool terrace all those months ago: 'I think you've forgotten what it's like to be wanted just for yourself.'

'You no waste my food,' Mrs Christos said ominously. 'You eat second helping.'

'My dear lady,' Sir Humphrey said weakly, 'splendid though it was, I couldn't possibly . . .'

'Skinny old man.' Mrs Christos wagged a wooden spoon at him. 'How you stay on stage for three hours if you no eat?'

Sir Humphrey stood his ground. 'Every good thespian knows the hazards of gorging himself before a performance.'

'You no eat,' Mrs Christos threatened, 'I no cook.' She retreated to the utility room with the satisfied air of one who has had the last word.

'Pay no attention to her,' Humphrey told the others. 'She adores me, really. I am making great progress in liberating her from the stranglehold of the Catholic Church.'

'What I want to know,' Becky said, 'is how on earth you persuaded her to start working late just to cook your dinner.'

'There's nothing she wouldn't do for me,' Humphrey declared. 'I'm going to teach her the Queen's English next . . .'

'This is rather delicious,' Anthea said, chewing appreciatively. 'What is it?'

'Feijoada – the national dish of Brazil.' Humphrey was clearly revelling in the sharing of his new-found knowledge. 'It's basically pork with black beans and rice and greens. The orange segments are to counteract the fattiness of the dish.'

'Marvellous,' Anthea said, swallowing her mouthful. 'Such a pity I can't be fagged to learn how to cook.'

'It used to be a slave dish – the leftovers from the master's table – which is why they include all sorts of parts from the pig, from the ears to the tail.'

Anthea began to look a little green. Humphrey didn't notice. 'Damn good, isn't it? Almost as tasty as Indian . . . You're supposed to eat it with some lethal alcoholic drink called *caipirinha*, made from sugar cane and mixed with a lot of lime and sugar. Didn't dare try it before I go on stage, but Mrs C has promised to make some for me next time. I dare say I'll get her to take a glass or two of it with me. She's becoming quite an abandoned woman, you know.'

'Now, Humphrey, don't you go scaring off the staff,' Becky warned mildly.

'What about this play of yours, then?' Anthea asked, pushing her plate surreptitiously to one side. 'Becky's promised to come and see it with me.'

'I can't,' Becky said a little sheepishly. 'Rupert's already bought tickets for the two of us.'

Anthea eyed her darkly. 'I don't like the sound of "the two of us". You're not letting him cosy up to you again?'

Becky stood abruptly and began to clear the plates. 'It's no big deal. We both wanted to see Humphrey, that's all.'

'Jolly good of you,' Humphrey said.

'I just hope you know what you're doing,' Anthea snorted.

'Never fear – I'll arrange other tickets for you,' Humphrey promised. 'You can always come with that man-hating housemate of yours. Just mind she doesn't start groping you the minute the lights go down.'

'Now, Humphrey, you mustn't be prejudiced towards Henri . . .'

'Prejudice be damned,' Humphrey said. 'If anyone's going to grope you in the dark, I'd rather it was me.'

Juliette prowled round Alex's sitting room, looking at the cream curtains with elaborate tiebacks, and the matching cream sofas with enormous puffy cushions that looked as though they had never borne the imprint of anyone's weight. 'There isn't much here that's really you,' she said.

'No,' Alex acknowledged.

'Why is that?' She jumped onto one of the cream cushions, making a large dent in it. 'Is it because you don't want anyone to know who you are?'

He laughed. 'Not really. I never invite people here anyway.'

'Then why did you ask me?'

He wasn't ready yet to answer that. He sat down opposite her, and made a play of adjusting the creases in his trousers. Juliette, curled up on her cushion, wore a big loose silk shirt and leggings and ankle boots. She allowed the boots to rest, quite deliberately, on the cream fabric.

'Weren't you married once?' she asked curiously.

'Briefly – a while ago.'

'What about her, then? Didn't she make a home for you?'

'She never felt as though London was her home,' Alex said without bitterness. 'She always behaved like a tourist – as though she were just passing through.'

'And left nothing of herself behind?'

'Not even a photograph.'

Juliette crossed her legs and propped her pretty chin in her hands. 'I don't understand women like that. I would want to leave my mark.'

'Lara just wanted to leave.'

'And what happened,' she asked, 'after Lara?'

'Nothing, really.'

He didn't want to tell her that he had put his life on hold, that he had been waiting for the miracle that would allow him to start living again. He had an uncomfortable feeling that she already knew.

She turned huge brown eyes on him, warm as melting chocolate. 'It's not much fun being alone, is it?'

He shrugged. 'I've kept myself busy—'

'To fill all the empty spaces.'

Under her intense gaze Alex shifted his eyes to his watch. 'I'd better phone a restaurant. I didn't pre-book – I wasn't sure if you were in the mood for Italian or Chinese . . .'

'Alex,' she said firmly, 'I'm not some teenager you have to woo with flowers and candlelight. I'm here because I know what I want.'

She stood up and began to walk towards him, and he stayed where he was because he couldn't trust his own legs to hold him.

'Let's just skip the hors d'oeuvres,' Juliette said, 'and go straight to the main course.'

There were all sorts of things Rupert seemed to know now that Becky couldn't remember him knowing before – things like where to park the Range Rover within walking distance of a West End theatre so they didn't have to fight for a taxi, and the names of little-known restaurants with wonderful menus where well known faces could dine afterwards without attracting unwelcome curiosity.

They were in one of these eateries now, a small art deco room tiled in black and white, with a menu offering a range of Sezhuan Chinese specialities.

'I thought Sir Humphrey was marvellous,' Rupert said, as he nibbled on seaweed and sesame prawn toast.

'When I see him on stage I forget how old he is,' Becky said. 'Then I catch sight of him sometimes, at breakfast, with the morning sun on his face, and it makes me cold with fear.'

Rupert patted her hand. 'You've grown quite attached to the old boy, haven't you?'

She nodded, and for a moment she couldn't speak past the lump in her throat. 'He's been so good to Adam – and me – when there was no one else.'

'Then I owe him one too.' He drew her hand towards him, and smiled when he saw that she was still wearing the eternity ring.

'Talking of Adam,' Becky said a little too quickly, 'he's decided he wants a football party for his birthday, and enough kids to make up two teams.'

'Heavens,' Rupert said, 'is he turning seven already?'

'I'll have to arrange several cars to ferry the children over to Battersea Park for the game, and then back to World's End for tea. Your Range Rover would come in handy.'

'Of course,' Rupert said, 'count me in.'

Becky eyed him warily over her wine glass. 'Don't say that if you're going to be up to your eyes in work and won't be able to get away. I don't want to tell Adam you're coming if you have to cancel at the last minute. It would spoil everything for him.'

Rupert looked offended. He put his hand over his heart. 'I swear to you, I will make a plan to get off work for my son's birthday. What do you take me for?'

'OK,' Becky said, reminding herself, as she sometimes still had to, that this was not the old Rupert she was dealing with. 'I'll count you in.'

The waiter came with crisp, fluffy Peking duck, and deboned it with a flourish at the table, and then Rupert took over from him, and rolled the meat into pancakes with cucumber and spring onion and plum sauce. He passed a couple over to Becky on a plate. She bit into one, and the delicious plum sauce spilled onto her tongue. She smiled at Rupert.

'To us,' he said, smiling back, clinking his glass against hers. 'And to Adam . . . and one day, maybe, a whole football team of our own.'

Becky's fingers, holding the neatly rolled pancake, froze halfway to her mouth. Rupert took it from her, and laid it gently on the plate. 'You know what I want. I want us to be a real family again. And now we're both earning decent money, why not make it a bigger family?'

She thought of Adam's old crib, now up in the attic, and the baby clothes she had folded away so carefully in mothballs for the day she had given up believing would ever come.

'Rupert,' she said, 'that's not fair.'

'Why?' He seemed genuinely puzzled. 'I thought that was what you wanted too.'

'It's not fair to bribe me with what I always wanted.'

'It's not a bribe, Becky,' he said, kissing her lightly on the cheek. 'It's an option we should consider . . . Now let's not waste all this wickedly expensive food.'

She picked up her pancake and tentatively probed it with her tongue. Rupert finished off the last of his, and expertly began to roll some more.

'I heard some rather good gossip the other day,' he said conversationally. 'You know I go to the same gym as Juliette Winters? Well, she told me she's having a wild affair with Alex Goddard.'

Becky continued to chew mechanically on her pancake, but all the taste had gone out of it.

'About time he took the plunge again,' Rupert said. 'He was becoming a bit of an old monk. But if any woman can cure him of those tendencies, it's Juliette. You should see her in a leotard.'

Becky had the very firm conviction that she didn't ever want to see Juliette Winters in a leotard or anything else. She took a rather large gulp of wine.

'You've gone very quiet,' Rupert said, his eyes boring into her. 'Aren't you happy for old Alex?'

Becky took another swallow, and tried not to flinch under Rupert's gaze. 'I am if it's what he wants . . . and if Juliette's telling the truth.'

'No doubt about that,' Rupert laughed. 'She looks like the cat that got the cream.' His face suddenly became more serious. 'It made me quite envious, really – made me think about what she's got that I haven't.' He refilled both their glasses. 'How long are you going to make me wait, Becky?'

She took another quick sip of wine, though it was making her quite light-headed. She tried to put the image of Alex and Juliette out of her mind and focus instead on Rupert, on his features that were so familiar to her she could close her eyes and still see their contours. She wondered rather hazily why she didn't just accept the inevitable – the fact that it was only Rupert who really wanted her, and he was certain to have his way sooner or later, so why not now?

He was watching her, waiting for her answer, and his face swam dizzily in front of her. 'Rupert, I think I want to go home now,' she said.

All the way back to World's End, Becky's head was filled with superstitious incantations. 'If he doesn't ask to come in I'll know the time isn't right, but if he does I won't fight it.' And then, 'If there's no parking outside the house, I'll take that as a sign that it isn't meant to be, but if there is . . .'

There was a space right outside her front door, just as there had been on that long-ago day when she'd found Rupert in bed with Lolly and didn't want to go back inside. Rupert manoeuvred easily into it, and got out without asking, and Becky felt the inevitability of her fate.

They didn't speak as they climbed the stairs to the bedroom they had shared for all those years. There was no need. They both knew the pact had been sealed between them.

She watched as he stripped off his clothes, and there was no detail of his perfectly sculpted body that she had forgotten. She felt his hands on her, touching her in all the places he knew she liked to be touched, and experienced the reassurance of being in well-charted waters. Her own involuntary responses took over, the patterns of ten years of intimacy that were printed into her very bones.

She wasn't surprised that the sex was still good between them. At some level she had always known it would be, whatever he had put her through, like the feeling of a limb still being there even after brutal amputation. There was comfort in the irony, as though loss were not really loss after all.

'I love you,' Rupert said afterwards as she lay in his arms, and he fell into a comfortable sleep in her new bed, her new life, without even waiting for a response.

There was another incantation going through Becky's mind as she lay in the dark, with Rupert breathing evenly beside her, unable to succumb to sleep herself. Since Jeremy she had not taken any form of contraception, had not foreseen the need. 'If I'm pregnant,' she said to herself, 'then the decision will have been taken for me.'

Becky was nibbling absently on a piece of toast, remembering how in the early months of carrying Adam she had eaten doughnuts for breakfast to ward off the morning sickness. Unconsciously she touched her flat stomach, trying to remember what it had felt like as it swelled with the growth of the child within her. The ringing of the phone didn't penetrate her reverie until Mrs Christos called her to take it.

'What a *co-incidence* – bumping into you the other night,' a familiar voice boomed down the line.

Becky didn't believe in coincidence. 'What can I do for you, Stanley?'

'You can allow me,' Stanley said in a surprisingly abject tone, 'to say how *sorry* I am about the way we parted company. You can, I hope, find it in your heart to *forgive* me. You can—'

'Stanley,' Becky said wearily, 'what do you want?'

'You know your trouble? You were always too *suspicious*. You've never given me credit for just being your *friend*.'

She waited patiently, reminding herself how Stanley always got to the point in his own good time. To help it pass, she hummed a nursery rhyme under her breath.

'A little dicky bird told me,' Stanley was saying, 'that Pantheon Pictures bought that screenplay you wrote. Harry Widmark himself is very *impressed* with you.'

She had got successfully through 'Incy Wincy Spider' and was trying to remember the words of 'The Teddy Bear's Picnic'.

'I always *knew* you had it in you. Wasn't I the one who gave you your first *break*?'

'We're covering old ground here, Stanley,' Becky said.

'OK, so maybe I'm hoping you'll do me just a *tiny* favour – for old times' sake.'

She smiled. She hadn't even got to the second verse.

'Pantheon *fired* Letitia,' Stanley announced mournfully. 'I had to go along with it – the woman just wasn't ready to go it alone as a producer on a picture that size.'

'You surprise me,' Becky said demurely.

'Don't say "I told you so". You're too *big* for that.'

'I told you so,' she said gleefully.

'So you got the last laugh. I can take that. What I *can't* take is if this picture falls apart. Becky, we want *you* to come on board and pick up the pieces.'

Becky smiled secretly to herself. She looked down at her breasts, and imagined them heavy with milk.

'*Becky*, are you still there . . . ?'

'I'm here, Stanley, and this is where I'm staying. I'm not going to tear around the country trying to rescue some over-budget catastrophe that probably isn't worth saving. I'm not in that game any more, haven't you heard? You and Letitia elbowed me out of it – and you know what? You probably did me the biggest favour of my life!'

'So don't you think you *owe* me one?'

Becky almost laughed. 'If you really want to be friends – which somehow I doubt – that's fine by me. But I'm not planning on producing any more films right now. And even if I were, it wouldn't be for you.'

Stanley sighed theatrically. 'Can't blame me for *trying*.'

Becky put the phone down, still smiling to herself, and wondered if she should go up to the attic to check on the condition of the crib.

Everyone was having tea at the wooden table out in Becky's garden. Jeremy had brought Akiko again, and Anthea had come with Henri, Joshua having returned to his boarding school while Hugo had started his course at the London School of Economics. 'Following in his father's footsteps,' Anthea said mournfully.

'Shame neither of your boys shows any leanings towards the arts,' Humphrey said wistfully, having quickly established that neither of them were interested in joining the home theatricals, Joshua's sole passions being rugby, cricket and girls.

Anthea was frowning at Becky's withered roses. 'I'll be round tomorrow to deadhead those. It really should have been done already – those poor bushes are just wasting all their energy producing seeds you have no room to plant.'

'I know – I've been meaning to get round to it,' Becky said sheepishly.

'You never get round to it, as you know perfectly well.'

The leaves on the trees, Becky noticed, were beginning to turn from their full autumn glory to wither and fade. The evenings were shorter now, returning to darkness. There was change in the air, and it made her restless.

'What I want to know,' Henri was saying to Akiko, 'is why you've turned your back on your own traditional theatre and come to work here in a foreign culture.'

Akiko laughed. 'I've made a study of Noh and Kabuki, but I can't perform it. All the female roles are taken by male impersonators.'

'That's outrageous,' Henri said heatedly.

'It's a waste of talent,' Jeremy agreed, looking adoringly at Akiko. Since their arrival, he hadn't let go of her hand.

'It wasn't always like that,' Akiko explained. 'Noh is more aristocratic and was reserved for men from the start. But Kabuki began as mass entertainment performed in the open air by troupes of women who were also prostitutes. They attracted large audiences, but the authorities obviously didn't approve because in 1629 they banned women from the stage.'

'I bet they didn't ban the prostitution, though,' Henri said angrily. 'I bet they thought women were only good for one thing.'

'Don't know what they're missing,' Jeremy said. 'You should have seen Akiko in *The Tempest*.'

'I enjoyed our little rehearsals very much,' Humphrey said to Akiko, while monopolising the plate of Extremely Jammy Doughnuts. 'I think we should try another Shakespeare, to improve your boyfriend's theatrical education.'

'*You* should try watching a few more films,' Jeremy said belligerently. 'That's the most significant performing art of today.'

'I thought *Romeo and Juliet*,' Humphrey continued, ignoring him. 'You two could play the young lovers – no great strain, from the looks of you. I might even persuade Mrs Christos to be the Nurse.'

Becky's mind boggled at the thought. Anthea turned towards Humphrey, and at once his eyes were on her cleavage.

'Can we perhaps persuade you,' he said to her longingly, 'to take the part of Lady Capulet? A fine bosom like yours would do credit to any stage . . .'

Anthea smiled coyly. Henri looked at her with exasperation. 'How can you let him speak to you in that disgustingly sexist way?'

'You're the sexist,' Humphrey said unrepentantly. 'You loathe all men.'

'Anthea,' Becky said quickly, 'how are you enjoying the start your own business course?'

Anthea turned away from Humphrey's ogling gaze. 'Funnily enough, I'm quite taken with it. Not nearly as much of a bore as I feared.'

Humphrey turned regretfully back to Akiko. 'The only problem with *Romeo and Juliet* is the lack of a suitable part for Adam. I must find some way of including my boy.'

Adam, his school tie hanging at half mast, was slumped on the piano stool, struggling to master the opening bars of 'Für Elise'. His music lessons with Mr Chubb had resumed shortly after the court case, but now it was Becky who took him every week.

She sat close by, listening to him practise, sewing the name and number of his favourite striker onto the back of his England football shirt so it would be ready in time for his birthday. She was becoming quite a dab hand at sewing. She wondered if she should try knitting next, and whether her fledgling skills would be equal to a pair of booties.

The music stopped abruptly, and Adam turned round on his stool. 'Todd's going back to America soon,' he announced out of the blue. 'He wants to sell the flat.'

'Oh,' Becky said, her voice neutral.

'Where's Daddy going to live?'

Was it, Becky wondered, another omen?

'I don't know,' she said carefully. 'He may buy his own place.'

But she knew that was not what Rupert wanted. What he did want, as he had made abundantly plain to her when he made love to her again a few nights ago, was to move back into his old home with his wife and his child – and possibly, a whole little football team.

Becky held up the shirt to check whether the lettering was straight. If Todd was selling the flat, then Rupert would have an even stronger excuse to mount the pressure on her, to insist she made a decision. But she knew she couldn't do that yet – not until the predictor test she'd bought at the pharmacy the other day (because, by her best reckoning, she was already a little late with her cycle) told her what she wanted to know.

It would be the final – and the most conclusive – omen of them all.

It was already past seven when Alex stirred from sleep, woken by light filtering through cream curtains. Normally it wouldn't have bothered him. He always rose anyway before the sun.

But not today. It was, in fact, becoming less and less of an entrenched habit for him to be at his desk by six. He stretched luxuriously. He was beginning to allow himself the indulgence of sleeping in till seven, since Juliette.

He turned to look at her, at her halo of cropped brown curls against his pillow, and the mischievous laugh lines smoothed out of her face by sleep. He almost bent to kiss the lashes that lay thickly against her cheekbone, but then stopped himself when he remembered that she didn't want to wake early. Juliette, he'd discovered, always loved a lie-in, but today she had a legitimate excuse. She was scheduled for night shooting, and would have to get her sleep during the day. There was a new producer taking over from Letitia Harker, Juliette had told him, with all the tensions such a change usually entailed.

Carefully Alex slid out from under the bedclothes, and padded softly to the bathroom on bare feet. He couldn't remember the last time he'd had to move quietly round his own flat because there was a girl in his bed – a girl he had allowed to stay the night. The consciousness of it gave him a sense of quiet satisfaction.

He hummed a few bars of Cole Porter as he stepped under the shower, enjoying the sensation of rivulets of hot water running down the length of his body. His mind, for once, did not circle endlessly around the problems of the L.A. office and the piles of paperwork on his desk. His mind, like his body, was at peace.

He stepped out of the shower and reached for his towel, only to find that Juliette had somehow managed to leave both hers and his draped over the side of the bath tub. Indulgently he replaced hers on the heated rail, and wrapped his own around his dripping body.

It was quite a feat to discover his razor amidst the clutter of Juliette's jars and bottles of cleanser and toner and make-up. He looked at his face in the mirror and his reflection, swathed in shaving foam, smiled back at him.

In the bedroom, he stepped over the clothes Juliette had dropped on the floor the night before. Mrs Bryce would pick them up later and find somewhere to put them. She was far too discreet to say anything, even if she felt disapproval, which Alex doubted after her years of cleaning London homes. But Mrs Bryce was used to banishing disorder in all its forms, and Juliette was quite the untidiest person Alex had ever tried to live with. Mrs Bryce would fight the tide of Juliette's chaos, and win a temporary victory, only to have to start all over again the next day.

Alex went through to the study, and fastened the lead to Wellington's collar. The dog dragged himself up and gamely followed his master to the door. As Alex closed it, he was filled with a deep contentment at knowing he was not leaving an empty home behind him.

The instructions on the back of the packaging were very explicit. Becky was to put the absorbent test stick into a sample of urine, and in just three minutes she would have her answer. She was to watch the two windows, the right hand one already containing a thin blue stripe. If a matching blue stripe appeared in the left window, then she was ninety-nine percent certain to be pregnant, the blurb on the packaging assured her.

With slightly trembling hands she followed the instructions. Just three minutes – three minutes in which her whole future would be decided.

She began to count the seconds off, watching like a hawk for the slightest change in colour, the faintest trace of blue. One minute gone, and as yet nothing.

Adam was longing for her to have another child. He was always asking why God hadn't sent them one, when Freddie Foley had more than his share – an older sister *and* a younger brother. Adam envied him the brother, but was inclined to remind God in his nightly prayers that he would really rather not have a *girl* in the house. There were very few girls who liked football, and besides, they always tried to boss you around.

Another minute had gone by, and still there was no change. Becky put a hand to her breast, where she could almost feel the tugging of a tiny mouth on her nipple. She also longed for another child, but she wasn't so sure she wanted what would inevitably go with it . . .

The three minutes were up. The left-hand window remained obstinately clear. There would be no sibling for Adam, no child for Becky. Fate had not intervened in her life to make the decision for her. Unlike that first time, almost eight years ago, there would be no outside factor forcing her hand when she made the choice of whether or not she wanted Rupert as her husband.

CHAPTER EIGHTEEN

Getting together over health shakes in the pastel-painted refreshment area of the Riverside had become a weekly ritual for Rupert and Juliette. It was here they were drawn together for a reprieve from the demands that governed both their lives – the need to maintain a physical edge in the most competitive of professions, a requirement to keep in shape and look their best that was more tyranny than choice, the willpower they had to exercise at all times to refuse sweet puddings and avoid late night parties and force down eight glasses of water a day, in itself a tedious activity. They had both had to learn self-discipline and denial, not qualities inherent in either of them, and while both enjoyed the rewards, neither was completely reconciled to the sacrifices.

'I managed a whole extra circuit today,' Juliette said, sounding anything but thrilled.

Rupert put down a glass lined with the froth of the pure whipped fruit juices he had gulped down to soothe his raging thirst. He had gone through a pretty rigorous routine himself.

'You're looking pretty good on it,' he said to Juliette, patting her slender thigh. 'Radiant, in fact. If it's not the exercise, it must be love.'

Juliette smiled lazily, fluffing up her feathery curls with her fingertips. 'From what I gather, you haven't got much to complain about in that department either.'

'No . . . except that Becky just won't commit herself to a decision about whether to let me move back in with her.'

'She probably wants to keep you on your toes. You can hardly blame her if she doesn't quite trust you yet.'

Rupert shook his head. 'That may be part of it – but I have the feeling there's something else too, something that's making her keep her options open.'

Juliette darted him a look of sympathy. 'I know what you mean. Alex is wonderful to me, we have a great time together, but there are moments when I feel there's a part of him he's holding back.'

They lapsed into silence, and though Rupert could not read Juliette's thoughts, he knew they were not dissimilar to his own. There were so many temptations they both had to deny themselves, the least each of them expected was to possess completely the heart of the person they loved.

'Rupert,' Juliette said suddenly, 'it's the London première of my Warner film next week, in the presence of the Prince of Wales. Should be a bit of a lark. I'll be taking Alex, of course. Maybe you'd like to come along too – and bring Becky.'

Their eyes met in a look of mutual understanding.

'I'd love to,' Rupert said. 'I'm sure she would too.'

He knew only too well what Juliette was trying to do. She wanted to mark out her territory, let Becky know once and for all that Alex was now hers. Rupert was not averse either to seeing his wife confronted with that particular reality.

There were more barriers in Leicester Square to hold back the fans, more ranks of photographers to get through, bristling with hi-tech equipment. This was becoming quite a pattern with Rupert, Becky reflected, as they waited for Prince Charles to move down the reception line, shaking hands with stars and theatre managers and assorted dignitaries. But she noticed that Rupert was taking it more in his stride. He no longer needed props like limousines to impress her or the fans. They had arrived in a taxi, walked the rest of the way when there was no access for vehicles, and Rupert had acknowledged the cries of recognition with no more than an almost absent-minded smile and a wave.

Amidst the throng in the cinema foyer, there was more than a scattering of well-known film faces, even some Hollywood imports like Juliette's co-star Brad Pitt. But the familiar face Becky was seeking, as she craned her neck this way and that, was nowhere to be seen.

'Just think how convenient all this is for you,' Rupert was saying. 'Through me you can stay in touch with the glamorous side of the film industry, the part you would have missed through being locked away at home doing your writing.'

Becky heard the edge of pride in his voice and couldn't tell him that it wasn't really the glamour she missed but the teamwork, the feeling of being in something together, the sense of achievement when you pulled it off. She had revelled in being an insider, and wasn't sure you could ever get the same thrill from the outside, simply by rubbing shoulders with those who weren't.

'There you both are.' Becky turned to see Juliette, dazzling in a figure-hugging gown shimmering with beadwork. 'I've just done my little curtsey for HRH, and very charming he was too. Alex, of course, made his escape – now where can he have got to?'

'I'm right here.'

He wore a dark dinner jacket with his hair curling softly on his wing collar, and too late Becky realised that no matter how she had tried to prepare herself psychologically for this moment, there was nothing she could have done to protect herself from the onslaught of feelings the sight of him aroused, standing companionably next to Juliette.

'It was sweet of you to invite us,' she said to the other woman, 'but don't let us keep you. This is your night – I'm sure you have to mingle.'

'If it's my night, I don't have to do anything I don't want. I'd rather stay here with friends.' She circled a hand through Alex's arm.

Why her? Becky longed to ask him. Why her and not me? But the sight of Juliette standing there in all her radiant beauty was answer enough.

'How are you?' Alex said to Becky in a tone that seemed to her no more than politely interested. 'I don't seem to have seen you in ages.'

'You're always too busy, that's why,' Juliette said playfully. 'I hardly ever see you myself.' She leaned confidentially towards Becky and Rupert. 'You won't believe it, but I've actually persuaded him to take me away for a weekend to the most romantic little country hotel, right near where I was born in Hampshire. I have high hopes of convincing him to leave his briefcase behind, and even to try a little clay pigeon shooting. Isn't it clever of me? I bet you can't remember the last time he actually took a whole weekend off.'

'He never had such a good reason to before,' Rupert said, eyeing her curves appreciatively.

'Do you mind,' Alex said rather irritably, 'not talking about me as though I weren't here.'

'But darling,' Juliette patted his hand. 'Of course we know you're here. That's exactly why we're teasing you.'

It seemed to Becky, though it may have been wishful thinking, that Alex wasn't enjoying Juliette's game quite as much as she was. He turned instead to Becky. 'How's the writing going? Any ideas for a second screenplay?'

'Not yet. I'm still doing a polish on the first one.'

She couldn't tell Alex that she wasn't ready yet to embark on a new journey, to open a fresh chapter before she knew the ending to the previous one. There were decisions to be made first, about her future with Rupert.

'It's worth playing around with some new ideas,' Alex said. 'Call me any time if you want to chat.'

'Honestly, Alex, do you always have to talk shop?' Juliette pretended to pout. 'I think we all deserve a drink. And I do hope you two are going to be joining us at the party afterwards.'

Becky was quietly determined that they would not.

When they pulled up outside the primrose four-storey house that Becky supposed was still technically the marital home, she said to Rupert, 'I'd rather not ask you in, if you don't mind. I just don't feel up to it.'

It was the same excuse she'd used when she said she really didn't want to go to the party on the top floor of a five star hotel on Piccadilly, with panoramic views over Green Park.

'OK,' Rupert said rather irritably, 'so you're not in the mood. But you could at least ask me in for a nightcap.'

The problem was, she didn't want to do that either, and Rupert, leaning on the steering wheel to get a better look at her, could see it in her face.

'This is ridiculous!' he exploded. 'I can't be sent off home like some member of staff whose services are no longer required.'

'I'm sorry—'

'*This* should be my home. Then there wouldn't be a problem. You could go straight to bed and I could fix a nightcap and potter around a bit and join you later. What I can't stand about the current arrangement is how inconvenient – how artificial – it all is.'

'I know,' Becky said. 'I know you've tried to be patient.'

'I can't for much longer.' He grabbed her hands, and held them a little too tightly, so that the stones of the eternity ring pressed uncomfortably against the adjacent fingers. 'Apart from anything else, Todd's found a buyer for his flat and I have to know where I'm going to be moving. You owe it to me to decide this thing one way or the other.'

Yes, Becky thought, I do – but I also owe it to all of us not to make another mistake. I can't risk having Rupert back if there's the slightest chance of it all falling apart again. It would be too hurtful for Adam, to destructive for me . . .

She looked Rupert full in the eye. 'We have to be sure – as sure as we can be – that we're doing the right thing. I just feel as though I need a few more days. Then, if we're both quite certain it's what we want, you can move back in on Adam's birthday.'

Rupert raised her hand to his lips – the hand on which his ring had cut into her flesh. 'I know what I want already,' he declared.

'You *are* still sure,' Becky said earnestly, 'that you can make Adam's birthday party?'

'I wouldn't miss it for anything – especially not now.'

'Good, because Adam's been asking. He's dying to show you off to all his schoolfriends who've seen you on TV.'

Rupert at last released her hands, and she cradled the painful one with the other. She would tell Adam his father was coming to his party, but no more than that until the day itself. Then, if everything had gone to plan, she could give him the best birthday present of all – the news that his father was coming home for good.

Alex sat at his study desk doodling blindly on a blank piece of paper. By his left elbow lay the fax upon which his thoughts of the last hour had settled in fierce concentration.

He heard but did not register footsteps coming towards him and stopping by the desk. A hand came into the circle of his vision, and placed a mug of coffee almost under his nose.

'I thought of playing a torch song and doing a striptease,' Juliette said. 'But I was afraid even then you wouldn't notice me.'

'Sorry.' Alex reached for her hand and patted it absently. 'Things on my mind.'

'Then how about sharing them with me, and unloading some of the burden?' She perched on the edge of his desk, swinging a slim leg in tightly fitting trousers, and looking at him expectantly.

He shook his head in an effort to clear his brain. 'It's just business problems – nothing for you to worry about.'

'But I *want* to worry – if you are,' she said with some exasperation. 'Don't you understand – I *want* to share your problems.'

He was mildly surprised by the ferocity of her tone. 'OK, if you're really that interested . . . Two more of our star clients have decided to leave IAM in Los Angeles. Two in one week!'

'Oh dear, no wonder you're in such a funk.' Her face was lively with sympathy. 'Any new recruits?'

'Too many – and none of any significance. That's the root of the whole problem. The reason the two left is because they felt the agency's resources were being overstrained and they weren't getting enough attention.'

Juliette eyed the offending fax with the IAM logo and gave a little grimace. 'Why do you think your father's allowing this to happen?'

'It isn't him – it's the guy he's put in charge. David Wiseman. Trying to compete with the big agencies when he only has half the resources.'

'Don't you think Frank will intervene and straighten things out?'

The worst part was Alex didn't think so, though he would have felt it disloyal to say so. Frank was anything but keen to take back the reins of power. On the contrary, despite the latest disaster, he was still telling Alex that they had to wait and see if David's ideas would work in the long term. They retained a healthy list of star clients, despite the recent defections, he said. There was no need yet for any real concern.

'Anyway, I'm thinking of taking Irene on a world cruise,' Frank had confessed as soon as he could change the subject. 'I owe her a proper honeymoon – Mexico was only a few days . . .'

'Do you really think this is a good time to be leaving everything to David?' Alex had objected. But Frank was already describing the attractions of the various cruise ships they were trying to decide between, and Alex doubted he had even heard him.

He had been lost in silent reverie for several minutes. Slowly he became aware of Juliette watching him with something like resentment.

'Since you're obviously not going to share all your thoughts with me,' she said finally, 'I might as well leave you to them.' She picked up Wellington's lead and pursed her pretty mouth in a cross between a pout and a whistle. 'Come on, boy, walkies.'

Shrieks and thuds came from the garden where Adam, in full English football gear down to trainers with studs, was practising his tackling and striking skills on Jeremy in preparation for the arrival of his birthday guests. In the kitchen Becky was putting icing faces on rows of cupcakes, assisted rather haphazardly by Anthea, and more expertly by Akiko and Mrs Christos, the latter smiling coyly at Humphrey and wearing a blouse with a dangerously scooped neckline and no sign of her regulation crucifix.

In a tantalisingly sealed white cardboard box was an enormous cake in the shape of a football, covered in pentagons of black and white icing. In the fridge were rows of scooped out orange halves filled with rainbow-coloured jellies.

As Becky piped on a smiling mouth, she noted with relief that the square of sky visible through the window was still an unclouded blue. Football in the park would not be cancelled due to rain, nor would they have to resort to the hazardous alternative of moving the table and the china out of the kitchen and using it as an indoor pitch. With luck, the good weather would even hold long enough for tea in the garden. Becky didn't relish the idea of trying to entertain sixteen small boys inside the house.

Nor was she entirely looking forward to their departure. That was the moment when she and Rupert, alone with their son, would break the news to him that they were all going to live together again. Now that the day had finally dawned, Becky wasn't at all sure how she felt about it. There were butterflies churning in her stomach that had little in common with Adam's as he waited with scarcely contained excitement for his friends and his father to arrive.

When the phone rang, Becky had to run to the hall and pick up the receiver with icing-coated fingers.

'It's me,' Rupert said. She could hear he was on the mobile in the car, and hoped he wasn't too far away. The other children would be arriving any minute.

'Something's come up – something very important,' he said in a rush, as though his explanation could forestall her objection. 'I've just been contacted by a top studio executive from Warner Brothers – put onto me by Juliette. He's in London for meetings for just twenty-four hours, but he thinks he can squeeze me in this afternoon. He's interested in me for one of their pictures.'

He paused for breath, but Becky just waited, saying nothing.

'Look, you of all people should know what this means. Every actor wants to be in feature films, but it's almost impossible to make the transition from television. This guy's offering me the chance. It's too important to miss.'

'And your son's birthday party?' Becky said quietly. 'Isn't that too important to miss?'

For a moment she thought they'd been cut off, and wondered if in the rage that was growing inside her she had done it herself. But then she heard his voice again, crackling urgently. 'We're not talking some small independent film here, Becky. It's a *studio* picture . . .'

Becky closed her eyes, and thought of the studio film she had been working on when Rupert suddenly threatened her with the loss of her son. She remembered the stark choice she had had to make between Adam and her career, and how there had never been any real contest.

'Rupert,' she said, 'I'm sure this man will reschedule the appointment if you just explain that it's your son's birthday party. I told you we need your car to ferry children to the football game.'

'Can't you call a car service?'

'Not at such short notice. And anyway, it's not the point. All Adam's friends are expecting to see you – the big TV star. If you don't come, they'll be disappointed and Adam will be embarrassed.'

'I'll make it up to him when I come later – when we tell him I'm moving back in.'

Becky took a deep breath. 'Rupert, you won't be moving back in.'

There was a moment's stunned silence before he exploded, 'You can't be serious! Just because I'm missing a kid's birthday party . . .'

'No, because you're missing the point. I only want you back if Adam and I come first in your life. But underneath all the window dressing, you haven't really changed at all, have you? You're still the same old selfish, self-centred Rupert.'

This time the connection really was broken, and this time Becky knew it was she who had cut him off.

Becky stood in the hall, her mind racing through the problem of what to do about transport for the children. She and Anthea and Jeremy could each take four in their cars, but that still left another four stranded.

She almost jumped as the doorbell rang. They were arriving already. She would have to think of something, and think fast.

She opened the door with a welcoming smile, and found herself face to face with the last person she had expected to see. On the doorstep, nervously clutching a brightly wrapped present, stood Lolly.

For a moment they just stared at each other, then Lolly said in a small voice, 'I hope you don't mind me coming. It's just . . . Adam's birthday . . .' Awkwardly she thrust out the present.

Becky looked at it without taking it. Then she said, 'Why don't you come in and give it to him yourself.'

Lolly's face lit up. 'Thank you. You don't know how much I've missed him.'

She followed Becky down the passage to the kitchen, and they both looked in through the doorway at Anthea and Akiko and Mrs Christos and Humphrey, all pulling together to get the birthday table ready. She and Adam were lucky, Becky thought, to have such friends.

'Lolly's here,' she announced quietly to the room. 'But I'm afraid Rupert isn't coming.'

They all stopped what they were doing and turned to stare at her and Lolly framed in the doorway, their faces registering various degrees of surprise and concern.

'I have to go and tell Adam,' Becky continued. 'If any guests arrive, can one of you please let them in?' She left Lolly standing there shyly, clutching the present like a protective charm, and moved purposefully to the French doors.

Becky stepped into the garden and looked around at its riot of

growth and was glad Anthea had never managed to tame order
from the chaos. There was too much order already inside the house,
where Rupert had martialled furniture into position like a bullying
sergeant getting new recruits into their ranks. But it needn't be
that way any more, not after she'd sent his half of the antiques to
whatever new home he purchased. Then she would have the space
and the freedom to make some changes.

Over near the back wall, Jeremy was throwing the ball to Adam
so he could practise his headers. 'He's a champ, your kid,' he said,
giving Becky a wink. 'Just like his mum.'

She winked back. 'And you're a true friend. Talking of which,
they need help inside shifting the table . . .'

He was off in a flash, and Becky was alone with Adam, just the
two of them, the way it would be from now on.

She looked at him, standing proud in his England kit. She had
no intention of patronising him, beating round the bush. He was
seven now, and he'd been through as much as she had. He deserved
the unadorned truth.

'Adam,' she said, 'Daddy isn't going to come to your party.'

He looked down at the studded trainers that were her birthday
present to him. 'Why not?'

'Because he's going to see a man about being in his film.'

Adam bounced the ball up and down a few times on the
flagstones, between which stubborn little weeds pushed out their
bright green heads. Then he looked up at her. 'Are you very angry
with him, Mummy?'

She was caught off guard. 'Me?'

'It's OK. You can be if you like.'

'I was wondering more whether *you* . . .'

'Oh, I don't mind all that much. Daddy often doesn't do what
he says.'

Becky looked at him in growing wonder. He was trying to
reassure her, in his not yet fully articulate way, that he had learned
to live with Rupert's failings and to love him in spite of them, that
his concern was more for her than for himself. She felt humbled
by the bottomless generosity of a child's heart.

'It's still going to be a lovely party,' Adam said, hugging her
fiercely round the legs. 'You're the best Mummy in the world.'

As she bent to enfold his body, grown a little taller now, in the circle of her arms, she thought that yes, she was becoming a rather better mother, learning a little every day – and it was always Adam who taught her.

He cocked his head at the sound of a bell ringing deep inside the house. 'Someone's arrived,' he squeaked, disentangling himself at once from Becky's bear-hug. 'I can't wait to see what present they brought.'

'Go on, then – and there's another surprise waiting inside for you as well.'

He raced across the grass, all excitement and delight, no shadow lingering over his day, just as no cloud spoiled the great reach of sky overhead.

As she looked up at its endless blue vista, Becky thought that yet again Adam had taught her something new. He had taught her how to accept.

The unexpected arrival of Lolly had been the solution to Becky's problem. She had her own car now, she said, pointing proudly to the little Italian model parked by the kerb – a twentieth birthday present from her parents. She could fit one child in front and squeeze three into the back, she assured Becky eagerly.

At Battersea Park the children played eight-a-side football, with Jeremy acting as referee, and the birthday boy's team managed to score the winning goal. Then they all returned, still full of bottomless energy, to tear around Becky's garden and devour every cupcake and jelly in sight.

Adam had been delighted to see Lolly, but there was also a sense in which he took it all in his stride. He was, Becky noticed, much less dependent on Lolly now, treating her more as a friend than the substitute mother Becky had almost allowed her to become. When he opened Lolly's present Becky saw that it was a train set, and knew at once it was a little babyish for him now, although Adam was careful not to say so. There were so many developments he had gone through in the past months, which Lolly had not been around to see but Becky had lived through with him day by day. Becky looked at Lolly, bending over the engine to show Adam how it puffed out steam, and realised that at last she had reclaimed from her her rightful place in Adam's life.

Mrs Christos mixed the long promised *caipirinhas* from white rum and lime and sugar and ice cubes for the small army of adult helpers. Becky had picked up a tray of pre-prepared snacks for them from the Italian deli, but she noticed Humphrey sneaking treats from the children's table whenever he thought no one was looking. After his third *caipirinha*, he pinched Mrs Christos's ample bottom, and her eyes twinkled beneath black brows that Becky only noticed now had been plucked to half their beetle-like prominence.

All the children were duly impressed with the enormous football cake. When Adam blew his seven candles out, all on the first go, Akiko led the singing of 'Happy Birthday' in a beautifully trained soprano accompanied by Humphrey's baritone, a little the worse for wear. None of the children had remarked, in Becky's hearing at least, on the absence of Adam's father, seeming too preoccupied with everything else on offer. Freddie Foley told Adam it was the coolest party he'd been to all year.

At the end of it all, mellowed by rum and tired out by boyish exuberance, the adults trailed round putting paper cups and plates and squashed orange halves into big bin liners. No one left until the last boy, carrying party pack and balloon, had been dragged off, complaining bitterly, by his parents, and the last half-eaten cupcake scraped off Becky's flagstones.

Becky allowed Adam to fall into bed, filthy and exhausted, still wearing his football kit. 'Thanks, Mum – it was wicked!' he said and was asleep even before she could kiss his chocolate-smeared cheek.

Humphrey had also retired, defeated by too much rum. As she saw the others off, Becky surprised herself by saying to Lolly, 'Would you like to stay for a coffee?'

Lolly seemed both pleased and taken aback by the invitation. She waited to one side while Becky said her thank-yous to the friends who had helped to make Adam's day.

The two of them returned alone to the kitchen. As Becky poured ground beans into the filter machine, she stole a glance at Lolly, noting that she seemed to have filled out slightly, and no longer wore her abundant hair in the girlish ponytail on top of her head. There was a different aura about her now, a sense of acquired maturity, of having experienced the knocks of life, which hadn't been there in the frightened adolescent she had fired in this very room all those months ago.

'Thank you for helping out today,' Becky said as she placed steaming mugs in front of them. 'I don't know what we'd have done without you.'

'It was a lovely party.' Lolly looked down into her dark brew. 'It's a shame Rupert couldn't make it.'

'His loss,' Becky said shortly.

'He's made quite a success of things, hasn't he? I watch him from time to time on *Laurel Close*.'

Without quite meaning to, Becky said, 'Are you still in love with him?'

'I suppose those kind of feelings take a while to die completely. But I don't see him as some sort of god any more.' Lolly smiled with a trace of bitterness. 'I've learned that much.'

Becky felt a sudden, inexplicable need to apologise on Rupert's behalf, since he had undoubtedly not done so himself. 'I'm sorry he hurt you so badly,' she said.

'He hurt us both.'

'He *has* changed, with success.'

'But not enough to avoid disappointing Adam.'

'No, not enough for that.'

It should have felt uncomfortable, disloyal, Becky thought, to be discussing Rupert with this other woman in his life. But instead, it simply felt like a relief.

'We were thinking of getting together again,' she confided to Lolly, 'after you left him, after his career took off and he felt better about himself and less bitter towards me. But it isn't going to work out.'

'No.' Lolly lifted her eyes from her coffee, and looked directly into Becky's. 'I used to think it was all my fault that your marriage broke up. I felt so bad about it, and of course I'm still guilty about what I did. But I've had a long time to think about it, and I know now there were things wrong between the two of you even before I came on the scene – things that had nothing to do with me.'

'The problem with Rupert is – he lets you down. He probably doesn't mean to, but he can't seem to help himself.'

'We were both too soft on him,' Lolly said frankly. 'We aren't the kind of women he needs.'

'You know, I do believe you're right,' Becky laughed, looking at Lolly with new respect.

She took their empty mugs over to the filter machine for a refill. She felt an incredible sense of release, like a condemned man who has been expecting a life sentence and gets instead a full pardon. 'Have you found another job?' she said to Lolly.

'I've been waitressing for the last few months.'

'And how do you like it?'

'I hate it. But I've just been marking time, till I could work out what I really want to do.'

'And what is that?'

'I miss working with children,' Lolly confessed, 'but I'm not sure I want to be a nanny for the rest of my life. I think it hit me when Rupert said something about me just being Adam's nanny to some girl he brought home. It made me feel so inferior. So I've decided to get my A-levels, and then go on to study part-time to be a social worker, specialising in children.'

'Good for you!'

'I'll have to keep on working, though, to pay for the courses.'

On a sudden impulse Becky said, 'How would you feel if I offered you your old job back?'

Lolly looked at her in blank astonishment.

'Well, not *exactly* your old job,' Becky hastily corrected herself. 'More on a part-time basis, so you'd have the time to study. I could do with a few hours' help a day with Adam so I can get my writing done, but I have no intention of handing over full responsibility for him to anyone else again.'

Lolly's new composure seemed, for the moment, to have deserted her and Becky caught a glimpse of the eager seventeen-year-old she remembered from the interview. 'Oh Becky, I'd love to – if the sums work out.'

'Half your old salary, plus accommodation. I can't offer you the nanny flat now that Humphrey's here, but you could have the spare room upstairs.'

'Done,' Lolly said with a grin.

Becky leaned back with a sense of calm amazement. It was not Rupert who would be moving in, but Lolly. Life had provided its own unexpected ending, as it nearly always does.

CHAPTER NINETEEN

If this was being alone, Becky thought, then it wasn't nearly as bad as she had feared. Above all, it wasn't the same as loneliness.

Of course she wasn't on her own as such, not with Adam and Humphrey and Lolly and Mrs Christos, and the usual visitors popping in and out. But there wasn't a man to share her thoughts and her burdens and her bed, and now that there wasn't, she found that she didn't altogether mind. At the very least, it was better than having the wrong man.

Which was part of what Alex had tried to tell her when he'd said she needed time, time to be on her own, and now that she finally had it, she was learning just what an invaluable commodity it really was. At last, with no one to answer to but herself and Adam, she was beginning to ask herself the right questions, the ones that would determine how to make the best life for herself and her son. Though she knew she didn't have all the answers yet, she also knew that they too would come with time.

She had started on her second screenplay, the ideas suddenly coming to her thick and fast. This time the circle of her fantasy was widening out to include events that were not directly within her experience or so personally painful. She was broadening the horizons of her imagination, expanding beyond the boundaries of her own world, heading into uncharted waters, and the thrill of it absorbed her working hours.

The Pantheon executives had scheduled her first screenplay for shooting the following year. She'd been flattered when Harry Widmark had asked her if she wanted to produce it herself, but on reflection she had negotiated instead an executive producer's role. That way she could help put the deal together, and the major cast, but avoid the hours on set that would entail long separations from

Adam. It was part of her growing awareness of what was best for herself and her son. Perhaps she would reconsider producing when he was older and more independent, but not in these childhood years when he needed her most. And in the meantime, her executive producer role would keep her in touch with the world beyond her study, and allow her to spread her wings again in readiness for the day when she might be ready to take on that world once more.

Lolly had moved back in as arranged, and the first thing Becky noticed was that her wardrobe had been ruthlessly pruned of its tartan miniskirts and lycra pedal pushers. She wore no-nonsense clothes for work, and glasses when she was studying at the table she had borrowed from Becky to turn into a desk, and sometimes at night a rather unglamorous pair of old pink slippers. Becky liked to see her making herself at home. An easy relationship, without rivalry, had grown up between the two women in their joint care of Adam. When Becky had work to do, Lolly stepped in. When she didn't, Lolly made herself scarce. It was, from Becky's point of view, the perfect partnership.

They had also tackled together the rearrangement of the furniture, after Rupert bought a large maisonette in Holland Park, with high corniced ceilings and a patio garden, and the delivery vans came to take away his share of the antiques. Becky had told him to make the choices himself, that she would be happy with whatever he left her. And afterwards she replaced only the necessities, preferring the barer, simpler, less cluttered look of the rooms.

There had been some awkward moments with Rupert, once it became clear to him that Becky meant what she said about not having him back. It was some weeks before he would speak to her, or come to terms with the added indignity of Lolly's presence in his former home. But it was Lolly, surprisingly, who brought him to an acceptance of the new status quo. She was serenely friendly when Rupert finally came to the house to fetch Adam for a visit, so that it was impossible for him to be anything but calm and polite in return, an attitude that gradually extended to Becky herself.

Over the weeks time began to work its magic, as Becky had come to believe it always would, and Rupert had learned to live with the blow of her rejection, and even to be philosophical in defeat.

'No reason why he shouldn't,' Humphrey grumbled. 'It was Kipling who exhorted us to "meet with triumph and disaster/ And treat those two imposters just the same" .' Becky was inclined to give Rupert more credit. She knew how she had damaged his delicate pride, but somehow they had survived to become, if not friends, then at least not enemies. And time would do the rest.

For her own part, she tried to live each day as it came, without false hopes or pointless regrets. At nights, when she was too tired to work, she would sit up chatting with Humphrey, or go to a movie with Anthea, or perhaps join Jeremy to watch Akiko in one of her student productions. She did not feel short of adult company, although she knew the time might come when she did. And if thoughts of Alex and Juliette were a cloud on her horizon, then she tried to look beyond it, to the day that would inevitably dawn when she would no longer feel the loss.

Juliette heard the key in the lock and hurried to greet Alex in the hallway, where he stood uncertainly in the half dark, the rain dripping off his Burberry coat and plastering his hair to his head. Even when she called out his name, he didn't move.

'What is it, Alex?'

He had taken Wellington to the vet, to get something for the pain in his joints that was making it difficult for the dog to walk any distance, despite the little pills Alex forced nightly down his reluctant throat. Now Alex held only the dog's worn old leather lead in his hand.

'Did they keep him in overnight?' Juliette said.

Alex shook his head. 'The vet said he was riddled with arthritis – and in terrible pain. He said it would be cruel to let him linger.'

'Oh, Alex!'

'I gave permission for him to be put down. It's already been done.'

She flew across the hall to hug him tightly, but he felt stiff and resisting in her arms. He seemed to be waiting, silently unresponsive, until she finally released him, then he said, 'Sorry.'

'It's all right.'

'I just feel . . . I can't bear too much sympathy right now.'

'You don't have to explain – I understand.'

They both stood there awkwardly for a few more moments, then

Alex said, 'I think I'll go and change out of these wet things.'

Juliette trailed slowly back the way she had come, and sat on one of the cream sofas in his impersonal sitting room, and thought that there was still a part of Alex she was no closer to reaching than that first day, when she had sat here asking him all those questions in the impossible desire to know him one day as well as she knew herself.

'You sound better. Got yourself another bloke, then?' Michael said down the phone in the teasing older brother tone Becky had long ago learned to ignore.

'The reason I sound better,' she said rather tartly, 'is because I don't have a bloke to bother me.'

'What happened to the happy families and the roses round the door?'

'We're trying the other version, where mother and son find happiness on their own.'

'Told you you could do it,' Michael said rather smugly.

But this was one of those days when she didn't really believe she could, when the greyness descended over her vision and she couldn't see the way ahead, when even Michael's well-meaning attempts to cheer her up only worsened the gloom.

'Statistically women over forty are more likely to be struck by lightning than find another husband,' Michael teased. 'So if you change your mind, you'd better get your skates on.'

But the mere thought of entering the dating game again, making all that effort with total strangers who meant nothing to her, in the hope that one day one of them would, made Becky feel weak with weariness.

'I'm sorry,' she said to Michael, 'but I don't feel up to the repartee. Mostly I'm fine, I promise, but today I'm having a bit of a sense of humour failure.'

At once his voice was warm with concern. 'Listen, Mae and I don't want you to be alone at Christmas. That's really why I phoned. We want you and Adam to come to us in Hong Kong.'

'It's sweet of you both,' Becky said. 'Let me think about it.'

She and Rupert had already reached agreement, without lawyers, that Adam would spend this first Christmas of the divorce with her, and the New Year with his father. Becky wondered a little guiltily what Rupert would do for Christmas, with no family to share it with.

Then she found herself trying not to wonder how Alex would be spending the festive season with Juliette.

Juliette strode along the river, her long red coat flying out behind her like a sail. She was too restless, she had told Rupert, to sit with him in the club restaurant. She needed air and something to look at. As he tried to keep pace, he wondered what was eating her.

She turned suddenly, and asked with a strange intensity, 'Have you met anyone yet? Anyone new?'

'Well, yes, as a matter of fact, I have.'

'Tell me about her.'

There was an urgency in her request that Rupert couldn't help feeling had little to do with his own situation. 'Her name,' he said none the less, 'is Caroline Hargreave. She's decent, attractive – a little older than me, but I seem to make a habit of that. She's also a widow.'

Juliette cocked her head, and he felt at last he had her real interest. 'What happened?'

'Her husband had a heart attack. He was a race horse trainer. She used to help out – now she's had to take over the whole show.'

'She must be quite a lady.'

'I suppose I also go for the ones with an independent spirit.'

They leaned on the parapet, and looked out at the sprawl of rather ugly industrial buildings on the south bank. Juliette frowned, but Rupert doubted it was the view that preoccupied her thoughts.

'Caroline lives in Lambourne,' he went on, from his own need to talk about it, now he had begun. 'So far we've only seen each other at weekends. And usually with her children. She has a son of fifteen called Harry, and a daughter of twelve called Emma.'

Juliette gave him a mocking smile. 'You must be keen, if you're already playing the step-papa.'

'They're nice kids – she's done a good job with them.'

'Has Adam met them yet?'

'It's a bit too soon for that.'

Juliette took off again, striding along by the parapet at a punishing pace. Rupert almost had to jog to keep up with her.

'Do you love her, this Caroline?' she said without breaking her stride.

'It's too soon for that too.'

'But tell me there *is* a life for you,' she cried, 'after Becky.'

Rupert took her by the arm and made her stop. There were bright spots of colour in her cheeks, and her breath came in ragged gasps. 'Juliette,' he said, 'this isn't about me or Becky, is it? Tell me what's really wrong.'

She slumped her shoulders in a gesture of defeat. 'I tried so hard,' she said, 'everything I know to make Alex fall in love with me . . . but he can't.'

She passed a hand across her eyes. Rupert waited silently for her to continue, to get it all off her chest.

Then she focused on him again with the same burning intensity. 'You know why he can't?' she said almost angrily.

Suddenly Rupert wasn't at all sure he wanted to hear.

Lolly was gently insisting that Adam concentrate on his homework, though he was far more interested in the football he was surreptitiously rolling between his feet under cover of the kitchen table. He was doing a topic book on 'Animals and Insects', and Lolly was patiently explaining the lifecycle of the grasshopper, from egg to nymph to adult.

At the other end of the table, Humphrey was giving Mrs Christos her bi-weekly English grammar lesson. She wore a look of pained concentration and a brightly coloured floral blouse.

'One does not go somewhere quick, but quick*ly*,' Humphrey explained. 'It is the adverb you must use, not the adjective.'

'I learn quick*ly*,' Mrs Christos said, smiling at her little joke.

'So you do, Branca. You are a *quick* pupil.'

She blushed at the compliment. Humphrey, looking up, saw Anthea watching them with amused disbelief, and winked.

'What's that delicious smell?' Anthea wrinkled her nose in the direction of the Rayburn.

'I do love a woman with an appetite,' Humphrey said with a twinkle of appreciation in his eye. 'Branca is cooking us some *mariscada* – a Brazilian fish stew – aren't you, my dear?'

'He still too skinny,' Mrs Christos declared.

'He *is* still too skinny,' Humphrey corrected her. 'And if you have anything to do with it, he won't be for long.'

'Well, it's certainly making *my* mouth water,' Anthea said.

'Why don't you join us for dinner, then?'

'You know, I just might. Henri has some discussion thing on at my place – the exclusion of women from the Japanese theatrical tradition, or some such high-brow stuff. I don't think I can face it.'

'That settles it.' As Becky wandered in for her tea break, Humphrey informed her, 'Anthea's staying for dinner.'

Becky stretched her chair-bound limbs. 'First you can have a cuppa with me in the garden. I need some oxygen to the brain.'

'Mummy,' Adam cried, grabbing her hand as she passed like a drowning man clinging to a lifebelt, 'can I come out too and play football?'

Becky gave Lolly an enquiring look.

'He's got another paragraph to write before he's done,' she said.

'Mummy, *please*—'

'You finish your paragraph,' Becky said firmly, 'and then you can come out and play.'

As she and Anthea carried their mugs out beneath a chilly grey early winter sky, Anthea said under her breath, 'What's with the English lessons?'

'It's quite sweet, really. Humphrey is determined to improve dear old Mrs C's lot in life, and she's positively blossoming under all the attention. He won't let her pay him, so she cooks us a meal almost every night now. She also seems to work more days than she did before, but it's Humphrey who slips her the extra money on the side. He's just landed a big part in a new BBC costume drama, so he tells me he's very flush.'

'He's an old softie, that man, though he'd kill me if he thought I'd said so,' Anthea said fondly, stamping her feet on the paving stones to keep them warm. 'Honestly, Becky, we're going to freeze our posteriors off out here.'

'We'll go back inside in a minute,' Becky said. 'I want to tell you first about Rupert's new girlfriend.'

'Oh, in *that* case . . .'

Becky explained about the widow who trained race horses and lived in Lambourne with her two children.

'Heavens,' Anthea said, perching warily on a cushionless garden chair. 'I don't know how Rupert always manages to attract women who are so obviously his superior.'

'Lolly thinks he needs someone tough. Perhaps a race horse trainer is just the answer.'

'Hmmm. Either she'll whip him into shape or he'll get her to mother him and spoil him rotten, like you did, which is exactly why he goes for older women in the first place.'

Becky blew on her hands, and watched her breath make silvery trails in the air. 'Do you think we're all condemned to repeat our old mistakes?'

'Oh, I wouldn't go that far. Even I'm learning a thing or two in my old age – and you know how thick I am! In fact, I've got a piece of news of my own.'

'What's that?' Becky said, perching opposite her.

'I've decided to try and earn a bit of money. I can't rely on beastly old Simon forever, and I suppose, in a way, it isn't fair to. So I've decided to start my own business.'

'Doing what?' Becky said in a tone she hoped wasn't discouraging.

'Creating town gardens. It's the one thing I'd be an absolute whizz at.'

'Yes,' Becky said slowly, 'I suppose you would. And the business side of things?'

'Oh, they've drummed some of that into me on this course I've been doing, but I'm not optimistic enough to think I'd be any good at it on my own. So Henri's going to set up systems and do the books in her spare time.'

The door burst open, and Adam's football sailed through it, followed by Adam himself. 'I've finished, Mummy. Now Lolly has to do *her* homework,' he said in a tone that implied there was justice in the world after all.

The ball thudded again and again against the back garden wall as Adam scored practice goals. Becky said to Anthea, 'Does this mean I'll have to pay you in future when you come over to rescue my poor little patch?'

'Darling, I wouldn't dream of it. I think of yours as a charity case.'

Becky aimed a mock kick at her ankle, then broke into a smile. 'I can't see why you and Henri shouldn't make a go of it. Gardening is what you know and love, and Henri never fails at anything she sets her mind on.'

'I owe her a lot, you know. I didn't quite realise how short I was on confidence till she showed me how to get some of it back. I'd never have thought of going into business before I met her . . . But I must say, I'm getting a bit tired of all the meetings. I know most of what they say about women having a raw deal is true, but there's a limit to how often I want to talk about it. You know me – I just want to get on with things. It's reaching a point where I'd really like to have my house back to myself again.'

'Perhaps,' Becky said, 'you've hit on a way of doing just that.'

Juliette looked beautiful tonight, Alex thought as he let them back into his flat – beautiful but also driven by a sort of determined cheerfulness he didn't quite understand. She wore a black lace dress that was daringly see-through in places, and she had chatted and laughed relentlessly with almost everyone at the wrap party for her Pantheon film, practically having to be dragged away when the doors were closing.

'Would you like a nightcap?' he said and she accepted brightly as she followed him to his study.

'I've never been a fan of Letitia's,' Alex said as he poured them both a cognac, 'but she seems positively sweet-natured compared with that harridan they hired to finish the picture.'

'True,' Juliette said almost absentmindedly, 'but she got the job done. At least it's all over.'

Alex put the glass of cognac in her hand, touching it lightly with his fingertips. 'This film hasn't been a very pleasant experience for you, has it? But you can unwind now it's finished – and you'll forget all about it as soon as you move on to the next one.'

She raised her eyes to his, and though there was a sparkle in them, it wasn't the playful one he was used to. 'Alex,' she said, 'I'm thinking of accepting a role in Hollywood next.'

'You should.' He moved away from her, to the chair behind his desk. 'It's very important to keep up your profile there.'

'I don't mean just the one film. I've decided to move there – to make Los Angeles my base.'

He was beginning, now, to understand her mood. He waited, knowing there was more to come.

'It's been wonderful, hasn't it – you and I?'

'Yes,' he said, 'it has.'

'But we both know it isn't going to go any further . . . is it?'

He considered his answer very carefully, before saying, in a voice filled with regret, 'No, I don't suppose it is.'

She closed her eyes for a moment, then she said, 'Thank you – for being honest with me. And for some wonderful times . . .'

'Juliette—'

'I would say I'll go and pack my things, but I never really unpacked them properly, did I? I'm sorry I turned your tidy world so upside down.'

He went to her then, and drew her tightly against him. 'I'm not. I'll never be sorry for that.'

She gripped him with all the strength in her slender frame. Then she pulled back and looked into his face. 'Alex, I did leave my mark, didn't I? It won't seem afterwards as though I was never here?'

'Oh, no,' he said. 'There'll be no going back to the way it was before.'

She nodded, then walked unsteadily to the door and kept on going until even the sound of her heels on the passage floorboards had faded away.

Alex sat down again on his chair and looked at the empty space where Wellington's basket used to be, the basket he had donated to the RSPCA. There were no more ties now. It was time he started asking himself where he wanted his life to go.

It was a long time since Becky had seen Rupert in such a state. He was pacing nervously up and down as he used to do when he was an unknown actor preparing to audition for a make-or-break role. All he was actually going to do now was take Adam to meet his new girlfriend for the first time.

Caroline had arranged to come up from Lambourne, leaving the children with a neighbour in case meeting all three of them at once proved too intimidating for Adam. They planned to take him for a cream tea in a London hotel, after which Caroline would drive back, and Adam would spend the night with his father in Holland Park.

'It'll be fine,' Becky said quietly to Rupert, while Adam was deciding whether or not to pack his Gameboy. 'If you relax, then so will he.'

But she was quite incapable of following her own sound advice. She was equally anxious about the outcome of this first meeting between Adam and a woman who, from the way Rupert was behaving, seemed a likely candidate for his future stepmother.

'Dad, can we rent a video for tonight?' Adam said as he zipped up his suitcase.

'Fine – as long as you're on your best behaviour at tea.'

Adam pulled a face. Becky caught Rupert's eye and gave a slight shake of her head. If he wanted to win his son over to Caroline's side, the way to do it was *not* to tell him to be on his best behaviour.

'What are we going to do on Sunday?' Adam said. 'It'll be boring if there's no one to play with.'

'Do you want to invite a friend over?' Rupert said.

'No – I want to go ice skating with Freddie Foley and his parents.'

'That's all right with me, if your mother doesn't mind.'

'I'll give you the Foleys' phone number,' Becky said, with a little inward sigh of relief that Adam was able to sort these things out directly with his father now, without involving her as a go-between. He was also starting to make it plain to both his parents that he had his own life to lead, his own friends to see, his sporting passions like football and karate to cater for, and they could not simply carve up his time between the two of them, without considering these other needs.

Rupert glanced nervously at his watch. 'Are you ready to go?' he asked Adam with an almost pleading look in his eye.

'Yup. I just have to say goodbye to Bogey.'

While he buried his face in the dog's neck, and mumbled softly in his ear, Rupert turned to Becky and said, 'I don't know if you've heard the news yet, but Juliette's leaving town – going to live in L.A. It seems things didn't work out between her and Alex.'

'Oh dear – poor Alex,' Becky said at once.

'I think it's more a case of poor Juliette.'

Alex opened the door to her in a tartan silk dressing gown tied at the waist with a plaited red cord. On his feet he wore brown leather slippers. She looked at his face, as serene as if it had been hewn from marble, and wondered how she was going to read from it the answers she was seeking.

'You were going to have an early night,' she said apologetically.

'A lazy one, anyway.'

He stood aside to let her in, and she saw beyond him in the hall rows of stiff new cardboard packing boxes stacked against the walls. They gave the place a mournful, unsettled look. She walked past them, saying nothing.

She would let him do the talking, she told herself as she followed Alex to the drawing room. She would leave him to take the initiative, to tell her whatever he chose to reveal about the changes in his life. Above all, she would make no move towards him. She was determined, this time at least, not to make a fool of herself.

'I'm glad you're here,' he said. 'I was going to call you anyway.'

Her heart gave a little leap of hope, but she sat down carefully on the over-stuffed cream sofa and kept her silence.

'There's something I wanted to ask you . . .'

'Yes?'

'If I leave London, will you still want me to represent you?'

She had been listening with all her attention, but now she repeated stupidly, 'Leave London . . .'

'I'm thinking of moving back to L.A.'

'You too!' she cried.

'Oh,' he said, understanding her assumption, 'not with Juliette. This is another matter entirely. I have to go and salvage IAM head office, while we still have some good clients left. Frank's had enough, he wants to spend time with his new wife, and the guy he's left in charge doesn't have what it takes. So it's up to me, Becky. My father gave me everything I have, including my start in business. I owe him a decent retirement.'

He was playing with the fringes of his dressing gown cord, and she watched the movements of his long fingers, trying to focus on them and not his words.

'You of all people,' he said, 'must understand why I have to do this – after what you've just been through with your own father.'

'Yes,' she said quietly.

'So you see, my decision is made – and now you must make yours.'

But it wasn't the one she had been hoping for, and she wasn't ready to face this new reality just yet. 'What will you do with your flat?' she asked dully.

'I'll rent it out until I know for sure whether I'm coming back or not.' He looked round it with a rueful half-smile. 'It always looked like rented accommodation anyway, except when Juliette was here.'

'I'm sorry about Juliette.'

'Thank you.'

'And Wellington too, of course.'

'When the decks have been cleared,' Alex said, 'however painfully, it's sometimes easier to see where you're heading.'

Becky wondered if it would be that way for her too. When Alex was gone, when she was truly alone, would she find herself steering towards some distant point she had never made out clearly before? Or would she simply flounder in a void of loneliness?

'I can't imagine you being happy in L.A.,' she said.

'It's not a question of my personal happiness. My first priority is my father's financial security. He worked all his life to build up the agency. I'm not going to let some hired gun run it into the ground, now that he's too tired to stay on top of things himself. But we might decide we're better off selling head office, and letting Dad take the capital, while I turn the London branch independent and go it alone. In which case, I'll be back.'

Becky was afraid to hope for an outcome that was beyond her control. Instead, she tried to keep her mind on the practical. 'What will happen to your office here while you're gone?'

'I'll leave someone else in charge, and supervise it from L.A.'

'In that case, I want to stick with you. I don't want to be turned over to someone I don't know. Anyway,' she said, trying to smile, 'you're the only agent I've ever trusted.'

He grinned back. 'L.A. is only a fax or a phone call away.'

She tried to think of that and not the distance. It was an unsatisfactory link, this impersonal one between agent and client, but it was better than no link at all.

'Alex,' she said, 'I'm really going to miss you. You're the best friend I ever had.'

'Don't talk as though it's in the past. When I'm in L.A., I'll still be your friend.'

But they both knew it wouldn't be the same.

CHAPTER TWENTY

Becky had never heard the voice on the other end of the phone before, but somehow she would have known who it was even without the confident introduction.

'This is Caroline Hargreave. I thought it was time we spoke.'

Becky put aside the figures she had been running through for her accountant. Now that she was working from home, he had told her, a percentage of her household bills were tax deductible.

'It's about this weekend,' Caroline went on. 'Or rather, about Adam's visits here in general.'

The plan was that Adam would go with Rupert to Lambourne for the first time this coming Saturday. He was filled with nervous excitement, bombarding Rupert with endless questions about what Harry and Emma were like. The prospect of meeting children so vastly older filled him with awe. He didn't seem too bothered about Caroline herself, having met her that time at tea and decided she was 'not bad' when she told him she had kept a pet mouse as a child and was not afraid of snakes. It was Becky who felt uncomfortable at the prospect of another woman taking care of her child, assuming her own mothering role – and a woman she had never met, at that.

'I've been thinking how difficult all this must be for you,' Caroline said now, bringing a guilty flush to Becky's cheeks. 'It could be for Adam too. Which is why I'd like you to help me get it right.'

'That's very kind of you,' Becky said. 'But there's nothing to worry about. Adam's very much looking forward to coming.'

'I'm glad, but there's more to it than that, isn't there? This extended family business can be awkward for everyone. We grown-ups are big enough and ugly enough to handle it on our own, but we're responsible for making sure the little ones don't suffer.'

'What is it you want to know?' Becky said.

'Anything that will help make the visit easier for Adam – what he likes to eat and whether he's afraid of the dark and would he prefer to sleep with the other children or alone . . . Of course, I've already asked Rupert, but frankly, it's the mothers who really know these things, isn't it?'

Becky found herself smiling. 'Frankly, yes it is.'

'I thought you'd agree,' Caroline said with satisfaction, as though a pact had been sealed between them. 'So tell me how *you'd* like me to play this, chapter and verse.'

Becky suddenly found herself sharing with this stranger a mother's intimate knowledge of her child, and as she spoke the thought crossed her mind that even Rupert had never voluntarily consulted her on what Adam might need when he was away from her, although it was usually she who saw to his daily care.

'And what time,' Caroline said finally, picking up on the one point Becky had missed out, 'do you like Adam to go to bed?'

'On weekends, nine at the latest, but I'm not sure what Rupert—'

'I haven't even bothered to ask him,' Caroline said dismissively. 'In my experience, men are hopelessly irresponsible about that sort of thing.'

'Well, Adam does get rather tearful and grumpy when he hasn't had enough sleep . . .'

'Of course he does. But don't worry – that's not going to happen under my roof. And we won't all get on top of him either. I know he needs to spend a little time on his own with his father. They can take the dogs for a walk in the woods, or something.'

'Sounds idyllic,' Becky said almost envyingly.

'Oh, my dear, it's anything but. This is a working stable, and mostly we have to slave away all day. My children know they have to help out, but fortunately they love it. Rupert also has to lend a hand when he's down here – I've told him there's no room for passengers. But of course that doesn't apply to Adam – he's just a child, and not even mine.'

'He'll probably enjoy getting involved. He's never had much to do with horses before,' Becky said, giggling to herself at the thought that Rupert hadn't either, not since he was a child – until now. Caroline, by all accounts, was far from mothering him or spoiling him rotten, as Anthea had prophesied – but she *did* appear to be whipping him into shape.

'Well,' Caroline said, 'I'll get back to you afterwards and let you know how it all went. And it would be nice to meet you too one of these days.'

Becky had the feeling she would like that very much indeed.

With Becky's blessing, Lolly had turned her upstairs bedroom into a little corner of the Mediterranean, painting the walls a vibrant blue with the ceiling and skirting boards a brilliant white. She had hung up posters of all the places she had never been and planned to go – Greece, Sardinia, Seville – when she had finished her studies and was earning full-time again. Once she had the room the way she wanted it, it didn't feel like a part of Becky's house any more, but a place of her own.

'It looks really good,' Hugo Brockenhurst said, peering round through his fringe. The back of his hair was longer too now that boarding school was finally behind him – longer even than Lolly's, since she'd had all hers cut off into one of the new spiky styles. Hugo said it suited her.

He had also told her all about his new course at the London School of Economics.

'What a shame you have your father's stuffy old financial genes,' his mother had remarked when he told her his choice of career. 'But at least you also inherited his brains, not mine, so I suppose we should be thankful for small mercies.'

Mostly, he was just thankful that his parents didn't row so much any more. His mother pretended she was still furious with his father, but that was just her way, and when they spoke they seemed to get along just fine. In fact, his father was treating her with a whole new respect. He had been astounded when she announced she was starting her own business, and had predicted instant ruin, but as the weeks went by, he was forced to concede that she was making a go of it after all. Now he looked at her as though discovering hidden depths he had not suspected before. His new wife, Daphne, had given up work at the bank as soon as she fell pregnant.

'What's your baby sister like?' Lolly broke into his thoughts.

'OK. She screams a lot, but I guess she'll grow out of that. I quite like giving her a burp after her bottle.'

'That's always been one of my best bits too,' Lolly grinned. 'But now I find I like the studying more.'

'I think it's so cool what you're doing – going back to school, and all that.'

'Yes,' Lolly said with an edge of pride. 'I'm a bit behind you, but I'm catching up.'

'I wish I could slow down.' Hugo stared longingly at a poster of a Mykonos beach. 'I wanted to take a year off after A-levels and hitch-hike round the world. But then I got into the LSE, and Dad said he'd pay the fees, and Mum said I had to take him up on it or she'd personally wring my neck.'

'She's great, your mum,' Lolly said. 'She doesn't mean all that stuff.'

'I know, but I can't rock the boat when she and Dad are agreeing for once. So maybe I'll take that year off at the end of my course. And in the meantime, some mates of mine and I are saving up to take a van to France for the whole of summer next year. We can sleep in it, and club together for petrol and food . . . Fancy coming along?'

Lolly stood beside him, and imagined herself into that picture. It would happen one day, she knew it would. 'I can't while I have this job looking after Adam, and my studies to pay for. But when I qualify, when I'm earning a decent salary, then I'll start seeing the world.'

There was so much to look forward to, she thought, and so much that was good about the here and now. She smiled up at Hugo, and he blushed.

'Perhaps you'd like to go to the movies one night,' he mumbled.

She was glad she hadn't been wearing her reading glasses when he came in. Surreptitiously, with one foot, she kicked her grubby pink slippers under the bed. 'I'd love to,' she said.

Adam came back from Lambourne with a lucky horse shoe and a fund of stories for his mother. 'I missed you, Mummy,' he said, clinging round her legs, but there was a sparkle of excitement in his eyes that told her it wasn't the painful, lonely kind of missing.

'Harry and Emma,' he said, as soon as he had let her go, 'have ponies of their own. Harry wants to be a jump jockey. Caroline says over her dead body. Harry says he's going to be too tall for flat racing. What's flat racing, Mummy?'

But before she could answer, Adam was chattering on. 'Daddy says if I like riding, he'll buy me a pony too. Caroline says she'll teach me – if you say it's OK. Is it OK, Mummy?'

'I don't see why not. I'm sure Caroline's a very good teacher. But don't go asking Daddy for a pony till you're sure you want to stick with it.'

'I like ponies,' Adam said, swooping on Bogey's basket and giving the dog a giant bear-hug. 'But not as much as Bogey. Caroline says I can bring Bogey next time, but I'm not sure he'd behave himself. Their cat's just had kittens. They're going to keep one.'

'Did you get on well with Harry and Emma?' Becky asked as she sifted through the fridge, trying to decide on supper. Sunday evenings were among the few when Mrs Christos left them to fend for themselves.

'I slept with Harry in his attic room. It was so cool. Emma's OK – she's a bit more like a boy than a girl. She helps with the horses and she didn't boss me around.'

'Caroline's very nice too, isn't she?' Becky said, settling on the no-cooking option of ham and cheese baguettes.

'She let me help her get the eggs from the henhouse. I only dropped one. She says they taste better than the ones from the supermarket, but I couldn't really tell.'

'And did you have a nice time with Daddy?'

'Daddy's much more fun there. He doesn't moan when I put my feet on the furniture. Caroline's dogs sleep on the furniture all the time.'

Becky smiled secretly to herself as she buttered the baguettes. In all their years together, she hadn't been able to change Rupert's finicky ways. But perhaps they were not beyond changing after all . . .

'Next time,' Adam said contentedly, leaning on Bogey like a pillow, 'Harry and Emma are going to teach me how to groom a pony. I'll need to know that, in case I get my own.'

Becky thought back to previous ordeals before visits to Rupert, when Adam had cried or complained of having no one to play with or hidden under the bunk bed in protest against going. She had the feeling that at last those painful times were behind them.

*   *   *

Was he really going to go through with this? Alex wondered as he climbed out of the taxi and looked up at the primrose-painted house that was so woven into the fabric of his life he hardly knew where to begin to disentangle all the threads that bound him to it. Was he really going to walk away from what had become his life, this city he loved and the people he loved, knowing that where he was going he couldn't hope to replace them?

He had asked himself the same questions, looking down at the Strand from the window of the office where he had worked day and night to build up the thriving agency it was today, and sitting on the bench by Cleopatra's needle, where he used to take Wellington for his walks and pause to gaze out over the broad sweep of the Thames. He had asked himself, but he hadn't been able to answer.

He paid off the driver and mounted the steps to the black door with its brass knocker. A chilly wind cut through his thin jacket. How he was going to miss the cold, and a wind that brought the promise of early snow.

When he thought of Becky in the long days ahead, he would always picture her here, in this house which she had nearly lost but fought so hard to keep. This was where she and Adam belonged, with their friends nearby, and Adam's father, and his school. They had found their own life here, and now Alex must find his.

He paused for a moment, his hand on the knocker, his courage almost deserting him. He didn't know where he was going to find the strength to say goodbye. He only knew that he couldn't have done it without the certainty he felt in his heart that Becky would be all right now, even if he wasn't there. She was facing life alone with all the courage he had known her capable of, and finding her own joy in her son and her work and the people around her. There was no danger of Rupert dragging her down, now that he had found another path. Even Adam, sensitive to the peace between his parents, was thriving as much as could be expected in the aftermath of their divorce, finding his own feet, making his own friends. Alex thanked the Almighty for this one slim comfort, that he wouldn't have to worry about Becky and Adam when he was gone.

It was Lolly who opened the door with a teasing smile. 'Don't think you've seen the last of us,' she said. 'You're not going to get rid of us that easily. I'm going to drive across America one day, from coast to coast, and when I get to L.A. I'll look you up.'

Alex smiled down at her, looking for the love-struck girl who had run off with Rupert, and saw she had become a confident young woman with a mind of her own. Becky's instincts had been right when she had invited her to rejoin the household. With Lolly back in the fold, the process of reconciliation was complete.

He followed Lolly down to the kitchen, where Adam was sticking his tongue out in elaborate concentration over his maths homework. Alex looked at the serious blond head bent over his books, and was carried back on a sudden wave of nostalgia to the day he had rushed round to the hospital with an armful of flowers to see the tiny newborn creature, with a single blond curl on top of its head, nestling in its mother's arms, and had been knocked almost sideways by the force of his longing that the baby had been his.

'I came to say goodbye,' he said simply.

Adam looked up at him with Rupert's eyes. 'I wish you weren't going. Did you bring me a present?'

'Adam!' Lolly scolded.

'It wouldn't be a proper goodbye without a present.' Alex drew a small package from his pocket, and Adam fell on it with indecent haste and tore the wrapping off.

'Co-ol!' He held up to the light the watch with a big round football face, carefully marked off with different coloured numerals for the big and small hands.

'I'm going to ask you what time it is whenever I call up from the States,' Alex threatened.

'It's dead good,' Adam said. 'But I'd still rather you weren't going.'

Alex blinked hastily. 'You keep up with the chess, do you hear? By the time I next visit, I expect you to beat me hollow.'

'And when will that be?' Becky said from behind him.

He turned and saw her standing there, so slight her head could have tucked comfortably beneath his chin, her blond hair falling softly now to her shoulders, her green eyes dancing with the pleasure of seeing him, and tried to imprint the image on his memory so he could carry it with him wherever he went.

'Adam,' Lolly said firmly, 'let's go and play football in the garden.'

'You never play it with me, you don't like breaking your nails—'

'I'll do it just this once. Come on.'

'Will you be in goal?' Adam demanded as he trailed suspiciously after her.

'I suppose so,' Lolly sighed, and followed a whooping Adam out into the cold, shutting the garden door firmly behind them.

Alex looked around the kitchen, which Rupert had left intact despite his love of the Clarice Cliff china, in a tacit acknowledgement that it had always been Becky's room. 'When I think of you,' Alex said, 'I'll always picture you in here.'

She smiled wryly. 'So many of the important things in my life seem to have happened in this room. And now this . . .'

He reached into his jacket pocket. 'I brought you something to remember me by.'

'I don't need reminding,' she said softly, but she took the brightly wrapped package and slid her nails under the Sellotape to prise the paper open.

'It's memento jewellery,' he explained as she took out the small exquisite gold Georgian locket with an appliquéed flower made of gemstones. 'Rather quaint. The first letters of each gem in the flower spell out the word "REGARD" – see there – Ruby, Emerald, Garnet, Amethyst, Ruby and Diamond . . .'

She looked up at him, and her eyes were bright with unshed tears. 'You should have someone of your own,' his father had said to him all those months ago, and 'promise me you'll live a little.' But he couldn't live only for himself. Frank hadn't, when Alex was just a boy and his mother had walked away from all her responsibilities. Frank had stayed and provided a home and worked all hours so Alex could have a good education and a start in life. And Alex, mourning his absent mother, had never appreciated enough the father who was always there and so easy to take for granted. It was time to get to know him, now, before it was too late. It was time to repay a debt of gratitude.

'I would have put a lock of my hair in the back,' Alex said lightly to pass over the moment, 'but I thought that was a bit on the morbid side.'

'At your age, you probably thought you couldn't spare any,'

Becky teased, because that was how he chose to play it. She didn't
say that she wanted to remember his hair just as it was now, curling
softly on his collar.

'Well, I'd better be going. Things to do . . .' He drew her to him,
and held her close, and when the time came Becky was glad it was
he who found the strength to break away.

As she watched his familiar upright figure walking away from
her down the pavement, and finally turning the corner into the
New King's Road, she found she was gripping the locket so tightly
that the stones had made an imprint on her palm. Looking down at
them, she reminded herself firmly that the word they spelled was
'regard', not 'love'.

In the long days after Alex had left, Becky took energetic walks
with Bogey in Battersea Park, almost relishing the cold air that
stung her cheeks because it made her feel, despite the numbness,
that she was still gloriously alive. In the late afternoons when the
dark had closed in and it was too chilly for football, she persuaded
Adam to teach her chess as Alex had taught him, and they played
hard-fought games against Humphrey in front of the kitchen fire,
and if anyone missed the presence that was no longer among them,
no one spoke of it. When she was alone, she worked on her screenplay with a fierce concentration that left no room for thoughts of
'what if'.

So that when she was looking into the dying embers of the fire
one night, and her mother phoned to ask after her and Adam, she
was able to answer truthfully that they were both fine.

'And how is Daddy?' Becky asked with the anxiety that would
never again be absent from her voice when referring to her father.

'His health is holding up,' Alice replied. 'But his spirits have
never been the same since the attack. Nor, to be honest, have mine.
I think we feel too isolated out here now, like exiles instead of
expatriates.'

'Do you want Adam and I to come and visit you?' Becky offered
immediately.

'We'd rather come to you. We were thinking of Christmas . . .'

Becky imagined her house filled with the comings and goings
of family. 'Michael and Mae invited us to Hong Kong, but I might
be able to persuade them to come here instead.'

'I don't want to drag your father as far as Hong Kong,' Alice said firmly. 'Besides, we have other matters to see to in England. We're going to look at country houses.' There was a brief pause. 'We're thinking of moving back home.'

For a moment, Becky was at a loss for words. 'I never thought I'd hear those words pass your lips. I thought you hated the climate.'

'Frankly, darling, the winters in this place are absolutely bloody . . . cold and wet. We might just as well be in England. We can always hop abroad for a few weeks' sunshine when we feel the need.'

Becky curled contentedly against the sofa cushions. 'It would be wonderful for Adam and me to have you here.'

'That's the whole point. At our time of life, we want our family around us. I know we wouldn't be in London itself, but you and Adam could come down for weekends, and we could have Adam to stay any time you and Rupert were busy with your work. Now that you're not just writing any more, that might come in very handy.'

Unbidden, thoughts of Alex came into Becky's mind. He had moved thousands of miles, to an alien life, because of family ties, and now her parents too were feeling their pull. 'Where will you look for a house?' she said to her mother.

'We thought somewhere on the south coast. Your father will want to be near the sea, and I'll want him close to a good . . .'

She paused, but Becky could fill in the gap for herself. She knew it would be a great weight off her mother's mind to have her father within driving distance of a respected British hospital.

'Nowhere too remote, anyway,' Alice continued. 'Somewhere easy for you and Adam to get to. And of course, it'll be better for Michael too, being able to take just one flight from Hong Kong to Heathrow . . .'

'Well,' Becky said cheerfully, 'I'd better get on to Michael . . . and the estate agents . . . And I'll also have to see what I can do to move around my lodgers so I can fit you all in.'

Wrapped in anoraks and scarves, Becky and Rupert sat uncomfortably on hard bleachers overlooking the playing fields where Adam's school was holding its end-of-term house football match. It was one of those late November days when the sky actually showed blue in patches. They could count their blessings, Becky thought, that their parental devotion did not have to extend to sitting here in the expected drizzle.

It was one of those events that always brought together, either with great awkwardness or the acceptance of long habit, parents who were in various stages of divorce. Glancing around her, Becky played a game of trying to pick them out. They were usually the ones who sat apart, saying little, staring stonily at the game, or the others who spoke too much and kissed too heartily when saying their goodbyes.

She and Rupert, thankfully, had arrived at a different sort of truce. Becky was glad that Rupert was making more of an effort to be there for events that might otherwise seem unimportant but which mattered a great deal to Adam. He seemed at last to be taking on board what he owed to his son, and how proud Adam was of showing off his famous father to his friends.

He had been quite frank one day, of his own accord, about the painful subject of missing Adam's birthday party. 'I don't blame you for cutting me loose after that,' he had said to Becky. 'I know I let you both down.'

'At least you know,' Becky had replied.

'And all for nothing. That film offer never materialised.'

'They seldom do.'

'The trouble is,' he said candidly, 'if the same opportunity presented itself again, I'd behave in exactly the same way.'

It was the honesty of his admission that at last helped Becky to forgive him. 'If you know that,' she said, 'at least you may not make any more promises you can't keep.'

Now, as they cheered Adam on for a brave tackle against a boy almost twice his size, Rupert suddenly announced, 'I want to sign my half of the house over into your name, and I don't want any money for it.'

'That's very sweet,' she said, 'but you don't have to worry about my financial situation. I'm solvent again, now that I've been paid for my first screenplay. I've even managed to repay all the loans.'

'That's not the point,' Rupert insisted, his eyes never leaving his son. 'It's the least I can do to pay you back, after you supported me for all those years.'

'Then I accept – with thanks.'

'I'm also prepared to increase the child support – if you need it.'

'I don't. You've been quite generous enough.'

The overweight boy on the opposition team, with surprising agility, scored a sudden goal, and Adam's face was a picture of misery. Rupert gave him an encouraging thumbs-up sign.

'I'd like to buy Adam a pony for Christmas,' he said, 'but Caroline quite rightly pointed out that I should clear it with you first.'

'I told Adam I don't mind – as long as he's serious about the riding and it isn't just a fad.'

'I don't think so. He's becoming quite the country boy. Caroline says he tries very hard in his lessons. He's quite good, in fact.'

Becky touched Rupert's arm and said with sincerity, 'I appreciate everything Caroline's doing for Adam, more than I can say. She seems so genuinely nice. I'm very happy for you.'

For the first time Rupert took his eyes off the game, and looked at her. 'You could be happy too – you and Alex . . .'

'Come off it, Rupert. He's thousands of miles away.'

'That doesn't mean you aren't in his thoughts.'

There was a roar of applause from the parents, and Becky and Rupert turned back guiltily to the game, to see that Adam's team had equalised and their son was doing an elaborate war dance with Freddie Foley.

'Do you know what Juliette told me the last time I saw her?' Rupert said as the clapping subsided. 'She said the reason Alex could never fall in love with her was because he's always been in love with you.'

Becky glanced down at the Georgian locket, which she always wore now on a slim gold chain around her neck. 'How does Juliette know? Did he tell her?'

'He didn't have to. She could see it – and so could I. I think it was one of the things that spurred me on to try and get you back.'

Becky closed her hand over Rupert's, in silent acknowledgement of what this admission had cost him. Then she touched the locket on its chain, feeling the gems of the flower stand out hard against her fingertips. At some level she had always sensed it too – this love of Alex's that never faltered. But by a perverse trick of circumstance their timing had never been right. And then, when the moment came to fight for him, she had let pride get in the way, and fear of rejection, and meekly allowed him to walk out of her life.

Becky tried to warm her frozen hands on the teapot while she waited for the fire to take the chill out of her bones. Across the table Anthea was tucking into Jaffa cakes. Upstairs, Adam and Freddie were happily playing computer games, quite recovered from their despondency that the other team had scored the winning goal.

'I finally plucked up the courage,' Anthea said through a mouthful of chocolate sponge, 'to tell Henri I want my spare room back. She was perfectly sweet about it. She's going to shack up with the new girlfriend in Fulham, and carry on doing my books.'

'Can you manage without the rent money?' Becky said as she poured mugs of tea.

'Perfectly. My business is doing a nice little turnover now. Only yesterday Major Foggerty asked me to redo his garden in Chiswick . . . Anyway, money isn't the only consideration. All those fearsome feminists were frightening the wits out of Hugo, now he's living at home again, and trying to spread his wings a bit with the opposite sex.'

'If Henri's going,' Becky said hopefully, 'do you think you might have some space in your house over Christmas? My family are arriving *en masse*, and I simply don't have room for them. Lolly's going to her parents in Kent, thank goodness, so I'll have the Mediterranean room for Michael and Mae, and Adam can share with me so the twins can have his bunk beds, but the only place I can put my parents is in Humphrey's basement flat, if you wouldn't mind having him at your place for just ten days or so . . .'

'Funny you should ask,' Anthea said, looking decidedly guilty. 'I've been meaning to have a word with you about Humphrey. The thing is, I *do* want him to move in with me, and not just for ten days.'

Becky looked shell-shocked. 'You can't mean . . .'

'Why not? I've grown very fond of him.'

'But surely he's too old to . . .'

'There are other ways of doing it, you know.'

'Anthea!' Becky said, feigning shock.

'Well, he kept inviting me to visit him in his basement, and finally curiosity got the better of me.' At Becky's fit of giggles, she went on rather crossly, 'Anyway, it's not the sex at our age, is it, it's the company.'

'This is going to break poor old Mrs Christos's heart,' Becky warned.

'The old charmer's already been at work on her, persuading her to come and cook for us next door when she's not needed here. He says he can't risk having me poison him, so Mrs C's taken pity on him and agreed to come.'

'Am I the last to know about you two, then?'

'I haven't dared tell the boys yet,' Anthea confessed. 'Or Simon . . . I'll just have to say it's the title that's turned my head – I simply can't resist the idea of being the next Lady Humes.'

'Don't count your chickens,' Humphrey snorted from the doorway. 'I haven't asked you yet.'

'That's only because you're scared of going down on one knee in case you can't get up again!'

'Come, come,' Becky said. 'No premarital arguments. We should be cracking open the bubbly and celebrating.'

'I purchased a bottle,' Humphrey said, bringing it out from behind his back, 'for just such an eventuality.'

While Becky popped the cork, and poured out glasses, she tried to reassure them that no, she wasn't the least bit upset that Humphrey was moving out, and yes, she could manage perfectly well without the extra money, and truly, she was delighted for them both.

'I'll just be a stone's throw away,' Humphrey kept saying, 'if you or my boy ever need anything.'

Becky thought of the cheerless rented flat from which she had rescued him. 'No time to make a home,' he had told her, 'no one to come home to.' And now he would be living in Anthea's chaotic, cluttered house stuffed with furniture and boys and gardening tools and Anthea's overflowing personality. On impulse, she leaned over and kissed him on the cheek.

'You're a lucky man,' she said.

'She's the one who got lucky,' he grumbled, but there was a twinkle in his eye.

'When do you want to move out, then?'

'As soon as I finish shooting for the BBC. And you won't believe what I've got lined up next. That young philistine Jeremy has finally seen the light, and decided to produce a film version of *King Lear*. He wants to do it all in the style of the Noh theatre, with ornamental masks. Of course he has Akiko in mind for Cordelia, and he's bamboozled me into playing Lear – but I said only on condition that Becky's the executive producer. Which, of course, is exactly what the crafty young whipper-snapper had in mind all along.'

'I'm sure he'll take all of five minutes to talk me into it,' Becky said wryly. 'I know just how persuasive he can be.'

'Yes, well he's not the only fish in the sea,' Anthea intervened, 'and nor is Rupert. It's high time you found yourself someone nice.'

Becky looked at the tiny bubbles struggling to the surface of the amber liquid in her glass. 'I suppose I *am* the odd one out at the moment,' she admitted, 'what with everyone else finding their other halves: you two, Jeremy and Akiko, Rupert and Caroline . . .'

'Your turn next,' Anthea said firmly.

'It's not that I think happiness can only be found in pairs . . .'

'Nevertheless, that is often the case,' Humphrey said, his eyes on Anthea's breasts.

'. . . but I do think I had the chance, with Alex, and I let it slip away.'

'In that case,' Humphrey said, 'you must remember what our old friend T. S. Eliot said about success: it's all a question of what we can make of the mess we've already made of our lives!'

CHAPTER TWENTY-ONE

Becky knelt amidst pine needles on the drawing room carpet and gently lifted the delicate angels and Santas and ribbon bows off the branches of the Christmas tree, placing them carefully in boxes between layers of tissue paper, as she had watched Alice do when she was a child. The silence seemed strange after days of family and laughter and celebration in which she had finally understood that the contentment she now felt was real and enduring and built on foundations that would not crumble, whatever the future held.

It had been an almost perfect Christmas, with all the Haydon family under one roof, and her father in such high spirits, now that the decision to move back to England had been made, that the years seemed to fall away from him, and Becky could at last hope his recovery might be complete. Alice had arrived with her specially hoarded solid silver sixpences to hide in the pre-made Christmas pudding that had been maturing for months in her Tuscan larder, and which they would eat with her famous and lethal brandy butter. Michael and Mae had come with their usual suitcase full of extravagant presents, and Adam spent the days trying to make the twins pea-green with envy at tales of his promised pony.

Becky had invited Humphrey and Anthea and her boys to join them for Christmas lunch, and regretted it almost immediately when Humphrey began to tinker with her menu, being unable to resist persuading Mrs Christos to cook them turkey with a *sarosa* stuffing of fried manioc flour and eggs and onions and bananas, so that Becky was obliged to provide an additional sausage and sage one for the traditionalists. For good measure, Humphrey had also ordered a *rabanada* pudding to satisfy his perennial sweet tooth – fried white bread dipped in milk and egg, then covered with cinnamon and sugar. Mrs C obliged in dignified silence.

Though she could refuse him nothing, she had reverted to her widow's black in protest against his defection to Anthea.

At times Joshua seemed visibly embarrassed by Humphrey's attentions to his mother, and Hugo appeared to avoid noticing by taking refuge behind his fringe. But Becky, knowing the warmth of Humphrey's heart and the ease with which he had won Adam over, was willing to bet that it wouldn't be long before they were both eating out of his hand.

When Adam was told their news, he asked Anthea with great seriousness, 'Is Humphrey a castrated nude, then?'

'Whatever do you mean?'

'You told me that's the only sort of man you would marry again.'

'We really must get rid of those damn silly statues,' Humphrey snapped.

'Of course, darling,' Anthea meekly agreed.

For her part, Becky found the obvious mutual adoration between them endearingly touching. They were planning to go off shortly after Christmas, when the boys would be with their father and Daphne, to a rather grand country hotel for a sort of pre-wedding honeymoon – a trial run, as Anthea referred to it. Humphrey liked to pretend that she had bullied him into it.

In the days after Christmas, Becky's parents had scoured the home counties for a suitable house, and settled on one with a sea view in a West Sussex coastal village.

'It's as far south as we can go without crossing the Channel,' her mother had said. 'But you should be able to get there in under two hours from London, and it's perfect for Adam – horses everywhere – Goodwood and Cowdray Park right on our doorstep.' What she didn't say was that it was also very close to the excellent hospital in Chichester.

'Maybe you and Dad will take up sailing,' Becky said when she went to give the house her seal of approval, and saw all the boats in Chichester harbour. 'I'm sure it's a very good form of relaxation.'

'I suppose one is never too old to learn,' Alice said enigmatically, so that Becky wasn't quite sure whether it was the sailing or the relaxation she was referring to.

Now Hugh and Alice had returned to Tuscany to pack up the farmhouse, and Michael and Mae and the twins had flown back to Hong Kong, and Rupert had arrived in the four-wheel drive to take Adam and Bogey down to Lambourne for a week over the New Year. Adam had driven off with hardly a backward glance, knowing that what awaited him at the other end was the Welsh pony which Caroline had personally picked out, with the intimidating breeder's name of Forsythe Cambrian Nelson. Even before seeing him, Adam had nicknamed him Nellie, and was in a fever of excitement to get a saddle on him for the first time.

Becky had been down to Lambourne one Sunday, at Caroline's invitation, so that, in Caroline's words, she could 'see where your child spends every other weekend'. She was given an enthusiastic welcome by the mistress of the house and assorted dogs and cats, and a guided tour of the stables by Harry and Emma, and was duly impressed with the organisation and sheer hard work it all required. If anyone could handle Rupert, Becky couldn't help reflecting, it was the woman at the helm of this remarkable operation.

Caroline herself said something along the same lines when they had a private chat after lunch, Becky drying the dishes while Caroline washed. 'I know what you're wondering,' Caroline said. 'Why would I take on someone as spoiled and selfish as Rupert, when I have so much else on my plate? But men like him are really quite easy to handle, if you just remember they were all brought up by nannies and need a good spanking when they get out of hand – or at any rate, a smart slap on the wrist.'

'You're obviously a lot more successful at it than I was,' Becky said, impressed with how Rupert seemed to pull his weight in Lambourne.

Caroline laughed. 'Perhaps it's just that we both work so hard, we don't spend enough time together to get on each other's nerves.'

Becky was relieved to see the relaxed friendliness with which Caroline treated Adam, so that as the real mother, she need feel neither apprehension nor jealousy. She left Lambourne believing that she had found a firm ally – maybe even a friend – and one she could certainly trust with Adam's welfare while she took the trip she had booked to Los Angeles for the New Year.

It would be her chance, she told anyone who asked, to discuss with the Pantheon executives the final polish to her first screenplay, and the casting of the lead roles. It would be her first return to Hollywood since her producing days. It would not, she told herself firmly, be simply an excuse to see Alex.

There had been letters from him over the weeks, letters in which he described Frank's delight in having him home, and Irene's warm welcome and earthy sense of humour, which made her a joy to be with and a perfect companion for his father. There was a sense of contentment in these pages, as though Alex felt he had done the right thing, and Becky had tried to put all hope of his return behind her.

But gradually the tenor of the letters began to change. On a sudden impulse Frank sold the house in Beverly Hills and moved with Irene to Santa Barbara, where the lifestyle was more congenial for a couple in retirement. Alex was left in sole charge of IAM, with little time on his hands to visit his father, and a sense that his desire for a greater family closeness would come to nothing. Frank, it seemed, though devoted to his only son, was used to the independent lives they had always led, and content with the company of his new wife. Alex had spent a rather uneventful Christmas with them, lamenting what to him was the incongruous midwinter sight of sun on palm trees.

He had forgotten, he wrote to Becky, how much he disliked playing the Hollywood game – the single-minded obsession with movies that dominated every conversation, the insincere friendships, the power breakfasts, the petty rivalries, the concern with image. He still loved films, he said, but not the shallowness of the film world. And Frank had simply walked away from it, showing no interest in the agency he had built beyond as a source of current revenue for him and a future inheritance for his son. Becky knew that Alex's deep sense of indebtedness to his father would keep him at his desk in downtown Los Angeles, holding his other longings at bay. But a little of her hope began to blossom again.

It was a question, she would say to him, of balance. He had his obligations to Frank, as she had had to Adam and her first marriage. But ultimately, they also owed it to themselves to lead their own lives.

Long ago in Tuscany, she had stood before Marcovaldo's painting of the *Crucified Christ* and vowed that she would not be a sacrificial lamb. Now, if it was within her power to do so, she would persuade Alex that neither should he. His father would understand if he proposed the sale of the L.A. agency, the giving up of his birthright. Frank would want Alex to find his own destiny, not just the one that had been mapped out for him in advance, when he wasn't yet old enough to embrace it out of choice.

There had been so many changes that Becky had had to make to the path she had thought she was destined to follow. She looked back on them now as she reached up to take the star from the top of the tree – a tinsel echo of the guiding light the wise men had followed to Bethlehem. There had been, for her, such compromises and leaps of faith, and it was Alex who had given her the support and the time to herself to enable her to make them. But perhaps it was she who now saw more clearly what the future could hold. She was no longer part of the problem, she would tell him, she was part of the solution – a new woman who knew what she wanted from her life. And part of what she wanted was to share that life with Alex.

But if she could not make him see it as she did, if Alex was set on some other path that didn't include her, then she also knew with absolute certainty that all she had gained would not be lost, that it would not be the end of hope. And if she couldn't have Alex's children, as she longed to do, then at least Adam now had Harry and Emma, who might soon be a second family. Life would go on for both of them in some form she could not yet imagine, but which would be rich with promise. It was that conviction that would give her the courage to speak her mind.

She put the last of the brightly coloured decorations back in their box and closed the lid. She looked up at the uncluttered simplicity of the tree. Then her gaze shifted to the window, and the blanket of snow that covered the tiny garden outside. It had been a white Christmas – a rare treat in London. Adam and the twins had spent hours building fantastical ice creatures and hurling frozen missiles at each other, while Hugh, sitting safely inside by the fire, grumbled unconvincingly about the cold.

But Becky had loved waking to the lacy drapery of snow on the trees outside her bedroom window, and stored the sight in her memory so she could describe it to Alex in all its glory when they met beneath tropical palms. In a year when there was a white Christmas, you could believe that almost anything was possible.